Robert Cameron is a retired professor of evolutionary biology, living in Sheffield. His studies have taken him around the world, and he has written many scientific papers and non-fiction books. Robert's taste for fantasy, SF and dystopian fiction have seduced him into his own distinctive pattern of storytelling—stories that have a twist—that reflects his professional interests.

Robert Cameron

BESTOWAL

AUSTIN MACAULEY PUBLISHERS™
LONDON · CAMBRIDGE · NEW YORK · SHARJAH

Copyright © Robert Cameron 2024

The right of Robert Cameron to be identified as author of this work has been asserted by the author in accordance with sections 77 and 78 of the Copyright, Designs and Patents Act 1988.

All rights reserved. No part of this publication may be reproduced, stored in a retrieval system, or transmitted in any form or by any means, electronic, mechanical, photocopying, recording, or otherwise, without the prior permission of the publishers.

Any person who commits any unauthorised act in relation to this publication may be liable to criminal prosecution and civil claims for damages.

This is a work of fiction. Names, characters, businesses, places, events, locales, and incidents are either the products of the author's imagination or used in a fictitious manner. Any resemblance to actual persons, living or dead, or actual events is purely coincidental.

A CIP catalogue record for this title is available from the British Library.

ISBN 9781035847426 (Paperback)
ISBN 9781035847433 (ePub e-book)

www.austinmacauley.com

First Published 2024
Austin Macauley Publishers Ltd®
1 Canada Square
Canary Wharf
London
E14 5AA

Once again, my debt to my friend and colleague, Ann Hurman, is beyond measure. To read and to reread what I have written before and after her gentle but powerful strictures was a labour of love, for which I am eternally grateful. Plot holes ruthlessly exposed, obscurities highlighted, but also the necessary encouragement poured at every step. An early version of a part of this story was also greeted with enthusiasm by the late Jack Cohen, who has advised many of the great writers of SF.

It is with great sadness that I have to say that my two additional readers for *Ground,* Julia Macdonald Ogilvie and Beata Pokryszko, died while this book was being written, and sickness prevented their comments on the sets of chapters I sent them. I have declined to make a formal dedication, but their memory will stay with me forever.

When you have eliminated the impossible, whatever remains, however improbable, must be the truth.

Sir Arthur Conan Doyle: *The Case Book of Sherlock Holmes*

Table of Contents

Epilogue	11
In the Beginning	16
1. The Scholar and the Sea Captain	18
2. The Policeman	36
3. The Expedition	51
4. The Acolyte	69
5. The Westerlander	82
6. The Refugee	101
7. The Conference	111
8. The Archaeologist	128
9. The Historian	149
10. Colonel and Doc	163
11. The Seigneur	171
12. The Physicists	185
13. The Students	199
14. Power and Paradox	212
15. Gathering Pace	226
16. Consie Concerns	242
17. The Priest	256
18. Yes!	270

19. No!	**287**
20. Encyclopaedia Kindlandica	**303**
Prologue	**309**

Epilogue

Arthur, I'm dumping this on you as insurance. They will have no reason to come calling, and good old-fashioned snail mail escapes their notice, especially up here. Too much of it, these days. I've cleared my files, because, sure as hell, they are going to grab them. There needs to be a record. Sorry, mate, I'm rambling. It's that Savernake pagan rites story, from back in November. Maybe you caught it? The tabloids were screaming about it for a week, then shut up rather suddenly. Even passed *Private Eye* by. Then there was the breaching of the Thames Barrier just before Christmas and the wave of cyberattacks that followed, and everything since. Looked like a natural death, news-wise.

First, it was just a strange forest fire. Then those Wiccans started babbling, and it was all pagan rituals. New Agers and animal sacrifice. Then there was the inquest and the official account: accidental detonation of an ammo store from WW 2. The place is still sealed off. I'm told they are going to landscape it. The thing is, Arthur, that explanation won't wash, despite the inquest. I was inclined to drop it after that, like everybody else, and the boss agreed. Then I started getting messages; messages from a Wiccan who'd been at the scene. No proper name, just 'John'. Actually, 'John' was a guy called Matthew Franks. I know this because he was the only Wiccan they held, and who appeared at the inquest. I could tell he was unhappy, and gave him my number after. Pagan rites always titivate and there's always scope for another weirdo story.

He was dodging about from phone to phone, short texts and the rare conversation. It didn't make much sense, what he told me. A group of them going into the forest to celebrate Samhain. No, me neither, but it's the same day as Halloween, not that they'll thank you for saying so. Some kind of sacred spot; it had vibes (my word, not his). I asked about that later; seems one of them was into detectoring. They dug about and found a whole lot of metal something or others; even a cannonball. Badly corroded, but it started some story about a lost civilisation. A little got out from their babbling, but when we were told about an ammo dump, it got forgotten. That's why they chose the spot.

Anyway, they'd made a small clearing and built a fire. Sounds as though they were going to sacrifice a cow, for heaven's sake. It was around midnight. They were assembling in a car park off the A346, while two of them had gone ahead to get the fire going. Clear sky, and it was damned cold.

Here's where it gets weird. There was a clap of thunder, and a kind of whooshing noise. They couldn't see anything, but it came from their sacred spot, about half a mile away. John seems to have been some kind of leader. He and a guy called James went to see what was happening. I'll quote John's words.

The sodding clearing was huge, hundred yards across at least. Like a giant crop circle. Trees all cut off at about a foot high just where we were standing. The fire was still burning, what was left of it. No sign of Pete and Jeff. I stopped at the edge, gobsmacked, when there was another whoosh, and a pile of stuff dropped from the sky. Something hit James, who'd walked in a way. Like a crate.

I'll condense the rest, because it took several exchanges to make any kind of sense at all. It seems to have been mostly wooden crates, perhaps some pallets. They fell hard, and broke. Some must have had petrol or diesel, because the fire spread like crazy. He ran for his life. When I mentioned James, it was clear he was killed outright, crushed. Naturally, I wondered about a bomb or something like that, and something dropped from a plane. That wasn't it. We went over the same points over and over. Those tree stumps left. It wasn't so much that they were cut off at a foot; they were all at the same height though the ground wasn't.

You see, Mr Gordon, they were the same height. I mean, you could have put a table top on them. Across the other side was bare ground, like it had been bulldozed. And the final puzzle: *If they removed all those trees, Mr Gordon, where did they put them?* Planes overhead? They heard nothing. I wondered about a balloon, later, but judging by the amount of stuff, which I learnt about later, it would have had to have been a bloody Zeppelin.

That was all the real sense I got out of him. The ones in the car park didn't take in much besides something going wrong. They scarpered. Fires in the forest, never mind animal sacrifice, they'd be arrested. There was a cow wandering about in the car park when the fire brigade came. The blaze was visible from a distance. I don't know if anyone phoned, but the fire brigade and the police were there not long after, by John's account, so I guess he hung around. They got the fires out fast enough, but the police cordoned the area off pretty quick. There was a woman inspector in charge. They carted John off for an interview. As I recall, they had him in a hospital until the inquest; PTSD, it was said. The coroner was oozing sympathy, as I remember, but was always telling the lad to answer questions directly. He got clipped if he tried to expand. Otherwise, there was just the pathologist's report on James. Crushed under a huge weight of wood. It was badly burnt, as was his body. Nobody could point a finger at John; whatever had crushed him could not have been lifted by a single man, probably not by ten.

Of course, it was just the fire that attracted attention at first. A few local reporters and sightseers went out, and were faced by barriers and a big cordon. Then, of course, there were all those anonymous Wiccans talking about fire from the gods, and the coming apocalypse. That's why Henley sent me to the inquest. I went to have a look just before. When I got there, there were big DANGER EXPLOSIVES notices all around the site, and the army were still poking about. Car park sealed off; you couldn't get within 200 yards.

I'd have left it, Arthur, if John hadn't started texting. *Wood, Mr Gordon? It was an effing crate, not a pile of logs.* It went from there, like I said. It set me wondering. He didn't spout mumbo jumbo about ancient gods. Not the type to be hysterical. Trees shaved off like a giant razor? If there had been an explosion, you'd expect a bloody great crater. Another thing; what about those two starting the fire? No bodies reported. The coroner had asked. No trace, was the answer. I should have spotted something strange right there, because it was not followed up. I did put it to John. *I wasn't going to grass them up. Gave false names, Wiccan, like, but not the ones they used. I guess if they'd found bodies, I'd have had to confess.* Of course, the police had asked for more. *Didn't know where they lived, I said. Kind of secret society rules and so on.* Didn't they press you? *For a while. Then they lost interest. Surprised me a bit.*

Seemed to me the story was getting legs. I said as much to old Henley. He gave me a look, told me to drop it and shoved me off to Chipping Norton. Satanic Abuse, big names in the frame. You might remember that one. Load of bollocks, of course, some disgruntled old Trot stirring it. A bit of a rush, now I think of it, and it was pretty open and shut from the start. When I got back, a couple of weeks later, I asked Henley again. He gave me another look. Downright shifty it was.

You have some leads, Jimmy? He messed about with his keyboard and turned the screen. Little item in the local press. *Matthew Franks, found dead in his burnt-out camper van, suspected overdose. Police would like to interview anyone who saw him last week, etc., etc.* You don't need the whole lot, Arthur. *Drop it, Jimmy,* that's all he said. He left me to add two and two, as it were.

Well, what would you do? Obviously, something big was being covered up, something worth killing for. Did they have any of the phones? If so, I'd be next on the list. Maybe his went up in the blaze? Clever lad, thank God. When I checked back, I'd been called from a whole lot of numbers. Burners, for sure, that lot have reason enough to be paranoid. Got the lot on a stick, it's here with this letter. Trashed my phone, and reported it stolen. Got a grim smile from Henley. Nothing more. Lose stuff and you usually get a bollocking.

It faded. Out of our league if it's some kind of security stuff, and I didn't like the sound of what had happened to Matthew. Nor did Henley, and he'd made it plain enough. Then I got a piece of snail mail. Address all in capitals. Typical Green Ink Brigade stuff. Just two pages inside. The first was the usual stuff. Letters cut out of newspapers. *Why don't you ask about the missing overcoat?* I had to think before I twigged what that referred to. A paedophile case that had ended with a not guilty verdict. A month previous. The other was different. No details, Arthur, just in case. I filed the first under Nutters, and destroyed the second. Let's just say I had a brief meeting with a young woman. Pretty sure there was no CCTV. Handed a letter.

It was from that inspector, the one at the inquest. You can imagine, that got burnt pdq, Here's the gist. She'd seen me talking to Matthew, 'John' as far as the messages were concerned. Then heard of his death. I think she thought she was next on the list, though there were enough coppers and firemen who'd been there. They can't kill the lot of them. Wanted to get something off her chest. Now I think of it, I think she was warning me too.

They'd all been read the Act. National Security, blah. All sounded like some kind of secret weapon gone wrong. Ours? Theirs? Nobody liked to ask. Sounded like teleportation to me, Arthur, in which case it'd scarcely be one of theirs. SF territory anyway. And why dump a lot of machinery in hostile territory? If it was ours, surely, they would know where it was supposed to land, and would have chosen somewhere safe? Obviously, a balls-up either way. What she said about the scene matched what Matthew had told me. Shattered crates all over, many burnt, seemed to have a lot of gear inside. But she added two things. The two who were on site? Feet and calves. Burnt, but clear enough to her and the pathologist. Cut off at the same level as all those trees, by the sound of it. No trace of bodies. That certainly did not come out at the inquest.

The other thing was stranger still. She walked round the edge with her torch, and came upon a body, slumped against a tree. Pool of blood beneath him, but untouched in front, bar a few scratches. Called the police pathologist over. Male, probably in his twenties, dark but clearly white, sort of Mediterranean, she thought. Pathologist turned him over; half his arse and upper thighs sliced away. Like a guillotine, she said. That was not the strangest thing. The guy was dressed in what she took to be wool and leather, Like something mediaeval. But it was skimpy. As she said, what idiot would be out in that kit on a cold night in November. Even those Wiccans would have more sense. *Was he there when whatever it was happened, or did he come with it?* Good question, lady.

Oh, there was a huge medallion round the body's neck. She took a picture, and it was in the envelope. Here it is. Some kind of dark hardwood, like mahogany, she said. Looks like a palm tree to me, but I showed it to a botanist I bumped into in one of those endangered species cases. More like a tree-fern, he told me. All over the tropics. Too stylised to say any more. If it is a badge of membership, no one can recognise it, and I've tried quite a few hobbyists. Not inclined to push it online. You could, if you've the time.

Anyway, it seems she and the pathologist were given a very special talking to. Before the goons arrived, it was only the two of them had seen the body. Hearing about Matthew had scared her.

I didn't dare make any enquiries. Any hint that she and I were in contact, and we were both in the shit. I learnt later she'd been sent on some kind of exchange, Botswana, I think. I relaxed; too much. Henley called me up to his office. There was a tight-lipped suit with him. Turns out they'd picked up a phone from one of those damned Wiccans. My old number in there. Oh, it blew over. I gave him the story about pagan rites and all that. He just gave me a look. If they found a message, it can't have been much.

But I got to thinking: God knows how many of those bloody phones are still out there. What might be on them? If they don't trust a guy like Matthew to keep his mouth shut, are they going to trust a bloody hack? Bless old Henley. He may not be one for taking risks, but I think that guy was told in no uncertain terms that my death would raise a lot of questions.

But just in case, Arthur, here it is.

In the Beginning

The world was in the power of the Adversary. A world corrupted and unpleasing in the sight of the Bestower.

The Bestower took thought. He created his people and the means for their sustenance.

And the Bestower said to them, I have prepared a place for you, with all good things that are wholesome.

Eat only of the wholesome, that I have bestowed on the world for your comfort.

Cultivate and preserve only that which is wholesome, your crops, your animals, your trees.

That which was living there beforehand is not of My making. Replace it with the gifts from My hands, that the world may be fashioned according to My will.

He opened His hands, and placed the people in a boat on the waters. But the people were afraid, and asked, how shall we find the place prepared for us?

And the Bestower said, follow Colonel. I will guide his voyage and his steps to the place appointed.

Long was that voyage, and great the doubts. But Colonel held faith in his Bestower.

And after thirty days, they saw land. On the shore, Colonel summoned them around him, saying, the Bestower has shown me the way.

And they marched for four days. They passed through the unclean and aboriginal. And on the evening of the fourth day, they arrived at Rehine.

And they saw that it was as the Bestower had promised.

And Colonel said, do you not see, all that is needful has been granted in what he provided.

And they named the land Kindland, to acknowledge the Bestower's gift.

From the Declaration of Faith as authorised by the Supreme Temple of High City, Westerland, in the year 2987 After Bestowal. The earliest written version, differing little, dates from 892 AB. Other versions have contested passages.

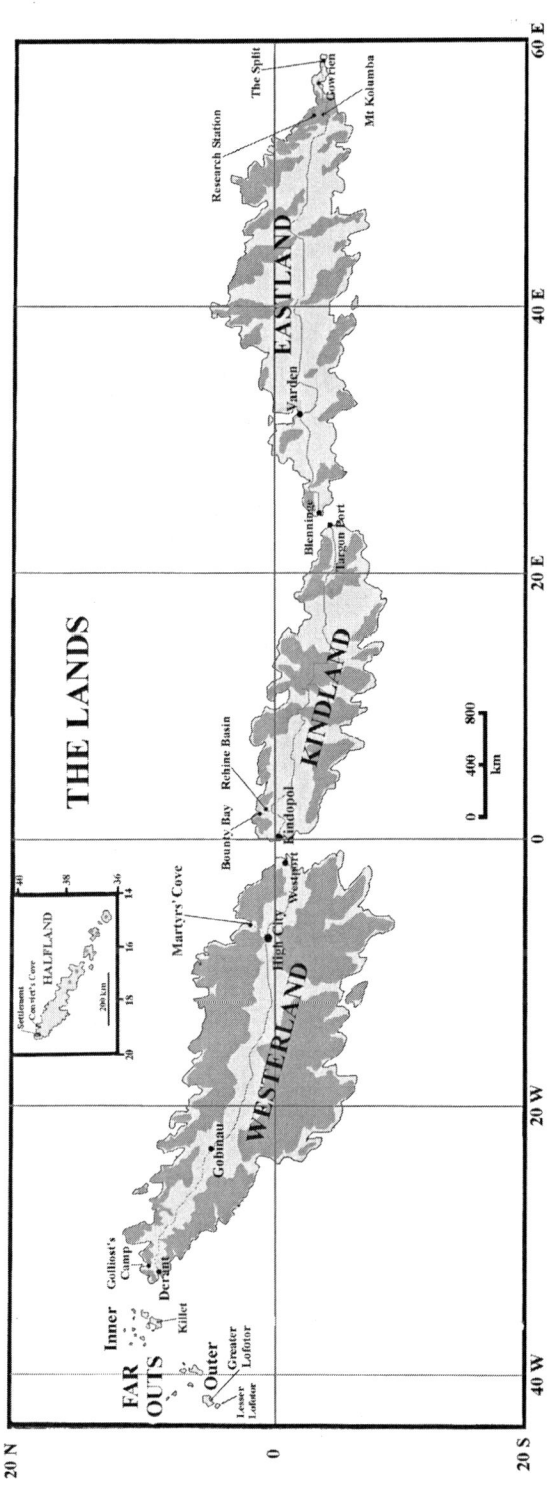

1. The Scholar and the Sea Captain

The *Golden Nodule's* horn gave two blasts. Soon, a line of parents, brothers, sisters and friends were descending the gangplank to Killet Harbour, their finery showing as a glittering and colourful spot near the gangplank's base amid the duller mass of the crowd gathered at the quayside. As the gangplank was drawn in, a crowd of young men and women lined the rails on the deck above, waving to those below. Three blasts, hawsers freed, and with black smoke issuing from its two funnels, the ship pulled away slowly. A band on the quayside competed with cheers from both ship and shore.

The Grand Tour had begun; the scions of the noble, of the Masters and Seigneurs of more than thirty islands, were embarking on the final stage of their education. To traverse the whole length of the Lands; to take in the vastness of the three great continents to which their island homes were but a tiny appendage at the western edge of the inhabitable world.

"I wonder," remarked Noris Denno, the Seigneur of the Lofotors, as he walked back towards the harbourmaster's lodging with his host, "how many more such tours are left to us, Moran? What would we do if Westerland impounded our ship, complete with the next generation?"

"They'd not dare," replied Moran Ombro, the Master of Killet, with a scowl. "A bunch of landlubbers using our cast-offs for what they are pleased to call a fleet. Take Master Duggor along with them and there'd be more than an international incident."

"Cast-offs with guns, so the Kindlanders report. Some detained and inspected. Fined, or so the Westies claim, but it is mere extortion. *Territorial Waters, Forbidden Goods*. Rubbish, of course, but they don't argue with a gun aimed point blank at their waterline."

"Kindlanders need more spine, that's my view, Noris. Anyway, Captain Gerrichen has a gun mounted. Under cover, for now. Duggor knows how to play the strong man, and they'd not want to lose his trade. The *Nodule* will take the southern passage out to Kindopol. Nothing much on the south coast of Westerland, and they'll not land. On the return, let's see. Any damned politics going on, and they'll wait in 'Pol until we can mount a convoy. Any trouble, and we'll sail straight past the whole damned continent. Best part of 3000 kilometres of bugger all but soggy moors and their lunatic clearances anyway."

"A pity if so. There was nothing like a few days in High City to turn me away from those damned clerics when I was doing my tour. Others felt the same."

"Anyway, they value our trade too much. They'd starve in the far west without our grains and meat. From what I hear, they are often starving anyway."

Seigneur Denno departed for his own lands, Greater and Lesser Lofotor, the following day, in what, in honesty, was a private yacht, despite its registration. The richest man in all the Far Outs, his fleets depended far more on trade with Kindland and Eastland, as did all those of the Outer Outs. It was the Inners, of which Killet and its Master were the greatest, who depended more on the short haul trade with Westerland, and its nearest ports like Derant.

Colours his view, thought Denno. Days gone by, before steam, such tours were individual and far fewer. Risking an heir away for three years, often enough, and wrecks frequent, was not that well thought of. Now, it was a coming-of-age tradition. Charter a whole ship, kitted out for the style of life suited for the young ladies and gentlemen, complete with tutor and assistants, and a Master to maintain discipline. The round trip would be less than a year, a mere couple of hundreds or a bit over. Not every year, though; get a worthwhile number willing and able to pay. Westie militancy had waxed and waned, but it was certainly greater now. Do we have to revert to earlier ways? A shame if so, for the bonding of the next generation that took place on such tours had mitigated the frequently violent clashes between Seigneurs and Masters prickly over matters of honour and prestige. Feuds could start from a mere trifle of precedence at a dinner table.

*****

Captain Gerrichen was an old hand at the game; the *Golden Nodule* had been chartered for the tour three times in the last ten years, and he was well used to providing high class passengers with luxury. Himself an Outer, from the Dark Isle, he had spent far more time at sea or in foreign ports than at home. If anything, his home had been in Madam Forliggen's House in 'Pol. Poor woman had been busted, he found out on one visit; married some yokel in the sticks to escape.

He looked across at the Tour's tutor as they sat together in the captain's quarters with Master Duggor. Stary Ropuch was indeed well-travelled for a landsman, for with scholarships and exchanges he had spent time in both Kindland and Eastland. He had even paid a visit to Westerland's High City, a visit that had converted him to a markedly Conservationist turn of mind. A dangerous enthusiasm, in the captain's mind, but that was not the greatest of potential problems. The man had returned to Killet with prestige. Now retired, he had been Principal of the college at Killet Port, the nearest the Far Outs could get to the great Academies of Kindopol and Varden. He was favoured by Ombro, and tutored his children and their cousins. A man of scholarship indeed, with more to him than the previous tutors. But totally inexperienced when it came to the business of controlling a gaggle of young men and women confined in close quarters for weeks at a time. His crew and the assistants provided would have a hard time unless Duggor knew what he was about.

"Another two days, Dr Ropuch, and we will close in on the Westerland coast. I've kept us out of sight so far. Not that it matters much, but it's all to the good if folk at Derant don't know we are at sea. There's little but wormers in the way of Westie vessels until we're near Westport."

The captain pulled a chart closer to his companions.

"We sail close in when we can, for the water's safer, deeper, than further out, unless you go two hundred or more kilometres further out. Right hundred in the year for it too, for there's a northerly shift to the winds in the middle two. Any storm, and we have a little shelter. Your young people will get a close-up view of desolation, for what it's worth."

"Wormers, Captain? I thought the trade was almost dead. What oil we cannot extract ourselves, Kindland can supply in abundance."

"Kindland has it, Westerland does not, or nearly so," said Master Duggor.

"They have little enough to trade for it, either. It's the rendering season, isn't it, Captain? Will the fleets be out?"

"Unless the weather turns, yes. But not the tankers that collect. First half of fourth hundred, usually, before the south-westerlies threaten to drive them on the rocks or have them stuck in harbours." *A lesson the young would have learnt, though the consequences for oilworm harvesting would have escaped them. That tiny tilt in the planet's axis, that heated the north a little more in mid-year and the south at either end, the change that gave a twist to the everlasting westerlies that girdled the world. A twist, Ropuch had thought, a Bestower's little joke, that the year was 401 days, not 400. Calendars of confusion, indeed. Four quarters to the year, hundreds, and a day left over.* Bestower's Blessing Day *in High City, neatly at the beginning of the year, but* Victory Day *in Kindland for more than 200 years, 58th day of second hundred, when the last Westie forces had been expelled back in 2735. Reverted, of course, after much argument, and known throughout the Lands simply as New Year's Day to all but the most pious.*

*****

The young lining the rails as the *Nodule* passed along the Westerland shore were silent. Silent in the face of what they passed, small cliffs topped by bare, gullied slopes, or hillsides covered in dense, low, grey-green vegetation. The untouched aboriginal, with no trace of the Bestowed. Untouched, that is, except where the pious had exterminated it. Low cloud and frequent squalls did nothing to improve the view. They passed a small cove, the inner shore of which was a mass of debris. Behind it, a steep-sided valley disappeared upwards into mist. The slopes were bare, save for a few patches of the dismal, aboriginal, grey-green shrubs familiar to them in parts of their island homes.

Ropuch and Duggor passed around telescopes.

"Look to the left, just above the valley bottom, near the shore. Buildings, or what is left of them. It was inhabited, once."

"A worming station?" asked one.

"No. A settlement. They tried to grow crops here. Then stripped the hillsides of abos to please the Bestower. The hills came down to meet them. Lousy climate anyway. According to the captain there are more like this. An exercise in futility."

"Does anyone live along this coast, then, sir?"

"Wormers, that's all. Their stations are mostly further east, within easy sailing to Westport. We'll see them in a few days."

The young corralled below, Ropuch held one of his seminars. Most had at least a rudimentary knowledge of geography and the distinction between the Aboriginal and the Bestowed, the crucial separation of life-forms on which their survival depended. A few, sons and daughters of the prominent families like the Dennos and Ombros, had taken in a smattering of politics too, but with a twist that reflected their fathers' interests.

Why are our islands more fertile? Rocks, sedimentary, not the acid volcanics that made up most of Westerland. Landscape, lower and flatter, so less rainfall, and easier, much easier to clear and plant, and not with the massive erosion you saw this morning.

Why are we richer, richer by far than those poor Westies? More fertile land, certainly, but we have ore and nodules, they do not, or not enough. In return? Some coals from their far east. Machinery, of course, though we can make our own and buy from Kindland and Eastland too.

There were other reasons, of course, for the difference. More contentious ones at that.

"My mother says it's because they breed like the rats from Halfland, sir, whether there's food on the table or not. There was that plague in Kindopol."

"That's not true," another broke in. "It's all those monks and nuns and priests that don't get married. They all need feeding. Still, I suppose they don't have children."

"Not have children? Who told you that? You don't need a certificate. Worse than the rats, my uncle said. He went to High City as an envoy. Told us a thing or two about those monasteries."

There was a burst of embarrassed laughter and a few blushes. As well, thought Ropuch at first, that Duggor was beside him. But after his frown had silenced the room, the man launched into a diatribe.

"Never mind children, children who are put to work in a way even your lowest subjects would resent. It's soldiers, snoops like the Zaggara, besides the religious. They are all working in their way, just not on growing food or making something useful. Those that make are as likely to make cannons as trucks or trains. Clearing more land than they can convert too, more labour to no good purpose. Damned religion, that's their problem."

There was a hubbub. Many hands were raised. Ropuch cursed silently. Not that he disagreed, not at all, but many families took a different view. On the tour, he had been instructed, any discussion of religion, and especially of the Ultra tendency in Westerland was to be carefully avoided until the party had experienced High City for themselves, and listened to those oh-so-rational arguments on the other side that they would hear from the elite Varrenians in Kindopol. Now, he would have to deal with questions that he would have left till much later.

Zaggara? The religious police, dedicated to dealing with heresy and unbelief. Yes, Drann, unbelief means Evolutionism. No, Gelia, it's only about the Bestowed, but there are those who deny evolution of the aboriginal too; the devil's Bestowal, some call it. Hence the desire to destroy it. Punishments? Death or a lifetime of clearance in chain gangs on the western moors.

Even Duggor, surprisingly outspoken for an Inner, whose trade was mainly with Westerland, refrained from telling them the manner of death inflicted. Some would have heard, but perhaps not believed. A country where stoning was a merciful death. Ropuch left for his cabin. It was the perennial, unresolved issue. The sharp distinction between the Aboriginal and the Bestowed, the bestowed poor in species. The Bestowed that lacked a fossil record, the Bestowed that held only that which aided survival, *except for those creatures on Halfland,* an inner voice reminded him.

It had been bad enough even in the old days before the Evolutionist idea had occurred and accumulated evidence. The practical approach acknowledged Bestowal, for how could you not. But the aboriginal had its uses as timber, as fuel, *including those deposits hundreds of millions of years old,* and, with careful treatment, a source of medicines and even of drink. If it was strange that no life in the sea was edible, at the least it, and the aboriginal life on land, served to maintain the atmosphere or prevent erosion. Until those first Ultras, the Martyrs of sacred memory, had fled to Westerland to fulfil the Bestower's will and beat the devil.

Well, these Outers would get an education, that was for certain. More than they could imagine once they met Eastlanders in Blenninge or Varden. Ropuch gave up his circling thoughts, and prepared for dinner. Among the captain and his officers, there were always good stories to hear. This time, it was a little different.

"I think you are all in for a spectacle tonight, Dr Ropuch. The mate on duty reported a few worms passing us. It's the season. There will be many more in an hour or two."

"It will be dark, though, and I thought they went deep."

"It will be dark, certainly, all to the good. The creatures are luminescent, and they come nearer the surface at night. There's some think they go deep in the daytime to avoid the wormers. If so, it's maybe a case of that evolution you scholars argue about."

"The season?" Ropuch, like nearly all, had paid scant attention to sea life.

"They circle the globe. Against the current, always westwards. It's annual, that's to say they pass a place at the same time each year, but there are those say it takes them three to go around. Whatever, they are at their largest as they pass the Far Outs, and smallest when they pass Eastland's tip. They breed, we suppose, somewhere in Anasman's seas."

There was a spectacle. Gerrichen stilled the engines, so that no wake disturbed the quiet sea. The vast worms passed; almost transparent forms outlined by flickering lights across their skin: green, blue, even mauve or violet. First a few, but the numbers increased. Great, flickering backs broke the surface, and the undulating skirts flashed in pulses as they propelled the beasts forward.

There seemed no end, but eventually Gerrichen had to get underway. The propellers and the wake had immediate effect, for those nearby descended into the deep, while many moved away from the ship. The watchers dispersed.

"Such beauty, such size. Twenty metres or more, surely. Hunted for oil?"

"The beauty does not show in daylight. When we still depended on them, twenty-seven metres was the largest," said Duggor. "A big one would yield oil to keep a family in funds for half a year. He'd not like it said now, but that's how the Denno family made their first fortune. Centuries ago, mind."

The morning provided a demonstration. Ahead were a fleet of small boats, sails and oars only, tacking to and fro across the mouth of a bay. On shore were intact buildings, evidently in use, for from the largest, two tall chimneys belched a thick black smoke. A small steamer was tied up against a single jetty. Captain Gerrichen slowed, keeping just enough movement to avoid the shallows further off.

"They'll be cursing us," he said. "The engines will drive them deeper. Yes, they are wormers, and that's their rendering factory, burn oil to get oil, the poor bastards will not get coal, even peat, or if they do it will not last the season. They need that steamer, though to land the catch. No sign of life there."

He was wrong about cursing. A single boat sailed alongside and a shout came up. A ladder came down, and a man came aboard. On the bridge, his conversation with Gerrichen was incomprehensible to Ropuch, and nearly so to Duggor, even with more experience of the harsh dialect of Westies from the wilderness. Whatever was said, the man was not angry, and he departed with bows and grins to all.

"We are saviours, as it happens. Their ship has broken down. They were merely quartering the channel, for without power, no number of rowers will bring a worm to shore. I'm to back a bit and anchor. He's shown me the spot where the tanker sits. There are many down there; it's a good year, he says."

The *Nodule* backed slowly, then dropped anchor closer to the shore. All but two of the small boats formed into a straggling line at right angles to the shore, tacking to and fro to maintain position. The two took up stations down current. One fired a flare; both threw off a container attached to a line. As the lines went taut, there was a muffled roar, and columns of water shot upwards. The effect was instant, for the sea became a churning mass of worms, colliding with each other but all trying to move west. As they reached the line, harpoon after harpoon was hurled. In the thrashing crowd, two boats were overturned.

The mob, Ropuch could think of no better word, passed, but three were held, each with many harpoons at their head. They appeared stunned, for the boats were able to close round each and twine the lines of the harpoons. In his absorption in the spectacle, he did not, at first, notice that the *Nodule* was underway, turning so that her stern faced the boats, now being towed westward by the recovering worms. More explosive canisters were thrown, keeping the worms from diving.

It was a scramble, for the *Nodule* could approach only one victim and its conquerors at a time. A line was thrown. Thrown again and again until caught. Line hitched to line, and the boats disengaged. Only after an hour, and nearly three kilometres west was the last worm tethered. The ship turned, heading back to the cove.

To Ropuch's surprise, it soon became apparent that the worms no longer fought; indeed, they appeared to be lifeless. The *Nodule* edged gingerly towards the jetty, stern first, a sailor calling the soundings repeatedly. A sharp change of tone, and the ship edged forward again and dropped anchor. Boats and men were busy, taking the lines from the ship towards the shore. Ropuch saw a huge winch, and watched as the first worm was hauled ashore, to be attacked at once by men armed with huge knives.

"The modern way," said the captain, wryly, seeing the look of distaste on Duggor's face. "Your lot used proper ships in the old days, big enough not to be pulled under, and with enough sail, given wind, to turn for home. No ships like that today, least of all in Westerland. Abo trees were an abomination unto the Bestower. Use them, yes, replant or harvest? Fancy a painbush beating?"

"They went flaccid, those worms. Do the harpoons kill?" asked Ropuch.

"No. There's one thing kills them, not headed against the current. Can't breathe, so I'm told. Get them turned, and they are helpless in minutes."

There was a call, boat approaching. Three men boarded each with a backpack. One was more smartly dressed, and evidently in charge. There was a quiet conversation with the captain, who turned to Ropuch.

"Get your bunch assembled in the mess. Mr Triast has something to say to all of us, and I think it is educational. Don't worry, he speaks clearly enough."

Triast, that's a Martyrson's name, thought Ropuch. Not a priest, for no priest would visit a bunch of foreigners without his robes. He rounded up his charges, who had been enthralled by the spectacle. Many were asking about the upturned boats, and Ropuch put the question as soon as all were quiet. It received a smile, and then a laugh.

"Your concern does you credit. Fear not, for none were lost. The boats salvaged too, while your captain was dealing with our catch. All can swim, and all know the risk. It is a frequent occurrence."

"Are the worms not dangerous?"

"By accident only." He held up his hand. "Their food is at most the size of my thumbnail. Imagine feeding by swimming through soup with your mouth open. Rather thin soup, mind, but there's enough if you feed all day."

"I have already thanked your captain," he continued, "for his assistance, without which we would have caught nothing today, nor for some time, as our ship is in need of more repair than we imagined. And the worms' passage may soon be over. Three in one day has never before been achieved. We have brought a small token of thanks, bottles of oil subtly distilled and infused with herbs. Used in lamps, it has a pleasing effect on those nearby. I hope there is at least one for each of you."

It was Master Ombro's daughter, Melie, who jumped to her feet.

"Mr Triast, may we ask some questions? Herbs, Mr Triast. I have heard of such, but are they not abo?"

Triast grinned. "Well now, a pertinent question, if you are of a very particular religious persuasion. Here in our little backwater, we tend to take all that we find as the gift of the Bestower. Anything that is useful was surely given to us. It remains only to find the right use. Are worms themselves not abo?"

There was something about that grin, something that suggested anything could be asked. Melie plunged in.

"Please pardon me, Mr Triast, but your name? We learnt even at school that those who were Martyrsons held the places of honour and distinction in Westerland. Is the running of such a place as this so regarded?"

The grin became enormous, and Triast laughed out loud.

"I congratulate you, and your teachers. I wish we were as well taught about the ways of those abroad. No, young lady, it is not so regarded. It is indeed banishment for my sins. Sins that involved a dispute with a priest. Sins that might have condemned me to much worse. *In danger of heresy* is the charge. Notice, not heresy itself, a mercy since I would long since been restored to the bosom of the Bestower or his Enemy."

"You are here for life?" This was Duggor.

"Yes, Master, or perhaps Seigneur, I beg pardon for ignorance, for life. As are those I manage. Our labour is valued, but our company is not; we are deemed infectious. We get new recruits from time to time. Perhaps, seeing the outrage in your face, I should say that most are glad to be here, for there are many worse fates for those who fall from grace."

"All, always, for life?" Duggor was incredulous.

"There is an alternative, also for life. A really sincere confession, a total abasement, may earn you a place as a servant in a closed monastery. Surrounded by the piety you so thoughtlessly dismissed, and with ample opportunity to do penance. Here, we may indulge our little eccentricities without disturbance."

"Escape? There are no guards?"

"Where to? Desolation on all sides. Reach habitation and you will likely be handed over. There is no need for guards. Indeed, their souls might be imperilled by service among us. Rather a lot of us to take refuge in some foreign vessel, and a few empty stations might indeed bring down guards, here and elsewhere. Believe it or not, there are worse lives to be led among the faithful."

"You are all men?"

"Yes." Triast regarded the mixed company before him. "Men are far more likely to offend than women. A couple condemned will always be parted, for *sin feeds on sin and turns from repentance.* The Bestower has other uses for women who fall from grace; service is needful in so many monasteries and chapters. It is, though, our choice, if a hard one. Equality of numbers, the provision of married quarters, these are out of reach. No place for children. My apologies if I offend, ladies, but I think you are old enough to imagine the fate of a small number among us. It is offered and rejected."

"You are not visited? Where does your food come from?"

"The steamer is with us for the season. The tanker comes twice a year. There is also another supply ship. We have a tiny garden for the bestowed. By land? Nearly never. Four day's march to the nearest approach to a track, and that washed away often enough by storms. A track that could sustain a bullock cart at most. Another three days to any habitation, and that worse than our own. It may have been abandoned, for none of us have been there in years."

Triast looked hard at the company.

"Have any of you, by chance, visited Eastland?" The captain and Ropuch nodded.

"You may know that they have ways of improving our ability to grow aboriginal plants that we can use. They even have ways to ferment the aboriginal so that it may be consumed, usually in liquid form. We learn. Alcohol is certainly a gift of the Bestower. Even the archpriests indulge."

"Are you not inspected?"

"In the most casual manner. Deliver the oil, that is all that matters. No priest on the steamer is going to disembark in such godless territory. A few hundred metres inland, and any other pious person will turn away. The Easties love our perfumed lamps. Fair trade is no robbery, so they say. Yours is not the first foreign vessel to anchor in our bay."

Educational, the captain had said. It most certainly was, thought Ropuch. They have learnt more here than in a week in High City and at Martyrs' Cove.

*****

The silence among the young as the *Golden Nodule* docked at Kindopol was one of shock. Here before them was a city so vast, with buildings so grand as to take the breath away. Twice the population of all the Far Outs put together. A city of gilded domes and fretted towers, over which there lay a haze of smoke from hearths, factories and workshops. A dockland with ten, no, more than ten great quays, each armed with massive cranes, and alive with activity.

It took Ropuch to give them a touch of insular pride.

"Take a look at the ships. Use the telescope. Regard the ensigns."

Sure enough, nearly half the ships bore the colours of Far Out fleets. There was Lofotor, Carrig, the Dark Isle. The largest, the smartest, of the vessels bore their colours. Others carried the flags of Eastland. The Kindlanders themselves were fewer, smaller, and decidedly scruffier. Only two Westerlanders were to be seen, the spread hands of the Bestower marking their origin.

There was no band to greet their arrival, but an assemblage of notables all too obviously aware of their status. There were speeches, largely inaudible to the bemused party still taking in the size and bustle of their surroundings. Some recognised the Far Out ambassador, Master Barkenwhitsson of Least Infolding, famous for having the longest name and the smallest domain in all the Far Outs.

"Always a problem," Duggor said to Ropuch. "All of us fear what will happen in our absence, and the Kindlanders would not take kindly to any lesser mortal, for all they sneer at our openly hereditary ways. Barko is able enough, and no one is going to make a grab for his island. Most of it is undisturbed abo. Octopods galore. Talk of milking them for poison arrows in the past."

To the resentment of the usual occupants, the wing of a student hostel had been cleared for their use. For Ropuch, the programme was both familiar and rather boring. The statutory visits: Congress, the Academy, a selection of Temples, the National Museum and Gallery. He was only too happy to hand over to Duggor and his assistants to deal with free days and the dangerous evenings and nights.

Dangerous they were, though not, Ropuch thought, in any mortal way. Outers were known for their appetite for fun. If their clothes did not betray them, their accents and mannerisms most certainly did. Wealthy with it, and certainly not mean, for pride would not allow it, even to the point of serious debt. A Tour meant five, six or more times as many young Outer nobility out on the town than normal; five or six times more naïve than the old hands as well.

At first, there were the usual problems: drunk and disorderly, a few mugged when they ventured a little too far from the major streets, a few indecent proposals. They soon learnt to roam in packs, unaware that the police kept up a discreet watch. International incidents were to avoided. It was Ropuch, not Duggor, who had to handle the most serious incident. It was in the Barol Temple, famed for its strict, fundamentalist faith in the Bestower, and the fiery rhetoric of its priests.

There was, of course, no service when Ropuch took them in. In a quiet voice, he pointed to its antiquity, one of the few buildings to be spared by the great sack of 2735; he directed their attention to the huge mosaic of Bestower the All-Powerful, probably made in the early 2000s. He barely noticed the priests and acolytes regarding the party with anger.

It was as they emerged, blinking, from the gloom of the interior into the bright sunshine of Deliverance Square, that the assault began. A crowd of acolytes jostled them, then started shouting, the shouts coalescing into a menacing chant.

"Consie Scum. Devil's disciples, Abo-lovers, Heretics."

A priest singled out Ropuch, grabbing him by his coat, glaring into his face, rage in his own.

"Desecration. Filth. The day is coming, Abo lover, the day is coming. Even Halfland will be no refuge."

The young were in confusion. Already accustomed to smiles and welcome wherever they went, they were slow off the mark. As Ropuch struggled to free himself from the spitting and now incoherent priest, however, he saw that the natural, self-confident aggression of aristocrats was asserting itself. Outnumbered they might be, but against the pasty-faced acolytes, they were dealing blows with enthusiasm. Three girls saw their tutor's predicament; as two dragged the priest away, the third delivered a kick that had the man curled up on the ground. The party now formed a phalanx that withdrew slowly from the Temple doors. Only when they were separated from their attackers by some distance did Ropuch realise that a crowd had gathered. Not only gathered, but already starting fights of their own. There was a riot.

His hopes of leading, or being led by his flock to safety were thwarted, for there was now the blare of police sirens and the blowing of many whistles. The scene changed rapidly as those in the crowd not caught and handcuffed by the police melted away into the streets leading from the square. Acolytes and priest had vanished into the Temple. The police did not lay hands on the Outers, but made it very clear that they were not to move. In the emptying square, an inspector approached them.

"A nice little international incident. Dr Ropuch, I presume. I take it you were showing your charges the Temple. A gaggle of Outers, in Barol. Petrol, matches and a child spring to mind. What in hell were you thinking of?"

"The temples are always open, Inspector. Many visit them for cultural reasons. I have visited it in the past, several times, with no problems. We were quiet and respectful. Only when we left were we assaulted by acolytes, even by a priest. Had we been asked to leave we would have done so at once. Unprovoked assault, Inspector."

Inspector Gornik just managed to avoid rolling his eyes.

"When were you last here, Dr Ropuch?"

"Twelve, no, thirteen years ago, Inspector."

"Things are just a little different now. What is the word? Oh yes, things are more polarised. Those sympathetic to a Westerland view of belief are more numerous, and more prone to violence. Those who fear that destruction of the aboriginal will harm us all, likewise."

"You mean Conservationist, I think. I am of that number, but I have never resorted to violence. A common enough view for us Outers, Inspector."

"No doubt. I hear that there are even reserves for your giant octopods. Those with such a view here show less self-control, though they are provoked in a way you Outers are not. As you have discovered."

The inspector looked over the crowd of young Outers. Dishevelled, yes, and a few bruises appearing. Nothing serious.

"Your opponents: any damage done beyond what you yourselves have suffered?"

"That priest, Mr Policeman," said Melie, who was the closest to Ropuch. "He was attacking Dr Ropuch. We dragged him off and gave him a kick, where it hurts. On the ground he was."

The inspector gave a long sigh. Trouble, and lots of it. He escorted the crowd to the Varden Street Station, where they crowded into the reception. Statements were taken and signed. He turned finally to Ropuch.

"You are all free to go. There are no charges. I think you will be leaving for the east in a few days? No harm in speeding it up if you can. When you return, I would recommend spending the nights on board. While you are here, I suggest you ask your embassy for a little guidance as to where not to go."

"No charges? I should damned well think not," said young Devo Denno. "What about those little bastards lying in wait for us, Inspector? Common assault where we come from."

"Welcome to Kindopol, young man," replied Gornik. "I did not follow them into the temple, and most will be long gone for a while. Barge in there on the word of an Outer, and there'd be more riots. Just suppose I arrest some. It might just as well be you, for they will all say the same thing, that you insulted the Bestower inside the Temple itself. They tried to make you leave. They were provoked. Either way, you'll be stuck in Kindopol to give evidence. Fifty-fifty what kind of magistrate you get. Even a Consie might not think it was open and shut. Verdict either way? More riots, even when the trial is underway. I think carrying with your tour is a better choice."

Another unplanned lesson, Ropuch reflected, and one more potent than the waffling of Kindland Seniors and the bloodless debates of Varrenians. A lesson for him too, upsetting the complacency of his previous visits. The next two days were spent mainly indoors, listening to the wisdom of Kindland scholars in many disciplines, before bags were packed for the next leg of the tour.

The train, a marvel indeed to islanders who had no need for such things. A train with twelve coaches, leaving from a station surely larger than any building at home. A train going, so Ropuch told them, at more than sixty kilometres an hour in places.

"One end of the continent to the other in less than four days, and that includes stops on the way. You'd need a racer like Denno's *Anasman Adventurer* to match it by sea; the norm is six or seven days with a cargo."

Their journey, however, was a few hours only, as they left the train at High Rehine, overlooking that strange and circular plain that was the Rehine Basin, the near legendary site of Bestowal, where Colonel and Doc had found the gifts bestowed upon our ancestors. The bright greens of field and forest alike contrasted vividly with the familiar grey-green hues of the low hills around.

"It is said that you cannot find an aboriginal plant anywhere in the basin," Ropuch told his charges. "Nor any animals, except for a few kinds of higgies that can eat Bestowed plants. There are trees here that we can grow nowhere else, however hard we work at conditioning the soil."

The two open-top coaches that carried them the fifteen kilometres across the basin made frequent stops and diversions. It was a working land, dotted with farms and vineyards, but also with shrines and attractions. A guide showed them the ruins of Old Rehine, only just preserved from clearance in the name of production. Tumbled walls surrounded now by neat lawns on which sheep grazed; sheep not reluctant to butt those who failed to deliver offerings to vary their diet. As the group wandered over the ruins, there was a cry of triumph.

"No abo plants? What is this then?" A handful of grey-green fronds was waved in the guide's face.

"Take a look around you, sir. What do you see?" The guide was amused rather than disconcerted.

"Just the ruins. And so?"

"Ruins made of stone. There are no rocks in the basin, at least down several metres. It is flat and unbroken below. Those stones were quarried at the edge, where there are small cliffs. Brought by bullock cart, we think, as timber buildings were replaced. Some maybe more than 2000 years ago. Excavated, they lack the soil that the aboriginal cannot stand. Wind and spores do the rest. We do not count what is found here."

He did not add that it was, nevertheless, an affront to the most ardent Bestowalists, and most notably to Westie pilgrims, Exterminators, who would set up camps to weed the site, while scouring the whole basin to destroy higgies. There had even been a petition to clear the site or to bury it again under soil from the basin.

The evening saw them taken in to the miniature city that was the pilgrim's centre at the northernmost point of the basin. Placed by necessity in a hostel that also held those ascending on their journey from Bounty Bay, they found an atmosphere akin to that of the Barol Temple. Pilgrims, from whichever continent, who had walked the hundred or so kilometres from the fabled landing place. They looked with hostility on the smartly dressed Outers, suspect for that alone, and the more so for perversely travelling in the wrong direction. Tourists, gawpers, in this holy place. It led to a change of plan.

"I've asked around," said Duggor. "There's a large party from High City staying several nights at the Doubter's Ravine, the Temple of Faith Restored. No knowing when they'll move on, but they are a pain in the backside to others already. We'll have a battle if we pass them, and no police to break it up. Bounty Bay is out, Ropuch."

"So, we must let the *Nodule* know. Where should Gerrichen make for?"

"Blenninge, surely, not Targon Port. Safely with the Easties. I'll see to it. You will have to get things sorted to travel by train, then the ferry to Blenninge."

An unsatisfactory journey. Ropuch had made all the arrangements for the outward journey to be from Bounty Bay to Blenninge in the *Nodule*. The train was to accommodate the return. Now, he and his charges were distributed among many carriages. Some could not travel the same day. The reassembly at Targon Port was spread over three days. His carefully prepared discourses on history, geology and biology were put away. The only gain, if such it could be called, was a heightened if arrogant patriotism among the party. He was forced to turn to the Consulate at Targon.

"All this rearrangement, Consul. I have exhausted my credit and my cash. Without help, we must summon the *Nodule* from Blenninge and head straight for home. Kindland is not what it was."

"Your misadventures are known, Dr Ropuch."

The consul handed him copies of the most Ultra Kindland pops. The incident at Barol was still reverberating, and the retreat from Rehine hailed as a victory for piety and decency.

"Westies have been busy, as have their friends here. We cannot allow them a victory. You will cross to Blenninge, and go on to Varden. Easties will be more accommodating. You will lead everyone up Kolumba. There will be a reporter with you. The expenses have been arranged, Dr Ropuch."

"And the return?"

"To Kindopol direct from Varden. The captain will be given orders there."

As the consul had said, Eastland was altogether easier. The ancient linkages, down to the discovery and colonisation of the Far Outs by Easties more than 1500 years ago, made for a common, sceptical culture. Varden might be half the size of Kindopol, but it had several times the number of Outer expatriates. The train took them to the *Wild East,* the domain of nodule prospectors and giant octopods; the realm of landscapes and rocks that had a familiar feel. Photo after photo of all at the summit of Kolumba, the highest peak in all the lands.

It was with sadness, but a sense of pride that they waved to friends on shore as the *Nodule* left the docks at Varden, down the sheltered Founder's Sea to the open ocean.

*****

The second stay at Kindopol was brief and frustrating. There had been riots. Easties and Outers were attacked on the streets. Factions in the Kindland Congress were shouting across the hallowed Hall of Assembly. They were confined to the ship, and the dockside was thick with police. Gerrichen had been summoned to the embassy, accompanied by police. His return was unsettling.

"We are to leave at dawn, since we have taken fuel on board. We are to take the northern passage. There will be an escort, an Eastlander with several guns. We are likely to be intercepted."

"Why not the southern passage? And I take it that a visit to Martyr's Cove and High City is impossible?"

"Certainly impossible. It is not just the rabble, but the authorities themselves. You would become hostages without doubt. And as to the south, both Denno and Ombro are agreed: it is one thing not to walk into a trap. It is another to let the bastards think they rule the seas. We are to engage if challenged. The point of danger will be Martyr's Cove, the only decent port they have in the north."

Leaving port, the day was taken up with lifeboat drills. The gun was uncovered, and crew engaged in firing practice. The Eastlander escort stayed close, guns fore and aft prepared for action, then covered. As darkness fell, both ships travelled without lights, veering northwards to avoid a small ship moving east, a Westie headed for Westport or Kindopol.

Morning came. Reefs and shallows way offshore confined them to the grim Westerland coast. It was afternoon when they passed the mouth of Martyr's Cove. Two small craft moved out, approaching them at speed. To Ropuch's surprise, the *Nodule* and the Eastlander slowed. One of the two approached closely, within hailing distance.

"Heave to. These are our waters. Inspection will take place. You are to come to the Cove."

"This is the open sea, God botherer. Take a look behind you."

The Eastlander had uncovered its guns. A single shot raised a column of water 50 metres behind the second Westie ship. The *Nodule* gathered speed. For a while, the Westie kept pace, its captain undecided. A second shot from the Eastlander showered the deck of the second Westie. It turned away to escape.

A crowd suddenly appeared on the deck of the *Nodule.* There were jeers, and then forty arses were bared in contempt, while the ship's gun lowered to point at the Westie's waterline. The Eastlander was rapidly approaching the Westie's other side. There were no further exchanges; the Westie slowed while the convoy sailed on.

"More education, Dr Ropuch," said Gerrichen, dryly. "But next time, it would be as well if the young stayed below. Bullets and backsides are a bad combination."

2. The Policeman

Maccan Gornik was going to be a policeman. It was not that he was compelled, nor that he had made any definitive choice at an early age. Nevertheless, only a juvenile crime or terminal stupidity could have broken the delicate web spun by his mother. An only child, the product of a late and, in retrospect, a very odd marriage, he could see from the perspective of maturity the way his mother's ambition had been achieved, and, more significantly, why.

Home, a small town some thirty kilometres from the capital. Father, a bureaucrat, a humble one at that, a man of few words, whose post raised him only slightly higher than the shopkeepers, factory workers and farming families that made up most of the town's inhabitants. His mother, though, was something else; extravert to a degree, flamboyant in both dress and manner. As he grew, he detected the mix of envy and disapproval with which neighbours, women especially, regarded her. She held no regular job, but the income she brought in enabled the family to live in a style that matched that of the small coterie of professional people that the town supported.

The match in material things did not extend to membership of any social circle. Not that she was in any evident way ostracised. Her parties, from which her husband usually absented himself, attracted the young and the incomers, both alike bored by the mundane, prying character of the place. He learnt, soon enough, that her income came as royalties, earnings from the numerous books she had written. Books that he was not allowed to read until just before his departure, but books that had circulated among those older than him.

"Quite a goer, your mother," he was told, as he was shown lurid covers and had short, tantalising extracts read out to him. In a strange way, his status was enhanced by the whiff of scandal. Published under a pseudonym and advertised as romances, their contents were calculated to stir rather more than true love and a happy ever after marriage in domestic bliss.

It was only after he had left for the big city, first on a scholarship, then as a cadet in the Police College, that he had come to realise just how constrained was life at home, and how odd it was that his mother had settled to it with a degree of relish. For even this close to the great metropolis, life revolved around the agricultural. There was, of course, the combined fertiliser and decontaminant factory, the principal employer in the town itself. There were the minor trades that the mixture of aboriginal scrubland and hard-won fields around the town needed, and the many farmers that worked those fields. It was a town, and a way of life, replicated across the western plains of Kindland.

Replicated? Not quite. The town held a penal colony, the inmates of which were put to work on clearance and decontamination in the particularly tenacious aboriginal wastes close to the town. The guards that managed it were a common sight in the town's shops, and the most regular attenders at the Bestowalist Temple, a place studiously avoided by both his parents. Few of these guards were born and raised locally, and many came complete with families. Those that married in almost always chose brides from among the most assiduously Bestie families.

The colony was a low-level irritant to the community. Even as a small child, he had picked up that Guardie children were both ostracised by others and clannish among themselves. They were poor learners for the most part. Only later, when forced to listen to lectures in the Social Mechanics sessions, had he been told, reprovingly, that the teachers, overwhelmingly Evolutionist and often Consie in sympathy, had created a vicious circle of low expectations and low achievement. Even then the instructor herself had recited the 'theory' with a sardonic air, and his later experiences had led him to rather different conclusions.

The town differed from others in another way. It was close to the city. Poorer than many, the lure of work in the metropolis, even of a parasitic, scrounging and criminal existence was too great for some to resist. There would at least be excitement and opportunities, not dull, predictable respectability. Even the return of a few as convicts, and the shame it brought to their families, failed to stem the trickle of rebellious young who simply disappeared one day. There were always the stories of those who had prospered, who had sent money or gifts back to their parents. Stories, just that. No smartly dressed absconder ever drove up in his own motor to shower gifts on the family.

He was clever enough to warrant a scholarship in the city, but, as with others of the same ability, the costs of accommodation deterred most. It had been his mother who had seen to the matter, and more besides. There were visits to the city, visits never joined by his father, visits on which he was introduced to the many contacts she seemed to possess. All men, and mostly men of wealth and importance. He was coached before each interview; interviews, he realised, because he was on show, though to what end was obscure.

Mother had female friends too, but these were very different. Unmarried women, usually living together in houses rather far from the most fashionable districts. Women who addressed his mother as Auntie, women who discreetly withdrew when she received some of her contacts in a downstairs room, putting him in front of them for inspection. But when they stayed overnight, it was always in one of the rather shabby but comfortable hotels near the docks, never in the women's houses, though they had rooms to spare. Foreigners were among the other guests there, and he learnt to recognise both the clothing and accents associated with each of the other three nations.

It did not take him long to realise the nature of the relationships involved, but it was only when he was about to depart on his own to take up his scholarship that his mother had been completely open with him. Another auntie, *very much retired, dear,* was to be his landlady; in practice, she had been a surrogate mother. An auntie who had a husband whose occupation remained obscure for the whole of his stay with them, though he was out, somewhere, in daylight hours.

Auntie Gemna had shaped what might pass for his political opinions, and had explained the whys and wherefores of his mother's apparent exile.

"Your mother ran an honest business, Maccan. As did I. You don't have to approve, though it's thanks to her that you have a chance to escape that cursed backwater for good."

To the obvious questions as to why she had, as Gemna put it, retired to such a backwater, married a stolid but respectable man, *Yes Maccan, of course he is your real father, never doubt it,* and lived in what to his now opening eyes was poverty when contrasted with Aunt Gemna's life and housing, he got a story of blackmail and even a murder.

"One of her girls thought to be clever. The Besties got wind of a client's, a Consie client's interests. Asked around the Houses. Silly cow tried to touch him to keep her mouth shut. Next morning, her body in the river, and the pops making hay. That killed the house stone dead, Maccan. She did the decent thing by the girls, and that's why she was left with nothing. Your father? She responded to lonely hearts ads. Plenty of those from the sticks wanting a wife, just as many girls in the back of beyond would rather work for the likes of me than be stuck there forever. He was not the first one she interviewed."

He had believed it. Quiet though his father was, dull, almost, when set against his mother, he had never had reason to doubt the affection between his parents. The late marriage, and no brothers or sisters fell into place. The rather explicit nature of some of his mother's novels was also explained. His furtive readings had presented a sharp contrast with anything he could imagine in his parents' bedroom.

*****

Two years in senior school. Aunt Gemna had impressed on him the rare opportunity that his mother had obtained by calling in old favours. Varren School, the most famous, the most elite school in Kindland; arguably, therefore, at the summit in the whole inhabited world. The great families of the capital were represented, along with those who had gained scholarships on merit alone (rare), or, like him, by the kind of influence that money, power or return of favours conferred (the majority).

From king pin in his hometown school, he had found himself well in the lower half of attainment. No dunce, certainly, but keeping up required hard work and a lot of it, work over which Aunt Gemna exercised a fierce discipline. There was no subject at which he shone, and none that attracted him to a particular specialism. There were openings to be had in public service, service that promised, in the words of the pompous principal, *positions of considerable emolument.* These, though, necessitated both a formal academic education and a network of contacts in high places. He lacked the ability, or at least the enthusiasm, for the former, and both his mother and Aunt Gemna had steered him away from such thoughts. She had been frank.

"Your mother would not spell it out, Maccan. The bottom rungs are open to talent, but you need more than that to go higher. Connections of the kind she has tapped to get you here are not enough. Family is all. At best, the able are shipped out to manage some town or province at the back of beyond. Well-paid, certainly, but a lonely life, and a dull one."

Dull was the ultimate word of condemnation for both women. But he was hard put to it to think of a career that would match his abilities. Technical matters bored him, and the prospect of teaching ceased to appeal as he came to realise that of all professions, it was the most politically polarised. His junior school had indeed been run by Consies. Others, especially in the city, were equally Bestie oriented. Those lacking a predominant view were repeatedly in the pops over rioting, strikes and court cases over dismissal or suspension.

His distaste for such squabbles was reinforced at Varren. There was an atmosphere of disdain, carefully cultivated, for the increasing strife in the wider world. Bestie and Consie? Games for children of little brain, ladies and gentlemen, we deal in the practicalities of leadership. To believe in the Bestowal: fine, as was the opposite Evolutionist position. To argue the case, even to hear leading advocates debate before them? Most certainly, provided such people were known for their scholarly approach, and had not sullied their reputation with political agitation. What is beyond proof has little to do with practicalities. Debate with wit, ladies and gentlemen, not passion. Enthusiasm, other than in matters of sport, was not an emotion to be encouraged.

To his surprise, this was an approach heartily endorsed by Aunt Gemna, and indeed by all her friends and neighbours he encountered. Their language was more direct.

"Bloody shit-stirrers, the lot of them, Turn the place into a howling desert or have us in enclosures to save the grey-greens. Time they were sorted out up top, and stop the hooligans messing us about."

There were other mutterings about the crazies who would kill us all; about honest folk prevented from going about their business. This last did cause him some amusement, carefully concealed. It was the underworld who most resented the disruption and police raids that followed. The genuinely honest, the families hit by the periodic rises in food prices, were those most likely to adopt passionate beliefs in both directions. Prey for the demagogues that his teachers and fellow pupils regarded with contempt. Not, he noted, that it prevented the parents of some with famous names from fitting the description rather neatly. Scholarship boys and girls should keep their heads down.

As the end of schooldays approached, he was uncertain where to turn for his future. Able enough, but aimless, was the view of tutors and careers advisors. It was what seemed a chance meeting with a police inspector at Aunt Gemna's house that shifted his mood. A meeting that, unknown to him, had been planned and timed by Gemna and his mother. The Houses had a network of their own. Their trade was not illegal, but linked inevitably with those that were. Some clients were less than welcome, and some needed removal. Times past, and networks of criminals had held the Houses to ransom in the name of *services rendered*. Networks who had fought among themselves, while at the same time involving the police in unwanted raids. Gemna and his mother had broken the system by a direct alliance with the police. *Keep it in the family* had been a private joke between them when considering his future.

Then the Police College. By schooling and examination record, he was way beyond the norm. A fact that brought a degree of suspicion from fellow cadets, but which a quick wit and amiable character quickly diminished. Certainly, he had the same basic training, the same bruises when taking part in raids and arrests under supervision. It was not long, though, before he found himself, with a few others, selected for more specialist roles, roles that required brain rather than brawn.

It was public order that concerned the Seniors and Congress. Not the mere suppression of riots, but the networks of intelligence that neutralised the collections of madmen, agitators and extremists on either side who were at the root of troubles that threatened the civil order. His unacknowledged connections to Houses, and to the networks they maintained was the path by which he had found himself moving through the ranks at a speed that would have attracted more than a little resentment had he been among colleagues confined to more conventional duties.

It had not been easy. An early triumph, the arrest of a cell of Consies, planning to bomb decontaminant factories, had given him his first taste of killing. As the smoke cleared in the cellar where it had been kill or be killed, the bodies around him were mere kids. A girl summoned the last of her breath to spit defiance. The waste appalled him, and anger at the people who had recruited these innocents. It had not ended there. Others had traced the leak to a House. It had been fire-bombed in revenge. No deaths, but disfigurements and disabilities resulted. Some very unofficial conversations with Auntie Gemna had followed.

"Another like that," she had said, "and they'll all clam up. You have to be smarter, Maccan. At least three steps way from any of us, and protection if there is even a whisper of a connection."

It had turned his mind to the forensic arts, to evidence that did not rely on witness statements. As an inspector, he had developed a team of specialists. His search for irrefutable evidence did not always find favour: *A spot of terror would work wonders, Gornik, and a few less of the scum would please us all.* Nor did his sheltering of the Houses find favour with all. Politics did not divide neatly along Bestowalist or Evolutionist, but among the former, the profusion of Houses and a reluctance to breed were linked. The demands his unit made on police budgets did not go unnoticed.

His career seemed to be stalling. There were hints from on high to postings elsewhere, elsewhere where theft, rape and the occasional psychopathic or jealousy-inspired murder were the bread and butter of police work. It took the Eastland question to make his name and put him beyond risk.

Eastlanders were an easy-going lot, unlike the famously puritanical Westerlanders. In many ways, they had more in common with the wild Outies. They were few in number, for Kindopol was at the western end of Kindland, two thousand kilometres from the nearest Eastland shore. Those few comprised diplomats and those seconded for purposes of trade. They seldom stayed for more than a couple of years. As clients of the Houses, they were highly esteemed: *generous, fun, nothing too kinky, not like those Westie weirdos* as Gemna had put it. The worst that could be said, from a police perspective, was the issue of the merrily drunk who were robbed on their way home, a routine matter that Gornik could leave to others. Even the embassy was good-natured about bailing out its more foolish citizens.

Behaviour in the bedroom was matched by the political stance taken by Eastland. Reclamation? One step at a time. The country had far less of a problem with food supply than others. An underlying Evolutionist culture had led to investment in the slow business of selecting aboriginal plants to find palatable strains, an approach which earned them the disgust of both the most fervent Besties and the hardest Consies. Easties actually ate some of this stuff! Even in Kindopol, such items were imported only under restrictive licence; in Westerland, possession was a criminal offence. Easties had also discovered abo plants that, in small, carefully prepared doses, had some extremely interesting psychological effects. Although not notably addictive, their use merited the death penalty in Westerland. The entrepreneurs involved were largely ignored in Kindopol, much to the disgust of the Westerland government; just one of many grievances that accumulated.

It was Gemna who began picking up little stories from the aunties still in business. A few rather unlikely partygoers among the roistering Eastlanders; some rather persistent questions about Eastlanders' habits. She had been stern with Gornik.

"There's something up, Maccan. I have no idea what, but it smells. You're to get it sorted, and sorted without dragging us in. A massacre of Easties on our turf, or a House burnt down again, and there's some that will be back to the old ways."

And worse, as she did not have to tell him. Have the Houses associated with disorder, and there would be pressure to close them down. He did, at least, get some names. Some were false, of course, and it required shadowing some back to their homes. Others, less astute, were known members of Bestie congregations, congregations known for their extremist preachers. They moved around, and their contacts were added to the list. Gornik's office pinboards became a mass of names, places, dates and connections. His sergeants became frustrated. Mere suspicion was enough for a series of raids, the more so as some of the movements and contacts were manifestly surreptitious.

"We've got a whole set of idiot Bestie plotters, sir. Time to give them a seeing to, surely?"

"And if we find nothing, Sergeant, or just the usual tracts and the odd pistol and cudgel? A mass of bleating in the pops, questions in Congress, police brutality, religious discrimination? Don't you think it's all a bit too obvious? Not only that; the source of our information will be obvious too. I'm thinking we were meant to find all this out, Sergeant. You said it: idiot Besties. But there's someone with more brains behind it. Just go on keeping them watched."

Just a Bestie scheme to provoke him, he wondered. To provoke him and to end the protection of the Houses? Eastlanders a target? A fine fool he would look if there was no evidence of an attack in planning. He looked for the hundredth time at the maze of cards, coloured ribbons and pinned comments on the board. This time, a pattern emerged. Overwhelmingly, those identified attended one or more of five temples known for their fundamentalism. Just three attended the Barol Temple in Deliverance Square. It was known to him only for that Outie incident; not otherwise a nest of troublemakers. Between them, though, those three had visited all the others, often several times. Always openly, always in daylight, along with many who shopped around for the most invigorating sermons. He gave a small grunt of satisfaction; it was not only his sergeants who had resented the round the clock watch and the tracking of all visitors.

He inquired. *Very respectable. Even Congressmen attend it. Westerland bigwigs too, because it's pretty Ultra.* Certainly not a place to raid on suspicion, not that there was any reason to, nor did it seem that he was being provoked into it. Why not, he wondered? A raid there, and not only would his career be over, but the political outcry would shift things in the Bestie direction. His next moves caused his squad to mutter about his sanity.

"Ease off on the others, but play it clumsy. Be seen to be watching, but not too obviously. Halve the manpower, don't bother with daylight. Barol: not just those three. Anyone except the top drawer, I don't want a Congressman find he's being watched; not yet, anyway."

Weeks passed. Nothing happened. Even Sergeant Nikkon came round to Gornik's way of thinking.

"They're getting more and more blatant, sir. We've had cheek from a few who've spotted some of ours. We've given a few slaps, and they've acted disappointed. They want us to come down heavy."

Barol was more interesting. Fully a quarter of the congregation were Westerlanders. Further, in the name of charity, the temple ran a shelter for the homeless, those nearest to starvation. Among the desperate, deluded and often drugged-up residents, Westerland preachers won many converts. Gornik set up a watch. It was frustrating, for the rules were strict; few residents got to leave. No trouble that would justify a raid or interrogation took place. He was wondering how to plant an insider when he had a lucky break. He was told about Daft Jimmy.

"Here's a thing sir. Jimmy is a street food guy, with his little wagon. Bit simple, but honest with it; most of us have bought off him as we come off duty. He got robbed last week, and the bastards smashed the wagon too. Gave him a bit of tea and sympathy, patched him up. Hysterical, he was. That shelter had agreed to sell him supplies at prices he could not believe. *I'm fucked. It was the best deal I'd had in ages. No wagon, no business. Next thing, I'll be in that shelter for life. Or starve.*"

Gornik frowned. Street sellers had a precarious life. The police tried to catch the robbers, of course, but it was usually a lost cause. Victims were beyond police assistance.

"He was back in three days, sir. Full of the joys, and full of praise for Barol. Spanking new waggon supplied by them. But he was up and down High Avenue, not his usual haunts, and not a place you'd think would get him much trade. Didn't seem to bother him. They told him it would build, and the bigwigs and foreigners would take to him in time. Get in their face, and they'll make a joke of it, he was told."

High Avenue, where the big businesses had their offices; where the three embassies occupied stretches of the road; where diplomats condescended to walk with their entourages to the People's Palace at the end. And where the easy-going Eastlanders never took a motor or carriage. He called the Congressional offices. Big events, ceremonial events? Certainly, Inspector, they all troop up for the opening of Congress in their costumes.

It was but a few days away. His men noticed that the Eastlanders passing by were among Jimmy's best customers. Westies disdained his offerings. For certain, glad rags notwithstanding, the whole troop would gather round Jimmy to joke if not to buy on their way up the hill. *A big bang*, thought Gornik, and a bigger one as the consequences were felt. The question was how they would trigger the fateful blast, and how could he prevent it? Was Jimmy to be told to open up some section, specialities for selected customers, or was there a watcher able to transmit some radio message at the right time? The latter, and it would be his own men and passers-by that were blown away when Jimmy was intercepted.

The day came. Jimmy turned up at the refuge to collect his wagon. It was not long before he was in High Avenue. Parked a few houses up from the embassy, he did an intermittent trade with passers-by and those loitering to see the show. Just before eleven, the embassy doors opened, and a crowd emerged to cheers, jeers and catcalls from onlookers, to which there was the traditional Eastie response of bows, grins and the waving of feathered hats. Jimmy grasped his handles and moved towards them. He was halted by a shabbily-dressed man shouting at him that he had been swindled.

Gornik was not known by Jimmy, who struggled to move on, cursing his assailant. Gornik brought him down. Police rushed to engage and remove both; others emerged from the crowd, forming a barrier through which they firmly refused to let the diplomats pass. Others cleared the road downhill. Leaving a cursing Jimmy in the hands of two of his men, Gornik dodged behind two others and shed the coat that he had worn over his uniform. He walked to the line behind which the diplomats were showing signs of confusion and anger. He recognised the ambassador himself.

"My apologies, Your Excellency. Could I ask you to cross the road until you are past this little scene? We need to examine the vendor's goods."

"Very well, Inspector. We all have a great regard for Mr Jimmy. I trust that justice will be done, and that he will not be a victim of a false accusation, if that is what has happened. We will certainly stand bail if it is necessary."

The ambassador stared hard at Gornik, who was sweating and shaking.

"You will let us know the outcome, Inspector, won't you?"

Gornik nodded. The embassy crowd crossed over and made their way uphill, followed by most of the crowd. Behind a now complete cordon, clearing a space thirty metres across around the wagon, he let out a sigh. No radio signal, then. He turned to Jimmy, still restrained by two officers. Jimmy recognised his assailant's uniform, and calmed down.

"Bloody hell, Inspector, what did you do that for? Any policemen, they get the best bargains. You had a problem, you only had to ask. I've lost the best trade of the day with that lot; they tip as much as they pay."

"Tell me, Jimmy, did you have something special for the Easties, something you would dig out of a special compartment?"

Jimmy looked at Gornik in amazement.

"How the hell? Yes, Inspector. Never seen the like. Sealed compartment, Hot specials inside. Pull the lever and it opens up. Eastie delicacies, they told me. They looked good too. Pull the lever when you have their attention, not before, keeps them hot that way. I don't think there's a wagon like it in the city."

"You are right there, Jimmy. Pull that lever today and you would be shaking the hand of the great Bestower, along with some very distinguished company."

Jimmy went pale. Gornik turned to his men. *Get this man somewhere safe, spoil him rotten, but don't let him leave. He's dead meat if he's found.* Then orders: himself in the shafts and an escort a fair distance in all directions, he pulled the wagon into Havering Park. An army man was with him soon. One side off the wagon, and he ordered all at least fifty metres clear. Material was removed, placed in boxes and carried away.

"At least five kilos of the real stuff, Inspector, and another two or three of nails, nuts and bolts around them. As well for you that the lever needed a bit of force; they would not want it to go off on any bump in the road. I wonder where they got hold of it?"

*****

It had made his name. Hero Gornik to the pops; expressions of love and friendship for our Eastie brothers, solemn warnings about the rise of extremism. Even Westerland sent its congratulations. Promotion, a medal and an expanded unit followed fast. For now, at least, his position was secure. No one could doubt the importance of his work. Somehow, though, the full details were never revealed. Jimmy was said to have acted on his own, or with some cell of madmen. He was said to have committed suicide. The connection with the refuge and most of all with Barol were never revealed. In the outcry, the notional Bestie provocations quietly ceased. The mood was not going to be tolerant, for all knew that a blow against Eastland would be down to Besties, Besties and their Westerland allies. Nor, for all the smug satisfaction and blaring editorials, could Consies claim Gornik as their own when his early experiences were brought again to public attention.

The warmest congratulations came from the Houses. Strictly in private, of course. No hint of involvement attached to them. Just good police work, that was the universal story, and the probing of clients subsided. Gemna held a very special party, at which his mother appeared.

The outward show of a job well done, of the foiling of an insane plot, the product of disordered, pale fanatics no doubt living in cellars, disguised the concern that it caused at the very top. The easiest problems were solved by Gornik himself. Accompanied by an officer, getting on in years, but apparently uncomfortable in his uniform, his visit to the Eastland embassy to receive the official thanks of the nation was not as outsiders might imagine. Closeted with the ambassador and his closest aide, the elderly officer was formally introduced.

"Your Excellency, this is Mr Jimmy. I know you have met him in rather different circumstances. As we have told you, we are completely sure of his innocence. He is anxious to become an Eastlander."

Jimmy remained silent. It had taken a while to get him to realise that life in Kindopol was no longer possible. It had been very hard to coach him in a story as to how he had come by the lethal wagon. Gornik doubted it would hold for long, but let him at least be out of the country when it broke. The Eastlanders, many of them, had swallowed the story that he was one of a band filled with hatred for their country.

"Welcome to Eastland, Mr Jimmy," said the ambassador, extending his hand. "You are already on Eastland soil, and you are now a citizen. We will be taking you home shortly, and I can promise a better life and occupation when you arrive."

Jimmy looked blank. He was led away by the aide, leaving Gornik alone with the ambassador, who regarded the Chief Inspector with an air of sardonic amusement.

"I wonder, Chief Inspector, if you have found the rogues who commandeered poor Jimmy to do their dread work? These miserable plotters hiding in cellars? It was a remarkable achievement to have foiled the plot, yet failed to find its instigators. I gather Mr Jimmy was remarkably vague about the matter."

Gornik kept his face immobile. "Good police work, Your Excellency, nothing more. We naturally regard the safety of embassies as essential, and any odd behaviour near them attracts our attention. Jimmy is easily confused."

"If you say so. I am an amateur in these matters, of course, but I would have thought that the sophistication of the device alone might prompt the thought that it was planned by those with rather higher standing than a bunch of deluded extremists."

"You may be right, Your Excellency, but I have no evidence to support or refute the idea. Be assured, though, that we monitor known agitators very closely. You will admit that on this occasion we did our job."

"Indeed, indeed. Pardon my curiosity. You are here to be thanked and honoured, not subject to impertinent questions from civilians. A reception awaits you downstairs."

The ambassador gestured him to the door. As Gornik passed, he saw a wide grin on the man's face. A grin followed by a silent mouthing that surely said *Barol.* The man knows very well what happened. It is in no one's interest to acknowledge it. And why else would they be so willing to acknowledge Jimmy's innocence?

Dealing with his own superiors was a much tougher proposition. The High Commissioner had been reasonable. The evidence was laid out with a degree of editing to save the sources of information from the Houses. But Barol, the refuge, and the distractions in the various temples, all could be laid out. Notionally neutral, as his post required, the man was a known Bestowalist, though of the very abstract, theological kind. He had no time for those who sought the destruction of all things aboriginal. His loathing of Consies, though, was legendary, showing mainly by his profanity when those the police had apprehended were let off with light sentences. *What are those damned penal colonies for* would echo round headquarters when he got hold of the pops. So, naturally, he had tried to find a Consie angle.

"Don't you see, Gornik, what the game is? Murder a whole lot of Easties and stir up anti-Bestowalist feelings. Why would Barol or the Westerlanders want to do that? Is there no trace of Consies here? What about that refuge? Full of nutters of all persuasions, no doubt."

Gornik had not argued. Instead, he simply reiterated the evidence, in which Consies did not feature. The same idea had indeed occurred to him. The murders would certainly have poisoned relationships with Eastland, but might also have led to a purge of Besties, something they were clearly trying to provoke. Just upping the temperature? Some devious Westerland scheme? For all the glory now heaped on him, he felt a desire to be a simple sergeant in the remotest of all the Far Out islands.

His promotion and the wider responsibilities that went with it brought him to the attention of the Seniority for Security and a Congressional Committee, attention that strengthened that desire. Madam Senior, Almata Storr, had a fierce reputation for tough sentencing, to which the High Commissioner owed his promotion. She had no time for the nonsense of the extremes, but her peculiarity was a pronounced dislike of foreigners. Ambassadors, she had to admit, were a necessity, but the size of their staffs and the numerous foreign merchants and students were a constant source of annoyance.

Gornik's past and present roles caused her no worries. But in the short interview she gave him, she was probing again and again for evidence of foreign involvement. Westerland were clearly into the events, deeply in. Gornik, while agreeing with her, was obliged to admit lack of evidence, even against the merchants and executives that offered easier targets than the diplomats. She railed about Easties too, though with a certain lack of conviction.

"Degenerates, Chief Inspector, as you know very well. In and out your cells after drunken brawls, and if they were gone, half your precious whorehouses would be out of business. Oh, I know about all these cosy little arrangements. I could lay hands on your mother if I wished. Less said the better about how she earns her living."

He had stayed silent. All knew that her real animus was against Westerlanders, but that military necessity required a degree of caution in dealing with them. Her own spies were not up to much, and what little information they provided was pitiful when compared to police dossiers. She could only confirm his appointment, extracting only the concession that any foreign involvement in crime would be relayed to her office. He left with a sense of increased confidence. So long as police were seen to be on top, he was safe, as was she.

The Congressional Committee was a very different matter. For the first time, he was exposed to the whole range of views among his rulers. There was no prospect of them refusing to make the appropriations necessary for his new role. Hero Gornik was, for a while at least, the darling of the pops. Congressmen and women had queued up to be photographed with him. They could and did use his interrogation to launch attacks on each other, all the while calling on him to support their positions. These strayed wildly from the public order and anti-subversion mission with which he was charged. To each of the wilder schemes, he was obliged to give a non-committal answer. *We could do that, sir, but if we did then... Yes madam, you are right, but bear in mind that...* Sympathy moderated by technical or professional concerns, but with the sense that his answers were almost beside the point.

He left the meeting with a deep unease, but renewed determination. Any major incident, like the one he had just averted, and the extremes would pounce, only too willing to use it to their advantage. Just one succeeding, and there would be bloodshed. Even, as he realised, the possibility of war, war with Westerland, a nation seething with discontent and more xenophobic than anything that Madam Senior could manage. The Great War, the burning of their capital before the invaders were finally expelled, was embedded in the national consciousness.

3. The Expedition

Platform six at Grand Central Station was a scene of confusion. The regular passengers for the express train that would traverse Kindland were inconvenienced, if not downright jostled by the crowds around a single carriage. Bestie demonstrators had broken past the barriers; they were held back with difficulty by the police. Their shouting drowned out the speeches and farewells that accompanied the crowd around the carriage. There were parents, husbands, wives, lovers, bidding goodbye to the select few that entered the carriage. There were civic dignitaries and reporters too, and even Professor Hochast himself.

The whistle blew, but the train moved only a few metres. Those on the platform could see police running to the front. Then scuffles as two women dressed in the drab clothing of the Inheritance League were hauled off the tracks and carried away to the exit. The train started again. Soon, it was gone from the station, and the crowds dispersed, not entirely without further jostling and shouting.

Professor Galla Hort leant back in her seat. As the train rumbled towards the edge of the city, she smiled at her two companions, Tommo Galen, the geologist, and her ecologist colleague Becca Gronlow. Both were still rather stunned by the reception.

"Now you know what an expedition, a Hort expedition, entails. A bit different to setting out on your own, isn't it?"

"That delay, Professor; were there Besties on the track?" asked Tommo.

"We couldn't see, could we? But, yes, almost certainly. The police warned me it might happen. Damned Heritancers. They'd been tipped off. I was afraid there would be dozens of them. It gets worse each time. I'm always afraid the railway will refuse us one day, and it will be a bus and a convoy all the way. Take twice as long, and we would have to leave in secret, probably at dawn."

She left them for a while, and walked down the corridor. The coach had been specially fitted. A single compartment at the end contained two policemen, men who would change at each major station. Two more, one for the five young researchers, another for three technicians. Their own, then a larger area, three combined into an approximate dining car and kitchen. Toilets and washrooms, and finally compartments from which the seats had been taken, full of their gear and supplies. Connecting doors to carriages in front and behind were locked and bolted.

A Hort expedition in all its splendour. They were famous way beyond the Departments of Biology and Geology from which she recruited a select few each time. Expeditions that took years of planning and cost far more than any Departmental or even the Institute's funds could support. Congressional funds might come her way, but only after angry debates, and not always then; Bestowalists might dominate a committee. Increasingly, she had come to depend on the fundraising abilities of numerous Conservationist Societies. A problematic source, she was soon forced to recognise, as it cast doubts on her independence.

This one was a monster, downright heroic, for they were bound for the narrow, windswept, far east of Eastland itself, at least 5000 km away. A place scarcely touched, aboriginal to the core; a place also where there had been tremors, and where land was said to have sunk here and risen there. A place that interested her Eastland colleagues too, a saving grace, for they had provided funds to stretch her budget and military help to establish a base, a base more than 160 km from the nearest village.

She returned to the compartment. Becca was telling Tommo of her brief visit to Eastland, only to Varden and the west.

"You'll like it, Tom. They're fun, provided you don't rise to a bit of ribbing. They mock us for all the earnestness and Bestie and Consie stuff. They'll add abo food to your meals, and tell you afterwards. Some of our lot dash to the toilet or go green, but it does you no harm."

"A bit different to Westerland then," he replied. Visitors to that dour country were few, and most needed not only elaborate visas and registration, but a letter of recommendation from a reputable Bestowalist Temple. "I got the work done, and there were some good guys among the geologists. Catch you doing anything with aboriginal plants, though, and things turn nasty. At least that's what I was told. Petro Daedon died. Did you hear about it? An accident, it was said, but in my crowd, they said it in a funny way. They did not let me out on my own. You need looking after, they said. I didn't argue. Glad to get home."

"Did you get your letter, Tommo?" asked Hort. "I'd never be allowed, and if they found me, I'd probably be stoned if it was in a village. I had to go all the way by sea when I went to the Far Outs."

"No. Two years regular attendance at a Temple and their catechism was more than I could stand. There was some kind of exchange between the Academies. I got a letter from a Bestie neighbour attesting to my good behaviour. I've changed a bit since."

They all laughed. Tommo had returned from Westerland a raging Consie. His own professor had told him to ease off or risk expulsion.

The journey across Kindland, a journey they had all made in whole or in part, dragged by. Most of the west was flat; small towns, areas of crops and fields of cows passed by, separated by large areas of aboriginal scrub. The effects of inexpert clearance were all too obvious. Aboriginal cover removed, but little growing in its place. Only the flatness of the terrain had prevented massive erosion. They passed through two ranges of low, rounded hills. A few larger towns, and more frequent stops here, where there was mining, and even the extraction of oils from aboriginal deposits. Here, they encountered the toxic mists that these works produced, mists that left eastward trending swathes of sterile ground.

"Swamps once; there are still arguments about how old they are. But they got covered, and that must have been the sea. Things rose up later. No doubt the Bestower arranged it for our benefit." Tommo's tone was beyond sarcastic.

More grey-green lands beyond, and precious few signs of humanity. The east lands were desolate, nearly to the coast. Only in the morning of the third day out did things change, as they approached the hilly region along the final coast. There were towns, large areas of bestowed vegetation and many roads. Around noon, they arrived at Targon Port, the second city of the country. They did not leave the carriage, and once the train was emptied of its other passengers, it was shunted into sidings, alongside goods wagons and empty cattle trucks. A police inspector boarded.

"You will stay here till nightfall. The trucks will be here, and take you to the harbour. The *Vascon* will be loading cargo through the night, and you will go with it." He gave the group a rather sour look. He stamped their exit permits and left. Tommo turned to the professor.

"Don't the wagons get taken straight to the docks? I remember seeing pictures. Why are we shut up here?"

"I was warned, Tom. News travels. There will be a bunch of Besties at Border Control and the ones here are prone to violence, more so than back home, for all they are thinner on the ground. Our carriage would be seen. The *Vascon* is an Eastie ship, thank goodness. On board, and we can return to something like normal."

It was indeed a rather unorthodox embarkation, lifted aboard in crates, and released in the hold, where they were greeted by Eastlander sailors and led upstairs. The captain and an Eastie immigration officer were waiting.

"Welcome to Eastland, Professor. Our apologies for any discomfort, though it appears we have spared you the possibility of worse. Your police are remarkably tolerant, Professor."

Such protests, Galla Hort knew, would not be tolerated in Eastland, where Besties, or at least the most extreme, were a small and despised minority. She restricted herself to a smile. Entry documents stamped, they were confined to crew's quarters until the ship had departed.

It was a voyage of a few hours only. The feeling of freedom as they wandered round the decks lifted their spirits. Their fellow passengers were mostly Eastlanders returning home, and there were few of them. Soon, the hills around Blenninge could be seen on the horizon. The landing was rather different to their departure. First to disembark, they were welcomed by the mayor, academicians and a brass band. Open-top motors took them to an hotel, the likes of which were beyond the experience of any of them other than Hort herself. A hotel that had at its entrance a banner: *Welcome to our distinguished guests.*

The young were overwhelmed. Grey-haired Academicians talked to them almost as equals. Late in the evening, their Eastie equivalents treated them to a sample of Blenninge night life. Galla herself retired early, but not to sleep. Lights out, she watched the street from her window. In the pallid streetlight, she saw a number of men casually chatting in small groups. A party of women, to all appearances party goers, approached the hotel entrance below her. There was a sudden rush. The women were held, their bags removed. A few shouts, and they were led away out of sight. She gave a grunt of satisfaction, drew the curtain and switched on the light. Eastlanders knew their stuff; did the young, she wondered, have any idea of the overtime worked by the plain-clothed officers shadowing their erratic tour of the city?

Another train, and a longer journey through Eastland, a more relaxed one, for although they once again had a special carriage, it was not sealed from others.

No time in the capital, for their carriage was joined to another train at the moment of their arrival.

"Our apologies, Professor. I regret we do have crazies here, Heritancers, I think you call them. We have set a trap. The acting profession has shown some remarkable talents."

The policeman showed her a photograph, in which a party bearing an uncanny resemblance to Hort and her colleagues were assembled on a stage. A banging and a clattering; movement back and forth, and soon they were on their way.

As they travelled east, they saw a more varied scene, for the hillier continent rose as they travelled. The expected consequences made themselves apparent, and much of their journey was made through rainstorms. In the sunny intervals, they could see what amounted to aboriginal forests, twisted-trunk grey-greens fifteen metres or more high. At the summit of a long, slow haul through higher hills, the train halted at a tiny station, alongside which were stalls selling knick-knacks and trail guides. Young Easties with backpacks walked from the station towards a cluster of houses nearby.

"Look to the north," said Tommo. "See the far peak? That's Kolumba, the highest peak in all the Lands, all 2,100 metres of it. It's an attraction. Legend has it that the first adventurers saw snow on the summit. No evidence beyond that, though. Even on Halfland snow that settles below 500 is a once in a lifetime experience."

Galla said nothing. Many years ago, she had climbed the mountain with Eastland colleagues and the young Jana Polin, fresh from a stint on Halfland. A visit that had provoked a lively debate when they had exposed the relationship between the straggly grey-greens at the summit and the aboriginal flora of Halfland. A piece of the evolutionary jigsaw that related to the history of aboriginal life, but one that left Bestowalists unmoved.

The descent was rapid, and they soon arrived at the terminus, the town of Gowrien, sited at the base of the long peninsula down which they would travel. A place with an atmosphere not to be encountered back home, for it had a buccaneering air, full of freelance prospectors convinced that their next excursion would strike the magic lode of minerals that would make their fortune. Motors here, parked seemingly at random, were nearly all robust two-wheelers or the large, open-backed carry-alls that earnt derision when they appeared on the streets of Kindopol.

They were put up in a very rough and ready hotel, a square of one-story rooms around a dirt courtyard. In the morning, they assembled in the dining room to meet Captain Taline, the officer who had prepared their camp and was to escort them to it. He brought a civilian with him, a tall, slightly stooped man with grey showing in his hair and beard. *55 at least*, thought Galla. The man had a limp too.

"I took a liberty, Professor," said the captain. "I believe you expected a bus? Not a good idea. A few kilometres out of town and it's just dirt tracks beyond, and plenty of them leading to nowhere. I've a truck for your gear, and another with supplies, but even my drivers can get lost. You need a local, someone to stay with you as well as leading us there."

"This is Jo Hugcine, Professor. He's one of the few knows the far end well. It turns out there's not much joy for prospectors, but he kept trying. He has his own carry-all, and I can vouch for its reliability. Jo has pulled a few of ours out of holes in his time. I've signed him up, subject to your approval. He'll stay and ferry around any that needs it."

Galla nodded. A handshake, the signing of a contract, and Jo stood back and surveyed the group of city softies he would have to look after. No worse than some of the soldiers, he supposed, though enough of them had been invalided out after ignoring his instructions.

"Just one condition, ma'am. You've maybe heard that abo life this side of the mountains is bad-natured, as some would see it. Catch on a thorn, even brush past a certain plant, and you are out for weeks. Not just a rash, there have been deaths. Octopods too; they're larger, faster and nastier than any you've seen further west. It's do as you are told, and no arguments."

Jo left, having agreed to meet them the following morning. He would take the three of them, leading the convoy, while the rest would pile into the trucks. Galla turned to the captain.

"He's strong enough, Captain? That limp, and his age?"

"Believe it. An ace prospector in his day. He got bitten. I'm no expert, but I was told that it would have killed some and caused amputation in many more. No more pick and shovel for Jo after that, but there's many hire him as a guide. He's not lost any that I know of."

The journey to the camp was slow. A distance that on good roads and in a straight line would have taken little more than two hours took the best part of six. There were sink holes, some marked with flags. The track twisted past great patches of scarcely-vegetated, ragged rocks, lava fields, as Tommo told them. Where the track passed close to the shore, it ran on the summits of great cliffs plunging to the sea below. They passed two wrecked carry-alls, one upside down in a gully. Jo, mostly silent as he drove, had muttered *idiot, pissed, at night,* without further elaboration. A mid-journey break, *look before you do your business, ladies,* released two very tired truck drivers, and revealed a corpse on the side of the road. An octopod, hit by a passing motor. Twice the size of any seen in Kindland.

"Take a look at that bugger. One bite and you'll be missing something if not your life. They're fast but stupid. You're not food, just a nuisance. Look round you. Just back off and they lose interest."

"Can you kill them, Mr Hugcine?"

"Sure, but it's not easy. They've little in the way of a brain, and it takes a lot of bullets to take them down. A pike will hold them off you while they wriggle, and heaving a rock will slow them down. Best is flamethrower or an acid spray. Just think which way the wind is blowing before you loose off. Of course, we don't miss the chance to squash them if they are on the road."

Galla frowned. All quite true, Jo, she thought, but you know as well as I that these creatures are rare. Centuries of occupation had eliminated them from Westerland and Kindland altogether, and this was a last stand in the east. Only a few of the tinier Far Outs, protected reserves, held anything similar.

The camp, when they reached it, was a welcome relief. It was set in a rectangle of low, flat ground running from the north to the south coasts, coasts with shingle and sand, not the cliffs that marked the shore elsewhere. The land beyond, almost an island, was wider, and rose from a set of small cliffs. The winding track, down which they drove, cut through a similar line to the west. The flat land was mostly cleared of vegetation. A row of small tents faced a few much larger ones. There were recognisable latrines, and stores protected by tarpaulins. A small shack, the only solid building, belched thick black smoke from a metal flue: the all-important generator. An army truck, lacking a front wheel, was perched on a ramp. As they approached, they discovered an electric fence, pulled aside by a soldier who had seen their slow descent.

"Here we are," said the captain, as they left the motors and stretched their legs. "Welcome to the Split. A home from home at the world's end. Only 23,000 kilometres to go, and you'll sight the Far Outs."

They settled into a routine. The cliffs on either side were sedimentary, with strata as near horizontal as made no odds. Tommo and two of the youngsters set to the mapping and measuring, while Becca and the others started sifting or chiselling out the fossils in each layer. Galla herself climbed up the cliffs to the east with a technician and often with Jo himself.

"Your friends will find nothing worse than itchybush along those cliffs, Professor, but there's few have gone where you are going."

As it was, they went wearing the heavy over-trousers that the army had provided. There were gauntlets as well. Jo brought her to the plants he knew were dangerous and specimens were collected with much care and attention. He had a common name for most, but not all of what they found, and she could match most with Decassine's *Aboriginal Flora of Eastland,* the 80-year-old classic. Again, some but not all, though the resemblances to the known were great.

There were about ten days of mostly dry weather. Material in bags, on trays, soaking in bowls soon mounted up, unattended other than by a technician attempting to maintain order and indexing. It was fortunate, Galla thought, that a spell of steady rain later kept them all under canvas, and starting to examine their finds or draw up their profiles, else they would have more material than the Eastlanders might be inclined to ship all the way back to Kindland. After a week, she called a conference.

Tommo had a lot to say. There was a near perfect match of strata each side of the flat ground of the camp: colour, texture, depth, all correlated. A technician had been hard at work with camera and darkroom tent. Prints were circulated.

"I'm waiting a bit on Becca, but one thing is obvious: most of that face has been under the sea for ages. Under and out again, more than once. We'd not see strata like these otherwise." He looked round the gathering. "The question is, has the whole lot been raised, or has sea level changed, changed several times?"

"And the answer, Tom?" asked Galla, dryly.

"I said it was a question, Prof." There was laughter. "We need to compare this with other profiles, few though they are, and get some opinions on age. The top ones cannot be that old, though, they are crumbly enough for Becca's lot to use sieves rather than chisels. But, of course, there is another question. What about where we are sitting now? It's the inverse: has it sunk, or the others raised? In either case, there are faults. Nothing odd about that, though this is so perfect it will be in the textbooks, even in Westerland."

There was more laughter. There were some in Westerland, though not the majority, who doubted even the evolutionary changes well-known through aboriginal fossils, and were in consequence inclined to regard geology as among the black arts. Galla probed further.

"The top layers are young, you say, Tom. Any estimate?"

"No, Prof. We'd need the fossil identifications. Becca has a few, but she says it is difficult."

"As it is," said Becca. "There is always the problem with marine stuff because so few are interested. Dr Hachini told me that more than 90% of all sea life is effectively unknown. I recognise a few that are found elsewhere, and even alive, but as far as I can recall these are found in older strata too. Not conclusive, I am afraid, it will have to wait till we have all the material back home."

All of them understood the significance of Hort's question. If very young, meaning anything less than a hundred thousand years, then there had been earth movements in the lands since, and substantial ones at that. Equally, changes in sea level on the scale that might be responsible implied warmer climates in the past, and the possibility of life on the polar continents, or on others now beneath the waves.

There was still work to be done around the camp. Becca was immersed in the cleaning and packing of her fossils, and also supervising the preparation of the plants that Hort had collected. Tommo started to dig a pit straight down from the camp. In fact, he tried several, to no avail. Large rocks impeded his progress or threatened to fall on the diggers. There was no material with which to shore up the sides, and below about three metres the pits flooded with seawater seeping in.

"Whatever is down there, all the stuff at the top is a mix. It cannot be so long ago that the sea was over the whole of the flats here, and with some pretty big waves."

Galla returned to the east with Jo. Now, she turned her attention to animals. The smaller octopods she merely collected; it was for others to identify. When she sought a specimen of the large one, the one they had seen on the road, Jo surprised her.

"Interesting that, Prof. I've been looking about while you were dealing with those plants, partly to make sure the area was clear around you. Not a trace, ever. Most places here in the east, be out for a day or so and you see remains if not a live one. I'd put money on there being none this side, and the bottom back there, it's not to their liking, even without the camp goings-on."

"What do they eat, Jo?"

"Mostly those higgyback creatures, the flat ones with lots of legs. They hunt at night when the higgybacks come out."

"So maybe there are no higgybacks here either?"

"I've seen the small ones, just a few. It's the larger ones they go for. I saw a chase once. Old octopod missed his strike, and the higgyback was off like lightning. Sun was just setting." Jo was silent for a moment.

"Thing is," he said, rather hesitantly, "it's not like those octopods. Any higgy dies in the open, something eats it, armour and all. Those that die of old age or whatever, they are underground. I'd not put a stake on there being none."

Absence of evidence, evidence of absence, though Galla, the old, old conundrum, the chants of *under the ice* from mocking Besties. Her suggestion that they might search at night was emphatically rejected. He could not be sure they avoided the most harmful plants, and the smaller octopods could give a vicious bite. He had a suggestion, though.

"They'd be resting in boulder fields. There's space under some you could hide a body, never mind a higgy."

The following morning, therefore, it was quite a party that set out to scale the eastern cliffs. Not only Hort, Jo and a technician, but two soldiers armed with crowbars. A few boulders turned to no purpose, and they split into two teams, leaving a landscape littered with unearthed rocks and the holes from which they had been prised. Suddenly, there was a yell from Jo. Galla turned to see him throw himself on the ground, apparently wrestling with something. They rushed to the scene.

Something indeed: a huge higgy, at least a metre long. Jo had it on its back, and a multitude of legs were waving frantically in the air. They had nothing big enough to contain it. One of the soldiers was sent back to summon reinforcements and the largest sacks that could be found. Jo managed to get a tape around the creature's middle, an extension acting as a lead.

"By the Black Bestower's Backside, I've never seen one half the size. This one would knock you off your feet if it ran at you."

They all waited for the reinforcements, staring with fascination at the monster. Although the lead was loose, it remained on its back. Someone recalled hearing that higgies could not right themselves.

"This one, maybe, but it's not true of all. The larger ones can twist and turn. Entertainment for kids where I grew up, one of the few abos that brought no one out in a rash."

Jo heaved, and righted the higgy. The force with which it attempted to escape pulled him off balance, but he did not let go. Others rushed to upturn it yet again, while Jo got back on his feet. No swearing this time, and a calculating look appeared on his face.

"How do you kill these things when you want to study their insides?" he asked. "They are a bit of a pest, but we just cut the heads off or crush then with a stone or a sledgehammer. None the size of this one, though."

"Ether, or extract of poison leaf, usually, but we've no jars big enough for this. Cut it to bleed out, I guess."

Jo went to work with a knife, making cuts between the segments of the underbelly. By the time others arrived, the legs had stilled. Jo was waggling a leg up and down, stopping only to see the body placed in a sack. Then all set to work again heaving boulders. Soon three more had been caught and placed alive in sacks. When a fourth was caught, held on its back by the students, Jo spoke up.

"Would you do me a favour, Prof.? Put this one right side up and let it go. I've a hunch, and if I'm right, it will be easy to recapture."

Released, the higgy stayed still for a few moments, then it moved slowly away. Jo walked in front of it, prodding its head with his fist. The creature turned and lumbered off in a different direction. At best, the speed was no more than walking pace. After a while, it stopped. Antennae waved, and then it turned and headed towards a pile of boulders as yet unturned. Jo gave a signal, and students went to recapture it.

There was something absurd about the creature. A girl gave a whoop, and with a jump straddled its back. Low off the ground as it was, the width of the carapace was such that her feet barely touched the ground. A moment's pause, and the higgy resumed its journey. Her efforts to prevent it, digging her feet into the ground, had no effect. It unbalanced her, and she rolled off. The others moved fast to overturn it. Galla Hort was furious. She strode to the group and grabbed the girl by her shoulders, bringing her face right up against the student's.

"Idiot. What might that creature have dragged you through? What might it have secreted? And you without the over-trousers that we use here. These creatures are not toys for your amusement."

Normally, it was Jo who dished out the reprimands. This time, though, he waited until Hort's anger had subsided, and his words were more of a riddle than a reprimand.

"Any of you follow the dogs? No? You'll have seen pictures though, I'll be bound, all those race-hounds on the track. Go like the wind, faster than any athlete. Seen the Westerland tow-teams? Those monsters strong enough to pull a cart or a carriage?"

Some had seen exhibitions of the teams, on the rare occasions when Westerland put itself out to present a friendly face, most often at Bestowalist festivals. Only Galla got a glimpse of where Jo's thinking was going. All the others waited to see what Jo's point was.

"I told the prof. here, octopods go for higgies, and higgies run when they sense one near; run faster than any octopod. It's what you are all taught, being Evolutionists. The laggards get eaten. We do the same thing with the dogs, at least the racing ones. Have a winner, and you have a breeder. They don't know it, but they're running for their lives, just like higgies. A few late finishes, and they end up in someone's pies.

Now look at these. They are big, yes, but that wouldn't protect them from poison fangs. Get one of those big octopods here, and these higgies would be easy meat. Look at where we've dug them out: dig and push. Dig and push to make your home. As for Miss Niama, here, if they've no enemies, why bother to secrete anything? You've no itches, I trust?"

There was a little laughter, and Niama turned away. The party returned to camp with the one corpse and four sacks, each with a scrabbling higgy inside. Galla brought up the rear. There was more to Jo than she had realised. She was already turning over what he said. What else promoted size and strength? Fighting for mates was an obvious one, but there was metabolism too. How long for such differences to develop?

*****

There were a few more days of sorting, packing and cataloguing. Jo accompanied a truck back to Gowrien with some of the finds, and returned with a convoy of three trucks. When they moved out, most of the camp would be dismantled. Galla was looking forward to the next part of their studies, a part she had not detailed in full to those back home. Jo took her on one side.

"That Captain Taline, Prof., he'd ordered your samples sent to the barracks outside town, not to the hotel storerooms. He must have seen the look on my face, because he took me aside to explain. I was wondering if there was some politics, like orders to keep stuff here in Eastland, and send you back with less. Not that, he said; there's strangers in the hotel he doesn't like the smell of. No law against anyone staying if they can pay, but he didn't like it one bit. Least of all, he did not want them there when you got back."

"Besties? Here to do us some mischief?" Galla was alarmed. Not so much at the prospect of assault as the prospect of prying eyes watching her less than authorised trips into the mountains to the west.

Jo grinned. "He's a smart one, for all those soldiers get it easy. He had a little plan, he said. You can tell the prof. I'll have them out of the hotel and incapable of mischief, or be sure they are harmless. Let's see what's what when we return tomorrow."

Jo's carry-all and four trucks started the journey back, the damaged truck seen on their arrival having finally been equipped with a new wheel. It was coming close to dusk when they entered the town and drove into the hotel courtyard. There were soldiers waiting, and Galla's surprise, the remainder of their gear and samples were taken straight to the storerooms. The captain came up to her. If it were possible, she thought, to represent the essence, the core, of complacency, the look on his face would be framed and exhibited.

"Welcome back, Professor. I think Mr Hugcine told you we had some strangers lodging here? I am happy to tell you they are on their way west under guard, for we lack sufficient cells to detain them." His grin threatened to split his face. She knew what was expected.

"Really, Captain, such dangerous men? Of what were they guilty?"

"Dangerous but stupid, Professor. We returned to the hotel from our barracks with boxes, heavy boxes, which we placed in the storerooms here. Boxes that were then opened to release some of my men. An attempt was made to break in and set fire to the place. There were arrests, and some very bad language. No one hurt, I am happy to say. The searches showed each with the Scroll of Obedience sewn into their shirts. Not clever, Professor, for we searched all those still in their rooms. Leaguers, every one of them. Conspiracy to commit arson, now that's a serious crime."

Relief at the removal of the threat conflicted with Galla Hort's amusement as she congratulated the captain. Leaguers, I suppose he means the Heritancers, she thought, but it was worrying that they had travelled to and through Eastland without challenge. She kept things light.

"Well, Captain, justice will be done, but you may find them relishing a few years clearing grey-greens. *The Bestower moves in many ways to work his purpose,* they will say."

Taline laughed out loud. "Clearance, Professor? Oh no, we have better uses for malefactors. Have you ever smelled what cattle discharge when fed on abo food? And do you have any idea how much is produced? If I did not know better, I'd have thought more than they take in. Takes a while to rot down, too. Shit needs shovelling, Professor. Prison diet has a fair proportion of abo veggies in it too, and we don't do force feeding, if any are minded to be martyrs."

A few days were spent being ferried around the district in Jo's carry-all, making more plant and animal collections. Nothing dramatic emerged: things were much as they were to the west of their camp. It was the arrival of Eugon Mallabine that changed the tempo. Mallabine appeared at first to be rather withdrawn and formal. As the Eastlander geologist assigned to them, it would be his job to certify and approve all the specimens and data to be taken to Kindland. There was some nervousness about how he would interpret this duty, although all the Eastie dealings they had had been positive.

Once in the field, though, his detachment dissolved. As a party headed west along scarcely visible tracks, it was he rather than Jo that was the guide. They wound their way higher and higher into the mountains to the north-west, until they reached the tall cliffs that fell away to the sea. The motor would take them no further, and a camp was set up. The next day they tramped along the cliff tops until they reached a line of sheer cliffs forming their side of a flat-bottomed gorge, a gorge invaded by the sea for some distance at its mouth.

At first, it was the sight of the vegetation in the bottom that struck them. Real trees grew there, trees with gnarled, scaly trunks enveloped in lianas, trees with grey-green dissected fronds at their crowns, fronds encrusted with droopers. Trees at least twenty metres tall, massive beyond anything they had seen elsewhere. Galla was about to question Eugon, when Tommo let out a whoop.

"A massive fault. Look, the other side is lower, much lower. This has risen or that has sunk. Moved apart too, erosion cannot account for that bottom."

He turned to the Eastlander, who was smiling at the young man's excitement.

"We heard nothing of them, Professor. The Earth has moved, moved a lot. How long have they been known?"

"A couple of years, that's all. There was a prospector got this far. Nothing worth his effort in the ground, but he was a good photographer. His pictures got published, and I caught sight of them. It was the trees that caught the eye, and a bit of commercial attention too. Heard of ironwood? Fanciest furniture in all the Lands, and takes a polish like none of our bestowed species. He wasn't going to reveal location. A bit of a Consie at heart, old Mafferine, but with an eye to his own interest too. We paid him well to keep his mouth shut, and the whole region is a reserve, permits only, and we've issued none."

All of them knew the ironwood story. An Eastland species only, felled for timber and for fuel since time immemorial, and bad at regenerating. The remaining stands, none as grand as this, needed armed protection. Mallabine looked at his companions and grinned.

"And here you are, a bunch of foreign trespassers. Any word of this in the pops and I'll be shovelling shit like your Bestie friends. The government could be out; some heads would roll for certain. But it wasn't the trees that struck me. A few long shots in Mafferine's portfolio, and I saw just what Tommo has seen. I came out by myself with him, but I couldn't do a proper job of survey and measurements."

"Your professor," he nodded at Galla, "was a better security risk than my own students. So, here we are. I am sorry old Mafferine is not with us. Two old octopod bites started playing up, and he's barely mobile now."

The days that followed were arduous. A trek to and from the camp each day reduced the hours of work. Tommo and a technician worked their way south, spending a night in the open, only to find the fault extending beyond their reach, although the cliffs on either side shrank, and the bottom rose too. They returned to find the others already in the gorge, Jo having constructed a route down the cliffs. Galla and her team were busy with cameras and collecting gear. Tommo, though, made straight for the base of the cliffs and the talus that lined it. Mallabine did not join them, and remained on the cliff top. Walking was all very well, as he told them, but rope and tackle quite another at his age. He nevertheless bombarded Tommo with questions, and his frustration that the photographs would be developed only when they returned to town was evident. He wanted to know how long ago this massive disturbance had occurred.

Tommo was not able to satisfy him. The rocks were volcanic: no fossils. The talus was not massively thick, and the rocks showed little sign of erosion or weathering.

"It does not look ancient to me, Professor, but we have little to compare the accumulation with. Nearly all cliffs studied are coastal, at least those made of hard rock like this."

"As I expected. There are no faults between here and your site at the end, Tommo. You've fossils there." He looked at Galla. "You see why I was so keen?"

Hort nodded. Evidence of movement, movement in thousands rather than millions of years, evidence of sea level changes by emergence or subsidence, all strengthened the possibility that what was under the ice now might not have been in the not-so-distant past. Still just a possibility, she had to acknowledge.

Back at Gowrien, there was just a day to pack all material and load it onto a wagon. Before they departed, Hort sprung a surprise. There was to be a five day stop at that little station in the mountains.

"You all deserve a holiday," she said to her companions. "There is Kolumba to visit. The highest point in all the Lands, the highest anyone can climb short of a visit to Halfland. I've been there, and I have friends to see here. Have fun."

Directed to a hostel, the group found that all, even a guide, was paid for. Seeing them safely on their way, and checking that a police guard on the coach and wagon was in place, she headed for the police station itself, tucked into the side of the railway station. She was led to a small back room, where an elderly man rose to greet her. They hugged.

"Dear Galla!"

"Dear Stoppen!"

They moved apart, and stared appraisingly at each other, both grinning at the changes time had brought.

"How long is it? At least twenty years?" Stoppen Hildin, asked, returning to a chair by the window. *At least.* He knew very well that it was twenty-two years, years since they had parted as rather more than mere colleagues. Years in which both had ascended the greasy poles of their professions. She was now not merely a full professor, but the most notorious to remain in post. He, once a humble assistant, was now the soon to retire director of the Nottogine Research Station, that Eastland establishment that enthused some and enraged others, with its attempts to breed aboriginal plants edible to the bestowed, and bestowed animals capable of digesting the aboriginal.

When Galla had visited, and stayed, the Station was still mostly a collection of shacks and byres, the latter containing some rather emaciated cows. She had not seen it since, but its products were now known throughout the Lands. Products that, according to belief, were either the way to an abundant future or an abomination, a turning of the back on the Bestower's will.

Things had been arranged. To Galla's surprise, this long-awaited return visit was not a simple drive. Rather than a single carry-all with Stoppen at the wheel, it was a small convoy that set out, the car in which they travelled, with a soldier at the wheel, accompanied in front and behind by open-top motors with armed soldiers in each. The convoy stopped frequently on summits, awaiting signals from those miles away below.

"Things have changed, my dear. There has been sabotage. A murder, and more attempted. We never make it known, but even here we have the fanatics. Mines on the road, attempts to poison both the products we bring in and those we send out. There are more soldiers than workers here now."

It was not a long journey. Soon, they descended a gentle slope towards what was now a complex of houses, workshops and byres, surrounded by regular, high-fenced fields. In some, there were rows of grey-greens, evidently cultivated; in others, cows or sheep could be seen grazing on what seemed to be nothing but aboriginal plants. The scale was impressive to Galla. Even so, she thought, for abo food to be circulating, it cannot be the only source.

"No indeed," Stoppen replied to her question. "There are many swollen-bud grey-greens that we have bred to be toxin-free. Many farms use them. But they supply energy, no more. For proteins, for the traces of other necessities, we must rely on what was bestowed, or on a tedious set of fermentations that are scarcely economic."

"And animals, bestowed animals?" asked Hort.

"Much slower. There is variation, of course, but our animals produce so few young. We are working on microbial evolution as well. Maybe we will get those that can both break down aboriginal matter and survive in a rumen. There are some promising strains, but nothing that would be of economic value unless the scale was increased a hundredfold or more. They work, but they do not survive for long in the rumen. Out-bred by the original gut flora, but those are still needed too."

Galla Hort carried with her the letters of agreement from the Seniors in both countries. These were shown to Stoppen's staff, as small containers were prepared for her to take back. They were not all she took, for extra items were added after hours by the two of them alone, items to be handed over to Consie groups and sent to remote farms in Kindland. Seeds and dormant cultures were in both.

The parting was hard. Officially, she had not visited, and the likelihood of another was remote. Stoppen did not accompany her on the return journey, a journey interrupted at the sight of a frustrated ambush. The road, partly dug up; soldiers holding two young men captive. As they waited for the all-clear, she saw soldiers search the captives, and heard the shouts.

"Leaguers, damned leaguers, again."

The tell-tale talismans sewn into shirts, she realised. Not that such incriminating evidence was needed here, but a sign of the rising tide of Bestowalist fundamentalism as news of Eastland's moves towards integration of the two living systems advanced. Kids, kids now doomed to a life of shit-shovelling. She turned to a lieutenant.

"Eastlanders, lieutenant, or foreigners?"

"One of ours, one of yours, by the accent, madam," was the rather sour reply. "We should search all who cross in those ferry-boats, and not just for those damned sewn-in prayers."

The journey completed, Galla packed the official cargo in the wagon. The rest was stowed among her possessions in the carriage compartment. She was waiting when the rest returned from their excursion. Attached again to a train, they travelled back across Eastland. Unannounced, their ferry journey and arrival at Targon Port were conventional and unchallenged. Even when they arrived, at last, at Grand Central Station, there was little commotion. The wagon's contents were loaded onto trucks, which were escorted to the Institutes. Among the relatives and friends waiting to greet them was a young girl, unknown to any, who helped Professor Hort with her luggage, luggage just a little lighter when it was loaded with its owner into a taxi than when it had been on the train.

4. The Acolyte

As the congregation left the Temple, each family nodded or exchanged a few words with Father Decran and his assistants. When it came to the Striggan's turn, however, the priest held Artyn Striggan back.

"A word if I may, Mr Striggan? Can I part you from your family for a while?"

Striggan stood aside, and waved his family on. As the last of the congregation dispersed, the priest took him to the Residence next door, and into the study that few were privileged enough to enter.

"Sit, Mr Striggan, or may I say Artyn?"

Artyn Striggan glowed. It was a rare sign of trust if the priest addressed you informally. Not, he thought, as he waited for the priest to remove his robes and file away the text of his homily, that we do not deserve it. Years of regular attendance, wife and children involved in every activity, an exemplary record of piety and honest dealing. Not to mention four healthy and obedient children, a sure sign of the Bestower's grace. The priest sat behind his cluttered desk and regarded his parishioner carefully.

"Your son, Janis, Artyn, A clever boy, and a great help to us here. He will finish school next hundred, I think? Do you have any plans for his future?"

"No, Father." Striggan shook his head. Head of the household he might be, but what to do with a clever, pious child when all that was on offer was a life like his own, a warehouseman plagued with the ups and downs of employment as regular food shortages deprived him of work. He had even discussed it with his wife, much to her surprise. The eldest, no problem, now an apprentice builder; daughters, trained to be capable housewives, but a spindly lad with bookish tendencies?

"He is clever enough to merit high school, is he not? Had you considered it?"

For the first time in his life, Artyn Striggan looked at the priest in what was almost contempt. His words were bitter.

"No. How could the likes of us pay for such a thing? He is not some star pupil for whom a scholarship might be awarded. At best, we had thought he might apprentice as a clerk, though he has little appetite for keeping accounts. We have seen no openings."

"Calm, Artyn, calm. The Temple cares for its flock, and you and yours are more deserving than most. Most certainly, Janis can serve the Bestower in better ways than as a clerk to some petty shopkeeper. He has the makings of a priest, Artyn, and with your consent, he will be accepted for training."

"A priest? A priest from this parish? Father, has such a thing ever happened? May I be pardoned, Father, but you and those before you are not from among us."

The priest smiled. The seed had been planted.

"It is rare, yes, but not unknown. I will be frank with you, Artyn. You will remember Hortan, Mr Dellinger's son? A firebrand for the faith?"

"Him? That clown that ended up in prison after an affray with Consies? Brought nothing but shame to his family. All over the pops too; links to Westie agitators. Last I heard he was on clearance somewhere out east. Serves the Bestower's purpose, I guess, but I'd dump the lot of them in Westerland. What of him, Father? Our Janis is no troublemaker as you well know. Live and let live. You teach that, and we follow."

"Just so, Artyn. It is the problem that we face in all the parishes like this. The young, the clever, the idealistic, they go to the extremes. Too often, those gifted with a sharp mind and an ease of thought are deceived into arrogance. They lack humility and diligence. By the Bestower's grace and your own good discipline, Janis is different, he is not of their number. The Bestower has need of such servants, a need that takes them from family and friends, and generally from the comfort of marriage and children. A rarity, one to be treasured. With your consent, and his, he will be trained. He will not be far away."

The priest watched Striggan's face. Of course, he would have the final say, but the Commission would need to know that the boy was sincere, and that he understood the rigours that he would undergo. The ascetic, celibate life for many years; the acceptance of menial tasks alongside learning. There was no resistance. Striggan would put it to the boy. The boy would accept.

A model family, Father Decran thought, as Striggan left him. A family with a simple faith, not disturbed by any theological arguments or concern with politics. There were rules; there were loyalties. Consies were to be pitied rather than hated, and Evolutionists dismissed, almost humorously, as those who had fancy and foolish ideas put into their heads by those who should know better. Nothing in the neighbourhood had served to dispel this amiable outlook. And here was Janis, firm in faith and firm in discipline.

Janis had always obliged. The Temple school had suited his undemanding temperament, and the clerics who taught him sent him home with glowing reports on his piety and its evident sincerity. Further, he was quick to learn; faster indeed than his siblings, but totally lacking in pride or ambition. He had unthinkingly expected an apprenticeship like his older brother. You stayed near your family; few children left the district, and those mostly under a cloud.

When his father summoned him to what was labelled as *a serious talk, my son*. Janis was, for a moment, anxious: had he committed some sin, said something out of order at school? The anxiety was soon dispelled.

"Sit, my son. Have you considered your future in this stricken world? What the Bestower's will for you might be?"

"No, Father," he replied. "I did not doubt that you would guide me when the time came, as with Johan."

"A very proper answer, Janis. But it is not the likes of us, even of me, your father, to act without guidance from above. We each have gifts from the Bestower, but these may be hidden, even from ourselves and from our family. When they are revealed, we have a duty to put them at His disposal."

His father looked hard at Janis, but saw in his son's face the expected look of innocent bewilderment.

"As you saw, Father Decran took me on one side after temple this morning, Janis. He praised not only your piety, but your ability to think and to write. This is what he said to me, Janis: *too often, those gifted with a sharp mind and an ease of thought are deceived into arrogance. They lack humility and diligence. By the Bestower's grace and your own good discipline, Janis is not of their number. The Bestower has need of such servants, a need that takes them from family and friends, and generally from the comfort of marriage and children.*"

Janis realised at once what his father was saying. He had been picked out for the priesthood. And, innocent and untroubled as he was, the implications were well-known. An honour, certainly, but one that meant many years of service as an assistant, years in relative seclusion and poverty, with no certain progression. Not all families welcomed such a call, and some so chosen declined the offer, notionally without penalty.

"You mean to enter training for the priesthood, Father? To be transferred maybe far away, even to be sent to Westerland? Will you wish me to follow that route?"

"Yes, that is the message. But it is not quite as you might imagine. Father Decran, and our Temple, do not follow the rule of the Exterminators, the Westerlanders who are led astray by their enthusiasms. No, you would serve in a Temple or offices here. You would still see us regularly."

"It is your wish, Father? Then I am willing to do my duty, to serve the Bestower as best I can."

*****

The change had been rapid, and at first, painless and exciting. He remained in Kindopol, and no suggestion was made for a transfer. A few months were spent in a Temple not far from home, sharing a communal room with two others. Chores shared were no burden, and were mixed in with lessons from the chief priest, lessons designed both to strengthen their faith, but also to moderate any excess of zeal. Patience, patience and forgiveness, these were Father Coran's watchwords.

"The Bestower gave us brains as well as hearts, boys. We are fallible, even when we try to do His will. Destroying the aboriginal before we have the means to replace it creates deserts, and not the land shaped to His wish for our enjoyment. Evolutionists? Pity, not persecution. They are prey to the sin of pride, but those that do not obstruct the Bestower's work can be tolerated. They will change as the great work proceeds."

He was, though, less charitable about Conservationists, and about the Eastlanders that sought to merge the Bestowed and the Aboriginal. The message was in tune with all that Janis had learnt at home: do your duty, and all will be well. His companions were inclined to argue, or express surprise; both had attended Temples in which Westerland influence had been great. The idea of tolerance when there was the chance to beat up the unbelievers came hard. Gronde had even joined in the periodic, symbolic Exterminations, where a whole Temple congregation would spend a day cutting, uprooting and burning areas of grey-green wilderness. Father Coran had become sarcastic over this, pointing to the bare, unused, gullied ground that was the usual result, and its subsequent recolonisation by grey-greens.

"You learnt about the war, did you not, Gronde? And the damage done in all this part of our country, while those savages attempted to turn our homeland into a desert? Be sure they will try again if we let them."

Gronde had scowled and kept silent. A week after that rebuke, though, he went missing, and in due course Father Coran told them why.

"Prison, that's where, the idiot got into a fight with Consies and attacked a policeman. No doubt he'll be taken on by Froggen Street when he's released."

Froggen Street Temple was one of those famous for its Westerland sympathies. Several preachers had been expelled, and the sermons were always hovering on the verge of incitement. Janis had thought no more about it. His nonchalance was soon to be destroyed. Well before the usual year of humble service at a Temple, Father Coran called him to the priest's house.

"You are to move, Janis, with my blessing. There is a vacancy as clerk to Commissioner Nagren himself at Grade Street. You will start tomorrow. Take your things, and return to your family for tonight. You are to tell them of the move, but not for whom you will be working. Your opportunities to see them again will be very few, and you should warn them of this. May the Bestower be by your side."

Janis gasped as he knelt to receive the priest's blessing. Even among the most humble and little-informed the Office of Bestowal was recognised as the organising centre of the faith, and the three Commissioners as the ultimate authority, tenuous though it was. To come from Grade Street was to have a certain authority, conferred on even the lowliest of its occupants. Occupants who had generally spent years of faithful service elsewhere.

His induction was swift. Armed with the pass delivered by Father Coran, he found himself ushered past the throng of people who had business with the lower echelons on the ground floor. His bags were deposited, and he was guided upwards. Even one storey up, the hubbub vanished, and he was led along broad, carpeted corridors, passing only a few priests, heads bowed, clasping files or folders to their chests. Another flight, and the silence was profound. A central, circular hall was domed, and on the inside of the cupola there was a mosaic depicting the radiant Bestower showering on a huddle of grateful people the means of their survival. Withered grey-greens parted all around, as though a divine wind had parted them around the site of Bestowal. Armed guards stood to attention at each of three ornate doors at the far side. Janis was led to that at the centre. A succession of doors, each guarded, led to what Janis took as a waiting room, strewn almost at random with tables and ornate chairs.

He did not wait, however. At the moment of his arrival, a priest got up, knocked on yet another door, and ushered him in. The Commissioner had already risen to greet him. Janis had little time to assess the man before him, and now shaking his hand, just as Janis was about to kneel or bow his head. The awkwardness provoked a laugh from the Commissioner.

"No need for that, Janis Striggan, no need at all. Whatever I have been in the past, I am no priest now, merely a civil servant."

There was another, barking laugh, as the Commissioner waved Janis to a chair, taking another and turning it to face him. Only then was he able to take in the man in front of him. No priestly clothes, rather, the elegant attire typical of Seniors and the very rich. A mop of curly hair, certainly not trimmed in the sober clerical manner. A face that somehow radiated a mix of confidence and good humour, assisted by the presence of an elegantly barbered moustache. Only a Bestowalist medallion hanging over his chest gave any hint of his affiliation.

"Welcome to Grade Street, Janis. You come highly recommended. Firm of faith, and without the excess of zeal that marks out so many believers. A man who can keep his head, and his counsel in the service of the Bestower."

Janis was lost for words. He nodded, feeling at the same time that such a simple response was almost impertinent. Commissioner Nagren spelled out his duties. He had need of a confidential secretary. Janis would be trained to do the job. He would see, even deliver, the most secret of documents. He would prepare papers for the formal meetings of Convocation. Nagren even took him around the room, showing him the arrangement of documents in the numerous cupboards lining the office.

"Whenever you need to see me, you are merely to knock. Only in the most unlikely circumstances will entry be refused. In due time, you will have access to this office when I am absent."

*****

Weeks passed. Janis learnt the full extent of his duties. He had his own room, one better furnished than any he had occupied before. He learnt the correct mix of notional deference and actual superiority to be shown when he had to deal with the priests or lay people with whom he worked. He also learnt, rapidly, the art of office politics. In this, he was further educated by Nagren himself, who would quiz him, almost daily, on his exchanges with others.

"Learn to tell the difference between mere jealousy and a hostile agenda, Janis. You know already that we believers are not of one mind when we try to interpret the Bestower's will. Convocation contains those for whom the Westerland, the Exterminator, approach has appeal. There are those who would sanction action against the law, even a coup, to round up and extirpate Consies."

Janis did encounter these Ultras. Within the building, such differences were muted. A few attempts were made to convert him, to which he responded with a show of humble ignorance and the beliefs of his master. No one could expect him to engage in doctrinal debates. There were, however, rather less loaded conversations in which he was asked about matters of policy or action to which he was privy. Often, they seemed harmless, even trivial, but he rebuffed them all. He found himself fiercely defensive where his master's interests were concerned.

Life settled into a routine. While restricted in his movements, he could visit his family. Not in priest's or even noviitate's clothes, but those of a civil servant. He could even pass on money and presents. His position opened up the wider world of politics, and he was often in attendance when Seniors held confidential meetings with Nagren. The threat of disorder, even of war, with the inevitable famines that would follow, impressed itself on his mind.

But disorder there was, and it was growing, as a visit by the famous Chief Inspector Gornik made clear. Nagren was, in private, contemptuous of many of the Seniors, even those whose beliefs were similar to his own. Eastlanders had taken fright at what they saw as the growing influence of Westerland. Kindopol seemed in danger of becoming an arena for every faction on the planet to stage their battles. The policeman, Janis saw, was engaged in a never-ending struggle to prevent the arena widening.

It was after such a visit that Janis was summoned again. This time, the Commissioner remained behind his desk. The bonhomie was missing from his face. As he spoke, there was a certain weariness in his voice.

"Janis, do you remember Ritter and Hausred asking you for certain information?"

Janis thought back. Yes, those and others had asked for things, things notionally of no great import, and presenting no obvious risk. He nodded.

"They were tests. Tests that you passed, or you would long ago have been despatched elsewhere. Now there is a much harder test for you, one you are free to refuse. First, though, did you discover why I was in need of a confidential clerk?"

"Yes, sir. I was told that Gordo Niffen had an accident, that he was killed by falling in front of a car."

"That a car ran him over is true enough. That it was an accident is not. He was pushed, Janis, because he had infiltrated an Ultra cell and been found out. One too many tip-offs and they guessed. There are more of them now, and Gornik is desperate."

Nagren paused. He looked at Janis for a moment before continuing.

"We need you to do the same, with the same risk. To gain their confidence and get information to us. You will have to lie, Janis. You will be in danger. They need only suspicion to justify murder."

"How is that possible?" asked Janis. "I am known to be loyal, passionately so. The crazies have given up on me altogether. I cannot simply advertise a change of heart."

"Just so. It would mean time and patience. You should express a doubt here, a feeling there that some rioters have been harshly treated. You will be approached, be sure of that. You will express anguish at the position you are in. You will be asked for a favour, a significant one. We will give you details of a planned police raid. You will pass it on and they will evacuate, we will find nothing. It will be embarrassing for us, and they will be delighted. They will think we would not use such an important event as bait."

*****

Janis walked cautiously along the darkened street. It was as well it was empty, for his movements, the anxious glances behind and to the curtained windows on both sides, would have aroused suspicion in any observer. Eventually, he stopped and knocked in a pattern on a door. There was a short pause, a chink of light as the door was edged open, and then he was admitted. Another looked out, up and down the street, then closed the door behind him.

"You were not seen?" said a voice from behind a mask. Janis shook his head.

"Turn around," the voice continued. A blindfold was tied around his face, and the light switched off. He was led by the arm. There was the sound of a door opening, and he sensed that he was again outside. The route that he followed twisted and turned. He was led into houses and out again. Dim light penetrated his blindfold at times, at others, the darkness was total. There were stairs, up and down, even a ladder that caused him to stumble. Eventually, his guide knocked on another door. It was opened a chink, and there was a muttered conversation. He was led in.

The door being closed behind them, the blindfold was removed. He was in a small, dimly lit room, each window sealed firmly with thick black cloth. Four masked men were sat in chairs around a small table, on which there were the remains of a meal. The stuffy atmosphere reeked of its flavours. He was motioned to an empty chair, while his companion took another.

"Welcome, Janis Striggan," said a masked figure. "May the Bestower keep you and reward you."

"And on you also may his bounty rest."

"So, Janis, you are called to do the Bestower's work, we are told. There are those who have claimed the same and then betrayed his servants. Be aware that you are now known to us all. Remember that. We are unknown to you, and it will remain so until your faith is beyond question."

Janis nodded. As he had discovered after his conversation with Nagren, all who worked for the Office of Bestowal in Grade Street knew the score; the mysterious deaths and disappearances of the notionally pious that were attributed to Consies, but were the price of betrayal to the authorities. The voice, despite its formally correct pronunciation, had the unmistakeable twang of Westerland. The real thing, then, not a decoy.

"To business, then." The masked figure turned to his companions.

"I told you of Mr Striggan's employment. He has the confidence of Commissioner Nagren. He is trusted to prepare papers for Convocation and with Nagren's files. He has spared us a loss already, the Degranne Street cell. They found nothing." He laughed.

"That took the sainted Gornik down a peg. A few more fiascos like that, and we may get the bastard moved on."

"One tip-off," another, Kindland, voice interrupted. "An easy way to gain our confidence, with small loss to them. A couple more, and even they could not miss the source. Striggan will be taken out. And what will he know and tell when that happens?"

"Not such a small loss. Gornik had been planning that raid for weeks. In any case, what could he tell them? Come, we have discussed this already. Nagren is hostile, but he is sloppy and lazy. Striggan here can see nearly everything that passes through that office. Some have wanted us to silence the man, but feeding from his weakness is so much better. It is details of policy, of connections, that we need, not the place and time of a few raids. We have to ask questions and get Janis to provide answers. Answers memorised. More than that, we need him to recognise what is important."

Janis reacted, as rehearsed, with subdued anger to the Kindlander's imputation. Don't overdo it, he'd been told, show that you understand their suspicion. He calmly stated his convictions; he was dedicated to the eventual destruction of the aboriginal; he abhorred the dependence on aboriginal products; he looked forward to the overthrow of their compromising state and the start of rule based on that of Westerland. The masked faces remained inscrutable.

"Enough," the Westerlander said. "Janis will be passed questions, and told how to provide answers. He is here so that you will recognise him. He need know no one, and the briefing can occur whenever and wherever we want." He turned to Janis.

"The street outside the Commission, yes? There's a potato-seller does the rounds when folk come home from work, you've seen him?" Janis nodded.

"Buy at least twice a week. If we want you, there will be an address and a time written on the inside of the bag. If you have something to tell us, give him one of these in the price. We'll contact you afterwards." He handed over a few one-cent coins; each had a small, filed nick in the edge.

Janis was again blindfolded and led away. A route as long and as devious as that by which he had arrived, but clearly different. There was no formal farewell. He became aware that no hand was on his arm, and after a pause removed the cloth. He was in an unfamiliar street, one largely flanked by shuttered warehouses. It took him a while to find a familiar street and head home.

That first encounter was chewed over by Nagren and Gornik. Gornik had marked up a map. He could pinpoint the house of entry, but the exit was just a street, some four hundred metres away. Janis could not be sure of where he was released. A crowded slum, Gornik realised; at least a hundred households and as near as impossible to surround as made no odds.

"So, we raid, but however clever we are, we catch a doorkeeper at best. We might rescue the boy, but his cover is blown and he'd be a marked man. Another to be sent to the remotest part of Eastland? That costs us. Further in, and he'd be dead, while we ransacked a large area. Find a Westie? No law against a Westie entertaining his chums, unless he's an illegal. Find his body? Probably not, he'd be in a cellar or tunnel somewhere, while we put the whole neighbourhood in an uproar."

"There must be limits to the places where they can be so thorough, surely? A Bestie place, I guess, but still. And what about that potato seller?"

"Oh, we know about him. I think they know we know too. Not much use. He gets a lot of custom, and the punters are chatty. We've an eye on one or two regulars who aren't local, but we've nothing on them. Close him down, and they'll find another way, and we'll be left with small fish and nothing much to charge them with. As to places, they've more choice than you might think."

Nagren sat for a while, head in hands, after Gornik left. The boy would be expected to pass on information unasked, and to dig in the files. It was clear that it was not the rooting out of cells that interested them. They wanted political stuff: as background for those far above them, or for planning assassinations.

A week went by. Janis received no instructions. He worried that he had nothing to tell them. Nagren told him to provide details of a private meeting of Eastland and Far Out diplomats with a certain Senior. The place would be well-guarded. Nothing of great significance would be discussed, but the absence of any Westerlander would be the sort of thing they might expect Janis to report. Janis duly handed over his marked coin. A day later, his bag again gave an address and time.

The same routine was followed, though it was only a Kindlander that received his message. A brief thanks, and he was dismissed, and once again, he found himself on a different street. As Gornik remarked, however, it was not far from the first encounter. There were several more such visits, each initiated by Janis. A month went by, and the pattern remained the same. There was never a summons, never a request for specific information. The area narrowed down, but was still too large for a swoop. A solidly Bestie area too; Gornik had toyed with idea of moving some residents in, but decided against it. Any hint of surveillance and the boy would be dead.

Things changed suddenly. Gornik staged two very successful raids on cells planning to disrupt Consie demonstrations by violence. A bomb maker was caught, and a very public trial and execution followed. Nagren knew nothing about them, and the Bestowalist establishment, shocked, was issuing denials and condemnations. Soon after, Janis was summoned. The interview was terse and later terrifying.

"You had no knowledge? Really? Whose side are you on?"

This time, the Westerlander was present. Janis was beaten. Candle burns were made where clothing would cover them. Janis protested his innocence, as it happened, with complete sincerity. The debate that followed ignored his presence among them, such was the confidence of his persecutors.

"The brat is probably telling the truth. Gornik has no love for the Bestower, nor for His more weak-kneed followers."

"But he had the details of the Degranne cell. Gornik must have talked to Nagren about that."

"Yes, strange, isn't it? I wonder why." The Westerlander paused to kick the prostrate Janis. "Tell us again how you knew of it, you little creep."

"I told you, it was just a conversation." Janis thought fast. "I think some bigwig was involved, and Gornik was warning Nagren. I don't remember any names."

"We would have lost a lot of good people if that raid was sprung on us, Josh," said another voice. "Would they have given that up just as bait? What the kid has given us since has been right, though not of much use."

There was a roar of rage from the Westerlander, and some kind of fight took place over Janis' head. Only when order was restored did his sullen voice return.

"Idiot, idiot, idiot. No names, remember. This brat must disappear." He produced a pistol, only to be again restrained.

"Not so fast," said a much softer voice. "Not so fast. There are things we need to know, things that Nagren will know. We do have a task for this boy. Lose him, and we will never know. Get him back in a chair."

Janis was hauled up. Apart from dishevelment, no sign of injury was visible, though he was pale and shaking.

"Now, boy, listen well," the silky voice resumed. "Your beloved master is our greatest enemy. Yes, more so than any bunch of Consie scum or snooty Evolutionists. The great betrayer, the collaborator who keeps his arse warm while warning the likes of Gornik. They depend on him to frustrate the Bestower's purpose for us."

The masked man pulled Janis towards him. His breath penetrated Janis' nostrils. Strong arms gripped his shoulders.

"There is no such thing as trust, boy, where you are concerned. Were you fed the details of that raid as one of theirs, or did you overhear and act on your conscience? We don't know, and more to the point, we don't care. Results matter, nothing else. One false step, one piece of misinformation, and the Bestower will take you to your reward. With assistance, of course."

Janis recovered some composure. Scared, yes, but aware, more than ever before, of the evil before him.

"Have I lied to you? Is my life in your hands only? Detected, and I face my end as surely as if I betrayed you. You have asked nothing of me, but I have aided you as best I can."

"Martyrdom is the best sacrifice, don't you think?" Another voice, tinged with sarcasm broke in. "A hallowed memory rather than a disgrace."

"Now we do ask. Bestowalist priests, a weak brotherhood indeed. Your master knows who to trust, who to set the police on when things warm up. We need names, we need places, we need the planned actions. Not the easy ones, like your blessed Father Coran or Father Decran. No, the ones who compromise with us, but are in league with the establishment, the ones who will name names when the time comes."

They blindfolded him again, but when he tried to rise, the shaking of his knees betrayed him, and he fell. Carried, semi-conscious, he was eventually dumped in an alley far from the meeting place. Rescued, the story was put out that he had been mugged, and the pops started asking pointed questions about trainee priests found beaten up in areas notorious for loose living. Although off for a week to recover, he was not dismissed.

More correctly, he was not dismissed at once. Gornik and Nagren could use him no longer, but they had insight into what the Ultras were after. The truth, they could not disclose, lies meant certain death for Janis.

"He must vanish. Nowhere is safe in Kindland."

"Eastland will not welcome such a Bestowalist, and the few that are there might well betray him. Next ship to the Far Outs is the only way. I will talk to the Embassy."

So it was that a young Kindlander found himself on the tiny island of Thundia, the new clerk to the Seigneur. A few hundred inhabitants, and a place where any stranger's landing was to be regarded with deep suspicion. A place where the rigours of everyday life and an obsession with the welfare and diseases of sheep overrode any doctrinal niceties.

5. The Westerlander

All day, torrential rain had smothered Golliost's Camp. All the villagers stayed indoors, for there was no chance of working in the fields. The stream had risen rapidly then steadied, leading the elders to say that the rain must be ending in the hills to their west. It was to be expected; it had happened often enough. The Hochast family were assembling for the evening meal, the gloom scarcely lightened by a battered candelabra hoisted above the table.

Then there was a rumble, deepening to a roar. Grandpa Hochast was the first to react.

"Out, all of you, up the hill, now." As Mrs Hochast stopped to grab the precious chest of silverware, he dashed it from her hands and propelled her towards the door.

"Run, you fool. A minute or two and this place will be matchwood. A blockage has broken. Run."

As they clambered up the hillside, still bemused, the roar became deafening. Upstream, they saw a churning mass of mud, boulders and shattered grey-greens moving faster than any could run. It was at their height; no, it was higher and upon them. Grandpa was the first to disappear, but all but Almar followed. Even he was splattered and buffeted as he clung tight to a bush, a grey-green that had survived the periodic clearances.

The roar diminished and silence fell as the wave of water and debris reached the bay. Almar, paralysed by shock, remained gripping the bush's trunk. Not able to let go, nor to look around him. The rain stopped. Darkness became complete. Then the silence was broken by cries. He loosened his grip and stood up, but could see nothing. The cries came from the north, from nearer the bay where the valley widened out. He stumbled in that direction, but soon gave up. The rough ground tripped him repeatedly. Eventually, he lay back against a small crag, and waited for dawn. It was not cold, but he shivered, great waves of uncontrollable shaking racking his body as though in a fit.

The scene that faced him in the morning light was bleak indeed. Of the house, of the fields they had worked, there was no trace. Of the village below, nothing. A tumbled mass of boulders, uprooted plants and pools of mud extended right down to the bay, now changed in shape. The jetty? Gone, though where it had been was now some way from the shore. Only two houses, those built on the hillside above the bay, remained on his side. He made his way towards them, instinctively remaining above the scoured line that marked the flood's passage.

He approached the first house. There was no sound, no sign of life. He called out, afraid to enter unasked. There was no reply. He knocked on the door, and heard a faint moan from within. He waited, but no one came. He grasped the handle and entered. In the gloom, he at first saw nothing but the simple furniture of a family room. Then he noticed: the meal, the meal that had been his family's last, was on the table, half-eaten. The fire was out, the chairs disordered as those within had rushed to see what was happening.

He called again, even shouted, more as a release for his fear than in hope of a response. But response there was, a cry from behind a door. He pushed it open, and stood, still hesitant to enter another's bedroom. An old woman was sat on the edge of a large bed, a woman struggling to rise. Beside her was a man, lying still and fully dressed, his clothes covered in mud. Unthinking, Almar uttered the greeting to which he had been schooled.

"May the Bestower look kindly upon you, and guide your steps."

The woman looked up at him. Tear-stained though she was, it was rage, not grief that marked her face.

"Bestower? Bestower? That deceiver? That bringer of death and destruction? Did he guide my Fornon's steps last night?"

Almar took a step back, astonished. The woman was one of the few in the village he had seen only at a distance. He recalled his mother telling him and his sisters to avoid those two houses high on the hillside.

"Trouble, those Rettigasts and Nornens; don't go messing about near their place. Not company for right-thinking people."

Recalling the warning, the extent of his loss hit him. No mother, no Father, no sisters. No grandpa either. Even as the flood had passed, leaving him soaked and shocked, he had no doubt that his family were gone, but the needs of the moment, then the desire to find someone, anyone, alive had suppressed the grief. Now, he turned from the woman, sat in a chair in the main room, and cried. His sobs became gasps; elbows on the table still set with its unfinished meal, head in hands. Alone, with only a crazy, heretical woman, the only one alive, as far as he knew, in the whole village.

He might have remained like that for hours. The woman, however, emerged from her room and sat opposite him. She had put on more clothes, and wiped her face. He looked up as she sat down, seeing at once the features and dress of an Outer, an immigrant, a rare sight indeed.

"Almar Hochast, I think. I am Mrs Nornen. My husband? Went to save whom he might, achieved nothing, came home and died in our bed."

The flash of anger as she spoke was replaced by concern. A ten-year-old boy, here on his own. Was their house not up the hill?

"Your family, your home?"

"All gone, Mrs Nornen. Grandpa heard the noise and told us to run. He was too slow, and all the rest too. I was highest. I clutched a vantabush, and the wave just went over me. I heard a cry over here, but it was dark. I waited till dawn."

A believer saved by a grey-green, thought Lilah Nornen, with a twisted smile. She repressed the sharp retort, and stared silently at the boy. Him and me; are there any others? The Rettigasts? Not at home, and they had assumed that they had been in the village, to be swept away with all the rest. And my idiot husband, floundering in the dark in the hope of finding them, searching until he returned, his face blue and his breath in irregular gasps. Returned, lay down on the bed and died.

She summoned up enough energy to feed herself and the boy. Cold oatmeal, boiled the previous day, and the local cheese, hard and acid in their mouths. She led him outside, and together they scanned the scoured valley below them. At first, there was no sign of life. Then, a little convoy of cattle on the far side attracted their attention, a convoy accompanied by a single man. She shouted, to no avail, then turned to the house. Soon, she had a fire burning, to which she added damp peat, sending a column of smoke high into the air. She returned to find Almar sat where he had been, a blank look on his face.

"Has he seen the smoke? Has he waved?" The boy did not move or speak. She looked across the valley. The cows had halted, tethered, she supposed, but of the man there was no sign. There was a cluster of houses above the flood-line, where there had been no sign of life before. Now, however, several people emerged, and were looking in her direction. She waved a cloth at them, but there was no response. They disappeared indoors. She turned to Almar.

"There are people the other side, see those houses? We should cross to be with them."

Almar said nothing, nor did he stir from the stone on which he sat. Exasperation overcoming all else, she shook him by the shoulders, to no avail. She left him, and returned to the house. *What should I take*, she thought; come to that, what should I take from the Rettigast's, even if I return it to anyone who has a claim? For certain, they would be moved. Golliost's Camp, another name on a map with no meaning, another witness to the lunacy of Extermination. She walked the short distance to her neighbour's house. Memories of good times, times when they found their only Westerland friends, the only sceptics in a community of believers. She sat for a while, looking at the meagre possessions of their friends.

She was inside when she heard the sound of voices. She went to the door, to meet a row of hostile faces, including that of the priest, Father Steliast, who held Almar firmly by the arm.

"Robbing already, you heathen bitch?" The priest's voice was harsh. "Even from those backsliding neighbours? Not enough to bring down the Bestower's anger, but you must profit from it too."

Lilah stepped back towards the door. She got no further, as she was seized by two farmers and dragged out to the bare ground outside the entrance. She was flung to the ground. She struggled to sit upright, and faced the priest.

"Bestower's anger? On me? You know very well the cause of this disaster, Steliast. Strip the hills, hills where no bestowed plant can grow. And the hills come to the valley. Your work, Steliast, not mine, nor Rettigast's. You were warned. You paid no attention. This settlement is finished, and you know it."

"From her lips have you heard it," said the priest. "Heresy. We have paid the price of tolerance. Now we must redeem ourselves. Stone her."

The men hung back. Infuriated, the priest picked up a rock and threw, knocking her back to the ground. She lifted her bleeding head.

"In the name of mercy, take that boy out of sight and sound."

"What, and let him miss a lesson in piety?"

The priest adroitly kept hold of Almar, while stooping for another stone. She had covered her face with her arms, and the stone caught one. A change came over the men. One hurled a larger stone, hitting her back. It released a wave of anger, and the stones came fast. Lilah did not move. One approached and turned her over. She still breathed. Now all were concerned to finish it, the spectacle at once enraging and sickening. Another moved to find a larger rock, and brought it down on her face with all the force he could muster. It was over.

"Take the body into the house. Burn it, and her own too. The Bestower's work is done."

The priest held tight to Almar, but the boy was passive and silent. Bending down to the boy's level, the priest forced Almar to look at him, grasping him by the jaw.

"Your family is now avenged, boy. A good family. The Bestower looks kindly on those who have made such a sacrifice. You will be cared for."

Almar said nothing. His face was set in an impenetrable, blank gaze. A silent party crossed the valley of devastation, the men avoiding each other's eyes. Only the priest had a swing in his gait and a smile on his face. A case that would go beyond the commissioner, and propel him upwards. The Bestower be praised.

*****

The days that followed became blurred in Almar's memory. There was an official, a commissioner, he supposed. He was interviewed, and had answered in monosyllables. He ate what was put before him, and sat silent when not doing so. There was a walk to a road, quite a long one, in which the last part had been on the shoulders of a stranger. A car, the first he had seen, arrival at a town, a seaport he had later known as Derant-on-Sea, and then an orphanage, where the commissioner had dropped him.

Although austere, the place aimed to fit its residents into the wider society. The standard routines of communal living bothered him not at all, and the daily periods of worship could be undertaken automatically. It was the attempts to educate him that caused problems. In many other such places, his passivity and silence would have led to punishment. The warden, a widow herself, was more humane. There were many interviews, many attempts at understanding. Teachers' complaints were stalled, patience was required.

For all she knew, his mind might have remained locked, locked in a set of memories that drove out any dealings with the world around him. It was luck, an accident, that resolved the matter. He was, yet again, in the warden's office. A teacher was also there, once more to ask what was to be done about this silent, uncooperative child.

"We must have patience, Dragimer," the warden said. "I have only recently been told the full story. It was not just the loss of his family. He found another survivor, an Outer immigrant, who looked after him." She looked straight at the teacher.

"That woman was stoned to death in his sight. By order of a priest. The commissioner did not tell me the whole truth when the boy was brought here. Even by official standards, it was barbaric, but of course concealed. No trial, no evidence, nothing. It got out, of course, because that cleric boasted about it in Traggatun when he was transferred."

"I made some enquiries. There was a school in that village. The reports are filed here in Derant. Almar is gifted. Come his twelfth birthday and he would have been boarded at the Academy here. He can read and write better than any in your class. The family were bookish enough."

"No hint of heresy in the family?" asked Dragimer.

"No. All I learnt was that the Hochasts were well-respected, did their duty, and earned no reproach. Martyrsons, after all. What was in the mind of the priest, I cannot imagine."

"The priesthood?" asked Dragimer, drily. It provoked a scream. They turned, remembering the boy's presence. Almar was now sobbing, shaking his head and clenching his fists. Stuttered noes were interrupted by sobs.

Quite what happened next, Almar could not remember. The teacher had gone, that he did recall. Then an outpouring, an outpouring on paper, about which he remembered little, a jumbled set of words handed to the warden.

"It will stay with me, Almar. Now listen. Those with little talent have, to a degree, greater choices in this world, for there are many occupations where little intelligence is needed. For those with the talents, the options are less open, for the priests certainly try to enlist. They can compel. But there are other needs too, in the government or in the great Academy in High City. These cannot be challenged. But the priests know of your talent. Leave here apparently unskilled, and they will recruit you and break you. Appear middling, and you may end up as a teacher, a teacher under the watchful eyes of a priest. Only high achievement will free you from them."

The change had not been immediate, but it was enough. Withdrawn but studious, he had no difficulty in surpassing his peers. He was enrolled in the local academy, while remaining tied to the orphanage. His bent was scientific, and as a consequence he and his fellows enjoyed a certain notoriety, for, however useful such knowledge might be, it involved the aboriginal, and not simply to engage in its destruction. The hint of heresy hung over them, the more so as they mingled with the Outers, merchants and seamen both, who traded specimens, often alive, to the youngsters who pestered them at the harbour. There was even a consulate of sorts, dealing mainly with redeeming drunks and brawlers, or requests for emigration where a local girl had fallen for an Outer. Specimens were sold or bartered, and the Academy's museum was among the best in the country. The boys were always made welcome at the consulate, but had to run a gauntlet of hostile believers, often ostentatiously writing names in notebooks.

Indeed, the consulate was picketed regularly, the more so when rumour had it that a girl would be coming to collect her emigration papers. The local pops would carry articles questioning the value of such a presence, and it was the subject of many a fiery sermon. Outers were, if not unbelievers, at best half-hearted in their service to the Bestower. There would be many who would have welcomed a ban on contacts, were it not for the fact that the town's existence was dependent on the trade. Hence, such stirrings never resulted in action, other than the odd prosecution of the boldest students, who ventured to picket the pickets. Not that such prosecutions were regarded lightly; two or three years on clearance, and your card marked when it came to employment. Some skipped, being smuggled in and out of the consulate to their exile in the Far Outs, with which no extradition treaty existed.

Almar kept a low profile. The warden would talk to him often; any excuse, any misdemeanour, and he would be removed. At one meeting, he had raised a question.

"The ships are all from the Far Outs, never our own. Why do we not sail? Is there no consulate of ours at one of their ports?" The warden's explanation took him aback.

"Historically, it was only Outers who mastered sailing. A necessity to travel among the islands, and to catch the oilworms. *Unclean, Unclean,* the priests all say, but there's many in High City use the oil rather than be beholden to Kindland. At least the worms are killed. It's a penance now, being a wormer. With our nearly eternal westerlies, none of ours thought the journey worthwhile. Of course, with steamships there is not the same problem. A couple set up here, maybe forty years ago. They were closed down very quickly, because they lost half their crews to desertion. Avoiding the draft was one thing, but the life style of Outers was a draw too. The Temple acted at the highest level; better to supervise a few heretics here than shed population. The Outers need people, as do we; they certainly would not return any, other than the odd misguided missionary."

"Could we not conquer them?" Almar had asked. "From what I learnt, there are few of them, and all the made stuff, the smelted iron, comes from here."

"From here, but now from Kindland, even Eastland too, and it would mean war with them. The Outers have learnt, too; they make better ships than us. Oh, it's thought about, believe me. It would need a navy, which we don't have, and to what end, other than religious fervour? If you get to the Academy in High City, you'll hear such talk often enough. We can hope it stays that way and goes no further."

The time to leave came quickly enough. Priests and would be employers were in and out of the Academy, recruiting, while the teachers were finding places for the bright but less than pious. Many previous scoffers mysteriously followed the priests, and Almar learnt of the subtle pressures brought to bear. A family blessed with a vocation would prosper. As an orphan, he was shielded from some of these pressures, but, as he soon realised, he had been singled out. Father Steliast had not loosened his grip from afar. There were interviews, interviews that mostly pitted teacher against priest. Almar said as little as possible, conscious that a charge of heresy could be held over him for just a word out of place.

It was going badly. All claims of scientific promise were countered by the need of such talent in the Temple, for the better execution of the Bestower's will. Would he presume to put a mere personal preference before His will? The more the teacher brought forward Almar's special talents, the more the priests indicated the Temple's need of just such ability. That his interest was in biology, not extermination, was something to conceal, or he would be prey to a charge of heresy. He had already planned an escape, talking to the consul himself, and of course to the warden, for the orphanage would suffer from a defection. Both had promised to help.

Two things saved him. An offer of not just a place, but a scholarship at the Academy in High City itself, a rarity indeed, and only the second the tiny academy at Derant had won. Even the principal was now prepared to plead for Almar's release. That might not have been enough. Then came the shocking news: Steliast had committed suicide. The cause was never made clear, but rumours told of child molestation, the torturing of suspected heretics, even simple consorting with prostitutes. The pressure eased, and soon disappeared. Almar was to be on his way to High City, to the centre of all Westerland power, to the only institute that compared with the renowned Academy and colleges of Kindland.

His departure was a little out of the ordinary. Among his parting visits was one to the Outer's consulate, where he was summoned by the Far Out consul himself.

"A favour, if you please, Master Hochast. I have an old friend in the Academy, Professor Nornost. A biologist, indeed, I hope he comes to teach you. He visited the Far Outs many years ago for research, and I was his guide. Things change; such a visit is no longer possible, and I would be most unwelcome in High City. We have kept in touch, but the mail is so slow, and what is written is sometimes wilfully misconstrued by the Office of Communication. I have a letter. To be delivered in person, of course."

Almar looked at the consul. The face was held in a studied smile. Almar nodded, and a letter was handed over, the envelope conspicuously lacking the consul's seal and crest.

"I don't imagine you will be subject to any impertinence on your journey. If that is not the case, then please destroy the letter if at all possible. A simple message to the warden will suffice either way; just say *I arrived safely* or *sadly, I lost a few items on the way.*"

The journey was less than easy. For more than a thousand kilometres, there was no railway like those that ran from end to end in Kindland and Eastland, just a bad road along which a succession of wheezing buses, trucks and even bullock carts made their way from town to town. Buses edged to the side by monstrous, steam-powered road trains; towns that were often little more than a crossroads, a traveller's hotel, a few shops and, of course, a temple, often absurdly large and fresh looking amid the desolate countryside. A railway? Always promised, never delivered, as his fellow passengers grumbled. Iron must needs be imported.

And desolate it was. The high, flat central plain was often bare and gullied. Tiny patches of cultivation surrounded some of the settlements; larger areas were covered in the dark, grey-green scrub that clearance had not reached. Sometimes, there were signs of fresh burning, and just outside one village he saw people at work hacking at the scrub and carrying the cuttings to the fires. There were swamps too, covered in bluish-grey tussocks. It rained often.

Except for the flatness, the sight was familiar enough to Almar. The hills, he knew, were hundreds of kilometres distant on either side; they would be equally uninspiring. The buses were far from full, and, indeed, Almar could see little reason to travel from one remote outpost to another. Only as they approached the railhead at Gobinau did the buses fill up, and on the outskirts of the town he saw gangs working to extend the railway.

"At that rate, they'll reach Derant in the next millennium," a sour voice behind him said. It had taken four full days, for the buses did not travel at night. The traveller's hotels on the way had been grim, even by the standards of the orphanage, and the company he faced at table did not invite conversation. It was with relief that he left the last bus and found his way to the Railway Hotel, next door to the station itself, an imposing building to his rustic eyes.

He dipped into his bag for the booking. His room was paid for, as was a meal. The clerk looked at the docket, glanced around, then invited him behind the counter, bags and all, and into a room opening off one end. Behind a cluttered desk sat a thin, middle-aged man with a look on his face that told of innumerable disappointments.

"The scholar from Derant, sir," said the clerk, and left. The man did not rise from his seat.

"Mr Hochast? Please take a seat. I am the manager, Mr Hochast. A pleasure to welcome a scholar; they are a rarity in these parts." The manager fidgeted in his chair. Almar smiled and nodded. The booking would have been made by the Academy itself, he supposed, as would purchasing the train ticket he held in his bag.

"Mr Hochast, I have a favour to ask of you. We have a large party here tonight, a Temple conference; *Spirituality in the age of decadence*." The manager grimaced.

"There are many priests and novices among them, Mr Hochast, even a High Chosen One. They are aware of your intended presence, and are anxious to make your acquaintance. I fear that some are already in a mood for what they are pleased to call *jollity*. It pains me to say it, Mr Hochast, but a fair amount of drink has been consumed already. Those colleges have a way of living that is less than pious."

"You mean that I am in danger of assault, sir?"

"Rather more than that. Oh, not murder. They have, I suspect, another intention, to relieve you of all your belongings, or to disperse them, and leave you naked on the street. It has happened before. The police would take you in, and only you would face charges. You would have great difficulty in making your way to High City. Scholars are not popular among such people."

Almar stared at the man. Surely, an outrage of this sort would be investigated, be prosecuted. He thought of the letter. Then he recalled the manager's words, *I have a favour to ask of you.* It was not Almar's safety that concerned him, but the reputation of the hotel. So, I am to stay out of sight. And then what? Will they break into my room, then bombard the manager to reveal my whereabouts? And if they do not find me, will they attempt some disturbance at the station? Do they know which train?

Another man might have taken fright, but the memory of Steliast, of Lilah, surfaced with force. It was with steel in his voice that he answered.

"I thank you, sir, and I do not wish to be a cause of trouble. Indeed, I think we should avoid it altogether. The station is closed at night, I assume?"

The manager nodded.

"So now I have a favour to ask of you. You have a man of my size on the staff? A man who can be absent tomorrow morning? Called to a funeral, perhaps? You have bags? The uniform, then, and enough luggage to hold what I have here. I am sure you can arrange for the disposal of my own bags. Oh, and a black band for my arm."

The manager nodded, and disappeared in search of the items. Do they have photographs? Almar wondered. They would not expect to need them. A risk, for he could scarcely alter his face. Even as he waited, he heard a conversation at the desk, a bellowing voice.

"Well, Mr Clerk, has our beloved scholar arrived? We are so looking forward to making his acquaintance." There was a gust of laughter. Almar could not hear the clerk's response, but the next outburst relaxed him.

"Out drinking, you presume, even before checking in? Well, boys will be boys, hey lads, we know, don't we? One or two ourselves before we get to know him better."

The noise faded. The manager returned with clothes and two suitcases large enough to hold Almar's clothes as well as his other belongings. He drew a black band out of his pocket. A few minutes later, Almar was outside a service door and walking away. Now, he had only the problem of the night. He walked, purposefully, away from the station and hotel, in what he hoped was a poorer part of town. He was rewarded. An inn sign hung from a shabby building. Cash on the nail, sorry for your loss, breakfast at seven. At last, he could rest.

The morning went smoothly. Priests there were at the station, but there were many trains departing for the capital or smaller towns on the way. Several had departed already, and the priests, already bored, paid no attention to some liveried servant in mourning. The train was crowded, no chance to change unseen, but he grabbed a window seat and sighed as the train pulled out of the station.

It was an altogether smoother journey. The train could at least move faster, and through the night; only one would pass before they reached High City the following evening. The seats around him were filled, but, seeing the armband, and his expressionless face, none attempted to talk to him. He realised that he lacked food and drink. Worse, he had nothing to read, and had no wish to engage his neighbours in talk. For hours, he stared blankly out of the window, watching the still dismal landscape go by. Rain and heavy clouds did nothing to ease the scene.

The food and drink situation resolved itself, for at the larger towns the train would wait for twenty minutes or so, and the platform was full of vendors, passing their goods through the opened windows. His fellow passengers had to crowd over him to buy, and there was a little talk, if only by way of apologies or thanks as he passed food in and money out. He could also buy a newspaper, a rather dull looking one, far from the pops that most were reading and discussing. It attracted attention, and a first attempt at conversation.

"An educated man, then," said one woman sitting opposite. "Sorry to see of your loss. I suppose it inclines one to a more serious view of affairs. I couldn't be doing with all that politics stuff. It's the clever ones fall into heresy, they say."

Almar mentally cursed himself for not thinking. A servant reading the *Capital Courier* indeed. Out of character, unless he was a dangerous radical. He did his best.

"The Bestower preserves me, I hope, madam. It was the priest told me to be forewarned, for I have never been to the High City. He was concerned that my simple faith would be challenged. Be aware, my son, he said, that you may be spared the shock of hearing notions that are strange, even perverse, from the lips of those you meet."

Most of the passengers nodded vigorously at this affirmation of faith, but Almar noticed one young man, furthest from the window, who said nothing, but looked across the compartment with a sardonic smile. A young man noticeably better dressed than the others, who then turned to a book, a book with plain covers. The rest struck up a conversation about the iniquities of the capital; about how they were looking to conduct their business and return to the tranquillity of home. Almar remained silent. His reason for travel was evident. After a while, hidden behind his paper, it struck him that there was something shrill, something false, about the protestations of piety and dislike for the loose living of urban life.

The young man excused himself, and left the compartment. The change in the atmosphere was obvious. No actual sighs, but a sense of relaxation that was almost palpable. It happened that the train stopped briefly at a tiny station. There were shouts, and a banging of doors towards the end of the train. Almar moved to open the window to see what was happening.

"Don't do that, young man," came a gruff voice from the seats alongside him. "You have never made this journey before, I think. Best pay no attention."

Almar sat back in his seat, struck by the urgency in the man's tone. A moment later, a file of manacled prisoners was marched past just as the train started moving. There were mutterings of sympathy and a shaking of heads. He was about to ask questions when the young man returned, and the woman opposite put her finger to her lips. There was a long period of silence. Almar turned to his paper. Most of it was dull reading indeed, but the editorials were more revealing. Disturbances in Kindland; the expulsion of Westerlanders, including priests; the beastly experimentation in Eastland; the passage of Kindland steamers through *our own* waters as they made for the Far Outs. The tone was anything but heretical, indeed, it followed the pops Almar had seen at home, calling for a firmer response from the government, without the strident calls for retribution that bellowed from the pops themselves.

As dusk fell, Almar had to make another trip to the toilet. As he made his way back down the corridor, he met the smart, enigmatic young man on the same journey. The book was tucked under his arm. The man stopped him to talk.

"You are a stranger to these journeys, I think? You will have travelled far."

Unthinking, Almar nodded. "From Derant, yes, I have never been this far east before."

The man whistled in astonishment. He gave Almar a glance, almost of pity.

"A servant in livery, with two large cases, attending a funeral? Surely only an extreme of piety could make you take such a trip. I had no idea such an establishment existed in such a backwater. The cost alone must be a burden."

Almar shrunk back, cursing himself for his stupidity. The behaviour of his fellow passengers now made sense. Was this a sniffer-out of heresy, of draft evaders, travelling to detect and to inform?

The man was regarding him with an air of detached amusement. Without a word, he opened the book, and showed Almar the title page.

Evolutionary Principles Explained
With further reference to human origins and the case for the First Run
Professor Karl Northport
Director of the Institute of Biology, Kindopol

"I am no priest's sneak, lad, though your fellow travellers are convinced of it. Do the idiots think that such a one would dress as I do? You are not what you seem. And had there been such a spy, you would have been bundled off this train two stations back at the latest. I was half expecting it, for the bastards are well trained, and your disguise is less than convincing. That newspaper gave me certainty, for all it is the Ultra's rag of choice."

Almar stood dumb. They both had to stand aside as a woman brushed impatiently past them. Here was a real heretic. The book was famous and banned, for all it was a hundred years old. Back home, there were rumours that Outers smuggled copies into Derant, and the consul had vented his anger when his compatriots complained of searches and confiscations, though he had not heard of this book being among the seizures.

"You do not trust me? Very sensible. It would appear, though, that you fear being detained if recognised. In the city, I trust you have some permit, some letter of recommendation? The place is not as obedient as the powers would like. It is policed, if that is the right word. An oddity like yourself would be searched and questioned, almost as a matter of routine. I do not know your business, and I wish to keep it that way. If you have a change of clothes in those cases of yours, a change that matches your real reason for travel, I suggest you make straight for a toilet when the train arrives. There is one on each platform. It is expected that users take their luggage with them. Change; if possible, emerge with one case only, and go about your business."

The man did not even wait for an answer, but walked away down the corridor. Almar returned to his seat, and sat silently in the dark. Soon, uncomfortable though he was, he fell asleep. Morning came, and the scene outside was already changed. Here the small towns through which they passed were more prosperous. The countryside was less ravaged, with more cultivation, although there were still whole stretches of barren ground. By late afternoon, the settlement became continuous. His companions were packing things away, holding coats on their knees. Soon the train entered the central station, and the crowds descended. There were police on the platform, not appearing to look for anyone, and Almar made his way unhindered to a toilet. Armed with instructions, it was an obvious student that made his way to the hostel as darkness fell.

The aged porter registered his arrival, and gave him a key to his room. A package was placed in his hands, the porter weighing it in his hands as he lifted it from a box.

"Your instructions, Mr Hochast. Scholarship boy, from the weight of it. Good luck to you. There is a welcome downstairs at eight, to meet others and those ahead of you in your studies."

The room was tiny, but his own. There was scarcely room for a bed and a minute, almost toy-like desk, with a few cupboards lining one wall. For Almar, there was one huge luxury, electric light. He sat on the bed and spilled the contents of his package. The porter's remark became clear. As a scholarship boy there were books of vouchers for meals, and even an envelope of cash, *allowance per hundred, see instructions for future disbursements.* There was, however, a separate letter, addressed personally. He tore open the envelope.

Dear Mr Hochast,

It is our pleasure to welcome you to the Faculty of Biology. It is our custom to interview all scholars individually to determine the most appropriate programme of studies. Please present yourself at Professor Nornost's office in the Anniversary Building at nine o'clock tomorrow morning.

Yours,

Amna Herlmanost
Administrator

The maps, the instructions, the rules of the hostel, all were glanced at, but scarcely taken in. A meal was available at seven. Almar explored the corridor, found the washrooms and toilets, washed and changed his clothes. Pocketing the consul's letter, he ventured downstairs, soon recognising that there were many other newcomers looking anxiously around them for the place to go. It was a simple canteen, with little choice, and quite a long queue. When he presented his scholar's voucher, there was a whistle behind him.

"Well, well, a scholarship boy. Endangered species you are, if you'll excuse the Consie language. Hang on till I've paid and sit with me."

Almar did as he was bid. The man with him introduced himself, "Jehon Maderist, Geologist, Third year. No scholarship, worse luck, it's a penny-pinching existence, but I enjoy it. You?"

"Almar Hochast, Biologist, I hope, but I have to be interviewed. From Derant."

Jehon looked at Almar in frank astonishment. The back of the back of beyond. But sending a scholarship boy, to study biology at that. A thought struck him.

"Do you get to meet Outers then? I hear they have rather too much biology than is thought proper, if you get my meaning. But perhaps it is livestock or crops that are your concern?"

"No, it is the aboriginal stuff. And yes, we meet those that visit, but we cannot go there. Our academy gets material from them, for there's precious little left locally."

The conversation drifted off into other channels. But Jehon shepherded Almar into the welcome party, ensuring that he was among fellow scientists. The segregation by discipline was very noticeable, and among the historians and spiritualist students there were many wearing large Bestowalist medallions on silver chains. Young priests were among them. The party did not last long, and Almar returned to his room. It had been searched. Not that his possessions were scattered, just the slight rearrangements, especially of the papers he had left on his bed, revealed that they had been gone through. His hand felt for the letter safely tucked in his jacket.

His walk to the Anniversary Building next morning was uneventful. The invitation saw him directed to Professor Nornost's room. A room adorned with pictures, including photographs, of an amazing array of aboriginal life, both plant and animal. A room otherwise littered with boxes, files and stacks of books that threatened to topple. The professor rose from his chair, smiled, and told Almar to sit, an instruction that involved uncovering a chair smothered in papers.

So anxious was Almar to be relieved of his burden, that he pulled it out and handed it to the professor before the man had uttered a word more.

"It is from the Outer consul at Derant, sir. I was asked to deliver it personally. I think people have tried to steal it, sir. And others tried to prevent me reaching here at all."

It came out as a gabble, of which Almar was instantly ashamed. The professor pulled out a monocle, adjusted it in his eye, and turned the envelope over and over in his hands. He grunted, and put it to one side. He released the monocle, and regarded Almar in silence for a few seconds.

"It was wrong of Boone to give you such a task, though he could not have known the risks you ran. Most dangerously at Gobinau. We did not hear about that until too late."

He grinned.

"Boy, we don't know how you did it, but you should have seen the faces in Spiritual here. Boasting before the event that they would have a new recruit, or deny us one at least. Locked away in a monastery somewhere, and turning up here as a born-again Exterminator. Oh, you would have done, don't doubt it. There is evil worse than that bastard Steliast, for all he had an eye for talent. We heard, boy, no need to relive the day."

Almar was obliged, however, to give a full account of his journey, interrupted by chuckles from the professor at each little twist. He turned serious only when Almar described his encounter with the Evolutionist.

"Damn fool, though he gave you good advice. The likes of him get caught, and then confess, and another bunch of idealists are under the bush. He'd do better scarpering to Kindland. True? Who knows? Evolution is accepted, grudgingly, by most, for the aboriginal, but we have to keep at it. The notion of a diabolical Bestowal is what fuels Exterminationism, and you will have seen more than most where it leads."

*****

Almar's student days passed all too quickly. Quickly, and very congenially, for science students were, to a degree, sheltered from the religious enthusiasm that prevailed in the ruling factions in the city, and in the government. They stuck together.

"Never," he was told, "never go out on your own, especially at night. You will disappear. There will be a perfunctory search. There will be talk of loose living. Months, even years later, a new novice will be scurrying round the High Temple, or a monk will be ensuring that some hopeless villagers are doing their duty by the Bestower in the guise of the Destroyer."

He soon grasped the situation. Faith notwithstanding, geologists and biologists were necessary. Not merely as technical assistants in the Great Work, the removal of the aboriginal, but as those who understood the properties of soils and the biology of the fauna and flora. Diabolical in origin they might be, though it was not downright heretical to challenge that, but both the living and the fossil were needed by the economy. Needed for fuel, for fabrics, even for building and furnishing.

The consequences were strange. The biologists, forced to share a building, were divided to the point of silence by their chosen studies: the Bestowed and how to encourage their growth, or the Aboriginal. Even that was not the sum of their differences. It was at one of the rather formal research seminars that Almar learnt of still further tension. A student of the Bestowed reported on the attempts to find a strain of needle-leaf that would grow even in the sodden hills of the far west. The priest-professors were nodding with approval; seek, and we will find the Bestower's bounty.

"Others have gone further," the hapless student said. "They have grasses, grains, that will grow among the aboriginal. I hope to test this here, to avoid clearance before planting."

There was uproar, even hissing.

"Others? Speak plainly; you mean those deviant Easties, the ones feeding abo muck to animals. Not only animals, but to humans too. Who are looking for co-existence in despite of the Bestower. You stand in peril of your soul."

The student was left standing helpless at the podium, while professors and their students shouted at one another. A geologist managed to shout above the babble.

"Even a Bestowed needle-leaf will not grow on bare rock. That is what is left when you Exterminators have done your work."

Nornost interjected. "It works on Halfland. Why not here?"

He had no reply. The session ended in confusion. The student was not seen again. Two others, however, were abruptly transferred to Nornost's care, where they had protection.

Even within the section devoted to the aboriginal, there were sharp divisions. A whole laboratory was devoted to the development of poisons that would kill the aboriginal without the need to dig, slash and burn. A laboratory amply funded, but one having little to show for it, as Almar soon discovered. Nornost had him seconded as an assistant.

"It is a pet project. I have followed up where they have sprayed. The grey-greens come back within a year, and they grow fast." The professor smiled. "More than that, the abos are evolving. Already there are resistant strains. Ha, evolution in action. Keep notes, Almar. They know, but bluff with the authorities; they know we know too. Try to inform on us, to rat out the *infirm of faith,* and we present evidence."

6. The Refugee

"And so, as you can see, there are at least three lines of evolution among the Protopedatoidea, the octopods of common speech. The Megacheliceridae, from the Outer Far Outs and eastern Eastland, the Eunornostidae both here and on the Inner Far Outs, and the Macropedidae all over Kindland and the west of Eastland."

Almar Hochast, now Dr Hochast, was concluding his seminar. The results of ten years' work, work that had moved slowly, carefully, without any intrusion into his monitoring of the latest herbicides. Work that had taken him back to home, and more surreptitiously, to trades arranged by Consul Boone that brought material both living and fossil from the other continents, places he would never visit personally.

The audience was mixed, and he knew that some regarded such studies as at best frivolous, at worst, subversive. He was braced for some awkward questions, his anxiety only partly eased by the stern presence of Nornost in the chair. The first question was simple: *material from Halfland? No, regretfully, for octopods are unknown. There are First Run equivalents. I can hope, for the place is little studied.*

"Not our territory, I suppose. Do you think a, a eunornostid presence would justify a claim?"

There was laughter, for the ownership of Halfland, useless as it was, by Kindland, was the subject of grumpy editorials in newspapers of all kinds. Hochast smiled and made no reply. The next question was more penetrating.

"A group common to the Outers and Eastland? A common ancestor? With 23,000 km between them? And just next door, another group altogether? Carried by the great Anasman perhaps, feeding his crew to them one by one."

More laughter, for the Far Out adulation of the great circumnavigator, who had, after all, discovered nothing of use, was a source of amusement, of scorn, even, for the pious. It was, though, a question with a point.

"Well," replied Hochast, "there are always the lost continents. But more to the point, there is the geology, the movement of continents, an idea that gains increasing acceptance from our colleagues next door. Rocks match."

"Rather less acceptance from Temple Hill, I think." A rather low voice interjected. Nornost was quick to react.

"Doubted, certainly, but not proscribed. Many here will know of similar patterns among aboriginal plants, and the evidence from fossils. Plants, or their seeds and spores might, just might, be blown over such distances. Scarcely the largest octopods, though. Dr Hochast's work gives us stronger evidence than those plants."

A priest, a scholarly one, as shown by the silver edging in his robe, rose to his feet. A loud and artificial cough caused heads to turn, then look away. The atmosphere chilled.

"I do commend Dr Hochast for his perseverance. I have now seen more than I could wish of the anatomical peculiarities of creatures not merely of no utility, but an impediment to our fulfilment of the Bestower's Will. Creatures, I am glad to say, that are now a rarity in our nation. Peculiarities that, as I am sure you are aware, may be, in my view should be, attributed to other causes. That is by the way, however. I am more concerned to hear Dr Hochast's assessment of the practical use, if any, to which all this labour, this theorising might be put. Others labour as hard, no, harder, to claim for us what has been Bestowed."

A point anticipated, for Nornost had faced it in various forms for years. He sat back and let Hochast reply.

"Your most learned reverence, Father, I think you will know that among my duties, the most time-consuming has been to aid those attempting to find reliable means for the eradication of aboriginal vegetation?"

"A programme that has consumed both labour and resources to pitifully little effect. Yes, Dr Hochast, I am aware. Maybe a greater proportion of your effort and intellect devoted to it might have yielded more results. Oh, I beg pardon; please continue."

"On the contrary, Father. Your assessment of that programme is to the point. And there are two obstacles to its success. One is the rapid evolution of varieties that are resistant to our products; the other is that what may work on some will not work on others. We have lacked any explanation; trial and error are our only recourse. My work, work on animals that you yourself regard as harmful, suggests a more systematic approach: that those more closely-related might respond similarly. Correct identification of such groups might well reduce that error."

"Ingenious, Dr Hochast, ingenious. Yes, I have heard similar arguments from Professor Nornost, *we must understand before we can act, study interactions before we disrupt.* Fine words, and a passport to absorption in the devil's, the Deceiver's handiwork, whether it was done yesterday or a billion years ago makes no odds. So, you will now design poisons or parasites that will kill octopods? Creatures that in our continent, if not elsewhere, have been reduced to negligible numbers by rather more prosaic means?"

The priest slammed down his foot, twisting it, as though stamping on a bug.

"Numbers so low that we now have higgyback plagues, another case of evolution, Father, for they can eat most of our crops." Hochast was struggling to contain himself. The priest's face whitened, and his eyes narrowed. Nornost intervened.

"It is the principle, Father, not the creature or plant. Dr Hochast has not merely traced the evolution of a group of animals. He has developed the analytical methods that may be applied more widely, even to higgybacks."

"So, why not those contemptible creatures? That would certainly be of more use."

"I talked about three groups, Father. The matrices are tedious to compute. Higgybacks? There are probably ten, maybe fifteen such groups. A lifetime of dissections, measurements and calculations, Father. There is, of course, the great computer in Kindopol; it would take years off the time, as it would for grey-greens. An exchange, perhaps?"

"With that bunch of heretics, Hochast? Oh, I know well that you have asked, as has Nornost. No. Not merely no, but never. Only the most trusted, the most devout are permitted to travel to that sink."

The priest hitched up his robe and left. There were no more questions.

*****

"He's lying, of course," said Nornost, as they sat in his office afterwards. "Plenty of students get to study there, and our merchants and diplomats are anything but the most pious. Kindopol whorehouses will vouch for that. It's us that they will not abide, us and some of the geologists. We are liable to get *ideas,* and the brightest may decide not to return. Another investment in a good scholarship boy like yourself down the drain."

"Surely there have been some? What about Prof. Riciniast? He was there for two years."

"Riciniast has a family, Almar. A large family that was not allowed to accompany him. And no dubious connection to Outers, either, unlike us. Students have families too."

I have none, thought Hochast, *and neither does Nornost, widowed and childless*. And for all the curses thrown at Kindland, there was both envy of their prestige and a desire to field the equally able, not to see them depart. Besides, we need what they have, and it's not just ideas.

"The ideas get here anyway, Prof. Rather more than ideas, so I'm told. There's Eastie bacteria in some of the fertility trials, though those up the hill don't know it, officially at least. Working well, so Ballinest said."

"Ballinest? What did he say, and when? Who heard?" Nornost had gone pale.

"Just the other day. There was a seminar, improving crop yields. Dramatic results too, and he was evasive as to just what was done. There were jokes about new formulations that would make a few fortunes. He said no more until there was a group of us down at the *Crushed Higgy* afterwards. He rattled off a few names. They meant nothing to me, the terms those microbiologists use have passed me by. But a girl questioned one, and Ballinest smirked. *A little help from our friends, but it will be ours in the eyes of the world.* We all know who those friends might be, Prof. Even the Kindlanders get their cultures from the Easties."

"Idiot. Him, not you. It's as well you told me." Nornost sat silent for a while, his fingers arched in front of his face. Then he rose, and without a word walked around the room, touching this picture, that book, the piles of papers, the cabinets containing his collections. Almar did not dare to move from his chair. Nornost moved to stand behind him, his face invisible. Almar felt heavy hands on his shoulders.

"Those up the hill, Almar, they know very well where Ballinest got his bacteria from. What they do not know is how he got them. They will bring him in, Almar, and he will tell them. You know why and how they will persuade him. They came from me, Almar. The letter you brought me from Boone all those years ago is not all that has passed between us."

"If they know," started Almar.

"Why would they worry? Because on the one hand, there are some who want to claim a Westerland discovery, on the other, there are those that will denounce the whole project. Eastie muck, they will say, a product that might have been bred from abo matter. Whose ears will the wretch's blabbing reach first? Either way, those who know the truth are an obstacle. For once, there will be no argument about that, regardless of any attempts to continue with the cultures."

"But Ballinest was at my seminar, Prof. He's not been taken in. Maybe it has not been reported."

"Our, or rather your good luck, Almar. The wheels up there turn slowly; informants do not rush, but cover their tracks. They will think before they act, and there will be no breaking down of doors in the early hours where you or I are concerned. Just some very unfortunate accidents. I might even merit an obituary in the *Courier*. Ballinest will not be so lucky, nor those in the *Higgy* with you. And in whom else has he confided?"

"My luck, Prof.?"

Nornost returned to his seat, grabbing an old cloak as he passed the rack. He scribbled something on an old envelope, then looked up at Almar.

"Your luck, because you are going to disappear, now. I am going to escort you downstairs, and in front of the receptionist I will say that I am taking you home, unwell. In your apartment's lobby, you will cover yourself with this." Nornost waved the cloak. "You will go to this house." He named a street and number. "You will show them this envelope." He passed it to Almar. "In a week or two, with luck, you will be in Kindopol. You will not return."

The professor unlocked a drawer in his desk, and pulled out a purse, which he threw at Almar, who was shaking in his chair. It landed in his lap.

"Your guides may need the means to sustain you. A policeman may even accept a bribe. More to the point, the ship that carries you will demand a fee. Now give me the key to your apartment; I will spend a little time there, and be sure to tell any I meet on the way out that I have left you sick, and not to be disturbed. I will return here. Now repeat the address."

"But," Almar started, to be instantly interrupted.

"No but, Almar. But what about me, you would ask? There would be no grace period, no claim of sickness, were I to vanish. I am too old to run, and I still have some friends up the hill. I take my chances; you will do as you are told."

A knock on the door. A door opened a mere slit on its chains. An envelope passed in without words spoken. A hurried opening, and Almar almost dragged inside. He was led to a comfortably furnished room in which an elegantly dressed, middle-aged man rose to greet him.

"From Nornost, comrade," his escort said, and departed. The man waved him to a chair. For a while, he stared silently at his guest. Then a smile broke out.

"I wonder, comrade, if you remember a certain train journey, what would it be, eleven, twelve or more years ago? Where a certain youth, in not very convincing disguise, was given advice for his welfare. Advice that he appears to have taken, since he is now here with me."

"The Evolutionist? The one that struck terror into fellow passengers. Nornost swore that one so conspicuous would be taken. I remember. You are he?"

"Indeed. I am afraid comrade will have to do for an introduction, but you need none, Dr Hochast. Not because I follow your career, but because Professor Nornost made arrangements with us many years ago. I had assumed that the dangers were past, but it seems not so. Tell me."

The telling took longer than Almar had anticipated. Names, dates, homes or hostels, all written down on a single sheet.

"There are some we cannot save, your colleague Ballinest for one. For the rest, where all those unfortunate accidents happen, we can protect to a degree. Too many near misses on someone, and even our lapdog pops pay attention."

"My professor? He seemed almost resigned."

"By no means hopeless, Dr Hochast. There are those up the hill, pragmatists, willing enough to tolerate such imports, provided they can be claimed as the wonders of our Westerland science, free from the taint of aboriginal evil. It will be made known that should any mishap befall the professor, certain rumours will be started, certain investigations will be called for. It is not only the likes of us, Dr Hochast, who may fear interrogation."

*****

There were just three of them on the beach, already shivering in the night air. The drizzle had stopped, but the damp had penetrated their clothes. The silence, save for the swish of swell on the rocks, was unnerving. Almar sat apart, no longer looking, hopelessly, out to sea. His guides stood muttering to each other.

They were the third pair he had encountered, all taciturn to the point of sullenness.

The journey had started conventionally enough. Expertly disguised, he had been taken by train to the west, a short distance from City. Away from Kindland, he had thought, surprised, but his question had but a brief reply.

"Where do you think they will start looking, eh? Use your head."

Loaded into an ancient steam waggon, he had been bundled into the windowless cargo space the moment they were away from houses.

"Those that don't know, can't tell," was the curt observation, when he had asked. Two days on the road, two nights in houses where none but his guides appeared to live. Then three whole days and nights holed up in one place, one or other of his guides disappearing for hours. Days when he was confined in curtained rooms. Then two more days in a smaller wagon, where his container, for what else could it be called, was small enough to give him claustrophobia. Another day after in seclusion. In the evening, he was brought a copy of the *Courier*.

"In the news, then, comrade. Taken them a while to latch on, all the better for us. There'll be cops all over Westport, no doubt."

It was a short piece, accompanied by a very grainy image, one Almar realised had been lifted from some group photo.

Dr Almar Hochast, of the Institute of Biology was reported missing yesterday evening. He had been ill, and police were called when neighbours offering help had met with no response. His apartment was undisturbed, but his usual working clothes were missing. His superior, Professor Nornost, has told us that his young colleague 'was under considerable strain'. It is feared that Dr Hochast has lost his memory, and may be wandering about. He is not thought to be dangerous. The police are anxious to find Dr Hochast, and should be informed by anyone who sees him.

"Where does that paper circulate?" Almar asked. It was three days old.

"The same day? Only between City and Westport. Not seen by many ordinary folk. Be different if the pops get going. They'll think you are an easy find right now. Batty professors and all that."

Then there had been three days of night marches, marches in which he could see merely the outlines of hills and the distant light of a few farms. The vegetation at his feet, where there was any, was relentlessly grey-green. Daylight found them in bothies concealed in the taller grey-green scrub. It was only at dawn on the fourth day that they had allowed him to see; a bleak rocky beach between two headlands plunging straight to the shore.

"We wait. There will be a light, and we will reply. Under cover for now."

A day, a night, another day. A sharp wind, and driving rain, with no real protection and certainly no fire. And here they were again. Hours passed. His companions started raising their voices, and Almar sensed an argument. Seeing his attention, they moved further off, leaving him to stare out at the blackness ahead. Were they about to abandon him? To return the way they had come?

Then he caught it, a single bright flash far out. Then another. He gave a cry; the others turned; he pointed. One moved to the oilskin covered pack nearby. There were little sparks, muttered curses, and finally a bright light, shuttered behind and on both sides. A message was flashed.

It seemed to Almar an eternity before the heard the splash of oars, and then saw the outline of a boat, and the six men rowing.

"Wade out to that rock. They can't come closer with this swell."

Wet, cold and exhausted, Almar scarcely noticed the journey to the waiting steamer. He missed the continual bailing as waves broke over the boat. He was only half conscious as the boat swayed on its lift to the steamer's deck. The heat and the smell below decks, the stumbling down stairs, these were all he remembered.

Come morning, and he was shaken awake. Stripped to his underclothes, he was told to don the sailors' uniform laid out for him. Taking with him only the purse, he was led to the bridge. The captain was easily distinguished. A spy-glass in his left hand, he offered the other to Hochast.

"Welcome aboard the *Higgyback Castle,* Master Escapee. No, don't tell me. When we are safe in Kindland waters, then we can do introductions. First things first; you have the fare?"

Hochast handed over the purse, intact since it had landed in his lap. The captain tipped its contents out onto a small table. There was gold among the coins. He whistled.

"Bosom of the Beholder! Someone thinks a lot of you. We'd take ten, each in a separate voyage for this."

He looked hard at his guest, removed all but three gold coins and some coppers, which he replaced in the purse and handed back.

"A week or so at a hotel there, Mr Escapee, if you have no one expecting you. But we are not there yet." He pointed to the grim Westerland coast to their south. "We left from 'Pol, and we are returning as asked. It'll be noticed. We cleared their so-called sanitary inspection, but we were bound for the Far Outs by the manifest. Cheeky buggers, they'd not try it if we were an Outer ship. But see us coming back, and there'll be a visit. Engine trouble, of course, we make for home. That's why we are crawling now. There are watchers on those hills. They'll suspect anything, but there was nothing below of much interest to those holy creeps, and nothing's been shifted. We are not peddling Consie tracts or abo drugs."

"That's why the uniform? But I will not act very sailor-like, Captain."

"Damned right. We thought of that. You will be in the engine room, coal dust all over you, in the nearest equivalent of those holy buggers' idea of hell this side of the grave. They'll not spend too long down there. Especially if we vent a few valves and give them a dose of sulphuretted steam."

It was as the captain said. Almar felt the ship slow and halt. Deep in the bowels, he heard nothing of the notional inspection. A pair of smartly dressed Westie coastguards scarcely reached the base of the stairs, before they withdrew from the stink of the engine room. He emerged to see the small Westie vessel heading back to port. Out of sight, the *Higgy* developed a surprising turn of speed. Kindopol was ahead and in sight.

It had not taken long for Hochast to establish his credentials. Segregated from the other passengers, he had been taken to a police station, but it was not long before he was sat in front of two biologists and a Senior, Congressman Trefoilen. There had been a short exchange after he had been brought before them.

"You have no doubt as to his identity, Professor?"

"None whatsoever, Excellency. And we have a message from City, from Nornost himself, telling us to expect him."

"His value?"

"Beyond price. He is a master of systematic method."

"To be given citizenship? Publicly acknowledged?"

"As far as we are concerned, Excellency, yes. A doughty proponent of evolution. Nornost's messages hint at ways to trace the First-Run back in time."

Trefoilen smiled. It would anger the hard line Bestowalists, but the pops, and indeed, popular opinion, had turned against those friendly to Westerland. Ships held for inspection, preachers prosecuted for seditious sermons, these, and more had given the Evolutionists a temporary advantage in Congress. A spot of Westie outrage, if it came, would do no harm. He nodded, and left the biologists to deal with the details.

Hochast's naturalisation was turned to a spectacle. There were pictures, there were editorials. His escape, for which no real facts were given, was glamourised. Westie obstinacy was mocked. The man himself said little. The Westerland embassy advised against demanding his return, at least in public, and its official position was that of sorrow at the actions of a deluded and disappointed academic whose work had had little utility.

A year later, he received the news of Professor Nornost's death, a tragic road accident. What the papers did not reveal was that his office was surprisingly bare; even whole cabinets of specimens were missing. Somehow, the baggage of Far Out diplomats had been a little heavier than usual. Somehow, papers and materials accumulated in Hochast's keeping.

7. The Conference

Rarely, if ever, had the old Institute of Biology been so lively. Tucked away in the shabby genteel end of Blacken Street, its staff and visitors usually encountered only the mainly elderly and somewhat straightened residents of the four or five storey blocks that lined the rest of the street. Not today, though. A cordon of police guarded the entrance; many more stood in groups at intersections with the narrow lanes that joined the main street.

The street was already filling up with protesters. At the approach to the Institute, the police had some success in separating Besties from Consies. A tenuous, policed corridor ran for about a hundred metres in each direction. Down these narrow corridors, conference participants walked to the venue, escorted by police. Most passed without remark, but a few, well-known from the pops, provoked cheers from one side and jeers from the other. The corridor wavered and narrowed when such figures passed. The police lines held, but from the balcony above the main entrance Professor Hochast could see batons swinging and the fallen pulled back by their comrades. A few were dragged away by police to the nearest side street, where a line of waggons awaited. He turned to Chief Inspector Gornik, standing beside him.

"Under control at the moment, Chief. Thank you for the numbers. I was afraid we'd have one of those scenes we see outside the Academy."

"Don't relax too hastily, sir. I think some of your most notorious colleagues have yet to arrive. I wondered about bringing them under blankets, but I was advised it would be provocative. The downtown end of the street is still filling up and they are getting closer."

The whole thing was a pain, as far he was concerned. Why it had not been banned, he did not know. For heaven's sake: a conference called *Origins and Evolution*. Here, now, when the mood on the streets was darker by the day. Very well, as Hochast had explained, these things are planned a year or more in advance. Foreigners invited, a showcase for Kindland science. Be a fine thing, though, if one of them got beaten up by that mob; Westerland pops would have a field day.

As it was, all police complaints had been set aside by the Seniors. *We are an open society, Chief Inspector,* one had said, *and proud of it too.* The implication that others were not, that a point should be made and moral superiority asserted, did not need to be made explicit. That Hochast himself, for example, typical Westie, but a 'refugee' seeking asylum and academic freedom. Naturalised, even honoured, a long time ago. He'd have fewer problems back home now, though things were deteriorating again. Of course, Seniors and the Institute itself had been oh-so-proud about their lack of prejudice when he was elected director.

In fact, as Gornik could see for himself, the small gaggles of foreigners escorted to the entrance caused the crowds to quieten. No one really knew what side they took, and did not care either. There were even cheers when two Far Outers passed by; cheers from both sides. The two waved cheerfully at the crowds and were seen laughing with their escorts. It reflected, he thought, the rather favourable press given to those distant islands and their eccentric inhabitants.

Their silence, their relaxation, was soon shattered. Noise from the far end of the street increased. No clear view, but soon they heard the whoosh of tear gas canisters, and the hubbub got nearer to the more strictly controlled approaches to the entrance. The lines dissolved. Protesters in masks were fighting each other, while the Besties could be seen attempting to breach the phalanx of officers that surrounded a figure whose identity Gornik could not make out. To his relief, the Chief saw that his men, nevertheless, advanced steadily towards him, and more squads piled in from the side streets.

Hochast knew at once who it must be: that damned Hort woman. Bad enough that his colleagues were targeted for what they wrote in learned journals, bad enough that lectures were interrupted, labs vandalised by militant students. Hort, of course, had to go to the pops. Hort had to give interviews that stirred Besties into a fury, while making her face an icon, plastered on posters, clothing and even tattoos of the most ardent Consies.

There had been pressure on him, lots of it, to oust her by fair means or foul. Pressure that it would have been very tempting to give way to, if only to give the Institute and himself a little peace. He could not bring himself to do it. He himself, an agnostic on the matter of Bestowal, had fled his native land when Bestowalist fundamentalists had held power in Westerland. Fled, and given not only sanctuary, but feted and promoted in his new home. He was, he had come to realise, a soft touch as far as Hort was concerned. Any reprimand, any suggestion about discretion and restraint, and she played the liberty card, reminding him of his own past.

He left the Chief Inspector, hurrying down the stairs to greet her. In the lobby, both she and her escorts were removing gas masks.

"Such an ordeal, my dear Galla. I trust you are unhurt?"

"I am fine, Almar, fine. The police were better prepared than the last time I was attacked by a mob. Maybe we will actually manage to have a conference, not a melee?"

"I certainly hope so. The CI upstairs, Gornik, is clever for one of his trade. Seating is to be no free for all, Alternate Besties and Consies in each row. No blocks of the partisan to be allowed. The staff gave him lists."

"Which means policemen in some numbers at each presentation, I suppose." She scowled briefly. "Body searches as well? I have no bag, as you can see."

"No. Gornik was willing to do without. I think bags will be inspected, are being inspected, as participants register. Not the foreigners, of course. The OSS vetted all the applications, and none had anything on them."

Hort turned and went to the registration desk, where a team of anxious to please students were backed by a line of impassive police. Hochast returned to the balcony. The press around the entrance had eased.

"Is that the last of them?" asked Gornik. The police had now widened the gap between the rival crowds, who seemed content to chant, wave banners and utter obscenities. Getting nothing more than a shrug, he was about to go downstairs, to go out and congratulate the men on a job well done, when there was the sound of gunfire several hundreds of metres down the street. A second's silence, then screams and a crush as people ran or pushed towards side streets. He ran down the stairs and towards the scene. By the time he had arrived, pushing his way through a confused mass of protesters, police were already assisting the two injured and holding back the much-reduced crowd, mostly locals.

"Anyone else hit, Sergeant? Where did the shots come from?"

"Not that we can see, sir. From above, the buildings on the junction with Sepulchre Alley. They are being searched, but I doubt we'll catch anyone."

The injured were now in the hands of the ambulance staff. Neither was critically wounded. One was an old woman, spitting with rage. A bunch of neighbours were by her.

"Bloody thugs, the lot of them, Mr Policeman," said one. "They'd moved on, most of them. We'd things to do. A few years on clearance for the lot, I don't give a damn. Besties, Consies, they're all the same."

The other was a young man, who readily admitted to being a Consie.

"It was over, sir. We were dispersing. The locals were coming out. No Besties near me, and I'd have avoided them, not started a fight."

The injured were driven away. Baffled, Gornik left the scene and walked back towards the institute. The crowds had dispersed, the police were in control. First making sure that the cordon around the Institute was complete, he returned to East Side Station. A provocation? If so, a ham-fisted one, thankfully too late to enrage the rival mobs even more.

Hochast did not reveal to any inside what he had heard. Those inside had not heard the shots, and the few that had seen Gornik run out of the building were easily placated. *I don't know, nothing of significance, I think. The crowds will disperse.* No noise from outside now penetrated, participants were moving into the large theatre for his introduction and the first session. As he entered the room, he was faced by an assembly of muttering professors. To his amusement, they were already exchanging grumbles with their neighbours, neighbours whom they would normally shun or shout at. From the snippets that reached him, he could hardly suppress a grin. *Police in here? Told where to sit? It's an outrage. Do they think we are savages? That Westie has got above himself.* Nothing like a bit of offended academic privilege to unite. So far, so good.

It continued to his satisfaction for the whole morning. His first plenary speaker was a geologist from the Far Outs. She was opening, yet again, the issue of moving continents. The data were complex; fossils, aboriginal, of course, that seemed to suggest greater connections between the Inner Outs and the west end of Westerland itself than they had with the Outer Outs. The fossils that showed a connection between the latter and Eastland. Dates, *very tentative, colleagues,* bathymetric readings, the undersea ridges so laboriously mapped, the types of igneous rocks.

An idea regarded as ridiculous only fifty years ago, it was now less controversial. There might be no active volcanos other than on Halfland, but the evidence that there had been was more and more convincing. She fielded the numerous, rather technical questions with confidence. There was, of course, a hidden significance to the idea. If continents can move, even if only in the past, could not those icy realms around each pole have once basked in warmer waters, warm enough for the first-run to evolve. Bestowalists had seen a danger, adding force to their ridicule, while Evolutionists were reluctant to endorse an idea that suited them well, only to find it by some means discredited. Gradually the fear had subsided. Her evidence had strengthened the theory, but it related only to the equatorial belt, the Lands. It settled nothing.

There were questions. Questions about the undoubted volcanic nature of the rocks on Halfland. Questions about the absence of active volcanos elsewhere. Here, Hochast could bring the discussion to a close, for his next speaker was a weird cross between cosmologist and geologist. Reaching even further back in time, he discussed theories of the origins of planets. Yes, theory indicated that planetary cores could be very hot. Yes, molten rock would then reach the surface. Ours must be very old. No, we cannot give you a realistic time scale, just billions of years.

Junior speakers filled the remaining time before lunch. Technical papers on dating, detailed local studies of sedimentary rocks and their fossils. Experimental papers on the speed of erosion, and the putative heights of mountains in the past. Hochast had drifted into that one, and himself raised a question.

"The mountains on Halfland are volcanic, and they are much the highest we know of; nearly three times as high as any other. There are active volcanos. Is the whole place much younger than the Lands?"

The idea had not struck the speaker, a geographer, but the question provoked nods from the geologists. The lunch break came, leaving Hochast well pleased. Colleagues who would not pass the time of day were nodding sententiously together as they queued for lunch. The few who ventured out for fresh air found the street deserted bar two well-guarded groups of peaceful protesters holding up banners devoid of anything other than slogans. Those trying to pass the cordon while carrying inflammatory pictures and shouting personal insults had been arrested long since.

The afternoon sessions raised the temperature a little. A microbiologist from Eastland, already famous both for his ideas and for his very eccentric ideas about appropriate clothing and personal hygiene, tried again to persuade his listeners that not only bacteria, but some fungi too, could not be regarded as manifestly first- or second-run. There were mutterings, even a shout of *Bestowed and Aboriginal, you idiot.* What had passed unremarked when geologists had the floor was seized upon here, for if true, it demanded a single source for life.

It was not, exactly, that he could be disproved. Kindlanders, though, knew that their own leading micro-prof. (thank you, pops), Jana Polin, thought it wrong. Away on her tour of duty on Halfland, she had briefed an assistant to give a mild rebuff. Again, the Evolutionists kept quiet. If right, it would be a triumph, but the evidence, such as it was, gave the idea no real support. Bestowalists looked rather smug. Polin was a known Evolutionist: *Proper scientist, nevertheless, wish some of the others would as honest.* By break time, there was renewed segregation, and loud laughter and rolling of eyeballs with sideways looks at the opposition.

The remainder restored a little goodwill, in some cases a shared boredom as when an Eastie agronomist discussed trials of selectively bred aboriginal plants as fodder for cattle. A talk boycotted rather than heckled by Bestowalists. *Little pieces of a jigsaw puzzle, Hochast,* thought. Each true, or probably so, but none fitting together so that a picture emerged.

For the evening, he had consulted the Chief Inspector. In the normal run of such things, there would be a conference dinner, on site or in a hotel. Bibulous professors would then descend on the city's bars, while the novices went clubbing. It was rare to have a designated hotel. Now, the possible consequences of such freedom were obvious. However segregated, a conference dinner would descend into a brawl.

"My cells full of hungover Academicians with black eyes and missing teeth, not to mention the hospital cases. The pops would have a field day. And you would have a hefty bill for breakages too. Loose on the town? Worse still, and I am not providing an escort for each of them. Best case, they get a beating. Worst, someone gets killed, and the riots that would follow would make those round the Academy look like picnics."

So, again, Hochast had imposed a discipline that concentrated all disgruntlement on himself. As a Westie, he had by upbringing a more chaste, sober and altogether more puritanical approach to life, and it was with a certain satisfaction that he had allocated participants to three hotels, Evolutionists, Bestowalists, and the notionally less committed, the last containing most of the foreigners. Taken by cab, once there, no leaving. Events of the morning had blunted criticism when the time came. For himself, the apartment in the institute itself, one he rarely used. Neutrality must be preserved.

*****

The second morning brought no trouble like the day before. Gornik had acted fast after that. All participants to be bussed. Police escorts. The street to be closed off. Marksmen at the ready. In the event, there were few demonstrators lined up against the barriers. Silently, they waved placards. The buses' darkened windows obscured their occupants, and at the Institute's entrance they were far away, too far to be recognised. Gornik even ventured out to talk to some behind the barriers. He learnt something.

News of the shooting the previous day had chilled the spirits, the more so since neither side, even among the Ultras, claimed responsibility, nor, to his amazement, did they blame their opponents. Some wondered about the crazies who reversed the notion of Bestowal to look for elimination of all the bestowed, humans included. That thought had occurred to him, but it seemed unlikely. More to the point, the few on both sides who had ventured out to picket the barriers this morning had been shouted at, even chased and pelted by locals until they were within sight of the police. Satisfied, he returned to his station. No need to be around until the conference ended.

Inside, the atmosphere was more tense. It was the archaeologists' turn in the first session. More bones, more primitive cultivation sites. As always, the dating problem, but no evidence, anywhere, of anything that could be older than about three thousand years. Certainly, younger than most aboriginal fossils, some thought to be hundreds of millions of years old. Bestowalists grinned. They applauded the young, who truth be told, were adding little more than detail. The Evolutionists sat silent. The earliest human remains differed in no significant way from those who died mere decades ago. Of course, in the abstract, this proved nothing. Changes traced through aboriginal fossils were plotted over millions of years. But the standard chant: *Where are the ancestors? where are they? bring them on,* were mimed by Bestowalist lips; chanting out loud would be vulgar. Occasionally there would also be the mimed, ironic chant: *Under the ice, under the ice,* the standard Evolutionist retort that lost its bite when there was no evident hope of looking for them there.

The pattern that the bestowed remains revealed was consistent, and already guessed at. Dates might be uncertain, but all agreed that the earliest were here in Kindland; earliest of all at Rehine. Nothing to challenge the account of Foundation, with Bounty Bay as the landing place, and Rehine as the first settlement. Westerland and Eastland, all later, but with little geographical pattern. The Far Outs, it was known, had been found and colonised in historic times. The voyage of Goden Ironfist, Goden the Navigator, his discovery in 1479, had stood the test of dated remains. Nothing had been found earlier than that.

The atmosphere in the theatre persisted through the morning: satisfaction among Bestowalists, a dull indifference or frustration among the others, for whom these findings settled nothing. That the Lands had been colonised by humans, humans who had brought stock and seed with them, was uncontested. The question was where had they come from: evolved through natural causes elsewhere, or *mystically* deposited by a Bestower for whose existence there was no evidence at all. Hochast, attempting to point to the gaps in both arguments, had made things worse in the break, by asking, out loud, and of nobody in particular:

"If we can have a mystic Bestower, can we not have a mythic navigator, a proto-Goden, if you like? Leading his people out of misery to the promised land."

There were unconvincing laughs among the Evolutionists, and sardonic grins among the others. Let's have a statue in Foundation Square, one said. We'll subscribe if you can show us what he looked like. The jibe backfired, just a little, after the next presentation. A year ago, a remarkable find of preserved corpses had been found in the bogs of the Predassy Ranges, just above the city. Early, really early. Clothing, flesh, even stomach contents had been preserved. The pops had gone to town over *The Bog People.* Lurid tales of human sacrifice and mass burials petered out rather soon, and the chemists, medics and biologists had been silent about their findings. Now, they were prepared to talk, to make a sensation.

The human remains, announced Professor Galbas, were different from us. There were gasps as he paused for effect. No, not in their bones, the only substantial remains previously found. Rather, there were three differences that only the unique preservation could reveal. The liver was smaller, as were the kidneys. The skin was much paler, almost lacking pigment, and there was evidence of skin cancers in several bodies. He could link the last two; to the educated at least, the connection was well-known. Our dark skins offer us protection. Humans had indeed evolved, therefore, if only in subtle ways.

He was subject to a barrage of questions, questions anticipated and prepared for. Most tellingly, he had dug out the records from the penal colony on Halfland, the colony abandoned in a more enlightened age. Disease, disease associated with lack of sunlight in that cold, cloudy land where sunshine, sunshine weaker than in the Lands, was a rarity.

"What about that crazy Professor Badon? She's been there for years. Is she wasting away?"

"We know the substance that sunlight induces in the body." Galbas smiled triumphantly. "We have made it. Professor Badon was indeed suffering. The pills sent to her have relieved the symptoms."

There was a buzz around the theatre. Hochast was impressed, but saw immediately that, once again, the evidence could point either way. We came from a darker place, but where was it: In the north, or from an unknown source in the Bestower's gift. Only the clumsiness of bestowing by a dumping in the ocean told against the latter. And, as he knew, there were Bestowalists now convinced that the gift had been given to Halfland, to Halfland alone. Why that might be remained unknown, but not unanswered. A test of devotion? A winnowing out of the weak and undeserving? Even Westies prevaricated there; do not, Archpriest Donnidan had preached, presume to know the mind of the Bestower.

The last talk of the morning, from Mira Forgoil, seemed at the time something of an anticlimax. New methods of dating were being developed, several of them. To the majority of those in the theatre the technicalities were incomprehensible. *Half-lives, racemisation, calibration curves,* sounded more like witchcraft than science. But she showed that the earliest remains for which historic dates were assigned were accurately dated in blind trials. An anomalously early date assigned to the Braccet Enclosure on Eastland, a subject of endless arguments over the years, was unambiguously dismissed.

"Certainly not five thousand years old, of that we can be sure. No older than Rehine, for sure, but the errors are still huge. Nothing," she added, "that challenges our understanding of Foundation."

"Eastie wild men," shouted a voice from the back, to laughter. Folklore, this, generally reckoned to be outright fabrication or the rediscovery of isolated settlements. The orthodox story of humanity's spread from Kindland was not threatened. On any other occasion, her results would have been a sensation; even the pops would have featured it. All knew, though, that the afternoon was the crux, the jousting ground on which the champions would contest.

Lunch was thus unusually subdued. The truce observed the previous day had disappeared. Hochast noted the clear separation by tables of those dedicated to either cause, and the dithering and peripheral placement of the miscellany of agnostics, many looking round the refectory to find a place that did not signal an allegiance. He had been minded to place these champions, Hort and Quinton, at the start, hoping that the sober proceedings that followed would defuse passions. Gornik had dissuaded him.

"If you want a conference at all, Hochast, leave them to last. Some of your supposed intellectuals are thugs in suits, little more. I'll double the numbers of my men in the theatre, but I cannot guarantee there will not be a brawl. Put those two incendiaries on first, and half your participants will be in my cells by lunchtime, and the Directorate will tell me to close things down."

As the theatre filled up, all could see the impressive numbers of police that had been assembled. They were behind and below the podium, and, significantly, placed in strategic seats among the audience, always in groups of four. Masks were hung openly around their necks, canisters at their belts. Briefly, their presence induced some solidarity, a general feeling of outraged academia. The prescriptive seating, though, soon reduced the room to a rather sullen silence.

Hochast had thought hard about the arrangements. The session opened with three lesser luminaries. Dr Andri Sheer was the darling of the pops, with his uncanny ability to weave remains, written history and folklore into beguiling tales of the Kindland pioneers and their early struggles. Dr Nana Selin, the ecologist, worked in Hort's laboratory. She had worked shifts on Halfland, studying the rather rich first-run flora and fauna. No seeker after publicity, the implications of her work were known only to her fellow scholars and the dedicated band of Bestie witch hunters, who monitored all the doings of Hort's team.

Sheer delivered the usual, blustering, joke-laden account. Little was new, but he had a way with words. The legends of *Colonel* and *Doc*, the earliest evidence of writing, *in our alphabet, remember,* found on stones, the tale of arrival, the mythical voyages of those who had discovered Westerland and Eastland. Over dating, and the origins of the calendar, he was subject to some neutral, informed questioning. Even well into historic times, the length of a year had seemed uncertain. 401 days had been determined by the Congress of Westport in 998, a date that the Congress of the Lands itself had laid down as canonical. Earlier references to years varied between regarding them as shorter, or gave up entirely, counting days or thirties since the supposed arrival on Kindland. Why thirties? It made little sense. There were rather muted allusions to women's periods, though their timing was usually a few days short of thirty, and varied widely. There had been many arguments as attempts were made to recalibrate earlier dates in terms of canonical years.

Out of his depth here, but anticipating the problem, Sheer had gained Hochast's assent to call on Nigsby Polun, the astronomer and historian. The story was well-known, but often misunderstood. The axis on which we spin deviates just a little from that vertical to our orbit, he told them. Only with accurate timekeeping and detailed observation of the stars had it been detected and explained. We do, indeed, complete an orbit of the sun every 401 days, as you all know, ladies and gentlemen. Not, of course, that it is a matter of any practical significance, other than the inconvenience of dating in days, *we'd be well into the millions by now.* That raised a laugh.

The session had run over time. Hochast had looked questioningly at Dr Selin, who had signalled assent. Her talk, well-illustrated with stunning pictures from Halfland, was simple in its message. Halfland had a predominantly first-run flora and fauna. There was no sign of human life prior to Vascon's discovery. There is co-existence of first- and second-run. The unspoken conclusions: first-run is natural; it exists without human intervention. It clearly originates by evolution in a colder climate. These, surely, would be made explicit by Galla Hort.

It was a short talk. It elicited some muttering of *under the ice, under the ice, here we go again,* but only one question: how sure are you that humans were not there, there perhaps thousands of years before Vascon? What about those stories from the colony? Selin managed to avoid a shrug, and contented herself with pointing out the complete lack of evidence for humanity, and the apparently stable ecosystem, one containing many plants and animals that did not survive when transported to the Lands. Plants and animals of no use to us. Far from the Wholesome of the Bestowalist canon. The Besties held their fire; they had little doubt that Magestas Quinton would tear her to shreds after the break.

A final short, from Sellender Crocken, better known as a humourist than for his biological qualifications. It was the classic *which came first, the chicken or the wings,* a staple of his more light-hearted performances. It was though, an intriguing question, for chickens were the only animal among the Bestowed, among those with a backbone, to lay eggs. It was, though, the wings that mattered. Chickens could scarcely fly, yet all studies indicated that the wings were intended to fly. There were models; wind tunnel experiments confirmed them. Then there were the eggs. Their abundance could easily be a product of the Bestower's grace, for it conferred a usefulness that was recognised. But why would the Bestower bother with such useless appendages? Did it not imply evolution from some unknown ancestor?

It was a talk delivered lightly, for the argument, bar a few technical details, was well known. It did, however, provoke a whispered retaliation from the Evolutionists: *The Bestower moves in mysterious ways, his wonders to perform.* There were scowls and laughter.

Hochast had settled the order of the final presentations with the toss of a coin, and Quinton was first. It was familiar stuff indeed, but filled out with what had been said over the last two days. The clear difference between Bestowed and Aboriginal. The utility of the bestowed to us. Here his rhetoric found its home.

"Evolution, we are told, the blind winnowing of the fit and unfit, accounts for all living things. There is no purpose, we are told, just the judgment of nature on what is put before it. How miraculous, then, that the bestowed are useful, the aboriginal not. A miracle? Do not the Evolutionists, the supposed rationalists, pour scorn on such notions. Chance then, or the providence of the Bestower in his concern for our welfare?"

He paused and looked around.

"There are some, some even in this room, who reject that gift. Those who will protect the miserable, useless and often toxic products of a billion years or more of evolution when further clearance, more food, more places for our growing numbers can be found. Do I think evolution happened? Of course, I do. The evidence is undeniable. Evidence that over those aeons of time, it results in the miserable degraded life that we see all around. I will even credit those that first conceived of it, despite the notion being there in our earliest myths. Fossils? Certainly, they tell us a story, a story of false starts, a story of little progress over hundreds of millions of years.

Is there any evidence of the ancient bestowed? There is not. Nor, despite the interesting discoveries of Dr Galbas, is there any evidence of evolutionary change other than the trivial, perhaps a little more than that if the Bestowal took place on Halfland. Do we have to reject the forces of nature and their potential effects on our heredity? We do not, but we cannot but note the evidence that such changes occur over millions not thousands of years. And what changes, ladies and gentlemen? Changes where the highest forms of life resemble nothing so much as lumbering simulacra of the glorious insects that pollinate our crops."

There was more, of course. The gift of language, the gift of writing, attested by that on stone from even the earliest traces of humanity. An attempt to deflect an attack he predicted Hort would make, pointing out that the supposedly useless bestowed on Halfland had, in fact, been used for buildings and for fuel. He almost sang as he quoted the hymn:

"*Hast thou not seen, all that is needful has been, granted in what he ordaineth.*"

Contrast that, the argument went, with the toxicity of many aboriginal plants, the indigestibility of nearly all. Despite the *interesting and original* observations of our friend from the east, the clear, unambiguous distinction between the two categories, even at the level too small to see with the naked eye.

Then he turned his attention to the Evolutionist alternative. Where, he asked, are the ancestors?

Under the ice, under the ice. The chant from Besties rose to a shout, a chant that mocked the standard Evolutionist's defence. The police looked nervous. Hands went to belts and masks. But even as Quinton signalled the chants to cease, all noticed that the opposition had failed to be provoked. Some had indicated their indifference by reading conference programmes. Others had armed themselves with newspapers. One, next to a policeman, had ostentatiously started work on a crossword. There had been a caucus. There had been instructions. All at Hochast's suggestion. It had worked, but would it work when Hort had the platform?

"Come, come, we should not mock our colleagues," Quinton said with a grin that was visible from the back. "It is, after all, a possibility. Unless that ice melts, we may never know for certain. But, as we know, those few rocks exposed for us are volcanic. No hope of any fossils. Let us go further. Our opponents use these strange terms, first-run and second-run."

Bestowed, bestowed and aboriginal. Scarcely a chant, a rising tide of discordant shouts. Another grin, another wave of the hand for silence.

"Well now. We can all accept that there are two 'runs' if that is what some would call them. One that reached the finishing line as soon as it started. The other lumbering along, with whole teams disqualified for running down Congress Street and being eliminated. Despite having a billion-year start."

That got a laugh, even from the Evolutionists. The famous shambles of the Round the City race two years previously, where one team took a wrong turn and was followed mechanically by others. The stewards were held in contempt for weeks.

"Consider the words. First? So, our blessed bestowed were here first? Here in the icy wastes of Northland? A run that produced such manifestly superior beings? And then second, a second-run so inferior as to beggar belief, unless, as is clearly the case, that is the best that mere evolution and the passage of time, time beyond our comprehension, can achieve. We might hope, even expect, that nature would make a better fist of it than of the first. Not so. I wonder why, when the Lands are so agreeable to life."

Quinton had thought hard about a climax. The crux, the practical matter, of clearance, the rights, indeed the duties of true Bestowalists to eliminate the aboriginal and replace it with the bestowed, had left him uncertain. His contempt for the supposedly rational Evolutionists did not blind him to the difficulties of clearance, and the problems that would arise if aboriginal cover was stripped in quantities too great for the planters and landscapers to condition the soil in ways that would allow bestowed cover to prevent degradation and sterility. Look at Westerland. Hochast had begged him to steer clear: *Science, Professor, science, not politics. That's for others.* Tell that blasted Hort woman that, had been his immediate response, but he had seen the sense. His peroration was, in consequence, rather tame, a mere iteration, in rising tone, of the principal points he had touched on.

It nevertheless received a standing ovation, a strange one, since those standing were interleaved with those sitting, arms folded and eyes averted. Hochast had decided that no questions were to be allowed. These final talks were summaries. No doubt, he explained, they could be dissected at leisure in Institutes and Academies here and abroad. He called on Professor Hort. There was a slight sibilance, a detectible hissing as she climbed to the podium.

Galla Hort was not one to be intimidated. There were scars, deep scars, that bore witness to her active engagement in the politics of clearance. Seven police stations and two courts held records of her activities on the street. Fireworks were expected. She did not disappoint.

"Learned colleagues, distinguished visitors. We have been treated to the outward cover, the supposed scientific rationale, for destruction on a scale that none have witnessed. Destruction that threatens life on this planet. At best, to a mean and squalid ruin of a world which fortune, not a mystical being, bestowed on us. Clearance, the contempt for all things aboriginal, the life that coats most of our land, and occupies the seas uncontested. The life that balances our atmosphere."

Hochast had his head in his hands. He had expected little else, but this, up front? What could possibly follow.

"Yes, I will use those contested words: bestowed, aboriginal. For there is a sense in which they may rightly be used. Learned colleagues, all life on this planet is aboriginal. How could it be otherwise? From where else could it have come? Bestowed? Certainly, we have bestowed on us a world in which we can make our way, for good or ill. Bestowed by our own power, our intelligence, by a nature shaped by the same processes that give us the lowly grey-greens that maintain the planet's balance. Grey-greens that some wish to destroy, heedless of consequences. Destruction in the name of a mysterious Bestowal that runs counter to all we know, not only about our planet, but of the universe in which it moves."

Hissing started again. Gradually, its volume started to drown out her voice. Hochast rose, and Hort paused. The noise subsided.

"Professor, it is the evidence for or against the theories of origins that concern us, not the practical consequence that follow. These are matters for other assemblies. I trust that your talk will follow that rule."

There were mutterings: *Hear hear; well said, Hochast, quite right too.* Hort nodded, and the hubbub ceased. She had known very well that her words, some of them at least, would be deemed out of order. *Better to get them in early,* she had thought. Keep them for the end, and they might not be heard. She knew, also, that not all, even a majority of Besties favoured the wholesale destruction. But the numbers were growing. There had been food riots in the east. Poverty drove desperation; envy drove Westerland.

"Let us take the case for a supposed Bestowal. It is true, and all acknowledge, that our origins are unclear, as they are for the first-run as a whole. There are, though, at least possible, rational, explanations as to why that is so. Yes, *under the ice,* shouted in derision. I might add, under the ocean, for the evidence mounts that land and sea were once not as they are now."

"I concede, there are great questions unanswered. But we have climbed out of savagery by the application of rational thought. I ask you: on what basis do we claim a Bestower? A supernatural being, fashioning the first-run out of the dirt at our feet? From where else might we have come? Planets elsewhere? Our astronomers have found few, and we lack the means to determine their nature.

They may be sterile like Hommoz, or gas giants like Be-Alba. More to the point, they are billions, no, trillions of kilometres from us. Travel to or from them is the stuff of fantasy."

She had planned well. Start with a bang, then move down the scale. Move to the mundane, to matters capable of proof or disproof. The diseases of the first-run, themselves first-run, almost certainly. The work of a benevolent Bestower? The fauna and flora of Halfland, where, indeed, the needle-leaves had proved useful, but there were animals, certainly first-run, that were not merely useless but downright dangerous. A benevolent Bestower? The difficulties they had in rendering the Lands fit for cultivation, and the destructive erosion that often resulted. A benevolent Bestower?

At that, Hochast's face displayed his displeasure. She was, of course, correct. Correct, but these were matters for agronomists and soil scientists to deal with. He was about to rise, but Hort had moved quickly to the question of evolution among the first-run. The selective breeding, and the changes in animals and plants relative to those found at the earliest occupation sites. Changes far greater than those announced by Galbas. Changes that Quinton had foolishly glossed over, changes that he could have sneered at as artificial, and, above all as purposeful. And, to her delight, he had ignored the few first-run plants that had evolved to grow in unimproved soils, plants that now had the status of weeds. No crop could be won from them, nor were they palatable to first-run livestock, still inhibited by chemicals the weeds had evolved to tolerate. Nothing artificial there.

There was no grand peroration. The seeds of political doubt had been sown in the beginning. She ended tamely, as far as her audience were concerned, with the apparent integration of both life-forms on Halfland, the stability of the system over many years of study. Only in her final sentences did she hammer home the underlying principle.

"In the end, colleagues, rationality obliges us to limit ourselves to the known, the mechanisms that we can demonstrate. To posit entities for which we have no evidence to explain what can plausibly be explained more simply is to escape from reality into the realm of superstition, and all that follows from it."

There was again a standing ovation, perhaps less enthusiastic and certainly shorter. The overwhelming feeling among the Evolutionists was one of relief, for Quinton was feared and Hort regarded as a potential liability. She had held the line. Bestowalists could not claim an unambiguous victory, nor had the meeting ended in a shambles. The relief was all the greater for Hochast. The conference had ended peaceably and complete. For all her dedication to the Consie cause, Galla Hort had played a clever game. The published proceedings would not close the debate prematurely. The pops would play on the characters, and possibly on Galbas' findings. He bid farewell to the departing participants, who would endure another escorted journey to their hotels, dispersing in the morning. Too tired to return home, he spent the night in the Institute's apartment.

8. The Archaeologist

As the sun set, Mira felt a shiver as the cold penetrated her thin clothing. With a final glance at the choppy, grey ocean through which the ship passed, she went below to reach her cabin. As she passed a crewman clad in thick jerseys and an oilskin, she received a sardonic smile.

"It'll be colder yet, Dr Forgoil, before we reach Halfland. I hope you have better clothing for the landing."

She nodded, amiably enough. Already she was further north than she had ever been, further north, indeed, than the vast majority of her fellow beings. There was still three days voyage before their arrival, three days spent moving steadily north-west. She had indeed been kitted out for the visit, as had her two assistants, Junte and Figra. The briefing had been frightening. Often freezing at night, they were told, a phenomenon known to them only from school demonstrations and, of course, refrigerators of all sorts. The array of clothing with which they had been issued had been daunting. Most particularly, how to make the delicate examination of finds when wearing heavy gloves.

For once, Captain Offeren joined the junior officers and herself for the evening meal. Apart from the formal introduction before the ship departed from Kindopol Port, she had scarcely set eyes on the man. He lacked the robust, properly sailor-like characters, being slight, bespectacled and clean-shaven. But while he seemed incongruously small, almost effeminate, alongside his burly, bearded juniors, he radiated an air of authority; his juniors were in awe of him.

In the days before this appearance, the others had explained to her just why he was held in such esteem.

"You know about the icy lands towards the pole, Dr Forgoil? Lands that support no life. Do you know that the sea itself may freeze where it is shallow, and there is no knowing when that can happen; it takes you by surprise. The captain has made several voyages along that savage coast. The last, and their ship was wrecked, wrecked by collision with a huge floating block of ice. Icebergs, we call them. Just the boats left to them, and an open journey south. Just one made it to Halfland, and he the only survivor. Oh, there were two others with him, near death when they landed, and with blackened feet that were poisoning them. Dead in days. Even back home, they'd have been saved only at the cost of their feet."

Mira had shivered involuntarily. She vaguely remembered the tale of heroic survival, and the political wrangling that followed it. Of course, she knew her geography; those desolate lands around each pole that were good for nothing. Lands that were, for the most part, so thickly covered with ice that even the search for minerals was thought futile. Lands mapped, mainly, by intermittent voyages that sampled only fractions of those desolate coasts. Often, only the towering cliffs of ice showed that there was, indeed, land underneath. Lands usually visited only as a by-product, as it were, of the so far futile attempts to find any other lands in the vast oceans that circled the globe. They were now largely ignored. Halfland was the furthest north any regular traffic went, and that merely to service the biologists' research station. Traffic that was increasingly resented both by the authorities and by the sailors themselves.

Captain Offeren was, however, surprisingly affable.

"I'm glad of your journey, Dr Forgoil, truly. There's more to Halfland than those pinchpenny bosses back home are willing to admit. They only see the costs. But it is a strange place right enough. More bestowed life there than the aboriginal, if you'll pardon me for the prejudicial language. Much more. You'll find Professor Badon and her team worth talking to. Did you know there's a few bestowed plants from right at the equator grow and reproduce there? But nothing aboriginal will grow other than under glass and heating, except for the indigenous ones, and they are, as it is said, endemic. Nothing like them in the Lands we all inhabit."

"Is it just them that stay all year, Captain? Do they return home often?"

"The prof. has stayed there for five years now, give or take a few score days. The rest are in and out in rotation every two hundreds. A few may do two shifts, and stay a full year. The maintenance crowd, they change every hundred. The next shift is with the crew now. That's why you were kept waiting. The money men in Kindopol wouldn't sanction a special voyage."

"The professor; what is she like? It must be a strange way of life."

"Tough as old boots, and just as well. There have been assistants cracked well before their 200 days are up. We've had to bring a few back with the maintenance shift. Even indoors, the cold and the silence get to you. There are fogs too, that can last for days."

There had been more. The islands, for there were several, were volcanic. In the east, there were still eruptions and desolation in their wake. Only the persistent westerlies shielded the western half from the falls of ash that sterilised the land. Western end a few degrees north of the eastern one. The spine of mountains, towering three times the height of any in the Lands, made for a uniformly wet climate.

The west had supported a penal colony for more than a hundred years, an experiment abandoned on grounds of humanity and cost. Bestowed life there might be, but crops? Not enough, and add to that the insanity, disease and riots, and the enterprise had been shut down, what, seventy years or more ago.

"Plain cruel," said the captain, "but you'll see the abandoned workings no doubt. There were strange tales from some sent there who survived. Some said they were restoring earlier workings when they tried to grow crops. Nothing came of it, but you could ask the prof. to show you the remains. I guess that might interest you, seeing your profession."

"Indeed, Captain. There is speculation that people lived there back in prehistory. I am to look for any evidence. None has been produced so far, and the place is scarcely explored."

"And do you think that is true?" asked the captain.

"I have an open mind, Captain, as far as I can manage to keep it that way. As far as we know, the place was discovered by accident, way back more than 400 years ago, and there was nobody there, and hard to believe they'd survive anyway. Now we have accurate methods of dating, it might be a mystery we can solve. I think you know why so many think it is worth the trouble?"

The captain nodded, but said nothing. Bestowal or double evolution, the running sore from time immemorial, a sore that was now leading to trouble, not only in Kindland, but in Westerland, Eastland and even in the Far Outs.

Just two days later, there was a call from the bridge. Mira and her assistants emerged on deck, rather better dressed than she had been previously. On the far horizon was a small cloud, the only one in a clear sky. With the mate's binoculars, she made out the hazy shape of a mountain below. Most of it is below the horizon, he told her, those are higher than anything in Kindland. Indeed, as they approached, more and more appeared. The ship ran parallel to a daunting coast, far enough away to obscure any details. Dense cloud covered the mountains above. They were still far from shore when darkness fell.

"We will hold our course until dawn, Dr Forgoil," said the mate. "We've to round Desolation Point and turn south-east. It's a difficult place to dock, for all that it's sheltered. There are rocks and shallows, and no lights to guide us, just the markers to be seen in daylight."

As it happened, the morning was clear. As they closed in, Mira gasped as the true scale of the mountains was revealed. Four thousand metres at least, plunging steeply right down to the sea. The tops were white. Snow, she realised, snow that she had seen only in pictures. Below the snow, dense forests, dark green, almost black against the snowy backdrop. As the ship followed a devious course through a small inlet, the jetty and the small collection of huts, the Settlement, came into view. There were many chimneys. All were smoking, the fumes ascending vertically in the windless air. The area of flat land, cleared of forest, was tiny.

As the ship approached the jetty, people started to congregate along it. Some, the majority, were evidently maintenance workers each with a trunk or large backpack at their feet. The ship would turn around fast, to reach the open sea before dusk. Others, Mira supposed, were biologists coming merely to greet. Among them must surely be the professor, but their heavy outdoor clothing concealed both rank and gender. Both she and her assistants were similarly clothed. They descended the gangway as sailors swung mast-based cranes with the cases of equipment, supplies and personal belongings. It was cold indeed by the standards of home, but far from freezing.

As she reached the jetty, one of the anonymously clad people approached her.

"Dr Forgoil, am I right? I am Professor Badon; but please, Torla to you. We do not stand on ceremony here." A gloved hand was offered and taken.

"Mira, if you please." Mira looked at the face of the woman in front of her. A tanned and weather-beaten face, but one in which wrinkles had been subdued by a comfortably filled out form. Indeed, now she looked harder, the professor's frame was sturdy indeed, a sharp contrast to her own bony, ascetic look. The professor followed her gaze, and laughed.

"You will find that a layer of adipose tissue," she smiled, "is as good as two layers of clothing in this climate. Not to mention what some hard physical work may do for you."

The unloading was quickly done. The resident maintenance workers boarded, while those freshly disembarked were put to moving the cargo back towards the huts, aided by the biologists. The gangway was hauled in, there were blasts on the ship's horns, and it was soon backing away before turning and heading out. The two women walked together towards the settlement. Once in the relative warmth of the largest hut, evidently the communal space for meals and recreation, they shed their outer clothes, as did Mira's assistants and several others. Sat round a table, there were introductions. Four biologists were introduced.

"Dr Jana Polin, our microbiologist. Dr Tamon Guterri, botanist." She smiled. "For information, that includes both notionally bestowed and aboriginal plants. Tamon is a little sensitive on the issue."

The others laughed; Tamon scowled, but then gave a rueful grin.

"Dr Kallan Gort, zoologist. In practice, this means the bestowed, for short. The lesser animals," again a grimace from Tamon as well as Kallan, "are the province of Dr Jessa Reboud; she is in the field, with their student Bernica. Finally, Mish Flond. He is the student of Dr Becca Gronlow, our ecologist. There are others in the field, but this is surely enough to grasp in one go."

"Dr Junte Derro. Junte is our fossils man; he should have much to talk about with Kallan. Miss Figra Desanta is my personal assistant. As you know, perhaps, we have these new methods of dating remains. The technique is slow and meticulous, and she excels. We will get only a crude estimate on the spot. Anything out of the ordinary will be tested rigorously back home, and will have to wait for a conclusive result."

The newcomers were shown to quarters. Mira found herself in a spacious room. There was no fireplace, but huge pipes along two walls were hot to the touch. There was room not only for a bed, but a substantial desk and many shelves and cupboards. Bright electric lights were there in abundance. A maintenance man appeared with her belongings. After unpacking, she ventured out, to be shown a large room in a nearby hut; a room set up as a proper laboratory, complete with microscopes and other equipment. Her two companions were already unpacking and setting up the equipment that had come with them. She noticed two strange cages along a wall.

"What are these?" she asked.

"Rat traps. They have rats here, and mice too, so they tell us."

Rats and mice, thought Mira. The fabled Bestower's little jokes. An infestation had occurred in Kindopol, traced to a Halfland voyage, and exterminated only with great difficulty. The animals could eat some abo plants, abo animals if it came to it. What a kind Bestower, the Evolutionists had sneered, to give us pests as well as useful life. A punishment for our sins? *Perhaps*, she thought, *we'll find some bones.*

It was soon lunchtime. A democratic assembly lined up to help themselves, the kind of cafeteria Mira associated with her student days. Seating, though, was more segregated, with scientists and maintenance staff seeming to sit in separate clusters. As the meal ended, the maintenance staff went about their business, but the biologists hung back, evidently by arrangement. It was over coffee, remarkably good coffee, thought Mira, that the professor called them to order.

"Mira, we all know the official reason for your visit. It was very skimpy, and on the face of it, a wasted journey, as we know of no traces of human occupation other than the old penal colony. Is there reason to think otherwise?"

Straight in, then, thought Mira. This one does not do subtlety. It was the hottest of hot topics, even here, as Torla had made clear in her introductions.

"You all hear news on the radio, yes? Maxim and his Ultras among the Bestowalists calling for clearance to step up, even to plan for the great replacement: the Bestower's will be done? Even culturing diseases to that end? Follow the Westerlanders, though they've little to show for it?"

Tamon banged the table with his fist; plates and glasses rattled.

"Madness, pure and simple. Kill what is natural, and we will kill ourselves too, in the name of dogma, dogma alone. Why is live and let live not enough?"

The professor put her hand on Tamon's arm.

"Let Mira speak. She hasn't come here just on Bestowalist orders. The Academy sent her. Sent her to answer factual questions, as far as she can."

"It's the issue of origins," Mira continued. "Halfland has become central. The place where the Bestower installed us, so some say. Despite Colonel, Doc and the bestowed ship on which they sailed to Kindland. There is a logic behind it; you know the arguments, I'm sure: the absence of anything notionally bestowed in the fossil record more than a few thousand years old. And all associated with us. Not here, though. Here, bestowed live without human presence. Or without human presence as far as we know. That is the Evolutionist's, the Conservationist's, argument."

Both Tamon and Kallan were near bursting to speak. Only a stern look from Torla deterred them.

"Let her finish, for heaven's sake. Do you think she does not know the arguments on both sides?"

"Old stories from the penal colony have been dug out. There were convicts claiming that people had been there before them, though when Vascon discovered the place, it was certainly not inhabited. Our job is to find evidence. If we do find it, the next question will be its age. A few hundred years, even a thousand, and we might conclude an undocumented voyage. Even some relic of Vascon's landing. Much older, and the association of bestowed and ourselves is restored. It would strengthen the Bestowalist claim that we were placed here, with all the bestowed, to make what we can of our inheritance. Older still, though, and the account of Foundation falls. And why here, of all places?"

"People have been here, intermittently, for more than 250 years," said Tamon. "And our lot ever since the colony was closed down. I admit we have not been everywhere, but we would surely have seen some evidence. Those convicts went mad, most of them. Their stories have no merit. No one's come up with anything around their camp, though no one's been there for ages. A terrible place, I'm told, and only accessible by sea."

"I'm afraid getting us there will be one task to impose on you. We will need to be taken to any accessible point, even if only by sea. It's a problem if we find nothing, because, as they will say, absence of evidence is not the same as evidence for absence. The Evolutionists will be delighted if we find something, and it is less than a thousand years old. Bestowalists will be hoping it is around Foundation. Much older than that, and the Evolutionists are back in business."

"How long was that penal settlement around for?" asked Kallan.

"It's not simple," said Mira. "I asked the historians and archivists. The problem is that the great Westerland War destroyed many records. There was a proposal to send criminals there just before the war, but no evidence that any were sent. Absence of evidence, again, I'm afraid. The first documented landing for the convict camp was in 2789, that's 212 years after the notional discovery of the place at all. More than forty years after the war's end."

"So, there could have been bones or whatever around for forty years or more, and the convicts found them?" This from Jana. "It's a strange thing, but notionally bestowed remains here rot more rapidly than at home, despite the cold.

The bones, if that's what were found, would look much older than any they might have seen anywhere else."

"Well, if we find any, that's what the new techniques should settle for us. But the accounts did not mention bones. It was signs of digging or cultivation, just the work for us archaeologists. What brought the attention, though, was that we could date things. Now, there are a lot anxious people on both sides waiting on our results, though it will not stop the arguments." She smiled. "Yes, Tamon, I know, what might there be under those thousands of metres of ice?"

Torla had remained silent. She now excused herself, promising to return, while the others showed Mira and her assistants a map, a map notably short on detail much away from the coasts. The penal colony was pointed out, along with a few other inlets where landing was possible. The east? Sterile and eruptive.

"At least it's on the north coast, a little more sheltered, but it's at least 50 kilometres away, and we certainly can't reach it overland. We'll need watch the weather; our little boats won't take much of a battering. Maintenance will be very grumpy about it."

Torla returned, with a brand-new book.

"It's Gigas on sea levels," she explained. "All this work on Ice Ages and eccentric orbits. It's fed into the climate change debate, of course, with some small rises attributed to all our use of fossilised carbon and hydrocarbons. Not to mention that half Westerland is burnt to a crisp; bare soil captures no carbon. But his main claim is that perhaps 20 thousand years ago, even 10 thousand, sea levels were much lower than they are now, maybe even 30 metres lower. From what we know from the sailors, there is quite a shelf around Halfland."

"And so?" Kallan was puzzled.

"Think how difficult it is for us to move around. Anything approaching flat ground is worth its weight in gold. If there really were people here a very long time ago, maybe they were only near the shore. If so, any traces will be under water or washed away. As Mira says, absence of evidence."

"Do you have much in the way of tides?" asked Junte.

"No, very little, a metre or less, unless the tide and wind combine; even then, only 50 centimetres more. We've no long inlets facing westwards to build it up, as in the Far Outs. An astronomer told me we'd have huge ones if we had a satellite like Hommoz. Of course, that planet has no water, so it's not to the point."

The meeting broke up. The archaeologists returned to their laboratory, and started setting up the equipment in earnest. Figra went outside to collect living material for calibration. She returned with a cut branch, a branch from a tree. It had what seemed to all of them ridiculous leaves: tiny needles of dark green, that gave off a pungent, aromatic smell. Like nothing they had seen in the parks and plantations of home.

"What is that, Figra?" asked Junte, "Is it aboriginal?"

"No, it is bestowed. I met Tamon. It's a needle-leaf, he called it, like all those trees in the dark forests on the mountainsides. He really doesn't like the word, though. Aboriginal stuff is small and inconspicuous, so he says, and quite hard to spot."

"Perhaps it would be a good idea to talk about first-run and second-run with him," suggested Mira. "you've heard the terms, surely. The Evolutionists use them all the time."

The others nodded. First-run was the polite term for bestowed if you moved in evolutionary circles, but common speech ignored it, even among those who doubted or downright disbelieved in the Bestowal.

*****

In the morning, it was Tamon who showed them round the settlement. It lay at the base of a horizontally V-shaped valley, which narrowed to a ravine scarcely a kilometre from the shore. The valley itself was entirely cleared, but the dark, needle-leaved trees covered the steep slopes on either side, though cleared patches showed where the settlement had felled to provide fuel for the generators and the furnaces that powered and heated the huts. *Not, thought Mira, that I should think of huts, they are well-built wooden houses, alongside many sheds and outhouses.* There were several electric tractors, and many trailers parked alongside. Smoke was rising from several chimneys, but today a gentle west wind blew the smoke away.

Tamon showed them the workshops, the generators, *three, only two at once; we'd have trouble if we lost power,* and the array of glasshouses and beds in which various plants were growing. He walked them up to the head of the valley. Here, the river burst out of a terrifying ravine, cliffs rising at least 100 metres on each side.

"Inferno, we call it," he said, with a grin. "Not the way to get inland, for certain."

"Could you not do it with gear?" asked Junte, a keen climber. He was already regretting he had not brought his own.

"Yes. We lost two that way," said Tamon, deadpan. "Get some rain, and that gorge sweeps all away, and we never know when it's coming. We'll show you the paths we have made elsewhere. There, it's safe to get into the forest. There's even a path to the snowline, and huts on the way."

Figra had had her eyes downwards for most of the time. Now she pointed to clumps of greenish grey vegetation growing among the boulders that littered the exit from the ravine.

"Are these, these I might call mosses, second-run, Tamon?"

"Frigidophytes. Yes, they are." Tamon had the grace to smile as he spoke. "They have the right cellular arrangements, but they are like nothing in the homelands except on the summit of Kolumba. But they are here naturally, along with the first-run. Talk to Becca when she returns. There's a mixture here that seems stable. Just two pathways of evolution, not some mystical gift of the gods."

Figra collected some for her pouch. As the party turned to walk back to the settlement, Mira could see that Tamon had loosened up as the right words were used. She changed the subject.

"The power, our heating, it all comes from burning wood? This needle-leaf wood? In the city, that would be big trouble. Can the ships not bring oil, or even coal?"

The question served only to bring back Tamon's scowl of the day before. There was a gritty tone to his voice.

"They could, but they won't. Ask the prof. Money, that's why not. It's hard enough to get the supplies and people we need as it is. The harbour won't take anything much bigger than the ship you came in, and we'd need a delivery three times a hundred not once. Polluting? Most certainly, and when we have a certain calm, an inversion, you'll feel it; the fumes hang in the bay until the wind blows."

"Wind? Why not windmills? The Far Outs are covered in them."

"Money, what else. The Far Outs can afford them, and good for them. We produce nothing, so we get nothing, or just the crumbs the prof's friends can wheedle out of the bosses. Another year, and we may be closed down.

Bestowalists don't like what we do, though they might like you if you find what they want. Then this place will become some kind of temple."

Mira said no more, and the short walk back to the settlement continued in silence. Only when they were close did Tamon recover his composure, showing them glasshouses where various grasses were growing.

"We control the temperature, and the water. We find out the extremes within which various species can grow. There are species here that are missing in the Lands. They don't tolerate the temperatures."

Tamon glanced sideways at Mira. The woman appeared to be genuinely interested. When she glanced at him with raised eyebrows at a glasshouse open to the wind at both ends, he was prompted to explain.

"That's a new experiment. We had an accident last year, when a storm blew out the glass from one set of glasshouses. We were too busy to make repairs until a new maintenance crew arrived. Too many sick or slacking before that. The plants seemed to die. By chance, the glass was restored and the heaters checked out before we got round to clearing the ground. The plants sprung into life. Now, we are seeing how many others can do the same. And for how long they can stand the cold and recover."

"First-run, then?" asked Mira, Tamon nodded.

"Yes. It doesn't work with seconds from the lands. Even a day and night of exposure is enough to finish some of them. Even those from our highest mountains in the lands can't take more than a year, and then only if we don't have a frost. They don't reproduce."

The following morning provided ample evidence for Tamon's warning about pollution. Mira woke with a roughness in her throat, and the sour taste of fumes in her mouth. Outside, it was hard to tell what was fog and what smoke. The air was still, and colder than the day before. Indeed, as she stepped out to the dining hut, there were ice crystals building on the grass-like plants by the path. Frost, a thing known only from book learning; ice, known only as a curiosity. Dressed only for indoors, she was shivering by the time she had finished the short journey.

The prof. and a few others were already eating.

"A bad day, I'm afraid. Not one for taking a hike along the trails as I had hoped."

"Does it last?" asked Mira.

"Usually not more than a day or two," said Torla. "If it were not for the fog and our fumes, we'd be grateful for more. It's steady westerlies most of the time, and raining with it; you were lucky yesterday."

Back in their laboratory, Figra was already processing her calibration samples. Feeling superfluous, Mira went in search of Junte, whom she found in a lab with Kallan. A lab reeking of preservatives, and untidily littered with jars, trays of bones and racks of boxes of varying sizes.

"Kallan is introducing me to the fauna, boss. Plenty with bones we can use, and he can identify most species from single bones."

"Only the right ones," said Kallan, laughing. "But there are species here not known from the lands. Mostly carnivores and the smaller plant eaters. Not much in the way of forage for them in the lands, though farmers might say otherwise."

Junte, though, was bubbling with excitement.

"There are some the same, though. At least, Kallan gives them the same names. Cats, dogs, cattle of a sort; there are more too. But they are different nevertheless; larger, usually, and much furrier. And they are all wild."

"Evolution in action," said Kallan. "We could do with some of that in this climate ourselves. Small, thin and naked and the prospects are not good. Lap dogs and moggies wouldn't last long."

Mira pulled her jacket around her, even though the room was warm. Her thoughts, though, turned around Kallan's words.

"Evolution? In which direction, I wonder. The earliest finds we have in the lands are not that different from what we find alive. And how did any get from here to there or the other way round?"

Questions to which Kallan gave no reply. Instead, he started on a demonstration of all the fauna he knew, and their habits. There were hens, of a sort, but larger and with a thick layer of down under the feathers. No, they did not fly. There were hexapods. No bees, but a multitude of flies. Others, too the names of which meant nothing to Mira. It was the mammals that were the focus of Kallan's attention, for there were little carnivores as well as the rats and mice that she had heard of.

And the seconds? Mira had asked. Here Kallan paused, wishing that Jessa or Becca were with him. Holed up in a hut until the wind blew again, he thought. Not everything they found got reported back, when anything might be used in the great debate, and they would act as a team. But they could not conceal things now.

"That's strange. We can recognise some families, but they are mostly very small. The only large one is an octopod; just the one specimen. Long dead, for it was dug out when we were making cesspits. Like the giants on the Far Outs. We're hoping your Figra will put a date on it, because we are wondering if it was brought here. I heard a tale that Outie pirates would keep one or two on board to milk for poison for their arrows. Kept higgies to feed them on too. It matters, because we are left wondering how such a creature got here."

Hope away, thought Mira. Yes, Figra could get an approximate age, but anything for public consumption would need to come from the Academy's labs. Labs constrained for cash, as she was too; the number of samples she could afford to process were limited, and straying from the programme would make things worse. She could at least check the story about the Outies.

The next two weeks were spent, frankly, more in acclimatisation than in serious work. Figra was kept busy enough, using living plants and freshly killed animals of both runs to calibrate her instruments. The good news was that first or second-run made no difference. But her equipment could not discriminate between a cat freshly trapped, and the oldest cat bones in Kallan's collections, perhaps fifty years old.

"Did Vascon leave anything behind?" asked Mira, more or less rhetorically, for she had studied the explorer's notes and log more than any. "Do we know where he landed?"

The description could have applied to their own landing point, but as Kallan and Torla told her, there were several such bays. Burials had been recorded, but not their locations, at least not in such a way to lead people to them. The Settlement, as it was now, had been occupied only briefly, 170 years ago, simply as a safer harbour for the convict ships than the place at which they were landed.

"No ship stayed there," said Mira. "They were afraid the prisoners would overrun them. No ship, no escape, I gathered."

"True enough. There were a few places cleared inland, but the coast is mostly as near vertical as it can be, right up to the snowline. The clearings were reverting to forest even before they took the last of them away. Now, you'd be pushed to know it had been occupied. It's been three years since anyone went there. No reason to bother."

There was a hint of disapproval in Kallan's voice, which earned him a sharp look from Torla. Poor Elgid Gronet had been lost overboard on the last return, a return in storms that had gone down in legend. There was a memorial, but of course no grave. Mira had dropped the topic, and she and her team searched the valley for evidence of any occupation earlier than the settlement. It was mostly fruitless, until they discovered low humps, features Mira was sure were made by humans. Of course, they were within the Settlement itself. Some, she suspected, were actually under the present buildings. Dig, nevertheless, though she stopped short of asking for demolition or movement.

There was little to show for their efforts. Most appeared to be latrines, new ones dug when old were filled, she supposed. A few fragments of cloth were the only finds of significance. Otherwise, just a mush of peaty sludge.

"Did they have no bones to dispose of?" asked Kallan.

"Unlikely. Well, unlikely if we are seeing the remains of Vascon's voyage. Ships in those days carried salted or dried meat only, and little of it. Vascon lost many crewmen, but tradition was to bury them at sea, even if they were tied up in harbour. Later? It's not clear. They mostly stayed on board."

Figra did her best with the cloth, or with a part of it. As she expected, however, the range of possible dates was broad.

"It's wool, which is what you'd expect. Anywhere between 50 and 350 years old. I could narrow it down a bit by using the whole lot, but then there would not be enough for the labs back home. Best guess is those dealing with the convicts, but it could be at the establishment of the Settlement, or even from Vascon's visit."

"Not the Settlement," said Torla. "From the start, rubbish and latrines were marked clearly. Bodies? Mostly embalmed and returned home, except those lost at sea. Few, I'm glad to say."

*****

Work round the jetty and the Settlement revealed little else. There were hearths, and a few post-holes. All pointed to temporary occupation at the time of the penal colony. It was time to make the voyage there, a moment none looked forward to. One of the two boats the Settlement possessed was prepared. A sturdy boat, decked over and with a wheel-house and an oil-fired engine, it resembled the tugs that guided the big ships entering Kindopol harbour from Westerland or the Far Outs.

The day came. Forecasts from Kindopol or Westerland were of little use; it was the seat-of-the pants feelings of Torla and Becca, now returned from the mountains, that determined the departure. Four crew, Mira, Kallan, Becca and Junte the team. The weather was calm, and the voyage easy, a mere four hours. Landing was also easy, but all could see that any wind, and it would be near impossible. Gear was landed, food for ten days, and two tents. One of the crew, Bragen Montoern, was left with them, and the boat pulled away.

"Not safe to stay. We'll give you a week, and come the first good day after. Supplies if you decide to stay, be ready to come aboard if you have finished."

There were ruins near the landing place. Even these were now partly overgrown with needle-leaves, and it was hard to find spaces for the tents. As evening advanced, the silent gloom became oppressive. Massive needle-leaves overhung the small area of flat land. Under them, and on what was once a path, were thick tangles of some thorny plant, first-run for certain. After dark, as they prepared a meal, there were howls and screeches from inland.

"Dogs and wild cats," said Kallan. "They keep their distance, but Becca and I have rifles."

Neither Mira nor Junte were reassured; both slept uneasily, woken by noises too close to the tents. The morning came. Calm, yes, but they emerged from the tents to a thick, clammy fog that sucked the heat out of them. They set to work to clear the path inland, a path originally used by the convicts. Strangely, as it seemed to them, the work became easier as they moved uphill, and by late afternoon they had reached the first of many small terraces that had been carved out of the valley sides. Overgrown with scrub and small needle-leaves, it was, nevertheless, a manifestly artificially flattened area.

Kallan and Bragen continued upwards. Becca standing guard, Mira and Junte started quartering the ground. Downhill, the field was supported by a terrace wall, while against the valley side small cliffs and diggings showed where the material had been obtained. Dark came early as the fog thickened, and when the other two returned, they walked together back to their camp.

"It does get easier," said Kallan. "It matches what I read in the Settlement log. They came to the conclusion the poor sods had to work higher and higher up as the soil became exhausted. I think this was the first to be abandoned."

"So, how many more, how high do they go?" asked Mira.

"I think there were six known of, but nobody went higher. Only about 200 metres up, I think, and that was a guess."

The sun shone the next day, and the whole party climbed upwards. There were indeed six such terraces, the last larger and more open than any of the others. Here, there were some first-run grasses and sedges, the first they had seen. Becca started on them at once, saying nothing for a while. Mira examined the cliffs behind while the others attempted to advance further uphill. Soon, she called to Becca.

"Look at these cliffs. Smooth and vertical. Look at the curve in the hillside. It's nearly a complete circle. Could the convicts have achieved that? Vascon certainly couldn't."

Becca shook her head. She also had something to report.

"These grasses, Mira. They are not in the flora. It may not be significant, given how little of this place is known. The forests cover everything, though, till you are at the snowline or near it. But that's where the grey-greens thrive, it has been tramped over endlessly; if they were there they would have been found."

Mira descended the steps down the supporting terrace wall. The base was covered in thorny plants growing over rubble from the wall, which was bowed and collapsed in places. Seeking to see further down, she shifted a rock leaning against the wall. There was a hiss, and a small animal ran past her legs, moved a few metres away, turned and screeched at her. Becca came running, rifle at the ready. She stopped at the top of the wall and looked down. The two women stared back at the creature, its fur bristling, and its back arched. A cat, unmistakeably a cat, but far removed from those known in the Lands.

Mira turned to the space revealed by the rock's removal. On a mat of dry, long dead grey-green plants there were three kittens, now mewing and squinting in the unaccustomed light. It was not the kittens that caused a gasp, but the base of the wall behind them. It rested not on the spoil that might be expected, but on solid rock, the top of which was absolutely horizontal. She carefully restored the rock to its original position and returned to the terrace above.

"That edge, Becca, look at it. It does not follow the circle. It's truncated like a dent. And where is all the spoil? The wall cannot account for what has been removed."

They were discussing their discoveries when the rest returned from uphill. There was more news.

"There is a swamp, right across the valley floor," said Kallan. "It is not natural. I think the stream was dammed to make a reservoir, and it has silted up. It is draining, though. The stream is cutting through its centre. Stuff is exposed on the sides."

He took off his pack, and took from it several bones and a heavily-encrusted disc about five centimetres across.

"The big bone. That's from a cow. The others? I'll have to check. Nothing human. We'll have to clean this thing."

Back by the shore, there was a feeling of elation. Bones could be dated. The cow bone and the object, unquestionably indicating human presence. How old, that was one question. There were others: Those smooth cliffs: did the convicts have the means to carve them out? Where was the spoil? Where did the unknown grasses fit? As Mira explained, though, these questions led to another; was bestowed, first-run life, here before humans, or did it arrive with them? The cow, surely, came with them.

They went to bed, eager to get started, to explore this uppermost site. The weather defeated them, as a storm swept in as they awoke. It raged for three days, raining heavily and continuously all the time. The stream that passed by their camp grew ever larger. Then they heard a rumble and then a roar from the mountains above them. Minutes later, the roar was deafening, and a debris-laden wave passed downstream, threatening to overwhelm their camp. Its force carried boulders, uprooted trees and a mass of grey-green debris towards the sea. As it subsided, the water was stained brown. The sky cleared soon afterwards.

"That storm was fierce, but we've seen worse," said Kallan. "If this happened with every storm, those terraces and the swamp would not be here. Something gave way higher up. It's like a dam bursting."

"Some of this is from near the snowline," added Becca. "There are grey-greens in here," she prodded the debris at her feet, "that live 2000 metres up. There are lakes there."

"The Bestower looks kindly upon us," said Mira with a grin. "This will have exposed much. We must return, but we cannot be up and down every day. The boat will be here tomorrow if the weather holds. Becca, you will stay here and meet the boat. Another week, please, and take any supplies they have. We will carry supplies and tents and stay there for as long as necessary."

It was harder than Mira had imagined. The path was largely swept away, as were many of the terrace walls. At the first she had examined, the rock concealing the cat's lair had gone, and the edge of the flat base was exposed. The cat and her kittens passed briefly through her mind. It took them all day to haul their loads to a site close by, with Junte, Kallan and Bragen up and down sections of the climb to move it in batches. When morning came, they scrambled to the broken dam that held back the swamp.

The place was transformed. The wall remained on both sides, but there was now a gorge, almost a canyon, in the centre. It ran right through the once flat terrain, smaller, shallower branches running off to each side. The base was strewn with rocks, shattered trees and pools of grey-green sludge. The peaty sides were unstable; a large section slid down behind them, temporarily blocking the stream until cut through by the rising water.

There were bones. Bones and the peat-coloured remains of plants long dead. At least some were human. Soon, the accumulation of material became oppressive, as the thought of carrying it downhill weighed on their minds. Junte and Bragen started the process of carrying loads downhill, returning each evening. The boat had been and gone, and Becca was free to assist them. Eventually, Mira called a halt.

"We can date all this, or at least a sample. But everything will be mixed by the flood. I want to find material where it was buried, bottom oldest, top most recent."

The sides were searched, with anxious eyes on the peat walls looming over them. The topmost layers were gained only from the shallow gullies that opened up on either side. Mira herself went for the oldest layers at the base, layers that contained soil and rocks rather than peat. Sterile, empty, until she reached the upstream limit of the swamp. Here, the flood had washed through buildings, or at least the shaped blocks that were perhaps their foundations. Calling the others, there were soon shouts and whoops as one artifact after another was retrieved from the muddy sludge that the flood had left behind. Broken crockery, glass, what might pass for cutlery when cleaned, and a multitude of other metallic pieces whose function was obscure.

Things too elaborate for convicts' use? A guardhouse? The fragments matched nothing in Mira's experience, where early sites turned up more primitive ware. She had not studied the products of recent times, times when the convicts were present. Age, we must have age, but these things cannot give us that. Bones and wood were needed. All were put to digging and probing the area around, the layer that preceded the peat. The peat, after all, surely signified abandonment.

Two days went by, days with mist and drizzle, cold rain that chilled the spirit as well as the body. A note of triumph when an old grate was found, yielding a few handfuls of charcoal, but that was all. Becca started to worry; the rain might be light, but already more of the peat walls behind them were slumping into the newly created gorge. Mira was contemplating the retreat; it would be necessary to search each terrace on the way down, for surely convicts had died there. It was Junte's heading off into the woods that changed things. Squatting, he noticed a stone ahead of him, a stone clearly shaped by human hand. Carefully burying the reason for his journey, he cleared the base of the stone. A slab, a straight-sided stone with a semi-circular top, its base firmly in the ground. Eroded lettering was carved on its face, lettering he half recognised.

It was a grave. They found others. While Junte was busy with the camera, Mira cursed inwardly. Bones would be removed piecemeal, and they were fragile. A crude, unprofessional excavation, all that could be managed. There were more inscriptions, most less legible than the first.

"Does the style mean anything," asked Becca. "Did anyone back home have memorials like these?"

"The very earliest, yes, but not later," replied Mira. "After that, nearly always ironwood, and flat on the ground. Even now, only Seniors and other important folk have stone memorials, and they are elaborate things. Surely you've seen them?"

"Important like professors, you mean?" The sally provoked laughter, a release now that they had all, more than all, they could have hoped for. Such stones? Surely not for convicts or even their guards?

The return was uneventful. To Mira's delight, bones were found at two of the lower terraces, where the flood had undermined retaining walls. One was an intact skull, complete with bullet holes in front and behind. Most certainly a convict. The boat arrived in calm weather which lasted until they were safely back at the Settlement. It was decidedly crowded, for their material was copious.

Soon, the archaeological hut was awash with material, as Figra started the approximate dating and prepared samples for transport back home. Junte and Kallan were immured in books and Kallan's collections, while Mira and Becca pored over photographs and drawn profiles. She spared time, however, to talk to Jana Polin and Jessa Reboud. The two were keen to impress on her the natural, integrated nature of first-run life. She was a bit bemused by the talk of food chains and nutrient cycles, but jumped when she saw pictures of the first-run invertebrates.

"That's not a first-run," she said, pointing at a picture. "That's a higgyback. They are all over the Lands."

Jessa smiled, and opened the standard text on the fauna of the Lands. There were higgies, from the tiniest to the giants from the Far Outs and the east of Eastland. Step by step, Jessa took her through the differences.

"Pseudo-higgies, properly, but they end up as pseuds. Same ecology. Just that higgies usually need abo vegetation and pseuds go for the bestowed."

There was more. There were even bestowed pseudo-octopods, likewise equipped with poison fangs, though not so lethal, at least at first bite. Some developed an allergy from a second, but most could not penetrate the skin. They were more obviously distinct from their abo counterparts. Much smaller, and much cleverer, too. There were many more, a range of hexapods way outside Mira's knowledge. The slimaks, astonishing animals with soft, slimy bodies that slithered over the ground. She grimaced as Jessa allowed one to crawl over her hand.

"So, what of the aboriginals, the second-run?" she asked.

"They are around, but you'd be pushed to find them, except where the vegetation is mostly abo; that's mainly just below the snowline. Under the needle-leaves, virtually never."

Mira thought, remembering the request to date octopod remains. *Does one drive out the other? Why so much here, and so little in the Lands?*

"Have things changed? Are the second-runs doomed?"

"We'd like to know for sure," said Jana. "There are no octopods other than that specimen, which is why we want you to date the remains. It might be recent. Otherwise, we've no evidence. Things seem stable, and the microbiological life seems to be a mixture. Some will thrive on the remains of both runs, and it's a job to tell their origins."

There would have been time to explore other inlets, but it seemed to Mira that there was little to be gained. None had yielded evidence of human activity, and there would be no paths. The residents were only too happy to agree, as each voyage carried its risks. As it was, they had more material than the most optimistic had imagined at the start. Figra was able to get provisional ages for much of the material, only stopping when her supplies ran out. As a last gesture, she included pieces of the octopod exoskeleton she had been given. Junte had identified most of the bones, though some remained unknown. Even Kallan could only place them in families.

The picture that was emerging, provisional though it was, pleased nobody. It was at a final briefing, a day before the boat was due, that Mira had to produce a summary. Figra's dates had wide margins, but their import was clear. All human remains from the highest point were at least two thousand years old; they might be much older. How much? Could be as much as four thousand. Crucially, no first-run samples, animal or vegetable, were any older, but many were much younger. Cattle, domestic cattle, and sheep were contemporaneous with the human remains. The much smaller, stockier cattle, still present in small numbers, were present in younger layers, as were the familiar rats and mice. Kallan interrupted to say that the cat and dog remains also changed as time went on.

The human remains from the lower terraces had ages that supported the idea that they were those of convicts. No trace of Vascon. The octopod? Here there was some excitement, for the oldest date was a mere hundreds of years ago. Vascon's pet? Someone suggested, to laughs. Mira followed on with the analysis that showed few abo remains at the bottom of the peat, but more in the youngest deposits.

She could say little about the artifacts and the badly eroded lettering on the tombstones, only that they showed a level of sophistication greater than that of the earliest sites on Kindland. It was Torla that put into words what all were thinking.

"So, the Bestowalist case is not refuted, is it? Nothing first-run earlier than humans, and nothing more than a few thousand years, maybe less than on Kindland. What do we have left? The possibility of colonisation from the north, and its abandonment, after only a short while. The presence of animals and plants of no use to us, and their survival in our absence."

Mira nodded. "There is, of course, the poverty of first-run in the Lands. It is as though those reaching them left behind all but the immediately useful, and in the struggle to survive, much was lost in terms of technology. And why has it been such a struggle to claim land for our own, when it is the first-run that dominate here?"

The question was left unanswered. Bestowal? To a place, Halfland, where it seemed survival was not possible in the long term, and a move to the Lands, where life was a slow struggle against the odds. An irrational belief, but one that was not conclusively refuted. Two days later, the ship arrived. Kallan and Jana were both to be replaced, and joined them. Back to Kindopol, and the myriad of questions that would be asked on their return.

9. The Historian

The noise could be heard all down the corridor. *Kolchan's class again,* thought the principal, wearily, as he rose and marched with two porters to the classroom. There was uproar. Several children were fighting, and books and scrunched up paper were flying. Old Mr Kolchan sat at his desk, head in hands, tears lining his cheeks. At a signal, one of the porters fired a sports pistol. The children were shocked into silence.

"Yet again. You were warned. You will sit in silence until you are dismissed. Mr Bechtel and Mr Gorrifon will remain here. They have my authority to beat any child misbehaving."

There was a shuffling. A hand was raised.

"Please, sir, it was Marala that started—"

"Enough. I do not want to know. Absolute silence, or there will be worse consequences, for all of you."

The principal beckoned Kolchan to follow, and left the room, leaving the two porters facing the class, batons swinging from their hands. In his office, he kept Kolchan standing as he sat back in his chair.

"So, what was it this time, Kolchan? The third riot this term, isn't it?"

Kolchan looked down. There was a pause before he raised his head and spoke wearily.

"The usual, sir. It takes so little when we deal with beginnings. The parents egg them on, and the least spark and it's *cursed Consies,* even *heretic*, or *idiot Besties, foul Exterminators.* I wonder if history is right for some so young."

Principal Lagroen hesitated. Try as they might to be neutral, to teach only the facts, such as they were, about the arrival on Kindland, the question of origins was raised. The last teacher had been a devout Bestowalist, and he had been bombarded with complaints about indoctrination from Consie and Evolutionist parents. The woman had moved on, not without some pointed remarks about consulting the Commission, and he had tried hard to find a replacement who would avoid taking sides. Kolchan had seemed to fit, but the man was incapable of maintaining order. He would have to go, or both sides would be howling for blood. He took pity on the man.

"Sit, Kolchan, sit. What sparked this one off?"

"Marala Gollichan, sir. We were going through the standard text: the legend of Colonel and Doc. I said nothing about from whence they came. Lachlon Hendy raised a hand; *The Bestower delivered them, didn't he, sir?* I would have told him that we did not know, could not know, that it was a matter of belief. But Marala piped up before I could stop it. *There's evidence, if we choose to look for it, isn't there, sir?* A rationalist family, of course. The shouting started at once. Parents stuff more into their heads than we have time for, never mind any consideration of evidence."

"Committed Consies?"

"No, not at all. But Mr Gollichan is a sceptic, and that girl is clever. She's always asking how we know this and that."

It is fortunate, Mr Lagroen thought, as he dismissed the teacher, *that it is near the end of term.* Old Kolchan qualifies for a pension, especially if we plug ill health. I can only hope that we can find a replacement that will keep parents off my back. A misfortune to be saddled with a *mixed* school, though I would not have risen so far in a dedicated one, where those that try to steer a neutral course do not fare well.

It was at the end of term that his thoughts returned to Marala. No doubt, Kolchan's replacement would be better able to maintain discipline, but the girl was trouble. A clever one like her could move; there were specialist schools for the gifted. Perhaps even Varren College. He asked the parents to call.

"Excellent work your daughter does, Mr and Mrs Gollichan. A star pupil indeed. Had you thought of her future? Before she has grown up, of course; there are limits to what a humble place like this can provide."

Mr Gollichan smiled. His wife nudged him with a frown on her face. A frown that said *behave yourself, no mischief.*

"I confess that we had not, Principal. As you say, her progress has been good, and entirely to our satisfaction. We like to think that she has received an education that exposes her to the variety of beliefs that tear our country apart. Too many schools put belief ahead of reason."

He paused, and regarded Lagroen with a look of sardonic amusement.

"I imagine that such diversity is hard to manage. But we would hate to see Marala in some school or college that offered only a narrow view, be it Bestowalism or Evolutionism. A child with an open mind might find the atmosphere oppressive."

"Indeed it is, Mr Gollichan, indeed it is. But such children may find themselves at odds with the less gifted on both sides, even here."

"And a source of problems for those that teach them, perhaps? Never mind. But there are few places that seem better equipped to deal with such issues."

"Few, but they are there. Had you thought of Varren College?"

Gollichan stiffened in his chair. Varren? For the children of the elite, the Seniors, the magnates? For a tiny, token addition of scholars. Oh, it was open-minded, true, for it trained its pupils in the degree of detached superiority thought fitting for those destined to rule. Cost alone was sufficient to deter even the most able. Was the man making fun of him?

"There are ways and means, Mr Gollichan. We Principals are invited to propose candidates. An exam removes most, but it is not academic ability alone that they look for. Attitude of mind is prized above all. Those enthusiastic for a cause are not looked on with favour. As one of their tutors put it to me, *it takes too long to remove the rubbish before we can insert the sense.*"

"Such a scholarship is complete? No fees?"

"Yes, some are complete. You live not far away, I think, and would not have to find boarding fees. That is the barrier for many outside the city."

*****

Varren: the place that made or broke the scholars that mixed with the elite. It made Marala, whose sceptical, worldly approach matched the ethos to perfection. She won praise for her acuity in debate, her ability to argue first one side, then the other in any controversy. She was also attractive, but the lapdog attention she received from many did not impress. Too often, she found, the notional rationality, the scorn for partisan enthusiasm marked not a sceptical mind, but an unthinking acceptance of a certain manner. Unthinking, she concluded, not from idleness, but an actual lack of capacity.

It set her apart. A quick, incisive demolition of any view notionally the same as her own, but taken on trust, did not make her any friends. As for the other scholars, a post in government, superficially attractive, would lead eventually to a posting in some remote town. The more so, since her reputation passed upwards to the parents of the privileged, with all their powers of patronage. Her thoughts turned more and more towards the academic life, and the disputes about origins that had disturbed her at her previous school.

She sat the Institute of History's exam, and passed with ease. The change in atmosphere was great. Suddenly, she was confronted with the old, unthinking prejudices that had prevailed at school. There were Bestowalist and Evolutionist professors, each with their dedicated camp-followers among the students. Debates were unmannerly, texts disputed. Even the Westerland War, a mere two hundred and fifty years old, provoked dispute.

"Aggression, plain and simple, in the name of religion, and a perverted one at that," bellowed some.

"A war we provoked by our interference in their affairs, by our support of the unbelievers, the heretics," shouted others.

Both cited the outcome as evidence for their view. The Westerlanders had indeed been driven out, at the cost of the great sack of Kindopol itself. Liberty had been restored. But, thereafter, successive Kindland governments had been assiduous in preventing its citizens from provoking their increasingly fundamentalist neighbour. Deteriorating international relations only heightened the tension.

Marala had kept silent. She had soon learnt that, out of classes, her biologist and physicist contemporaries were more congenial company. Disputes were few, and in general, good-natured, as all admitted that evidence was scarce and ambiguous. It was a biologist that had provided ammunition for an incident that nearly saw her ousted. She had been recounting, humorously, the shouting match that had developed during a seminar on the war.

"I've always wondered about that war," said Galla Hort. "Westerland is a lousy place to convert the land, for all they go rooting out the aboriginal. Those sodden moors. It's easier for us, and we have much more in the way of minerals too. Eastland even more, for all they have less rainfall. And we have the Rehine Basin, the place where almost anything bestowed will grow without preparation. Never mind religion, if I were a Westerlander, I'd want a piece of that."

That had set Marala on a hunt. Documents relating to the war were scarce, other than the rather turgid military histories written after the event, and the account of the peace talks that had followed. Any written evidence from the period before the invasion had vanished in the Westerlander's savage destruction of Kindopol before they left or surrendered. What about Westerland archives? Their histories, not surprisingly, saw the setback as the Bestower's punishment for backsliding, though a few pointed virtuously to the evidence of Kindland interference as a cause. A crusade that failed.

Histories, just that. The original documents were housed in High City. Cited, but seen by few Kindlanders, and only those few whose Bestowalist credentials were beyond reproach. Even then, some admitted that their searches had been supervised, and that copies rather than originals were made available.

When she suggested in one seminar that the Westerlanders might have had less exalted motives for their invasion, there was a near repetition of the scene that had seen her move schools. On both sides, the axiom that the war was motivated by belief was being challenged. For a while, she was shunned, and had thought of withdrawing altogether. She was saved by Professor Noppendor, the elderly military historian. A one-time colonel in entirely peaceful times, his lectures were renowned for their tedium. War as politics, as religion, that appealed. Marches, tactics, casualties, tales of courage and cowardice did not. He attracted no graduates; it was even rumoured that he would not be replaced when he retired.

He had stopped Marala in a corridor.

"I hear you had some original observations on the war, young lady?"

Marala shrank a little. But there was no sarcasm in those words, *original observations.*

"Yes, sir, though they did not find favour with my classmates, nor with Professor Indigan. And I have to admit that I can provide no evidence, just the mere plausibility of the idea considered rationally."

"Come with me, if you have the time. I am not sure just what might be considered evidence, but your idea set me thinking. I'd like to show you something."

He led the way to his office, a room lined with the massive tomes of past commanders and with the traditional maps marking the course of battles. Above the window, a huge musket hung from wires. He saw her glance.

"That was used in the Westerland War. Not much damned use. Kicked the man back about six feet when discharged, and had an effective range of twenty feet or less. Fifty pellets at once, but the targets would be on you with their bayonets before they knew they were hit."

He turned to a table, on which there were several maps, some hand drawn. There were a couple of file boxes alongside.

"Look here. These show the Battle of Brund. A glorious victory, the turn of the tide, indeed. It may even have been mentioned in your lectures, though I doubt with anything more information than *we won*." There was a tinge of anger in his voice.

Marala stared at the map on which his finger pointed. A name sprang out at her, Rehine. She saw the large, flat, circular basin, the famous site of the first settlement, the Foundation. The military positions were shown by little squares and rectangles. They faced each other in hilly country to the north.

"The Westerlanders outnumbered us; not by much, admittedly, but it meant they could outflank us. See, there and there." His finger moved across the map. The enemy's right flank was right on the edge of the great basin.

"They attacked on both wings. That on their left was strong, but not enough. It was repelled, though General Iggeston had to reinforce his right. On the right, they had much more success. They broke through. Now look at this." He turned to the next map.

"They had the men. They had the chance. It's a classic. You turn to your left and roll up the opposition. All the easier since you've made them commit their reserves elsewhere. They went straight on. Look, ran for miles southwards and eastwards."

"Why, sir, if the tactics are so obvious?"

"Why indeed." He showed her a third map. The left of the Westerlander army had been routed. The Kindlanders had moved to fill the gap left by the Westerland right, and were now chasing them further and further from territory they controlled. Tiny arrows pointed east, and split as the Kindland army chased after scattered opponents.

"There were prisoners, of course, though the commanders escaped. That basin was full of tall crops. There was a lot of hide and seek. It turned out none of the prisoners really knew what the strategy was. But they were told that our lot would be smashed or forced to retreat by the attack on their left. We were picking up stragglers for a week."

He regarded Marala solemnly.

"As the simple history has it, General Iggeston was a genius, especially in his own eyes, who let the enemy split their forces, and demolished each part in turn. Let them through and then chased them. The regimental diaries say otherwise. Most thought the game was up when their left flank was turned. That the Westerlanders went charging on east and south was totally unexpected."

"Then I heard what you had said. It set me to thinking. They wanted that basin, and they wanted it badly and undamaged. On any other grounds, chasing us up there made no strategic sense. They thought that their left would overwhelm us while their right took possession. Lose, as they did, and the whole enterprise comes down for them. But in any peace, possession is nine tenths of the law. You, or your biologist friend, have the right of it. Religion may stir passion, but it does not feed empty bellies."

He said nothing more, but shook her hand. She saw a watery look in his eyes and diplomatically left in silence. It was a conversation she recorded in a diary, but repeated to none. Never again did she venture an unorthodox opinion in the presence of her peers.

*****

Two years passed. Marala obtained a junior position in the Institute, an achievement that owed much to her diligence, and to her careful cultivation of archaeologists and the rapidly developing band of folklorists. The latter in particular were, almost to a man and woman, devout Bestowalists, and although their accounts of lore varied, almost all reflected the devoutness of the various communities from whom they gathered their stories. Some hoped that she would achieve a synthesis, an account that might reinforce this or that variant of Bestowalist belief; others hoped that she would reveal a rational explanation for what they regarded as a ragbag of superstition.

Her notebooks filled. She had many adventures among the remote communities of the north and east, those that had had, until very recently, very little contact with the outside world. From the archaeologists, she learnt what little evidence there was of the earliest human settlements. Leave aside the issue of dating, a still contentious field, she learnt something of the attempts to understand the orthography. A significant study, because the earliest remains indicated a literate society, for all that the evidence for later, notionally prehistoric, periods was sparse in the extreme. Often it was little more than abbreviated inscriptions carved on gravestones.

The starting point, of course, was the well-known tale of Colonel and Doc. Of their landing on Kindland, named because there, they discovered, was the means of survival. It was a dramatic story indeed, for it told how a single ship carried them to the shores of the continent, with barely forty companions. How they were near starving on arrival with little in the way of food, seed or livestock. How Colonel had led them, unerringly, to what was now Rehine. How the Bestowed flourished there, almost to the exclusion of the aboriginal.

The bare bones of the story, thus laid out, did not do justice to the many and various versions that circulated both in Kindland and Westerland. Where had the boat come from? Who was Doc? Who milked the cows that lived in Rehine? Were there forty companions or four hundred? Why was Rehine so suited to the Bestowed, when elsewhere the land needed such management, such engineering, to make it useful? In what year did it happen? For each question, there was always more than one answer, and the earliest written accounts, from centuries later, showed already the seeds of later disputes. Folklore added yet more variety.

Marala learnt the art of discretion. She would talk about each new discovery in neutral terms, refusing to be drawn on which account she favoured. Her files and notebooks were locked away each evening, and some things were taken home. Despite her increasingly accepted status, she found her fellow historians to be uncongenial companions, and the self-styled folklorists even worse. There was, in their eyes, in their anxious questioning, a desire for the killer blow, the finding that would confirm their own certainty.

It was a relief to maintain her friendships with biologists and physicists. The former certainly took her interest in Rehine to heart. The young Jana Polin, a microbiologist, had made repeated visits.

"There is a wealth of Bestowed micro-organisms there. Species that are not found on Halfland, though there are more there than here. It is a source for reclamation, though we now have lab cultures on a large scale. It's a puzzle, for certain. It seems your beloved Colonel knew where to go."

"Not only the micros," said another. "There's not much there now, just crops, but most of the trees we have cannot survive on Halfland, it's too damned cold. A boatload from there cannot have carried all those with them."

"Unless it was warmer then," yet another broke in, "but direct from the far north is not credible under any climate we can imagine."

The conversations tended to be repetitive. Halfland did not feature in any account, but how could it? The name itself was a coinage perhaps more than two millennia later. It seemed, though, to be the only place from which the settlers could have come, unless, of course, the Bestower had plonked them out of nowhere into a boat in mid-ocean. Why not in Rehine itself?

For all that they were good company, she often became bored. There was tension, the familiar tension, among these biologist friends. Talk about evolution of the aboriginal, and they were of one mind. On the bestowed, there were differences. Most accepted the logic of first-run, of the evolution of what was called the bestowed, on that great north continent now covered in ice, and their escape to the warmer equatorial zone. Most, but not all, for those trained in agriculture tended towards a Bestowalist stance. Never vicious, the arguments failed to convince, for there was no conclusive evidence either way.

Among the physicists, things were different. They were, almost to the last man, and they were nearly all men, completely indifferent to the whole issue.

"There are rules, Marala, it's as simple as that. Not simple to discover them, of course, but they just are, and they work, every time. If they don't, we've not found them. Steam engines work, electricity works, the orbits of the planets follow a rule. We don't need magic, or a Bestower."

"You do not believe, then?" she had asked.

"Does it matter? Can the Commissioners or the priests prove his existence? Can those Evolutionists prove he does not? Did he wind up the celestial clock and let it run? Maybe, maybe not. Did he make the rules? Who cares?"

Nevertheless, they listened to her retelling of folk stories, of the latest archaeological finds. There was a certain fascination in all these confused accounts, and they amused themselves constructing elaborate explanations in materialist terms, always ending with the refrain, *of course, it's untestable, but you never know.*

Then she met Torren, Torren Galben. Flamboyant, argumentative, and given to wild speculations way beyond any practical means of the testing so beloved of his colleagues. A cosmologist, *of the worst sort, always going on about the origin of everything, treats time as a dimension, crazy as an abo addict,* was the rough description. A joker, a court jester, loved for his good humour, and admired, even a little feared, for his mathematical ability, which none could match.

The arguments, which left her miles adrift, seem to go round in circles. The paradoxes of time travel were raised, then Torren would wave his hands and conjure up alternate universes, each taking a different turn as exchanges took place between them. The classic was the Westerland War.

"What if we sent an army back, Torren? Saved Kindopol?"

"How do you know we did not? At some time in the future?"

"Because Kindopol was sacked. No magic armies appeared."

"But in a parallel universe? One where the sack never happened. Things diverge."

"So how do we know that some other buggers did not mess up ours?"

"Well done," Torren grinned. "We don't."

The others remained unconvinced; an infinity of universes then, at least in theory. It hurt their heads. After a few such sessions, Marala had intervened.

"The same arguments, between the same people, in the same place. I think you have proved that time travel is real. It just goes round in circles."

There was a short silence, for they were all used to taking everything about their discipline seriously. Torren was the first to smile.

"A hit, a hit indeed, Mara. We do go round in circles. Somewhere, there must be a tangent, a means of escape. I'm working on it."

The last words were accompanied by a broad grin, and a mock puffing up of importance. Everyone laughed, and the talk turned to other things. Torren, though, now glanced across the table at Marala, a look in his eyes that brought a flush of colour to her cheeks.

*****

Somehow, the gatherings around the bar room table faded away. Torren's absence matched Marala's, and conversations without him lacked zest. When the pair were sighted, which was rarely, they took evasive action. They had an appointment here, a performance there, to which they were duty-bound to attend. It came as no surprise a few weeks later when they reappeared, hand in hand, to announce their engagement.

It was an unconventional marriage. The physical attraction was, at times, overwhelming. *Can't keep their hands off each other* was the standard refrain, and their colleagues became concerned at the lack of attention that conventional duties required. There were long periods of leave, stretching tolerance to the limits. The places they went to were strange indeed; out of the way, often primitive. There was even a prolonged visit to the Far Outs, a visit that held no obvious appeal to Torren, while Marala could claim her work required a sabbatical to collect oral traditions from the many island communities.

There were no children. It was only a few years before their lives appeared to outsiders to have drifted apart. Apart, but without rancour or any hint of dissatisfaction. Torren became more and more a recluse, although he attracted the most gifted of the juniors. Marala became famous for her dogged pursuit of each and every tale she encountered. Her travels continued, now alone or with students.

"Who did you hear it from? And from whom did they hear?" Students would recount the trailing round villages, the occasional brushes with priests faced with what they regarded as deviant versions from their parishioners. The files in her office multiplied, but no grand synthesis emerged. Her seminars were factual; the story went like this, in this place, she would say. Occasionally, she would condescend to trace a connection, a lineage, for a slowly changing story as new places opened up to farming and folk from different places mingled.

The years passed. Although the study of legends was maintained, she rarely mentioned them, and her research and teaching centred on the establishment of early settlements, and the gradual replacement of folk tales and the more concrete evidence of archaeologists with actual written records. There were visits to Eastland, where her work was more highly regarded than at home. None to Westerland, and that had not been for want of trying. The interview with a junior official at the embassy was both demeaning and revealing.

"I regret, Mrs Galben," the slight was deliberate and sneering, "that we see no need for your visit. All matters relevant to your studies have already been documented and published. You have the books, we know."

"Books that have been edited. Books that show a surprising uniformity in the Foundation Story. Very much unlike the variation here and in Eastland, never mind the Far Outs."

She saw the look on the young man's face; anger and contempt in equal measure.

"No offence intended. But there are variants in the far west of your country. The accounts are mentioned almost in passing. If there are no originals in High City, I would like to examine those in the communities in which they were passed down."

"Ha, as we expected. You have been remarkably silent about your extensive travels, travels even to that cesspit of heresy, Eastland. Not that your own country is free of taint, still less are the Far Outs. Do you think we do not know the nature of your findings? We retain the correct, the true story of Foundation. No, Mrs

Galben, you will not go to the far west, to stir up trouble among those that consort with Outers. You will not be able to offer a distorted view of our scholarly work. Those Easties are beyond redemption, but your authorities have been lax, far too lax, in dealing with the stupid distortions that malign the true account of Foundation."

There had been no further visits. Her appeal to the Foreign Affairs Commission to intercede made it clear that the Westerlanders were not to be persuaded.

"I am sorry, Professor. Only those with the purest of Bestowalist credentials are admitted, and certainly not those who are suspected of deviancy. We have problems even with the accreditation of embassy staff."

The official looked her in the eye.

"There is something else, Professor. We cannot say so in public, but should you actually visit, even if only to High City, we cannot guarantee your safety. They might, of course, use some excuse to expel you, but that is not the only risk. An exchange student met a tragic but *accidental* death. The circumstances were never made entirely clear. A blameless lad, as far as we know. I would have been more concerned if they had allowed your visit. I fear the tenor of your work is too well known."

Marala gave up the attempt. Any final account, should she ever publish it, would have to exclude the Westerland versions. She returned to her studies of settlement patterns. They led her once more to the site of Foundation, the Rehine Basin. Settlement had, of course, been continuous, and some of the earliest written records came from its neighbourhood. Very soon, the pilgrim route from Bounty Bay to the basin had become the basis for prosperity, fuelled by a steady stream of Westerlanders. The grant of land for the monastery was known, and the records showed Westerlanders among the monks. A way-station, a hospice, for weary pilgrims. A racket, her husband had said, dismissively, what's changed?

It was her undoing. Pressed for details on her early work on the Foundation Myth, she had agreed to give a seminar. Bravely entitled *The Pilgrim's Trail: History and Prehistory,* she had responded to a question.

"Professor, some folklore versions do not mention Doubter's Ravine, others do. Is the any connection with the monastery?"

She had hesitated. The idea had not occurred to her, since she had stuck in the rut of assuming the versions that she had recorded were little influenced by events after writing became commonplace. The monastery, it was thought, arose from the legend. The other way round?

"A neat suggestion. I confess I had not made the connection. We have no means of knowing when variants arose. The monastery archives were mostly destroyed in the war, but there is correspondence in High City for certain. Perhaps even in our own Commission. I will ask. Some survived the sack; temples and their offices were often spared."

There were other questions. Marala did not notice a muttering among a clique of Bestowalist colleagues. That night, however, a certain nagging fear led her to review her notes and put them in order. She slipped a file into her husband's disordered papers a few days later, knowing that he would be unlikely to find it.

A week after the seminar, she was walking from the Institute along the river bank towards home. She had worked late, as usual, and the street was feebly lit by gas lamps. Revellers, many the worse for drink, were moving in crowds along the bankside. There was an altercation; shouts of *Bestie scum, Consie traitors* degenerated into inarticulate jeers. Fights broke out. Marala tried hard to edge around the scrum, but one band of Besties had isolated a few Consies, and were more or less carrying them to the river.

The shouting mob surged over her. There were splashes as their hapless victims were thrown into the river. Marala lay trampled underfoot. A larger band of Consies charged for revenge. There were more splashes. Then police sirens. The mobs fled leaving only the injured and the lifeless bodies of Marala and others behind. Those struggling from the river were duly arrested.

Even in a city becoming accustomed to violence, the incident provoked outrage, the more so since Marala herself was obviously *an innocent bystander.* Citizens are not safe, screamed the *Planet;* Alcohol-fuelled madness, yelled the *Temperance Herald.* Where were the police, demanded the *Courier,* where was our famous Inspector Gornik?

There were interviews of the arrested, and autopsies on the dead. Stab wounds on the rioters' bodies, but not on Marala's. She had been trampled. But the police doctor had attached a note to his report. *I draw attention to the injuries to the victim's skull, themselves sufficient to kill. The force used is not compatible with mere trampling by a mob.*

Gornik had been inclined to see the incident as outside his rather special remit; a drunken brawl, even if inflamed by partisans, was a matter for others. Piqued by the attacks in the pops, however, he reviewed the case notes. A few familiar names appeared. In particular, a Westie student, Findus Forrost. He inquired. *Arrested and charged with affray. Released on bail.* And, of course, sheltered in the Westie embassy, and shipped home on the next steamer. *Don't stir it, Gornik,* was the reaction from on high. Marala's death? Manslaughter by person or persons unknown, a tragic consequence of disorder.

The hubbub died away. Gornik remained unsatisfied, but without anything to warrant further inquiries, he turned to other matters. Then there was the Institute of History fire. A trivial matter at first glance, for it had been rapidly extinguished. But the perpetrator was yet another Westie, and the target had been the cupboards in which Marala's papers had been stored. A sullen lad, who had played dumb when interrogated. Of course, charged, found guilty and expelled, the standard treatment for Westie militants. *Keep them locked up here,* he had been told, *and they start making converts among the clearance gangs.*

Anything to keep the peace, he had thought, bitterly. Do the Seniors really think an idiot like that would act alone? Even know that Marala Galben existed, never mind where her records were kept? What was it that mattered among that rather obscure historian's papers? He commissioned a review, using funds that were free from the tedious necessity of being accounted for. A review that removed the papers to an obscure office with the unrevealing nameplate: *Boggis & Sons, Accountants.* In due course, a report was delivered. A report to which there was a significant addition. He added a couple of comments, and filed it away.

10. Colonel and Doc

Extracts from the notebooks of Marala Galben

Note for C. I. Gornik: This is our best effort: Marala Galben's writing is at first hard to follow, because she inserts queries and citations in a rather haphazard manner. We have placed these as footnotes along with our own where it seems appropriate. A few names mentioned are also further identified. We think you will be familiar with most. This seems to be her summary.

Another try at making a synthesis. I'm excluding all those records from Westerland; the priests did too good a job with those insertions, *and the Bestower said to Colonel...* Bollocks. Somewhere in High City, there must be a template, though nobody will admit it. More than a hundred accounts collected, and almost identical[1]. A few from here are much the same, but at least I can tell when they stem from a priest's instruction[2].

What is the core here, the things that all[3] agree on?

1. A boat (s?) landed on the north shore of Kindland (Bounty Bay).
2. It contained at least forty people, among whom were Colonel and Doc.
3. They had very little with them. It was an escape of sorts.
4. Somehow, Colonel knew that there was a place inland where the Bestowed flourished.
5. He led them directly there.
6. There was a wealth of Bestowed life there, crops, trees, animals.

---

[1] *Goliast, P. J. (2945), Origins, a compendium of early days, HCP, does record some variants from the far west, attributed to Outer influence. They are dismissed. No first-hand accounts. The rest seem to follow the order of service.*

[2] *Box 12 has the best evidence of this. Those three villages near Ootersfold, and the parish diary. They did a very thorough job there.*

[3] *There were a few nonsense ones. Not filed in order until we can clarify them.*

7. There were no people there[4].

8. Colonel told the people there were other places the same. They were not found in his lifetime[5].

I have tried to sort out some of the variants, and to cluster those with things in common.

Most accounts refer to a single boat, but its size varies immensely. Do we dismiss the claim that it was a steamship? Some have a whole flotilla, but I think I've nailed that. It comes from that mural in the Temple at Ardnort, with folk disembarking while waving banners. It's old, but everybody except the locals think it depicts the first landing on north-west Westerland. No date for that either, of course, but it was at least a thousand years later[6]. Connection with Martyr's Cove?

Where did it come from? That's the killer. The priests say, "The Bestower set it upon the waters, put the people in it, and said sail; sail to the land allotted to you." Deny that, and you are left with Halfland only[7]. No life, never mind us, in the icy Northland, surely? As for a sunken continent[8]! As much evidence as

---

[4] *I must deal with this properly later. Skeletons and burials in reports 122, 157 and 289. Archaeologists say no way to tell from later burials. Need pinpointing dates, NBG for now.*

[5] *Galla told me that there are places, small, scattered and hard to find, where they find a few Bestowed plants that hang on, and with no evidence of settlement. But soils vary a lot, and she was not convinced that they were in any way 'prepared'. There are a few in Eastland, too. As she says, seeds can travel, and we have often damaged the ground without preparing it. Opening for some to spread naturally, if they are tough. (Professor Galla Hort, biologist and notable conservationist.)*

[6] *See the later notes found in Professor Torren Galben's files. She appears to have changed her mind about this. Versions running 'and the fleet set sail' seem not to relate to Westerland.*

[7] *I asked some sailing enthusiasts. The steamship takes eight days from Kindopol, and it is about 4000 km. The wind is favourable going SE, and they reckoned anywhere between twelve days and twenty-five. Even longer from the Northland, even to Halfland. There was that Offeren guy made it to Halfland. Half dead, and his crew really dead. Even from Halfland, a small open boat would be a great risk.*

[8] *Marala has a lot of crossing out and hard to decipher scribbles here. She clarifies this later: "Professor Hochast tells me there are places where the sea is very shallow, often only ten metres or less. Not mapped in detail, but a few wrecks made it necessary to pinpoint some. Sea level could go up and down that much, but could is not the same as*

there is for the Bestower's munificence. What or who did that ship have on it? There's another puzzle. Most go with forty folk, but it seems to be almost a token number. There are no names apart from Colonel and Doc. I asked Loman[9]. He said forty was far too few, we would be victims of inbreeding. He was even a bit iffy about four hundred. But four hundred in one boat? Steamships, yes, but even Vascon's caravels would not hold so many. Ship or ships? Again.

Colonel? Kernel? Really a colonel as we use the term? Never 'the Colonel'. Of course, it got written down as 'Colonel' because it made sense for a commander, not spelled phonetically. Even a nickname, like 'His Serenity' for old Fegran[10]? Certainly always male. Death contested, some say of old age, some bitten by an octopod on a hunt. Plenty of murals of that death, even some as the protector of a bunch of women about to be devoured. Huh. Doc is worse. Seems it really did mean doctor, and some variants tell of cures and potions (23–28 and 177–195 all describe this). Asked Dr Colloman[11]. Strange diseases, not identifiable. But the treatments don't match, certainly for the period. As he says, any sickness in the early days was attributed to malign aboriginal contamination, and was met by wide-ranging culls. Long after he (she?) had gone (no account of death) there were mass burnings of higgybacks[12].

What's worse, though, is that Doc is a man in about two-thirds of the accounts, and all of those that toe the Westerland line. But nearly all Far Out versions have Doc as a woman, and nearly all their medics are women too. Come to that, there is no enumeration of men, women or children. Back to numbers again!

---

did, by a long way. On present showing such a place would be as grim as Halfland in terms of climate. Pester the geologists, but they are mostly uninterested in what is beneath the sea, never mind the ice." (Professor Almar Hochast is a refugee from Westerland, currently President of the Kindopol Institute of Biology.)

[9] *Professor Horod Loman. He was head of the animal breeding unit at Fornigfold, and a respected hereditarian. Now deeply retired.*

[10] *His Excellency Paroan Fegran SE (†3012) famous for both his imperturbable nature and immense girth.*

[11] *Dr Colloman, a district doctor, gave many popular talks on the history of medicine.*

[12] *Hochast tells me that he heard stories of higgyback festivals in Westerland villages before he came here. A ritual burning that followed on any setback. Not officially sanctioned, but certainly not prohibited.*

What did they bring with them? Well from what the archaeologists say, precious little, or precious little that mattered. All the early sites are downright primitive. Even stone tools in some graves, but they certainly had metals, even iron. It takes a high temperature to work or extract, but they knew how to do it[13].

Weapons? Engines? All the things you would think evacuation from a civilisation might take with them? A few disputed firearms[14]. Fragments of fabric none of our chemists can understand, still less make. Of course, explained if they left in a hurry, and Colonel told them there were good things to expect. Whatever they had, it was not enough to save them from barbarism. No trace of any ship; perhaps too much to expect. Beachcombing for centuries has turned up nothing.

What they did have, though was writing. Just nothing to write on except carving in stone, and that only on gravestones[15]. Again, though, paper would have rotted long ago. If things were better before, and the evidence supports it, they went downhill very fast among those pioneers. First writing not carved in stone? A fragment on crushed vantabush bark. And what does it say? What A**cra* would like to do to Heri**a when they meet! Of course, no date, but in context, I hear it is from around 400–500 AB[16].

---

[13] *Damn the lack of good dating. Those people knew how to write, and did not. Best I can find they had found ore within a few hundred years. When things really got moving. They must have done a lot of recycling. There is meteoric iron too. Must ask a geologist.*

[14] *A few collections of rust vaguely rifle-shaped. At least one lot a plant by Bestowalist idiots (Kindopol Courier, the cutting is in box 6).*

[15] *There are several loose sheets with Marala's thoughts here. They are now together in box 10. As she notes, the alphabet is recognisable, though we now write differently. She has several copies of inscriptions, and of course there are others in the Archaeological Museum. Mostly just names, often abbreviated. Some crudely chiselled. There are dates, and this attracted her interest. There were a cluster with notional dates that make no sense, running from 2086 to 2104. Days since they set out or landed? The rest seem to date from their arrival, often given as days. On some, these have been defaced, and a traditional, AB, date inserted. Because our ancestors seemed to have had some confusion about the length of a year, these have been of little use. Marala possessed a tattered copy of L. P. Maddonstrer (2899) Early inscriptions and the problem of chronology. Her annotations are mostly scatological, and the book, while not superseded, is widely regarded as unreliable.*

[16] *A copy of this fragment is on show in the Archaeological Museum. The reconstruction of the original text (in part disputed) is not literal. As Marala notes elsewhere, later writing was on skin, until better paper started appearing around 850 AB. By then,*

Now we come to the real crux. They went as directly as possible to Rehine. Not in a straight line, but in what was clearly the easiest route. Here most of the tales are entirely consistent.

Colonel knew where he was going. Four days march, always the route that any sensible person with a map would take. It's thanks to the accounts that we know where they landed (of course not a sign of anything there. The bastards might at least have left us an inscribed monolith)[17].

So, how did he know? No evidence of earlier occupation? Those bones? The man must have had a map, or very detailed instructions. From whom? Did the Bestower float down with a scroll? Or guide his steps from above. One thing is clear, no tales tell of any guiding light. Colonel just marched. The flock lost faith. There was a near mutiny[18]. Or perhaps not. If not the Bestower who led them, then the Evolutionists have a point. Occupied or not, Kindland was known and mapped, at least in part by someone. So why was it not colonised earlier? Especially Rehine, almost prepared for their arrival.

And then there's Rehine. What a place! Scarcely an abo plant to be seen. Unnaturally flat, unnaturally fertile. And stocked with the necessities. Who milked the cows? More than 150 square kilometres, crying out to be farmed. Trees, proper trees, not those miserable needle-leaves from Halfland. Then there are those few accounts that speak of graves, of skeletal remains. There are few,

---

Kindopol was already established, and colonists had settled on Westerland. The earliest written account of Colonel and Doc dates to 905 AB. A priestly account, in which nearly every event is followed by a homily on the beneficence of the Bestower.

[17] *Bounty Bay (strictly, Bestower's Bounty Bay) is now smothered in shrines, and in booths offering fake artifacts for sale. There is, of course, the Founder's Trail to Rehine. Unlikely as it might be that any relics of the original journey survive, all hope is now lost. Box 3 contains Marala's diary as she walked the trail.*

[18] *Doubter's Ravine. There is a monastery there, dedicated to the 'spiritual renewal' of those whose faith has wavered. It receives an annual subsidy from the Westerland Embassy. Marala evidently got caught up in an Evolutionist demo outside the walls, which got her into a spot of bother (Box 3 again). The mutiny or protest is not present in all early accounts. Marala added a later note to Box 3, expressing doubts about the authenticity of the event, which is uniformly present in all Westerland versions, but in very few elsewhere. She made a note to examine Westerland connections in those places, but seemingly did not get round to it. The monastery was burnt down by angry locals during the war, and only reopened several decades later. See also the later comments in Galben's envelope.*

and some of those read more like ghost stories. And I can see why they were needed. Where were the cow-herds, the shepherds, the reapers and sowers? Oh, there are graves, there are skeletons, but can we tell them from those coming with Colonel and Doc? No[19]. And trees? Mature trees? How long had it been there? It does not add up. There is something missing. Clear such an area, better than anywhere, and then land your colonists in Halfland, or on a sinking continent, or let them descend from heaven in a boat, miles from the promised land.

Finally, Colonel's statement that there were other places *prepared for us*. And there are such places that *could* qualify, both here and in Eastland. Galla doubts it, but it is not just the occasional plant. The soils have some strange features, and the micro-organisms too. It sounds like that fantasy of life on Hommoz[20].

Note for C. I. Gornik:

As we told you, Professor Galben handed us an unmarked envelope that he had found among his own papers. He had no idea how this had come to be there, and seeing that the contents were a part of Marala's studies, simply passed them on. The envelope has two sets of papers. One contained a number of accounts of the Arrival and Foundation, all from a cluster of rather isolated villages north of Blenninge, at the western end of Eastland. It appears that they had been collected over a period of many years by a Folklorist in Blenninge. Pinned to the back of one such account, there is a note in Marala's handwriting.

---

[19] *Marala's problem remains unsolved, as she was heard to admit much later than her writing here. Even the new dating techniques, still disputed, are unable to distinguish between items with only a few decades between them.*

[20] *Marala is referring to the popular novel,* Onward and Upward (*Abram Denisor, 2975*). *It coined the word 'Terraforming' in which colonists on Hommoz alter soils and cultivate crops. It attracted scorn from both Evolutionists (nothing could grow on a planet with an absurd axial tilt, and anyway, where's the water?) and Bestowalists (a blasphemous presumption, humans seeking to emulate the Bestower). It remained popular, nevertheless, although no government has been prepared to reach into space.*

All close together. But that Rogeron[21] is at best sloppy. I think she asked leading questions when she followed up on a confusing account sent in by someone else. She has an obsession with 'wild men', a folk tale that runs around Eastland. The main point is that the accounts from families that have lived there, time out of mind, all talk about a fleet, not a single ship. Of course, the standard version circulates as well. It has to, for it is taught in school, and many villagers have moved from elsewhere; the place is exceptionally easy to cultivate, even by Eastie standards. The wretched woman pestered them, as far as I can see, and they started correcting themselves. At least, no priests to drum orthodoxy into them. Nothing about the Bestower, just 'the fleet set sail'.

She is convinced that we have evidence of another landing besides the one at Bounty Bay, but even less successful, with a few illiterates being found by colonists advancing through Eastland. No historical account to back that up. As far as I can see, Easties discovered many amenable spots, and spread out in small groups. The standard view is that these were rediscovered as the population grew. Hence, 'wild men'.

Have to check this myself, though the locals will now have ideas put in their heads. I am certainly not going to use these stories until I have. An explosive revision if that woman is right, but where's the evidence[22]. But there is one oddity. Uniquely, one account seems to suggest that the Bestower had a name, but that people quarrelled about it; Tronto is one, Sliski is another (I think there were variants). Nowhere else: it is always 'the Bestower'.

We note that tales of 'wild men' are widespread in the western half of Eastland. Their isolation and subsequent rediscovery are attributed to the

---

[21] *Rogeron: A common name in Eastland. Possibly the folklorist Amana Rogeron (†3009) but there are other possibilities. There is a flourishing Folklore Society in Blenninge, which is not well-regarded by the Academy there.*

[22] *We are forced to the conclusion that Marala neither wished to use or comment on the material, nor to make it known, although the idea has apparently circulated among Eastland folklorists and been firmly rejected by their Academy. Placing these accounts in her husband's files reflects the searches that were made in her office before her untimely death.*

unidentified plague of 1235. Marala had good reason to be sceptical of Rogeron's claims, though she does not cite Hofferan[23].

Interesting question at the seminar. Ought to have thought of it. That Doubter's Ravine? Well, the ravine is real enough. Two days in, not hard going, though it must have been more overgrown then, I suppose. Why doubt? All the other versions suggest that Colonel knew where he was going, and it seems that everybody trusted him. It would really suit those Westies to have a story of doubt and redemption.

Trouble is, there is no way of telling how old those stories are. The only clue is that they all invoke the Bestower's mercy, and they are repeated in the Westerland compilation[24]. That's suspicious, for certain. No way will I ever see High City archives, and there are none in the monastery. Temple records? Not my field, and its likely to be one of those Westie-infested ones. Bit of subterfuge needed.

So, a motive for murder, and for destroying the wretched woman's files. I wonder what kind of boots Forrost wore. *Gornik.*

Another thing. Look at the records of our observers at Barol Temple. Two days after that seminar the woman gave. Waggon load of documents transferred to the Westie embassy. Didn't mean anything at the time. Didn't have time to sort the potentially revealing papers? So shifted the lot to be sure? Too damned late to do anything now. *Gornik, 58/3/3019.*

---

[23] *J. G. Hofferan (2966)* The Plague of 1235: Causes and effects on settlement. *Blenninge Academy.* The second document is in a smaller envelope. It is actually dated two days before her death.

[24] *This is a reference to Goliast, cited earlier.*

11. The Seigneur

The boys had climbed back up the cliffs, bags full of the nodules that recent erosion had exposed. A good haul after last week's storms. They coiled the ropes, dug out the massive rods that had held their weight and sat together on the plateau above, carpeted in real grass. A few sheep looked up briefly, and continued grazing. They opened the hamper that contained their midday meal. As Stogher unpacked, Lorcan cast his eyes idly towards the sea, towards that vast expanse that stretched, 20,000 kilometres or more, to Eastland, so it was said. A sea that held who knew what, a sea that none had traversed. The westerly breeze blew gently in his face.

It caught his eye; there was a speck out there. He stared; surely, a sail, a ship. He gave a shout and pointed. Spellbound, they watched as the speck grew larger; more sails, a hull below.

"The Peradventure? Anasman? Is it possible? The Seigneur said we should abandon hope. It's near four years."

"Who else? Does anyone head west from here?"

Impatient to be sure, they waited until the ship was scarce two hundred metres from the shore, now swinging to the north. The torn sails, the patches on the forecastle, escaped them; the banner of Greater Lofotor did not. With a whoop, leaving all behind them, they rushed down to Kullenport.

Their hysterical shouting as they came to the harbour made little impression at first. Anasman had been gone three years and more. Rumoured to have been seen off Eastland two years since. Long given up for lost. Gradually, the possibility sunk in. Old Engleton, the harbourmaster, ordered small boats out from the cove, to see beyond the point, the point that shielded it from the everlasting westerlies. The moment the first cleared the point, a rocket went up. A cheer from the harbour brought others out. By the time the Peradventure *rounded the point, half the population of Lesser Lofotor were crowding the dockside.*

The elation turned to a whispered horror. The ship that edged its way to the quay, now assisted by the smaller boats, was as near a wreck as could be imagined afloat. It was their own sailors that manned the sails, or what was left of them. Three crewmen could be seen feebly attempting to assist; three men whose emaciated figures and ragged clothes marked them out from those that had boarded. One other, bent over the wheel, sank to his knees as the ship ground against the dock.

Eager hands tied the berthing ropes. Eager hands pulled a gangplank into place. Engleton spoke softly to a few, who barred the crowd as he went aboard. The ten who had boarded were silent, shocked, save for one, doubled up and retching. The crew he saw: three blackened skeletons, staring at him with eyes that seemed focussed elsewhere. A body lay on the main deck, differing from the others only in lifelessness.

"The Captain? Any others?"

With a gesture only, a boarder pointed to the stern castle. The door hung open on one hinge. As he entered, the stench of decay made him pause. Cap held to his face, he made his way to the captain's cabin. On a bed lay Anasman, his left arm and leg strapped tightly. Dead? No, or not quite, for a pair of eyes followed his movements. There was a croak.

"Sea, just sea. We are home?"

"Yes, Captain you are home. This is Lofotor. You have been round the world. The first, the very first."

"To what end? To the death of many and the reward of none. Vanity."

There was a spasm of coughing. The harbourmaster looked in vain for water. When he turned again, there was no movement on the bed. After a while, the harbourmaster reverently closed the staring eyes.

*****

Seigneur Noris Denno regarded the assembled dignitaries with considerable satisfaction. Never before had such an assembly met on the Lofotors. Among the crowd of nobility were Master Ombro from Killet, most powerful of all the Inner Masters, with a retinue altogether too flashy for his taste, or for that of any from the Outer Isles. An ally, nevertheless, a man prepared to treat him as the *de facto* premier of the Outer Isles, a cut above Tremain of Skellin and Rottion of the Dark Isles.

To his delight, a steamer had brought a mixed bag of folk from Eastland and Kindland: two Seniors and their staff, ferried together in the Eastlander's newest ship, the *Colonel*. The huge vessel was necessarily at anchor in the bay, its draught too great for their small harbour. No Westerlanders, of course, although a formal invitation had been sent. The refusal had held no hint of apology or excuse: *No one is available to attend your festivities.*

No Westerlanders? Well, that was true up to a point. Among the lesser guests, there were certainly some devoted to the Ultras in High City, Kindlanders or even some from the Inner Isles. They would be watching, and, no doubt, the movements of the great would be reported.

The hall in which they were assembled was newly built. Under its high dome was something massive, now shrouded in huge sheets with drawstrings. The walls were similarly covered. Attendants were politely rebuffing those seeking to peep behind them. At Denno's signal, a piper struck up a lament, *Anasman's Return*. The room quietened; seats were taken. As the last notes died away, a priest mounted the ornate podium, a podium that would remain as the nearest thing an Outer could tolerate to a pulpit. He was brief and conventional.

"May the Bestower look with favour on you. May He guide your conduct to the fulfilment of His wishes. May this building and its purpose be blessed in His sight."

He descended the podium almost at a run, anxious to retreat into the crowd, a crowd he knew held his vocation in no high esteem, moderate and conciliatory though he was. Denno took his place, ascending slowly, and pausing before he spoke.

"Fellow Seigneurs and Masters, Gracious Seniors from our great continents, ladies and gentlemen. Today is the day, exactly the day, when, one thousand years ago, our great compatriot Captain Frencon Anasman returned to these shores from the first circumnavigation of our world. A voyage not repeated for over seven hundred years, a voyage next completed by our esteemed friends from the far east, the advantage of steam behind them."

Here he paused, bowing towards Senior Falkendine. The Senior bowed his head in return, his Eastlander retinue bobbing with him.

"You know the story, but it is fitting that we recall it. Our heroic Captain died even as his ship was tied to the quayside in Lesser Lofotor. Only three of his crew, out of the fifty who left this port nearly four years previously, survived to tell us of that terrible journey; of nearly seven hundred days with no sight of land; of the losses to hunger and to thirst; losses to the sea monsters that dragged men from the deck; to the injuries as they battled with storms the like of which none had seen."

"His body, of course, is not with us. The *Peradventure* was towed here, and then set adrift and aflame, with the captain and those of his crew found dead on board. She sank some few hundred metres from the quay at which many of you landed. There has been no memorial; no memorial other than in the stories, the songs and of course, his log, the only item to be removed from that noble ship. It is our way."

"But, one thousand years? Is it not time, we thought, for a more solid memorial? A thousand years in which no one, surely, has surpassed the achievement, the courage, the suffering of Captain Anasman and his crew. So here we are today. This hall will be, we hope, a memorial to last another thousand years."

Here, Denno paused. His body relaxed its formal stance, and his face showed just a trace of a smile.

"For us in these islands, benighted as we are, it is the nearest we aspire to the great Temples of Kindopol and Varden. Do not think we are unbelievers; rather, we wear our faith lightly, honouring those who revealed to us the extent of the Bestower's gifts."

There was a murmur, light-hearted indeed. The omission of the Great Temple of High City did not go unnoticed, nor did the subtle allusion to the lack of anything comparable on any of the Far Outs, a lack deplored from pulpits throughout Westerland. Denno turned and pulled on a tasselled cord. Down came the shrouds, revealing a monumental statue of Anasman, staring into a distant horizon, a hand shading his eyes. There was a burst of clapping. Denno raised a hand.

"There is, under this statue, a vault. It holds the captain's log. I alone hold the key."

He held up a huge key, that glittered as he turned it in his hand. "Each year, on this day, I or my successors will read from it. Each reading will be a day's entry. In one thousand years, we will reach the end, the day when writing was beyond them."

Denno descended the podium, and turned to a small door at the base of the statue. Soon, he returned with a book, just one of many in the vault.

"I shall not start at the very beginning, but one thousand days before the Captain could no longer write. That was but twenty days from home. The *Peradventure* one thousand days before was departing from Blenninge, after a much enjoyed stay at that hospitable city."

He nodded again at the Eastlanders. He read from a transcript, concealed on the podium, for neither his sight nor the captain's scrawl made for easy reading.

"Day eighty-four, first hundred, two thousand and sixteen. A late departure, thanks to those rogues Diclan and Naderrile. Drunk, and in custody. A Naderrile family as an excuse, though there is no proven connection bar the name. At least they paid for the damage, and we claimed the scoundrels. Ten days below for each, and a whipping. Damn those Eastie families. Wind a feeble south-westerly, so the indignity of a tow till we rounded Harbour Ness, when we caught more wind. Full sail, and a straight north-easterly passage. Passed the Oret lighthouse at dusk, fifty legs, then. Same course overnight, and we should be north of the Lannerstones by dawn."

"For our continental friends," Denno smiled, "a leg is nearly two kilometres. We have long since adapted to your ways, albeit with some reluctance. They made good going that day."

There was hesitant laughter. Was this a religious ceremony, or one in which levity was allowed? Denno descended, returned the book to the vault, returned to the podium and raised his hand. The sheets came off the walls to reveal a series of panels carved in ironwood, each one a representation of the world as they knew it at different times. The scale and the expense were designed to impress, and they did. As the crowd started to close in on the panels, there was a murmur of appreciation, music to Denno's ears.

There were nine panels. The first was but a reproduction of the earliest maps known: West Kindland alone, with Bounty Bay and Rehine given exaggerated size. The next revealed the whole of Kindland, and the nearest portions of Westerland and Eastland. There was little added to these panels, for scholars still argued about dates, and about the mythical accounts of discovery. The third was far more detailed and with dates inscribed: 1157, the Martyrs land at their cove; 1201, the founding of High City. The whole of each continent was shown.

As well, Denno had thought when talking to the carvers, that we lack the means of colouring, of delineating borders. The ending of Kindland rule in the east of Westerland, the Holy War of 1355, was not featured. Stick to geography and discovery, that was the safe course, the more so because it gave prominence to Outer sailors.

The fourth revealed the Far Outs, and engraved in the wood were the tracks of Goden Ironfist, Goden the Navigator, in 1479. The Lands as we know them, a craftily carved version that displayed the superior cartography of Outers. Goden the Eastlander, too, as the tracks made clear. Ends against the middle, what's new? The Eastlander party were congregated around it.

The fifth had pride of place. Twice the size, it tracked in detail the voyage of Anasman, with the Lofotors appearing at each end of the map. Truth be told, Denno had thought, he had added little to what was known before, other than the vastness of that empty space girdling more than half the globe. Here, and here only, he had resorted to something more than the plain wood, for both Lesser and Greater Lofotor, tiny spots on such a vast canvas, were highlighted in gold leaf.

The sixth, once again omitting the vast ocean, paid token tribute to Vascon, and the discovery of Halfland in 2577, the only addition to that of the fourth. The carvers had used a little licence, for, minutely, puffs of smoke were shown billowing from its eastern end. Naturally, it was the Kindlanders that congregated around it, to the amusement of others. It was well known that its discovery was an accident; the ship had been blown off course when returning from the Far Outs. Worse still, Vascon was born an Eastlander, a man willing to sell his services to the highest bidder. A place, Denno thought, of no use to any; a place closer to Westerland in terms of distance alone, a cause for war if its uselessness were not so obvious, and Westerland ships so feeble. *The seas are the Deceiver's,* said the Temple. *The Bestower bestowed nothing on them.* Except oilworms and fertiliser, thought Denno, those hypocrites are happy enough to use those.

The remaining panels were of less interest, resembling closely the printed maps and atlases in circulation. All based on the advent of steam. First, the discovery of Northland, with no knowledge of its extent. Then, its circumnavigation (2803–4), and finally, the great Southland, vaster even than its northern counterpart. Still not mapped all around, but why would anyone bother? Was there any other land out there? A question often asked. The ocean so huge, the distances so great. At best, what might be found, though, would be another Halfland. Anasman's achievement was surely this: the Lands, and they alone, were the living-space for humanity. The Lands divided by culture, by religion, and increasingly by the pressure of population.

The gathering in the Seigneur's Hall that evening was both highly selective and decidedly chaotic, to the frustration of both the Kindlanders and the Easties. Their visit had been prompted by more than homage to a hero. Westerland was once again descending into the grip of Ultras, as both nations knew them. People who called for more clearance, people not afraid to raise the prospect of holy war. A war in which the position of Outers was vital.

Outers, though, were a bloody-minded bunch. A nation they might be in the eyes of others, but among themselves each island group was a law unto itself. Denno might have pulled off a coup in terms of prestige, but in no way would Ombro, Killent, Tremain, Rottion, or many others allow him to speak on their behalf. Senior Falkendine, a mere two assistants by his side, stared despondently at the mass of petty Seigneurs, some ruling tiny islands with less than a thousand inhabitants. There was jostling round the table, and it seemed to him that the smaller the domain, the more aggressive its ruler.

At least, he reflected, Kindland is represented by Congresswoman Giffone. A lawyer, one famous for her spirited defence of Consies. Tipped to be the next Defence Minister. Not a regular attender at a temple either, unlike some, whose company on the long voyage from Kindopol he would have found hard to bear. A voyage tinged with both humour and threat, for they had been shadowed for some time by a Westerland vessel as they passed along that country's north coast. A ship over which the mighty *Colonel* had towered and opened its gun ports. The Westie had turned away and vanished southwards. No treaty defined a nation's waters; more than one small Kindlander been boarded, and effectively ransomed before release. Easties? No, for all went armed, and were not afraid to use them, to the disgust of the preachers in the High City Temples.

The voyage had not been idle. The two visitors had shared what they knew of Outer politics. The inner islands, a mere 250 km from the Westerland coast, made great profit from trade across the narrow sea. Ombro in particular ruled a domain grown rich on the trade, for Westerland had an insatiable demand for meat, for minerals and most especially for ore. In return, the islands received both luxuries and the refined metals that were assiduously converted into ships. It was a dependency that had induced Ombro to tolerate the few Westies working in his lands, Westies that were winning converts. Few in number, but increasingly a nuisance.

For the outer archipelago, they agreed, there was no such problem. Subordinate until the coming of steam, they had prospered on the long haul, and most of all with Eastland, from which the original colonists had come.

"Most certainly," said Chania Giffone, "they have no love for Westies. Bonny fighters too, but more often than not against each other, often in the streets of Kindopol. Do you have any knowledge? Can they be united, do you think?"

"We will see," replied Falkendine. "That Denno has pulled quite a trick with this memorial. He has the largest fleet, too, and he's rich as hell. The others will certainly not help Westies, but there is no guarantee they accept him as a leader. Sign him up alone to send his fleet to block the Westies from assaulting your city, and it is odds on some neighbour will pillage his realm. Not a runner; it must be a combined venture. Closer to home, though, he might disrupt the trade across the narrow sea. Ombro is all talk and no action, and we can offer some rewards for any dislocation of their trade."

Giffone turned that conversation to other matters. Unspoken was the difference in perspective, for all knew that Kindland, for all its wealth and population, was divided, as Eastland was not. It might fall to the Ultras with only minimal intervention from the west, and Eastland would be dependent on denying the Westies the means to make war across the seas. Even the mines of central Kindland were of less significance to Easties than the riches of the Far Outs. You can leave Kindopol, she reflected, but Kindopol does not leave you, and brings with it its murky and increasingly violent politics.

To the relief of both, the high chair was not disputed; Denno presided, though Ombro and his associates sat resolutely at the opposite end of the table.

"My friends," Denno said, "this occasion has brought to our shores these distinguished continental guests. They have things to say to us, matters in which all should be involved, for would we not reject any decisions made in our absence? And for what other reason would all assemble other than to celebrate the mark we have made on the world?"

Falkendine remained seated. This was no time for formal oratory.

"Friends, on our voyage here, we were intercepted by a Westerland ship." He paused. "An armed Westerland ship. On its approach, we opened our gun ports. I doubt we could have depressed the barrels enough, but I think the sight of *Colonel* ready for action caused a certain change of heart. Maybe even a dash to the heads?"

There was laughter. All had seen the massive ship at anchor.

"Friends, I am wondering if such impertinence has been tried with others, as it has with those of my Kindland colleague here. Any attempt to interfere with navigation, with the freedom of the seas?"

There was a muttering, even an argument, further down the table. Eventually, a man close to Ombro spoke up.

"Yes, your honour, we have cases. The Kindlanders get taken with our cargo, and get bankrupted paying a ransom. Our own, not so much."

Ombro frowned at his companion.

"More fool you, Duggor, you and your mates. Not enough of your own, and too cheap to hire from your neighbours. Kindies are a soft touch."

The noise from the far end was too mixed for Falkendine or Denno to follow. One man got to his feet, and Denno signalled him to speak. Those at the far end subsided, sitting with arms folded and scowls on their faces.

"Saving Master Ombro's presence, Your Excellency, it is not just Kindlanders who get stopped. Oh, we stand armed, and it's a war of words only. *Territorial waters,* they say. *Why trade so far when there is a market here,* they say. *What do you want from those heretic Easties, smuggling abo foods or their seeds, are you? There is an inspection regime in force.*"

"He's right," said Tremain. "Last trip to 'Pol, they tried it on me. Lucky we were a convoy, because there were two of the buggers. Damned near rammed one of them, and they let off a shot, not aimed, but enough for us to go battle stations. They backed off."

"You never passed that on," said Ombro, accusingly. "Anyway, why not sail out of sight of land? And they are not fast enough to catch you. Bloody Outers."

His comment provoked a shouting match. Fists banged on the table, and both Falkendine and Giffone were introduced to profanities from which their continental ears had been protected. Inners and Outers again. Denno managed to restore a kind of calm, though not without some growling from the Inners.

"Master Ombro, you know well enough why we sail close in. The Mermaid Reefs, for starters, and we don't know how far out they reach. We don't all have your little boats that skim the surface. If we did, are we going to go way out in the open sea with them? Get blown to Halfland if there's a storm? As to speed, Congresswoman Giffone has something to tell us."

"Thank you, Seigneur Denno. Indeed. Those of you who have visited Kindopol will know how little trade there is across the straits to Westerland. People, mostly, and few of them. A hundred or two ago, one of our diplomats returned early from High City. The railway passes along the coast a little way before it reaches the harbour at Holy Bay, at Westport as we call it. He saw a small ship moving faster than any, a ship with one great gun before the bridge."

"We cannot be sure, gentlemen, but we think it was moving at thirty or more kilometres an hour." She looked down for a moment. "Sixteen or seventeen legs, gentlemen, if I understand your measures correctly. There is more. His view was brief, for the train staff and others rushed to block the view. Seventeen legs, gentlemen, possibly more. Can any merchant vessel of yours match that speed?"

"We've seen nothing like that," a voice said. "Most of their boats are bought from us anyway, not that they look after them. Not exactly the pride of our fleets. Hand-me-downs, we'd say if it were clothes."

"Most," said Giffone, dryly. "They have the metal, do they not, from the ores and nodules you sell them? They have the means to make engines, the means to make arms. How many such boats would they need to subdue you?"

"Master Ombro," said Falkendine, breaking the silence that followed. "You, and many of your ships will have landed cargoes in Westerland. You have heard their preachers. For now, their words are not acted upon. Imagine if they were. They lack food, they lack ore, they lack nodules. Your soils yield more than their sodden moors, made worse by their fanatic clearances. In their eyes, you are heretics at best, atheists at worst. A conquest would reduce all to slavery or mere hired labour. Your Outer Island friends have as much to lose, should those preachers wish to cut you off from Eastland. How many fine ships would sink under the guns of such ships as Congresswoman Giffone has described to you? Guns that we judge could outrange anything you possess."

"Beg pardon, excellencies," came a voice from the centre. "There are many ifs and maybes in your words. The power to hurt, I do not doubt, the power to occupy us, I do. Westies? Landsmen for the most part. Would they not rather take Kindland? Second time lucky? Some to cheer them on by all accounts."

That raised a laugh, and Giffone's lips tightened. Before she or Falkendine could respond, the voice continued.

"Trade is our livelihood, trade and mining. Are you calling for us to cease? To beggar ourselves rather than have our living taken by others? Become a bunch of illiterate shepherds?"

"And if they do take Kindland," asked Falkendine, "do you think it will stop there? You are right, there are Ultras there too. There are ores and coals in the

Daugger Hills, food all over. They will not need you, but need is not necessary to the greedy. Six, seven thousands of hostile seas between us then, my friend."

Chania Giffone had bent down to retrieve something from her bag, a sheaf of papers clipped together. Now, she looked up.

"We do not ask that you cease trade, at least not until there is news of a real war. Westerland is not yet ready. We ask that you prevaricate; delays, mine workings exhausted; costs rising. We ask that you prepare yourselves. I have here," she flourished the sheaf of papers, "the plans for a ship like the one our envoys saw. They were not obtained without cost."

The look on her face made it clear what cost she meant.

"The *Colonel* is a big ship. In its hold are ten great guns and the ammunition to go with them. Two kilometres range, ten kilos of explosive. They are yours on only one condition, that you do not aid Westerland when war comes, if it comes. In the meantime, you might find a use for them in the face of any impertinent interference."

"Westerland will not go to war while your trade with others is unimpeded. They seek mainly to divert it to themselves." Falkendine added. He also pulled a paper, a single sheet from the case at his feet.

"A page from the High City Gazette. I will leave it here. It is from seventy-six days ago. Four were convicted of heresy. They were in fact Evolutionists caught distributing books, copies of Northport's treatise. Death, my friends, and not any death, even that of burning or stoning. Tied naked to stakes, they were beaten with painbush stalks and untied. Left in the street to die, slowly and in agony over days. The words of the paper: *A fate richly deserved, a reprimand to those who advocate mercy for the devil's agents. Death from the devil's own creation.* There were pictures, my friends, you can see them here. It is such as would be done to any who opposed these priests."

Silence. All knew of painbush. Rare, which was good, and easily recognised which was better. Brush past it with bare skin and you would survive, but the pain caused many to cry to be killed. A plant that had been sought out and destroyed whenever it was found, a plant that merited a whipping if found on your land. A plant cultivated with tender, loving care in certain monastery gardens in High City.

Denno looked round the room. The agreement was laid on the table. Only Ombro's face showed uncertainty, but he was among the first to sign, and the Inner Masters followed his example. Two copies. All signed, and the foreigners retired to Denno's private apartment. The rest dispersed, but Ombro left him a note as he left. Denno sat pensive in his chair, the treaty and the papers left by the foreigners on the table beside him. Tomorrow, no doubt, the guns would be unloaded, one at a time, from the *Colonel*. The day after, the ship would depart. He rang a bell, and was attended by a small, almost crouching figure, face hidden by a cowl. He gave whispered instructions, and handed over a small purse. The man departed. Denno made the sign of the Bestower across his face, rose, and collecting the papers, went to join his guests.

The body pulled out of the harbour the following morning was for a while unrecognised. Stunned by a fall, perhaps hitting a winch, then drowning. Eventually, he was identified, a Master from a small Inner Island. Denno reported it in neutral terms to Falkendine and Giffone. The Eastlander raised an eyebrow.

"Sad news indeed. I admit I was worried that Master Ombro might meet with an accident."

"Master Ombro as a young man was keen on theatricals, Excellency. Famous for it. He has had few opportunities to practice the craft since, but I have every reason to think he retains the skill. And for all his grumbling he is Far Out through and through. A man in whom others confide, not necessarily to their advantage."

*****

The watchers on the cliffs to the west had reported back. *Convoy has split. Three Outers have surged ahead. One Kindlander lumbering behind, four legs at most. Pass Martyrs' Cove around dawn.* The news percolated through the small town. With luck, the Kindlander would pass less than two kilometres offshore. A festive crowd gathered on the point as the sun rose. Below them, the *Holy Sword* was already marking time in the bay, for the interception could wait until the victim could be seen from shore.

The S*word's* arrival a week earlier had stirred the town, and most especially the pious. The sleek warship, with its massive gun mounted below the bridge was the latest affirmation of Westerland pride and determination. Never mind the fearsome armament, the crew had let slip that the vessel could make fourteen legs, a speed unheard of by any.

A cry went up. The slow ship was approaching. A signaller relayed the message, and the *Sword* moved gently towards the point. As the prey came in sight to those on board, Captain Mikklost barked an order, and the *Sword* leapt forward with a roar. He had a grin on his face; that battered tub was no doubt full of ore or nodules bound for 'Pol. Prize money as good as in his purse. Overloaded, too, he saw, with tarps covering mounds on deck. The Kindlander must have seen their approach, but it made no more speed, nor did it turn away. Confident of passing its bow, he slowed, and signalled: heave to for inspection.

The Kindlander paid no attention, though sailors could be seen on deck, and at its stern.

"Across their bows, master gunner, close, mind."

The shot was fired; the shell exploded as it hit the water, barely fifty metres in front of the lumbering vessel. To his astonishment, it made no move to heave to; the tarps were flung aside, and he had barely time to see the ensign of Lofotor raised before the great gun now exposed returned fire. Fire to hit, not to warn.

His ship was hit astern. He had the presence of mind to turn away, though doing so obscured the gunner's line of sight. For a brief moment, his stern scarce a hundred metres from the other's bow, he heard the cheers of his would-be captives. Turning further, headed for shore, his speed slowed to a crawl as water flooded his engines. There were no more shots; the supposed Kindlander sailed on, its speed increasing, while he and his crew fought to stem the flood.

It was a sorry *Holy Sword* that was towed back to harbour, while a muttering crowd returned from the point. A grim-faced Mikklost disembarked and walked to the harbourmaster's office, noticing that the quaysides had already been cleared by police and soldiers. As he was about to enter, a soldier emerged, holding the journalist, Joliast, who had interviewed him the previous day and had been shown round the *Sword*. Archpriest Finnest and Colonel Nassiter awaited him inside. The journalist's camera lay on a table behind them. No mayor; the man had been hustled away to deal with townsfolk.

"Casualties, Captain? And the ship?"

"Five dead, seven injured. They'll survive. The *Sword*? She can be patched up and make it to Westport for proper repairs; at five legs if we are lucky."

"Their gun, Captain? One shot, and so much damage."

"It was covered until they fired. Much the same as ours, though, judging by the damage. We knew Kindland had some, now the Outers do too." The captain looked hard at the priest.

"That Lofotor ensign was hidden too. We were tricked, weren't we, your reverence, tricked into revealing our strength and being made all too aware of theirs? Now we have a choice; let them pass or fire to cripple, most likely to sink and lose the cargo."

"You would beat them in a fight, though?" asked Finnest, not responding directly.

"Yes, because we have the advantage of speed. We would fire in earnest and move fast. We could have dealt with the three known Outers too, at the cost of sinking them if there was no surrender. Provided they were not equally well-armed, of course. That's war, though, isn't it? Not contraband inspection. And when this little story spreads, you'll face mutiny or sinkings if you send out anything less speedy and well-armed."

"As you can see," the colonel nodded towards the camera, "we can prevent any details emerging officially, and muddy things by talk of a boiler room explosion. It is easy for those watching from a distance to get a misleading impression, don't you think? You and your crew will be under guard until you are ready to leave, Captain. And when you reach Westport, it would be as well if all understand the penalties for spreading false rumours."

"Aiding and abetting heretics and unbelievers, Captain, I trust that is clear?" said the priest. Mikklost saluted, and left silently for his ship. The colonel picked up the camera and turned to leave. There was an edge in his voice.

"I take it, your reverence, that those magnificent pictures of *Holy Sword* in the bay will no longer be of use, lacking, as they do, the subsequent images of its prize in our hands? A shame that propaganda takes precedence over strategic sense. Their traffic will now be unimpeded until we are actually at war, if that is the object."

"I would take care, Colonel, about how you frame your thoughts. Even the most pious incomer, even in the tenth generation, is not granted the same degree of latitude as Martyrsons when it comes to questioning the wisdom of Convocation. Faith must be fortified, Colonel, so that it may remain stronger than mere confidence in force of arms."

A debate, thought Finnest, as he walked towards the mayor's office and telephone, *that will be repeated in High City, a debate in which even clergy were not of one mind.*

12. The Physicists

Torren Galben woke to the shrill tones of his alarm. As was becoming increasingly common, he stretched out his hand to silence it and went back to sleep. There was little reason, after all, to stick to any routine. It was more than an hour before he woke again, this time of necessity. In no good mood, he prepared himself for another day, a day that would be spent in a mixture of boredom, irritation and increasing contempt for his fellow citizens as the daily news told of yet more disturbances and riots. Consies and Besties, Besties and Consies, a struggle over trivia, the struggle that had claimed Marala's life.

Collateral damage, that lump of a coroner had called her death. Even now, five years on, the memory provoked a mixture of bilious contempt for the perpetrators and a strange mix of sorrow and self-appraisal. Passion spent, their lives had drifted apart over the years without rancour; more roommates than husband and wife. There was little left of her presence in their home; her papers he had gladly handed to the Institute of History and her pictures, wardrobe and even furniture had been gratefully taken by her family. He lived in austere simplicity. It had been something of a puzzle, later, to find an envelope of hers in his files, but he had scarcely looked at it before passing it on. The find had shaken him; how easy it had been for her absence to pass unnoticed as he became ever more reclusive and abstracted.

Reclusive, and increasingly depressed once retirement had been forced on him two years ago. Now, he was expected to turn to hobbies, walks in the park and the care of grandchildren, of which he had none. Visits to the Academy were frowned on for all but ceremonial occasions and old lags' lunches, lunches at which he would find himself surrounded by oafish biologists and geologists who inevitably ended up shouting at each other, even when, like himself, they had no standing. Shouting about the earthbound, the time-bound, while he contemplated the infinite. He had largely abandoned these occasions. Unless he could talk, talk intelligently, to fellow physicists, he would rather be alone. The few that he met there, mostly older than himself, were incapable of grasping the ideas that he and his team had developed.

Developed, yes, but so incompletely. Objects had disappeared, though not always consistently, and he had been struggling with the mathematics at the time of his departure. To all but his team, the events were thought of as a conjuring trick, or at best, a form of teleportation. *Not much use, Professor, if we don't know where they have gone.* When he had chided them, *not where, but when and where,* he had endured derision. *Time travel? You're nuts, Professor,* a reaction that showed in faces, and sometimes in laughter.

The team had been cut back even before his departure; he had Rollo to thank for that, damn him. Only the thought that disappearance might have a military application, if a way out one, had kept the project alive. A sordid concern with practicalities that did not require his mathematical skills. He had worked at home, but his notions could only be explored by repeated simulation, simulation that needed the power of the Academy's great computer, a machine now denied him and, as far as he knew, to his old team too. He could merely speculate.

He pulled himself together. Come on, he scolded himself, you cycle through the same thoughts every damned morning. How Marala would laugh. And it was you as much as any who wanted the retirement rules enforced, you who complained loudly about dead men's shoes and the degeneration of old age. Quite a party they had when victory came their way, with promotions following on.

He settled down to breakfast, and wondered how to occupy himself for the day. The radio told of yet more protests. Galla Hort, the biologist, had been assaulted by a gang of Besties. Your own fault, you stupid cow, that's what you get for loosing off in public. There had been riots around Barol Temple; twelve Consies arrested. At least, his district and the parks that adorned it seemed to be trouble free. He could at least take a walk safely.

He was just grasping for his shoes, when the doorbell rang. A messenger in Academy uniform bowed and handed him a letter, a letter stamped with the insignia of the Academy's President. Delivered, the messenger saluted, turned and went away. Abandoning his shoes, he returned to the living room to open it.

My dear Torren, esteemed colleague.

I apologise most humbly for disturbing your well-earned peace. There are matters relating to your work that are causing us some concern. Matters that affect all of us physicists. I would be grateful if you would come to my office at 10.00 promptly, so that we can discuss the matter further.

Yours in greatest respect,
Morlan Rollo
President, the Kindland Academy of Arts and Sciences

Rollo? There's a surprise. Galben looked at his watch: 08.25. Plenty of time, and a pleasant walk. Then he thought. The messenger had disappeared, not waiting for a reply. The letter, while courteous, had a certain peremptory tone; the possibility that he might decline was missing. Short notice, too, very short. He might have been out, even in hospital. Matters relating to my work? There had been cases, not among physicists of course, of faked results, of misappropriation of funds; of these he was entirely free, and he had never had any grounds to suspect his juniors. Nor had they been censured for political activity, more than could be said for some others.

He brushed these oddities aside. At least, he would be going to the Academy on business, going to meet at least one active colleague, rather than to listen to the idle chatter of the superannuated. He went to change into his suit; the casual clothes that were now his standard would not do.

He set off at 9.30. Time enough and to spare. Along the riverbank, past the spot where Marala had been trampled to death; to avoid it had seemed a foolish superstition. Then into Demiss Park, where he heard the sounds of shouting in the distance. At its end, he turned into Academy Prospect, the grand, tree-lined road that led straight to the Academy itself. Long before he was near its end, it was evident that a demonstration was on. Not just a demonstration, for there were clearly fights in progress. No police were in sight. At first, he encountered only a scatter of protesters, mostly the injured and those helping them to safety. He was ignored, and indeed, he would not have tolerated any interference.

But the crowd grew denser, and he was pushing his way through, attracting only the odd glance. The noise became deafening. Now, he saw banners and placards waving. In the distance, he could see some falling. He stepped past a young man on the ground, bruised and bleeding. A placard by his side, bearing the Bestowalist insignia, read *OUR DUTY. CLEAR OR STARVE*. A girl knelt beside him, dressed in the sober clothing, almost a uniform, adopted by the Inheritance League. The crowd, however, were pressing forward, and a backward glance showed him that here it was the Consies advancing, placards shaken up and down. Placards that read *EXTERMINATORS OUT* or *SAVE THE PLANET*. It seemed they were winning the battle here. They were too intent to notice the respectable old man squeezing slowly ahead of them, and Galben managed to reach the steps to the main doors of the Academy. Here, there were police, and barriers. The police were making free with their batons on any who pressed up against them. But it was obvious that this was no attempt to storm the Academy. It was a fight between factions, rival demonstrations. As he climbed the few steps before the barriers, he could see the mass of Besties further along, and the frontline of shouting, chanting and wrestling opponents.

He had no need to show his pass. A policeman needed only a sight of him to open the barrier and drag him through.

"You're a brave man, sir, though a trifle foolish. No place for a pensioner right now. You have business here?"

Galben showed his pass, and the letter. The policeman's tone altered at once.

"Sorry about that, sir. They should have told you to go round the back. This," he waved his hand at the mob, where it seemed the Besties were indeed in retreat, "sprang up rather suddenly, but they're not trying to storm the place. Both hoping to picket their hated academicians, and cheer their heroes. There were rumours of a meeting."

"It's a riot, nevertheless, officer. Shouldn't there be more of you, and clearing these thugs off the streets?" Galben, now safe, was full of the righteous indignation of the affronted citizen, a citizen detached from either cause. There had been too many incidents of this sort.

"Our orders are to stop the idiots getting into the building, sir. As you see, they have not, and they won't. It will clear soon enough."

The policeman took a look at Galben. A physicist, so his pass said. None on his list, the list that indicated that there were a few academicians who might mind their mouths if they got a few bruises. The word was that the bosses would be grateful if a few of them stopped fuelling the protests that were increasingly difficult to control.

"There's some of your colleagues, Professor, that stir the shit, pardon my language. Does no harm if they get the message that actions have consequences. But this lot did get out of control. There is no meeting, and any of your colleagues that saw that lot would have the sense to stay away. At least, I would hope so."

Galben had nothing to say. He turned and mounted the remaining steps to the entrance. Inside, and as the door closed behind him, the noise subsided. In the grand foyer, the portraits of the great academicians of old stared down at him. Folegrande, Epplinant, Maduran, Northport. Oh, and many others, so many others. As he approached the concierge, he felt his irritation, his tenseness, melting away. This was the sanctuary, the haven of reason for centuries. Imelda, he knew. Older than him, but the rules were relaxed for the staff. A stalwart.

"Good morning, Mrs Ecloss. I hope you are not disturbed by this stupid business outside. How long has it been going on?"

"Good morning, Professor, and thank you. No, we carry on as normal, thanks to our wonderful policemen. But it shames me that you should have to run such a gauntlet, just to come to see the president. The wretches were here before me, though in smaller numbers then. If I had my way…"

The sentence trailed off. The widow of a soldier, a soldier killed in the Mount Sallibeg rising, she had no time for rabbles. Galben guessed she would have a short way of dealing with the matter. He turned to mount the grand staircase that led to the first floor, the floor that housed the Academy's President and its senior officers. He had a brief wait in the assistants' antechamber, where a security guard was exchanging gossip with the assistants. Soon, he was admitted to the president's own office.

A physicist like himself, President Rollo had been contemptuous of his predecessor's taste in décor, and the room offered a stark contrast between the irremovable character of the architecture, and the sleek, ultramodern character of the furniture. No portraits adorned the walls, and Rollo had not bothered to hide the paler rectangles where once they had hung. Bloody historians, had been his remark when Galben had complimented him on the change a while back, before his retirement. First physicist in that office, and then only because of the factions and backstabbing among the rest.

A surprise, too. Both factions had thought a head in the clouds physicist would be easy to control. But Rollo was not just clever. He had a nose for the sordid business of academic politics, and a mind like a lawyer. He had realised years ago that he had little more to contribute in the field of cosmology, while having the thoroughgoing rationalist's contempt for those swayed by emotion or ideology. He would have snorted at being called a 'people person', but he was a shrewd analyst of human weakness. Installed, and the majority of his colleagues soon learnt to keep their heads down.

"Thank you for coming, Torren," he said, advancing to give Galben a firm, powerful handshake. "I can only apologise for the scene outside. Holdbo and

Frettici will be with us soon, and two of their best students, fully vetted. I'll save the reason for your summons until all are here. I think you will not be disappointed."

All physicists, physicists from my old team at that, then, thought Galben. By the sound of it, this was no ticking off, no reprimand. Just those involved in the time/space enigma, not anything more mundane, and certainly nothing to do with the crude disturbances outside, disturbances that had, he knew, split the biologists, geologists and historians into squabbling factions. Even the chemists had become involved. He grinned at the thought that any of them trying to enter the building as he had done would have received a mauling from one side or the other, with the police looking the other way. Names, pictures, both were known and displayed on banners, posters and placards. Children, that's all; the real work, the real talent would be confined to this room when the others arrived. His mood lightened; maybe there would even be work for him to do, regulations notwithstanding.

Others filed into the room. All were known to him, and Rollo wasted no time in pleasantries. He turned to Holdbo.

"Janis, tell Torren of our experiments. You need conceal nothing."

"We have moved an object back in time, Torren. We know where it was and when it was there." Seeing the look on Galben's face, he spelled it out. "The surface of Hommoz, seven days previous. Hommoz, Torren, but not quite Hommoz; *Hommoz two* as it were."

Galben said nothing. He knew that more would be forthcoming. Their previous attempts at time travel had simply resulted in disappearances. Things might have gone somewhere else in time and space, but they had no means of knowing when or where. A convenient assassin's tool, someone had joked, provided you could encase them without taking their surroundings with them. A lot had gone into this, he could see. They had moved something, and knew where it was.

"Look at these pictures, Torren. We could look at footage of Hommoz at the time. Look at the surface. The images from the sending, and from the Halidon telescope. They are different. Not very different, but clearly."

"It proves you right, Torren," said Frettici. "There is only one explanation. Not just time and space, time and a parallel universe, though one very similar to our own in this case. You always said that was the only explanation for disappearance. We simply had no means of knowing."

"We did it again, but set time for seven days later. More images in a brief transmission."

Another set of pictures were put before him. Again, there were differences, not only with Halidon pictures, bit with *Hommoz two. Hommoz three*? They had a camera; how?

"The settings, how did you make them?" Galben asked.

The theory could cope with time, he had established that beyond doubt. Alone, it was impossible. Space, though, had always been unknown. You could try all sorts, but all that happened was disappearance. Even time and space tied you up in knots. But, as he had argued, space in parallel, and the object would, in a sense, *always* have been there. The problem was the indeterminate relationship between space and those other, unknown parallels. How could you measure the distance between parallels? Did time have the same absolute value?

"It was the camera. I don't know how it manages, but once we had it installed, we got those momentary images. Mostly just space and unfamiliar stars. We tried thousands of settings, and got a few from places we could recognise. Even a few here, but of course not here at the same time, because it's not our here, assuming we are right. We were able to work out which settings would keep us somewhere close, and in a recognisable universe."

"Close?" said Galben. "So close that the orbits of our system must be nearly identical, or you would not have found a target. And how did you know the time?"

"From the position of Hommoz relative to the stars and ourselves," Frettici replied. "The second time was luck. We had several blanks in between, and we don't know why."

"Just so," said Rollo. "That's why we need you back, Torren. It's the mathematics. Can we choose where in time and space to go? Think of it. Planets beyond our reach. No need for those ludicrous rockets the engineers waffle on about. Set them up to return, too."

Does the man understand what he's saying? Does he understand the difficulties? Of course not. But it was work, it was his colleagues, it was the computer. He could not resist. As he nodded, though, Rollo looked hard at him.

"Be clear what this means, Torren. You will move. You will live here, right at the top. You will be disguised. There will be few people allowed to work with you. Any travel, and it will be incognito, and with armed escorts. Officially, you will have died here in my office in a few minutes time, a sudden seizure. There will be a state funeral, of course." He laughed. "There's not many get to read their own obituaries."

Galben sat silent, shocked. Rollo's iron will he had already experienced. Here it was, more powerful than ever. Had he refused, had he been minded to back out now, or to reject the conditions, his funeral would have been real. His colleagues would have said nothing. Even so, their lives would be at risk, their freedom restricted. The guard with the assistants: that was no casual visit. They had prepared. He knew too much, and yet they needed him.

He nodded again. A student left the room and returned with an academic security guard and a spare uniform. Changed, he was taken to his new quarters, home for an indefinite period. The door was locked from the outside, and from the window he looked down at the courtyard, ten floors below.

*****

In the months that followed, he found adjustment to his new life painless, indeed rewarding. Already solitary, scarcely leaving his house, the confinement was no great burden. And the occasional, less than pleasant assemblies of the grumpily retired were replaced by the renewed contact with his old team. There were outings, too, carefully managed, to the testing grounds where object after object were hurled into the unknown, and the images they sent back recorded and prepared for analysis.

Frettici was a wizard with the practical. The idea of installing a camera, not the right word, but they struggled for a better, had been an off the cuff idea. They had no idea why or how it worked. He was always experimenting. As he explained, the method was derived from the biologists.

"It's natural selection, or something like it. As they told me, there are random changes in our genes. Some, most, are for the worse, and the creature dies. Some have no effect, but others confer an advantage. These changes, mutations, spread. There's nothing behind it, no purpose. But so long as there are new forms generated, there is a change overall. We took the original design, and simply messed about with it. Some versions sent back nothing but others lasted longer before blinking out. So, we messed about with those. Now, we are up to five seconds. Not only that, we can send out a compound, so we get images from more than one angle."

Galben had been both impressed and annoyed. Given the great computer, it would be possible to cross-reference images, and relate them to the settings for each despatch. A strange map might emerge. But he was revolted by the lack of understanding of mechanism, and found himself unable to account for the findings. Frettici had clearly developed an intuitive sense of what changes were likely to be fruitful, but could give no analysis of why. No first principles here; he would have to wait for patterns to emerge in the mass of data that only the computer could handle, and then work backwards.

One result, however, came in rather quickly. There were two clusters of settings that always sent back nothing, regardless of the camera. One of them had plagued them by its frequency. It was Galben himself who noticed that other settings close to the cluster sent back images only of distant stars, and few of them.

"It's not a given that all universes have anything in them, or at least anything that can be seen from that point in time and space. The blanks might come even from one like our own, billions of years from now. From our now, I mean. The astronomers say the universe is expanding. If ours, why not others?"

Left unsaid was the possibility that it was their own. Galben's theory remained unchallenged in their minds: time travel in the same universe was impossible. At least, so theory told them, travel to our own past. Travel to the future, and it became *the* future, or there was more than one. The other cluster was minute in comparison. The settings were not that far removed from those that had spotted the surface of Hommoz. This time, it was Holdbo who proposed a solution.

"If our object materialised underground, or at the bottom of an ocean, there would be nothing to see, would there? Or in the middle of a star, for that matter, it would vaporise at once."

The others were not convinced. Fire off objects at random into time, space and universe; what were the chances of being inside a body? Surely vanishingly small. The issue remained unresolved, although Frettici pointed out that their settings were no longer random. Holdbo continued to fuss over the issue. As the launches mounted into the thousands, a task that was absorbing increasing amounts of money and manpower, he noticed that these small aggregations of blank images were becoming more frequent, but always associated with a set of good images, some tantalisingly close to planets. His conversations with Frettici and Galben himself were increasingly frustrating.

"Damn it, Frettici, how are you landing so many hits? And then a set of blanks as you bombard the setting matrix?"

"If I knew, I'd tell you. It's a feeling. There's an order there, but we need the computer to spot the pattern. One thing's for sure, those blanks are not just from materialising underground."

It was Galben who came up with another possibility.

"That early experiment you did, with Hommoz. The first was previous to now, but the second was later than now. They both showed images. Were they the same universe? What if we reversed the order? Reach a place, and it is as it is from then on. Perhaps reaching the same place again, earlier, means that it is no longer the same place."

"Possible, of course," said Frettici, "but why blanks rather than just another view of something on a similar path?"

The matter was unresolved, since which universe they entered was undetermined. Frettici spent more and more time at the launch site, intuitively messing with the settings. He said little. Galben's excursions to the site became less frequent, for there was little he could do there. Only the need for exercise drew him out, while the security, and the deceptions involved for the technicians became burdensome. He felt freer in his own secluded apartment, where those allowed to visit needed no pretence.

He gradually became so absorbed in the work that he ceased to think about the world outside. He had been amused by tales of his funeral, and secretly rather proud of his obituaries, behind which, however, he sensed Rollo's guiding hand. The news was repetitive, simply more trouble, and no resolution. The famous Origins conference and the disturbances that had accompanied it earned nothing but contempt. He had taken a passing interest in the departure of the archaeological trip to Halfland, but any conclusions would be months away, years if the archaeologists themselves started arguing, as they surely would.

*****

Morlan Rollo's mind had moved far beyond the mere recruitment of Galben. While his cosmological research had not been startling, it had, at least, impressed on his mind the vastness of the universe. The talk of exploring space, of colonising other worlds, was to him an absurdity, the stuff of fantasy fiction. They knew life on the other planets in their own system was impossible, at least in any form they might recognise. He resented even the plans to launch rockets, to set up satellites, never mind the idea of sending people to another planet. Even with elaborate, clumsy space suits, only on Hommoz could they escape immolation or instant flattening by gravity. Hommoz, with that ridiculous tilted axis, subjecting most of the surface to extreme annual variations in temperature and day-length. And its sodding great satellite, making it nearly a binary system. Give it water, of which there was no sign, and the tides would be colossal, maybe twenty or more metres. That is, of course, if the water was actually warm enough not to remain solid. Unlikely, his colleagues had told him, and certainly not all year round. That idiot novelist had put ideas into the minds of simpletons.

And beyond? Even more ridiculous. Apart from the fact that it had proved hard to find any planets on other systems, and those few still argued over, apart from the fact that we had no idea if they resembled home in any way, there were still those, even a few who should know better, lapping up ideas of massive vessels in which generations would live while they travelled the billions, the trillions of kilometres to reach their destination.

And yet, such fantasies gripped the public imagination. The more so as issues of population growth and the resulting clearances had provoked sets of environmental crises: erosion, loss of soil fertility, and the evidence, hotly contested, that human activity was heating us up and causing the sea to rise. Some nitwit had even suggested that this was a good idea, perhaps melting the great polar icecaps, and rendering their continents fit for living. That one had come crashing down soon enough; even Besties and Consies had combined to demolish it. Never mind the weak sunlight restricting productivity, a few calculations showed that sea level rise would submerge not only nearly 90% of the rather flat Lands around the equator, but also who knew how much of the polar continents themselves. He was told to go build himself a hut 1000 metres up on the near vertical slopes of Halfland.

The fact remained, however, that *something had to be done*, as the politicians, the Seniors, and all the rest kept saying, to no effect. To Rollo, rationalist to the core, as were his parents before him, the proposed solutions were anything but rational. The Bestowalist case seemed to him mere superstition. That we were ordained to put the planet to our use, and provided with the means, in the bestowed fauna and flora, seemed to fly in the face of the consequences of attempting it. But the Conservationists were little better. To seal off regions covered in the miserable, grey-green things that might pass as plants from any further development when food supply was a chronic worry was absurd. And few were willing to accept the consequences of rigid population control, or even, as suggested by the Ultra-Consies, a lottery-based cull. Good luck with that, he had thought, though the cynic in him had seen that a war with the same effects might result if it were tried. Westerland eyes were always turned to our soil's fertility, and even more to that of Eastland.

The squabbles among his fellow academicians left him cold. Did it matter whether all life originated here, or whether some was here and others were bestowed? Academically fascinating, no doubt, to those who liked such things, and some of the arguments were subtle. But if bestowed, by whom, or what? From where? Those questions alone could provoke fights among the Bestowalists themselves. If one set is bestowed, why not both? The Evolutionists had no explanation of how life originated, just a mass of hand-waving: possibly this and maybe that. Just that, bar our own survival, there was no reason to favour one life form over another; all were natural.

As a physicist, even more as a cosmologist, he had for years regarded these arguments as beneath him. Mess, inadequate evidence, speculation, even downright superstition, instead of the smooth operation of the great, inanimate rules of nature, and their logical expansion into engineering of all sorts. It had not been hard to stage the coup, legal though it was, that had landed him the Presidency, and the reallocation of funds that followed in its wake.

In the endless committee meetings that had followed, he pushed his agenda forward. The practical, the applied was what mattered, not useless speculation about origins. Even within his own discipline, he detected the same pursuit of mere *notions* of no practical value. Galben and his team, for example. Not expensive, as these things went, but equally another crackpot notion. On Galben's retirement, on grounds that the man had himself endorsed, he had at first cut back the programme. But there was something about the team that pulled attention back. Whatever they were doing, something happened, even if it was only disappearance without the theoretical release of vast quantities of energy. Not destroyed, Frettici had insisted, moved. And then he had proved it. Things can move between universes. As Galben had claimed, but been unable to prove. For a while, he had merely devoted funds, funds to mass produce the tiny cameras that would send signals back, to give Frettici the technical team he needed, and, above all to conceal the enterprise until he could see any practical application unstoppable.

He had not thought much of Galben himself. Head in the clouds, unlike Frettici, who got on with things. But the man had been firm; Galben is the only one who can do the maths. Not us. And we will need the computer's time, lots of it. Now, he had Galben. Progress? Slow but promising. Soon, though, they would need that computing power, and that would attract attention.

In the meantime, he had thought ahead. If we can travel to another universe, travel to an inhabitable planet, what was needed? Here he had been forced to consult biologists. He had recruited Galla Hort, for the hypothetical task. The woman was a pest, no doubt about it, but she was, at least, concerned with the practical. It had been an interesting conversation.

"Tell me, Professor, what might ensure our survival, supposing that we were faced with devastation, a wipe-out if you will? A pod, a craft, that was insulated from the catastrophe around it?"

Galla had, naturally enough, queried the assumption, and the thinking that laid behind it.

"How do you mean, Mr President? A climate disaster would be doom unless such a pod could last centuries until a possible recovery. A nuclear war?"

Here, Rollo had raised his eyebrows. The possibility had been raised in the highest quarters, but the whole area was one supposedly shrouded in secrecy. Kindland here had its reasons. To be safe from Westerland, to be ahead, was the aim. But the practicalities were too daunting; no tests had been attempted, nor other uses developed. Stories leaked, evidently.

"A bit speculative, Professor. No. As I understand it, the long-term damage might be as great as you assume for climate. And no one has such weapons. I was thinking of something that might have an immediate effect, but then burn itself out. A disease, perhaps, that carried off all the bestowed. Oh, I beg your pardon, perhaps I should say all the first-run?"

He had hit a nerve, Conservationist and Evolutionist though she was, Galla was well aware of the crazy fringe, the fringe that accepted Bestowal, accepted it as a crime to be redeemed. There had been suicides, suicides taking with them as many others as they could, and the police had famously raided what appeared to be an illicit microbiological laboratory attempting to culture diseases. A very amateur effort, as her colleague Jana Polin had reassured her. A disease that killed both men and crops was beyond possibility.

"Hardly likely, or even possible, Mr President. There might be a plague that destroyed us. My colleagues considered the matter. Even then, there are measures we could take. Halfland alone, well stocked, could ride out the storm if isolated. I do not see the need for a pod, or any kind of sealed unit. It would not be long before we developed a vaccine."

Galla regarded Rollo with some concern. All had learnt, rather fast, that his influence with the government was great. Was there some plot they knew of, something more sophisticated than the so-called laboratory at Rommidor Hill, or the testing grounds at Nordgroen.

The conversation thereafter had been less than satisfactory, but Galla had been persuaded to think through the requirements to deal with such a remote contingency. Money talks, as Rollo knew to perfection, as did its absence.

Of course, the blasted woman was involved in politics, and had become a public figure. No reason to think she would not deliver the goods, but harder to dispose of if she did not. She might leak if in a tight corner, even though the purpose would be obscure.

He made a call to Vanishing Hall. Not its proper name, of course, but the headquarters of National Security. To his surprise, he was transferred to Gornik. That policeman who had foiled the assassination attempt on the Eastlanders. At least, the man seemed to be intelligent, unlike the security captain to whom he spoke at first.

"What is the problem, Mr President? Professor Hort is already watched quite closely by my team. She stays the right side of the law, by a whisker. Of course, she travels, and we can't follow her all the way across Eastland, still less to the Far Outs. Westerland? No. For one thing, they would not let her in; for another, if she were there, her life would be measured in weeks, if that. Not a popular figure there, our gallant Galla."

There was a laugh. Rollo paused. The task he had given her would necessarily be shared with colleagues. It had no direct connection to the vulgar debate, but he could see that either side might make something of it, and before he had achieved his aim. Then that policeman would be watching him too.

"Thank you, Chief Inspector. We have made some small requests for information and research. They might be thought to have military importance, and I naturally turned to Security. If you know of any evidence that our work with Professor Hort is finding its way elsewhere, you will let us know."

13. The Students

In the half darkness and shadows of the hostel grounds, sparsely populated by rather dim streetlights along the paths, Jarpen Stagg made his way round to the backside of the main hostel building. Nervously, he pulled a piece of paper from his jacket, using the light from windows above. Looking around and seeing no one, he walked along the base of the building. At the eighth ground floor window, he stopped. Once again looking round, he picked up a handful of gravel, and threw it gently at the curtained window. The curtain was tweaked, and a silhouetted face looked down. The window was opened, clumsily, as the curtains remained drawn. A short rope ladder was lowered, and Jarpen was quickly up and inside. The ladder was withdrawn. Three metres up, the windows were too high to enter unassisted.

Jago and Thoren, the roommates, regarded their visitor with a degree of annoyance and apprehension. Unmonitored access, access avoiding signing in with the night porter, was, of course, a long-standing tradition, a tradition established to ensure that female company after hours was not detected in this segregated wing. The entry points were established each term by the drawing of lots among those assigned to the ground floor. A pain to be chosen, as it committed you to remaining available one night in ten. Now, not a romantic tryst, but a man, a man almost certainly involved with that gaggle of nutcases on the third floor.

Of course, there were raids, and the college watchmen patrolled the grounds. A woman involved, and there would be a tirade; nothing more unless the woman was visiting you, rather than passing through. Second offence, though, and you might be out on your ear, left to find a sordid, shared room in the decaying tenements to the south of the college. *Hostel is a privilege, not a right*; a mantra dinned into them at the start of each year. Few opted for the greater freedom outside, those few mostly the offspring of very rich parents who could install their darlings in civilised apartments.

Politics, though, that was a different matter. Nearly all the residents were basically disposed to be Consies, certainly to be Evolutionists. It was tough to be a Bestie there, and this term there had been none, at least none willing to declare their faith. Things were more mixed in the girl's wings. But activism in the Consie cause, going further than mere blathering or turning up to the occasional demo was dangerous. As tempers rose in the greater public world, there had been vandalism and violence. Students involved lost their place entirely. Charged and convicted, a penal colony waited, but guilt merely by association could have you out for good. No due process either.

"Not seen, I trust," said Jago. "This is getting too much. Tell those friends of yours upstairs to ease off or find somewhere else. Risk or not, the next man coming knocking and we'll not let him in, or throw him back out. Women old enough to be their mothers are less than welcome too. It's not hard for the college to work out that it's political, especially if the woman is known."

"I was not seen. The watch has a stupidly regular routine. You know why; a few notes in their hands, and the girls know when it's safe." Jarpen let the remark about women pass by; he had never met one in his visits upstairs.

"Until, suddenly, it isn't, because the police have had a tip-off. Neither of us is keen to end up in the Rocannor Clearance, thank you." Even as he spoke, though, Thoren rose to check that the corridor was clear. At the stairwell, he looked back and beckoned. Jarpen walked to join him. Clear above and below, and he walked quietly along the third-floor corridor. Windowless and dimly lit, its dun-coloured walls, *Statutory Shit-tone* was the preferred term, seemed to give off a reek of overboiled cabbage. Not that any cooking was done on the block; the smell was characteristic of paints derived from aboriginal plants. Besties had been complaining about it for years, some even claiming allergies. No Besties, no problem, the residents of the block had said, and cost inclined the college to agree.

Room 324. Jarpen knocked quietly. The door was closed quickly behind him. The rooms, for there were three here behind the single number on the outer door, were each smaller than the one he had left. A multiple; cheaper per head than the doubles that made up most, and less popular. As he removed his coat, he saw that a stranger was with the four residents, a woman, a woman much older than Nadder, Modon, Karno or Tragast. *So, that's what those whingers downstairs were on about,* he thought. Nadder herded them all into the tiny room he shared with Tragast. They sat, three each on Nadder and Tragast's beds, a table between them.

"Jarpen, this is Dr Nana Selin. She is an assistant to Professor Hort. Dr Selin, this is Jarpen Stagg. He is a doctoral student at the Institute of Physics. He gets to work with some of Rollo's team. He's been with us for a year."

Jarpen looked hard at Dr Selin. *Brave woman,* was his first thought. Get caught here, and that's your life down the plughole. A second thought was more sober and selfish. *Working with Hort? The known troublemaker?* Link us with her, and there will be a convoy of prisoners headed for Rocannor. *These four,* he thought, *are moving a lot faster than any others knew about. Faster and with much more risk.*

His stare was met by one much more penetrating. He was being summed up, judged, even. How old was she? Maybe forty, must be quite high up the greasy pole. I wonder why she's here, and not one of the students.

"Well, Jarpen, quite a surprise to see you," said Tragast. "Old Rollo and all the physicists have seemed pretty solid up to now. Certainly, an improvement on that Bestie Magdana as president. No planned purge on Besties, I guess, that would be too much to expect."

"No, nothing like that. It's something weird. He's working with Galben, or that's what I suspect."

All five looked at him in astonishment.

"Galben? He's dead, for heaven's sake. The funeral was in all the papers, and on the radio. All that stuff about the multiverse. Time travel. The pops kept up with that for ages, even cartoon strips. It never got anywhere, all that maths that no one else could get their heads round. You've surely not seen him?" Tragast laughed. The others looked baffled.

"Didn't Rollo sack half of his team after he retired?" said Modon. "What I heard, Rollo had been pretty fed up with the whole thing, and wanted the loot for other things. And you confirmed it, more or less, last year."

"Yes, he did, and I told you so. If you remember, I also told you that they were to be transferred to a new Centre of Cosmology. Rollo returning to his old love, so we all thought. What I didn't tell you, because it came later, and seemed irrelevant, it was set up right at the top of the Academy itself, not in the Institute of Physics. Rollo said it let him drop in when presidential duties allowed. There were some disgruntled archivists given the boot, much to the delight of the physicists: *Nest of damned Besties fumigated* they said."

"And so? Where does Galben, or his ghost, come into this?" asked Modon. Jarpen was useful enough where Rollo's politics were concerned, though they had other, more senior sources too. There was a touch of impatience in his voice, and he wondered if Jarpen was a safe repository for anything Dr Selin might say. Olden Nadder, though, was looking thoughtful.

"We'll get on to Galben in a minute, Jarpen. Tell me about this Cosmology Centre. Who is in it? Do they talk about their work? I guess they are off to the Halidon telescope pretty frequently, or is it all abstract stuff like old Galben dealt with?"

"Just what was left of Galben's old team, Frettici and Holdbo and a couple of new students. I think five at most. They never talk about the telescope. Oh, sorry, they did have some visits. Just before Galben had that seizure, if it really was one. Something to do with the orbit of Hommoz. Since then, I am not sure they have been there at all. Some are often away, though, but very silent about it. The only time we see much of them is when one or two are at the computer. Rollo has taken time away from many groups and given it to them."

"Any idea what they are doing with the computer?"

"They don't encourage questions, and it's not only me that would like to know. It looks like the sort of cosmological calculations you might expect: all relative positions, speeds, distances, star magnitudes. Hard to believe there's anything left there to do that's new in any way. But it eats up the time. It was increased only last week."

"Let's get back to Galben. Wasn't he able to make things disappear? Some kind of conjuring trick, everybody said."

"Yes, he did. At the military testing ground at Nordgroen. Lots of bigwigs to witness them. Even the ambassador from Westerland. The place is hush-hush normally."

"Hmm. Yes, I remember it now. More jokes in the pops, and the patriotic rags hoping it had put the fear of the Bestower into Westerland, while the Bestie press were wailing about the waste of money. Hasn't changed Westerland attitudes, as far as I can see. It all went quiet later. But what makes you think Galben is still with us?"

"They were pretty merry for once, a New Year's party, and started boasting a little, the students, that is; the staff showed up for all of ten minutes. At first, it was just the odd remark about *the five of us,* followed by some frowns and kicking under the table. Of course, we asked, and there was mention of *a senior consultant*, and the other burst in: *magical powers, we consult beyond the grave.* He laughed, but the other got angry. They both left rather quickly after that."

"I thought no more about it. Then the other day, I went to the Academy itself, and crossed paths with a soldier and an elderly man on the way out, accompanied by Dr Frettici. There was something about his face, something familiar. I asked Mrs Ecloss who he was."

There was a frown on Olden Nadder's face.

"Sorry, she is the head concierge. All visitors sign in with her, and all need an invitation. She's a good head for names, and signs them out when they leave without bothering them. I asked her who he was. She stumbled over it, and then said, *Dr Landon*. I said I'd never heard of him. She just shrugged. I wondered if he was some kind of crank, a spiritualist of some sort. You know, *beyond the grave*? Not like Rollo to go down that path, but the face nagged at me. When I got back to the lab, I asked if anyone knew any spiritualists or a Dr Landon. That raised some laughter. I did find some ridiculous magazine, *The Worlds Beyond* it was called. I called on the editor. A crazy old bat with about six necklaces hung with *mystic crystals*. No Landon known to her. It was an eye-opener. When I asked if there might be those not on her list, she gave me a downright evil grin: *Oh no, dear, we have a short way of dealing with imposters. Anyone of that name, I'd know about it. Perhaps, I would have known about it would be a better way of putting it.* She cackled."

Nadder pushed on. Jarpen was prone to ramble, and he wanted him out of the way before hearing what Dr Selin had to say.

"So, this Dr Landon was Galben, you think? You are sure?"

"It hit me while I was with that woman. She had a picture of Galben on the wall, and the likeness hit me. Identical, bar dark hair and a moustache. Galben was nearly bald."

Nadder was intrigued, despite his wish to thank Jarpen and send him on his way.

"Why on earth would she have a picture of a physicist on the wall?"

"The disappearances. I asked. There was another cackle: *He knew the truth. There are worlds beyond our ken. And those rationalists, they did away with him. Seizure, heart attack, in that Rollo's own office? Done away with, more like. There will be retribution, you'll see.* Scared me a bit, even though it must be rubbish. It seems he has become a kind of martyr to that crowd."

"Well, conclusive enough," said Nadder. "Thanks, Jarpen. Another little puzzle. Why would Rollo go to all this bother, I wonder? He seemed to have little time for Galben's abstractions." He rose to start the process of getting Jarpen out of the building unseen.

"We'll see you clear to get out in a moment." He looked at his watch. "Next patrol is round in 20 minutes; time for you to get clear. Don't come again, though, unless we get you a message through Hellica. Use her to get a message to us, word of mouth only."

"Hellica? Why not Delia? She knows the ropes."

Both girls were physics students, and any meetings with Jarpen or any other male student could be passed off as innocent, in a strange overturning of the word.

"We are resting Delia. She thinks she's being watched. They have not pounced on her, though, and she's being rather clever: all sorts of assignations that look fishy but aren't. Keeps their attention."

"The guys downstairs threatened to throw me out or not let me in. They made a fuss about older women too. Isn't there a better way to make contact?"

"Thanks. We'll let you know. Next term we may get some more committed men on the ground floor. It's the luck of the draw, more's the pity. We can't fix that."

The conversation stopped. Tragast and Moden went out to check the stairs. All clear, and it was not long before Jarpen was out the window, and onto the street.

*****

Jarpen's visit had come as a surprise, a not altogether welcome one. Dr Selin had arrived only a few minutes earlier, and they had barely started to hear her news. Now he was gone, though, there was a new look in her face, a grimmer, more determined expression.

"As I told you, Hort has received a commission from Rollo. It seemed mad to her, but he was very free with the funding. Tell us what would be needed to preserve life if something threatened to eliminate all first-run life, ourselves included. How much; what; for how long. That was the request. She told me the details, but simply put it out as an academic exercise to the rest. He seemed to be thinking of some kind of sealed unit. She suggested Halfland, but that did not satisfy him."

"What do you think is behind it, Dr Selin?" asked Moden. "Is he worried by those reverse Besties that want to do away with us? That strange lab that was in the pops?"

"I don't think so. Galla says it's a load of rubbish, and Jana Polin backs her up. She's the best when it comes to first-run micro-organisms. In Halfland herself now, and she's had many rotations working there. They are a way-out group, and most are cracked, according to her. I don't see ultra-rationalist Rollo doing much more than keeping an eye on them, or even just leaving it to the police. Not dishing out serious money to our team."

"So, what are you all doing?" asked Modon. "Anything serious?"

"It's been an armchair exercise so far, but it is theoretically interesting. We started off simply assuming we were here in a pod, as she was told by Rollo. All first-runs gone outside. How many people to avoid inbreeding for a start. And the sex ratio. That got us going. Few males, it was suggested, but if all your women are pregnant at once, or there are lots of babies the same age, who does the survival work. You get the idea?"

"Then there is the choice of species. Not all first-runs are directly useful; those we know of on Halfland we manage without, though we could use the timber. Again, quantities of those we take. What about micro-organisms? Technology? Are we simply reoccupying our empty cities and farms, or is it start from scratch?"

"Sounds like a Bestowalist's wet dream," said Nadder. "Provided, of course, that it was somewhere else, or he had eliminated all life here."

"That's what we thought, and why we rejected it. Destroy all life, and you'd have a terrible planet. Even if it was only the stuff on land. Erosion, climate change, even the atmosphere would change. There's a fancy word for it: terraforming. It would take millions of years, and a start with the micros only. There are places now where first-runs don't thrive, try as we may to improve the soil. Rollo, remember, not some Bestie Ultra. And there isn't somewhere else."

She paused for a moment. The whole thing had been a complete mystery, and Rollo's motives were unclear. It was the news that Jarpen had brought that had shaken her up.

"This Galben business, though. He was making things disappear, wasn't he? A fine trick, but logic says the stuff has gone somewhere, or we would have nuclear explosions. Has he found somewhere else after all? Or is he just looking?"

"Where, for heaven's sake? Another universe? Disappearances, all well and good, oddities," said Moden, "but that's fantasy. More likely some kind of teleportation; still fanciful, but perhaps a bit more likely. It was Rollo took the axe to Galben's project in the end."

Nadder was about to ask more, when there was a gentle knock on the door, a rat-a-tat-tat that meant Lorsen. He went to the door.

"There's a policewoman talking to old Haggi at the desk. And there's a waggon parked right outside. Could hold quite a lot of them. All seemed relaxed, and I got just a smile when I clocked in. Just thought you should know." Lorsen turned away immediately, almost running down the corridor. A raid, even a routine inspection, and it did not pay to be seen with that gang. How they had avoided expulsion or worse, he did not know. Had he seen Selin, he would have cursed them for fools.

Nadder moved fast. Familiar territory this, but never when they had such a guest. Tragast to knock up his fellow Westies and start a punch-up in the stairwells with locals roused by Moden. Karno downstairs to trigger Losia's exit just after the riot gained attention. Nadder himself leading Dr Selin to the room by which she had entered.

They waited there, ignoring the terrified Jago and Thoren. Soon, noise from the riot echoed through the corridor. There were shouts from policemen. Thoren peered briefly out into the corridor. Tear Gas. Selin was keen to climb down, but Nadder held her back. He switched off the lights and moved to the window.

"Not yet. Watch."

From a few windows further along, Selin saw a girl climb down a ladder like hers. She started out for the shade of the trees along the perimeter wall. Less than a third of the distance, and a squad of three emerged from the shadows of the building. She ran, but was soon tackled to the ground, handcuffed, and led off towards the front entrance.

"Now, Dr Selin, and good luck." Down the ladder, and away towards the edge. Plenty of gaps, she had been told, and you are on the street. As she vanished into the darkness, Nadder turned to go back to his room. Jago nearly spat at him.

"That's it, you maniac. No more of your living time bombs through this room, ever. Get out and stay out."

The stairs were clear, if still reeking. He got back to the multiple. Karno and Moden were already there, Moden drying himself after a shower, and rummaging for clothes. The gas-tainted discards already in a sealed bag, and the window wide open.

"They got Tragast," he said.

"Better him than you, that's for sure. What with his father in the embassy, and playing the persecuted foreigner, the worst will be a fine. Most likely, just sent home. Riots like that get played down; international goodwill and all that."

Nadder's voice turned to a patrician pitch at his last words. The drill had been rehearsed. Fines? There were funds for that. Losia? A superb actress. Her artfully disarranged dress, her pouting lips and long blonde hair made a story of a tryst and a panic when the riot started all too believable. Not a student, either, and her parents were right behind the cause. She would play the faithful lover, refusing to name her boy. Not a lot the powers could do. Mere trespass was about it.

As expected, it was not long before there was a hard knock on the door. Two basics and an inspector, no less. Their old friend, Lestran. He thumbed them into a huddle by the door, while his men did a thorough job of ransacking the rooms. Chaos complete, but nothing of note found, he turned to them.

"A proper little nest of innocents. Well, well, and what about your hot-headed room-mate? Why was he stirring up that little bit of theatre for our benefit?"

"He is a Westie, Inspector. He'd been with his friends a while. You know what they're like. Having him with us, we thought to civilise him; doing our bit for peace and harmony among nations. I gather he was involved in the little fracas downstairs."

Lestran stayed deadpan. He'd paid many such visits, sometimes with no excuse whatsoever. The little bastards played with him. Nadder had family connections, and they could not push too hard. Himself, he had no time for Besties. Crazy, the lot of them. But the other side were over the top. Violence, vandalism, protests that led to riots. And most with connections to this bunch.

There had been a tip-off. They'll have a guest, the distorted voice had said, a guest worth rather more than another young agitator. He'd played it cool, more fool he. He should have just rushed the place. That girl? They'd nabbed her once before, but it was a while back, and none of this squad had been briefed. Perfect decoy, damn them. It was a mere formality, almost an admission of defeat, when he asked:

"Miss Losia? Nothing to do with you, of course?"

"Losia, Inspector? The name is not familiar, I fear." Nadder repressed the smirk that pressed for release. "Do you have such a girl? Some assignation disturbed by the noise, no doubt."

The policemen left, saying nothing more. *Your time will come, boy*, thought Lestran, *your time will come*. One slip, and you will find out what interrogation means.

*****

In the days that followed, Nadder's sense of confidence evaporated. Frustrated, the authorities might be, but their reaction changed. Tragast was indeed released with a token fine. Released, but banned from the hostel. Then, all the other Westies were moved elsewhere. The pops had had a field day with nativism when the riot was reported. There had been anti-Westie demos, and counter-demos from what Lestran contemptuously called the Love and Brotherhood brigade. Moved for their safety, was the pious excuse. The thing became an issue for the college as a whole.

New residents were moved in, some of them reprieved sinners previously expelled. At one stage, they were threatened with an allocated room-mate for the rest of the year. Only Moden's family connections averted that disaster. For now, fees being paid, the three of them were left undisturbed.

It got worse. The nightly patrols became more frequent, and there were new faces among the security force. More frequent, and more irregular too. Girls were handed over to parents, students were exiled to the joys of tenement life. Now, there were very few on the ground floor willing to have their rooms used as *doorways to bliss* as one frustrated lover-boy put it. The mood of the wing changed. Never mind assignations, many missed their foreign friends. Some of the new arrivals had a distinctly Bestie air about them. Certainly, many were less than enthusiastic about even the peaceful Consie meetings and demos.

Even their family string-pulling was failing, Nadder realised. Too influential to be treated as Lestran would have wished, they were being isolated, contained. Meetings elsewhere would be watched. Few would take the risk unless secrecy was guaranteed. At the regular Wing Student Committee, he was left in no doubt. They wanted him and his friends out. Out, so that the easy-going ways of old would return. The Union President, an ardent Consie up for any demo going, had paid a visit, cordial on the surface.

"It's like this, Nadder," she'd said. "This hostel has our strongest groups. You've contributed so much, and we're grateful. But there's too much attention being paid. You'd do the cause more good by being elsewhere."

He'd stalled, of course, and she had not pressed it. But when the three talked it over, there seemed little choice. Come the end of term, they would need to find a new home, and new ways of getting information. The mood improved when they made it known that they would leave. Papers and recordings were retrieved from friends, a risk they had to take, unlikely though another raid might feel. As term approached its end, Nadder collated them, and planned for their sharing out when they went home. Another problem to solve. A notionally random search in the street, and the holder would be for Rocannor. The rest soon after, and a bunch of informants in the shit.

As he sifted through the papers, a thought struck him. The Academy accounts were public, and there were those who could get more detail if needed. He'd not bothered with them, but Jarpen's information was worth following up. He put Modon to the task.

It was worth it. Two days later, the three of them assembled. Modon had a few figures down, but most was in his head.

"As we might have guessed, Rollo really tore up the rule book. Legally, of course, or the figures would not be there. History, archaeology, chemistry, even some branches of biology; all cut heavily. Clever with it. He can't just sack the academicians themselves, but studentships, secretaries, equipment, all cut to the bone. And travel; cut most of all. No pay increases either."

"Yes, I forgot about all those protests. Even questions in the Chamber. All submerged by the wider debate. Didn't help that their slogan was *Rectify the Anomalies*. And, of course, it was Besties hit more than Consies. What did he spend it on?"

"To start with, it looks like a straight payback for support. All the engineers, the medics and some of the chemists. The physicists too, of course. It's the fine detail, and what came later that's interesting. Physics: You can see the closure of Galben's Unit and the revived cosmology setup. Salaries and staffing, academic staffing, that is. Just as Jarpen told us. But technical staff and equipment? Miscellaneous? Way larger than anything old Galben ever got. I say technical staff. There were no figures for personnel, all for outside contracts. The sums are huge. Whatever they are spending it on, it's not on the top floor of the Academy."

"Wasn't it queried?"

"Oh, yes. Even in the Chamber, there are some pretty vocal historians and accountants. I looked up the Record. Can you guess the answer?"

"These are commercially sensitive matters. We have confidentiality clauses in our contracts." Karno recited in a monotone.

"Just so. There was a call to put Rollo before a committee, even a closed session would have been accepted. Defeated. It was seen as a surreptitious Bestie ploy. That's not all. Electronic Engineering has been favoured over all the rest, and when I looked at the report of the Computer Centre, they and cosmology have nearly 70% of the time. Only 30% two years previously, including Galben's lot. I asked an ecology student I know; his professors are fuming. They have huge databases, and don't have the time to enter new data, never mind running models and analytics. Rollo keeps telling them he's investing in more capacity, even distributed terminals. Nothing so far, and I could find nothing set aside for the investment."

"Do you think you were watched?" asked Nadder.

"I did not feel anything," replied Modon. "There are all sorts in that Library. The stuff I wanted didn't need any special requests. Of course, I showed my card at the entrance, but they scarcely looked at it."

Left on his own, Nadder turned to other matters, to the military budget. Here, he was on much more dangerous ground, for the Academy's budgets were like glass compared to them. Anything useful had been gained illegally. It was as well he had got what he needed before the raid and restrictions had hit them. There was no open budget or accounts for Nordgroen itself, and the item on research and development was opaque. The amounts had certainly increased, yet the usually upbeat Senior for Defence had announced no new programmes. Questioned, of course, and getting the standard reply of national security.

He had also got hold of payroll lists by task force. Patiently gathered over the years, originally to arm any politician brave enough to challenge any drift towards war. Before Rollo, after Rollo: yes, both electrical and mechanical engineering teams increased. Even more strange, another bunch of civilian contracts for optical equipment. Large contracts for unspecified gear. There were a few company names, meaning little to him, and the source knew that they were not the only ones. He could not be exact, but the sums involved, the manpower used, seemed far larger than those dedicated to weapons research. Rollo again, as with Dr Selin's story. No figures there, but a very direct involvement. Hort had been set a task, a task no one could make sense of.

It was a puzzle indeed, but not one that related to the group's opponents, the Besties. Term ended, and back home, his father had news that inclined him to take it no further.

"Rollo has been pestering the Defence Committee, Olden. He knows that there are unofficial attempts to unravel his accounts. The police are not interested yet, and it's not clear that he has evidence for them. Drop it. You have attracted quite enough attention as it is."

Contact with his roommates was out of the question. Tragast had been duly sent home, together with his family; his association with Consies had been noted, and his father recalled in consequence. The next term was unsettled; where would he live, who could he contact? Would they live separate or apart? Nadder turned his mind to other approaches, to the Consie groups faced with growing militancy among their opponents.

14. Power and Paradox

Facing Rollo yet again, Galla Hort was full of doubt. Not just doubt, for the conversation seemed to verge on the surreal. It was impossible to pin the man down as to what conditions the pod's inhabitants would face when they emerged.

"He seems to think they will emerge onto a Rehine minus its flora and fauna." Jana Polin had observed earlier. "With all our technology intact. He's said nothing to you about the non-living stuff?"

"No, but maybe he has asked others about that. Otherwise, it's as though he is repeating the legend of Colonel and Doc. No bestowed, no first-run, and a thousand years of crawling back from the Stone Age. That's not Rollo."

"He's going to have to explain if he starts constructing something on that scale."

Galla had shrugged. The living contents of the pod had been challenging enough, in terms of quantity and the species involved. Micro-organisms? Soils? Rollo had been both dismissive and inclusive; *all contingencies, Professor, all contingencies.* Now, though, she was pressing him on the wider conditions those emerging from the pod would face.

"Is the aboriginal still here, Mr President? If so, it will encroach on land adapted for the bestowed faster than your survivors can breed to occupy it. If it too is destroyed, then the planet will be uninhabitable. No life other than that in your pod: no oxygen, soon enough. Save the seas, and erosion will destroy prepared and unprepared land alike."

She had not needed to point to Westerland, where unwise clearance had left bare rocks. Each time she raised such questions, Rollo was evasive. Sometimes, it seemed he wanted to start, as it were, from scratch; at others, he expressed no interest in the aboriginal, tacitly assuming it would be as it was. Did he fear those freaks intent on destroying the bestowed? As she had told him, they could be dismissed. There was no means of destroying the bestowed in all their diversity.

It had become a game. Her questions, designed to expose the contingency he anticipated, the better to tailor their conclusions, had been met with a degree of obfuscation that left her baffled but concerned. Where was the threat? Westerland was the obvious choice, but they would scarcely be intent on harming the bestowed. She had been left with the necessity of planning for a range of contingencies that ranged from the impossible to the improbable.

"All of them, if you please, Professor," the man had said when she pointed it out. "All of them." The hint of something military, of something hanging over their world, was made more and more evident. But even the improbable, the replacement of the bestowed in an otherwise unaltered world, required space, protected space, on a scale she could not imagine. Never mind the time.

Rollo sighed as she left. Being open with that woman was out of the question. Read his mind, and the Consies would be screaming for blood. The damned Westies would be alarmed too; they might even attack before he could do a thing. A sterile world to colonise? Did she think he was daft? Nevertheless, get what was needed, and she would have to go; not just her, since she had, of necessity, involved some of her colleagues.

*****

A week before, he had had a scarcely less frustrating meeting with Galben and the team. Frettici had been coming up with anomalies, and even Galben's maths could not explain them.

"Our transmitters are not going where we think they ought, at least not always," Frettici had told him. "In one sense, they are adrift. In another, they are too close, often almost on top of a previous sending."

"But later, later in that universe?" Rollo had asked. He was beginning to get his mind round the weird ways in which the team expressed themselves.

"Yes, always. That rule that a sending will not go to a universe earlier than a previous sending has never been broken, as far as we know. It's as though the place we reach has not been reached before. Therefore, it hasn't, and our sending goes somewhere else."

"So you say," said Galben, sourly. "Why cannot a place we send to have been sent to before? It always had been, as it were."

Rollo had looked around the team at that. Galben frowned, and left the room, shoulders hunched.

"He cannot explain it theoretically," said Holdbo. "It's just a matter of observation. He hates that. But we will have to abide by it when we have a target."

The next meeting, many days later, was much better. Even Galben was in a better mood.

"Those transmitters that go astray?" said Frettici. "We have spotted something, though Torren can't model it. They are attracted by the previous one. We have even had images of the previous one in the brief interval of transmission. That involved leaving a vector indeterminate. It is as though there is an attraction that operates if the settings allow freedom."

Vectors, multidimensional co-ordinates, language that Rollo had long since blanked out.

"And so?"

"There is another regularity. We are near, or even on, a planet far more often than by chance. Once we relax the constraints."

"Chance? That must be as close to zero as makes no odds." Even Rollo could see that at once.

"Yes. Of course, we don't know how many there are in any universe, but we are talking hits billions of times more likely than random. It gets better, though. The more like our planet, the more likely we are to hit it, and for the second sending to be close to the first."

It had taken more than ten thousand sendings for Galben to spot the pattern, and it had only become clear when the relaxed settings followed a find. Even now, he was on shaky ground with respect to the size of planet, for who knew the numbers of different kinds and sizes of planets? But it was obviously not to do with absolute mass.

"Signs of life?"

"No, but it means little at this stage. Where we are actually near the surface, the few we have images of are like Hommoz; that, or a ball of what we take to be ice."

The conversation that followed passed over Rollo's head. Holdbo and Galben were arguing. Holdbo seemed to be suggesting that all universes were versions of an original, and that, given few constraints in their settings, their sendings went to the nearest equivalent of their own world. Galben was more sceptical; the idea smacked of wishful thinking, and he looked to a more mechanical solution.

Nevertheless, Rollo thought with a degree of satisfaction, the equivalents of our own world, altered by the separate history of each universe? We have life, why not some of them? He turned the conversation into new channels.

"These sendings; how much energy do they require? What would it take to send much larger objects?"

Frettici grasped his point.

"Do you mean a spaceship? Perhaps I should say a transcosmos ship? More, for certain; how much more? We'd have to experiment, but if Torren is right, not vast amounts. He found a way round the early problems."

"No need for a ship," said Galben. "Provided you get the settings just right, you could shift a person or even a house just where you wanted it. Of course, there would need to be an atmosphere when you arrived."

"Could we transport the means to make a return journey? All the stuff you use at Nordgroen?"

"In principle, I suppose so. You'd need to shift a lot of stuff, but what works one way should work the other, provided you return later than you left. Get the settings wrong, and arrive before you left, and you simply vanish. Maybe you end up in another universe."

Galben took a long look a Rollo.

"In principle, I said. There's no way of testing it beforehand, other than sending back some of our tiny rovers. And if there is life, and it is elsewhere or else-time, it might not welcome the intrusion. Imagine bigger, fiercer octopods?" Rollo left the meeting satisfied. Well, partly satisfied, for as yet the team had found nowhere inhabitable. And they were eating up money and metals at a rate the Seniors were increasingly disposed to question. All very well, it was said, but when do we see something useful. Left unsaid, useful meant in repelling or deterring any Westerland aggression.

*****

The Committee Room, large and otherwise ornate though it was, retained a unique feature. One wall was bare stone, pockmarked and with the fading traces of burning showing in the charred stumps of rafters. A wall that had survived the sack of Kindopol. A wall preserved to remind all of their duties, for this was the room in which the Defence Committee held its increasingly frequent meetings.

The wall alone had provoked controversy. Fifteen years ago, when relations had been better, Bestowalist Seniors had argued for its covering up, to acknowledge the improved relationships. They had been rebuffed, and now the wall was a stark reminder of present danger.

Around the crescentic table was an assembly of military men and reliable Evolutionist Seniors, including the newly-appointed minister, Chania Giffone. A procedural device, contorted in its complexity, had excluded those Seniors most well-disposed to Westerland. Rollo was sat before them. The issue was the drain on military resources that *Project Evaporation* was consuming.

"Thank you for your presence, Mr President," a gruff voice in colonel's uniform spoke. *As though*, thought Rollo, *I have a choice.*

"We are anxious, Mr President, to have a progress report on your project, one which is now consuming a significant portion of our budget. A budget under strain, as I am sure you are aware, with current tensions."

"Practical progress, Mr President. Please do not take up our time with the abstractions that Dr Frettici has thrust upon us. Weapons, Mr President, weapons of a value comparable to the great guns which we share with our allies." This was Giffone herself, a hardliner where Westerland was concerned, but whose position, as Rollo well knew, was precarious.

"Progress, Madam Minister? Certainly. We have refined the apparatus for sending. It is more mobile; the field can be focussed, and is large enough to remove several tonnes. We would be happy to stage a demonstration."

"Which you have promised before. Oh, by all means give us a demonstration, but let us deal with practicalities. Range? Ability to move as the target does? Demolishing a stationary object, one that does not take you out with gunfire before you pull a switch is of little benefit, Mr President. And how many of such devices do you have? How many can you make in the next couple of hundreds or in a year?"

Rollo paused before answering. The military had initially gone wild, as the idea of teleportation had taken hold. *Drop a ton of rocks on High City; Place our fleet out of thin air behind theirs, disappear the harbour at Westport.* They had to be disabused, fanciful ideas, one at a time. It had taken ages to get into their heads that wherever the disappeared went, it was not *here*. And he was not able, initially, to say where, and was now reluctant to reveal their progress. Even a mention of parallel universes had them in a half-mocking, half baffled confusion. Putting Frettici before them had made things worse.

"Trials have been successful at 200 metres. The field can be swung in an arc through 30 degrees rapidly. More, and we would need to develop new mountings. How many? We have two prototypes only, but with enough labour and resources we could produce many more in two hundreds. At the cost of less secrecy, Madam Minister, for Nordgroen cannot accommodate mass production."

"Damn secrecy," General Morgenstrum said. "Westie agents hover round the place already. They know we are up to something. But if we go big, it will make them inclined to attack before we have built whatever infernal machine they think we are making."

He turned to his colleagues, rather than to Rollo.

"No practical use. 200 metres, when they have guns that can reach a kilometre? Can they be mounted on ships? No? As I thought. Guns, Madam Minister, even, may the Bestower be blessed, rockets, for all their inaccuracy. Not a disappearing act that requires the enemy to sit and wait to be eliminated at close range. Quantity, Madam Minister, not wonder-weapons that cost a fortune and lack mobility or range."

There were nods around the table. All looked expectantly at the Minister, expecting her to dismiss Rollo and cut his budget. Giffone surprised them, Rollo included.

"Food for thought, gentlemen. I am sure we will act on it after due consideration. It is our last item, I think, and any other business should not burden the president. I would, however, wish to discuss the consequences with him in private."

"No decision, Madam Minister? We need Nordgroen, we need it now."

"I have spoken, General." Her tone was icy. The committee left.

"Come closer, Rollo. I think we can dispense with formality. You have been less than frank with us. Do not deny it. Do you think I do not monitor what goes on, even if I fail to see to what purpose? Your prototypes? Playthings, using perhaps a tenth of your resources. Designed to keep the likes of Morgenstrum happy. That went well, didn't it? Just more and more of your little whatever you call them, things that send back snapshots. Snapshots of *somewhere else*, not of the Westerland fleet preparing to sail. Why, Rollo? What are you up to?"

Seeing the truculence, almost defiance, in Rollo's face, her voice became harsher.

"Termination of the project might be the least of your worries. Misappropriation of military funds, Rollo? A charge that would remove you from your cherished Presidency even before a verdict. Fancy seeing a Bestowalist historian in your place?"

Her tone softened.

"Come on, man. I do not suspect you of any subversive action. I do not doubt your patriotism. Your contempt for Ultras is well-known. But whatever it is that you are doing, it will stop unless I get the truth. I, Rollo, not the whole damned committee."

"Suppose," Rollo said, "suppose you could set up a base elsewhere. A base beyond the reach of any Ultras, or Consies, come to that. A base that could manufacture whatever was needed, a base that, in time, could supply men and materials, even food."

"Suppose? That we could, what is the word, teleport, such things from some hideaway in Eastland or even Halfland? You have told us often enough that we do not understand, that teleportation is impossible. It takes only Westerland to dominate, and their ships will be everywhere."

"I said *elsewhere,* Minister. Another world, a world that would support life."

Giffone stared at him. That the bunch of misfits had, so it seemed, discovered other universes, she had managed to comprehend. That they might travel and return was beyond her belief; the *objects* they had hurled into the void had been minute. None had returned.

"You have found such a world?"

"No, Minister. We have, though, found planets, lifeless so far. There is every reason to think that planets like ours exist. Our searches achieve better focus with each sending."

"And having arrived, arrived and developed, you can return?"

"In theory, yes. We cannot know until we try. It would necessarily be to a later time, but not much later. The right settings, and a hundred years there might be but a day here."

"And if Westerland overpower us, will they not use the same methods?"

"Destroy the computer, and it would take them centuries, assuming their priests allowed it. They have enough trouble accommodating aboriginal evolution and anything resembling rational geology. They lack Galben."

"Ah, Galben. You played a good trick there. It took us months to twig to that little caper."

Giffone looked at Rollo, thoughtfully. Pie in the sky, or a real possibility? If possible, though, it was at best a long-term strategy. Or was it? What if something set up next month returned the following day, having had a century of growth and rearmament? Her mind started spinning. Fantasy? Probably, but no less of one than that numbskull Morgenstrum's belief that weapons alone would protect them. Gornik and Security were more realistic; any attack from Westerland would be preceded by Ultra atrocities in Kindopol and elsewhere. Atrocities that would attract reprisals, and reprisals from Consies, among whom were some cleverly-planted Westie agents. What was it Gornik had said? *They know more about Consie cells than we do, Madam Minister. They have the means to stimulate mindless aggression.*

She had asked what he meant. Abo drugs, was the answer; tasteless, easily added to food or drink, even the fumes from a scented candle. *Hottie, Ragebush, Blaster,* all made in secret Heritancer cells in Eastland. *The Easties bust them, Madam Minister, but more spring up; it's too damned easy.*

How much use are your big guns in the slums of Kindopol, General? That had been her thought after that conversation. Chaos in the streets, even in the docks. Westerlanders coming as liberators, to free the faithful from terror and oppression. She raised her eyes to Rollo.

"Your budget will be protected, Mr President. But there are conditions. Those at Nordgroen will appear to be producing a weapon, of course a secret weapon, in quantities. Westerland will, of course, get to hear of it. We will arrange an appropriate demonstration. This is what will happen…"

*****

There was a festive atmosphere around the ornate stands set up alongside the range. A Nordgroen Open Day, a day when the army displayed its prowess to the world. And this one would be special. All had heard of the disappearing acts two years previously, and rumour had it they would be repeated in a more dramatic fashion. The crowds were dense and expectant.

In the VIP stand sat a collection of notables, Seniors, army officers, the great shipping magnates and, of course, the diplomats. Rollo was sat next to the Westerland delegation, while Gornik was standing at the back, and his officers were scattered among the guests. A choice target for an atrocity, although he was gradually relaxing.

The drill demos, the bands, even the sharpshooting contests and the destruction of targets by artillery, all failed to arouse the usual degree of enthusiasm and applause. All were waiting for the *Vanishing,* the *Evaporation.* In a break, Rollo took the Westerland Military Attaché right onto the range, where a team with hoists were unloading a pile of boulders, forming a cairn of sorts, some four metres tall.

"There is power to show you, Major Pollinast, power that can be put to civil use as well as military. Feel these rocks. They are real, yes?"

They returned to the stand. Below them, a team carried an array of incomprehensible equipment onto the field, about a hundred metres from the cairn. Frettici, unrecognisable to most in his borrowed major's uniform, fussed about as it was assembled. He peered through what appeared to be a sighting device. Eventually, he gave a signal; a trumpet sounded, and the crowd fell silent. He picked up a megaphone.

"Your Excellencies, ladies and gentlemen. I present to you the *Evaporator.* Lest it be thought that our work has purely military application, I invite you to watch the cairn we have built."

He pulled a switch, and a buzz could be heard from the equipment, He peered down the sight and pressed a button. There was a clap as of thunder, but no smoke. The cairn had all but vanished, only a few boulders remaining on either side, some sliced cleanly through. There was a cheer from the crowd. He picked up the megaphone.

"We could not arrange a cliff for you, but it can hole solid rock as well as loose boulders. Tunnels, ladies and gentlemen, cuttings, the creation of harbours."

He turned to the crew who had set up the equipment. They set to realigning it slightly. Rollo turned to the Attaché.

"There is more to come, Major. You might appreciate these field glasses. Look to the east. Do you see a road train parked? It is 900 metres from us."

The trumpet blew again. Frettici again raised the megaphone.

"Excellencies, ladies and gentlemen. What may be used in peace may also be used in war. Look to the east. There is a road train. It is empty, please do not be concerned for any crew. When I give the signal, it will be towed to the north. As it moves, it will be destroyed."

There were two blasts on the trumpet, and a flag was raised. The train moved, gathering speed. Frettici pressed his button. The engine and the first two wagons disappeared, the front of the engine, however, fell to the ground, and was dragged a few metres by the towing cable. The cheers were loud and sustained. The show was over. The Attaché turned to Rollo.

"I wonder, Mr President, if I might see what remains of that train? A remarkable achievement."

"But of course, Major. I will arrange a car for you. The range ahead has unexploded shells; it is not safe to walk."

Major Pollinast walked in the gap between the severed front of the engine and the third wagon. The train was real, not some trickery. Even the road in the space had been cleanly cut to the depth of his ankle. He looked around. Only a few battered huts were nearby, evidently erected for target practice. He was in thoughtful mood as he returned to the embassy.

*****

The Westerland Embassy reflected in its austere appearance the dour reputation of its citizens. To be fair, the high, windowless wall that surrounded its grounds were necessary to protect it from Consie missile-throwing, but the external walls of the mansion inside were equally devoid of décor.

The ambassador's office, however, was different, for the walls were hung with lurid tapestries depicting the Bestowal, the arrival of the Martyrs in Westerland, the glories of High City, and even the raising of the High Temple Banner over liberated Westport. His predecessor, Archpriest Bokiniost, had, briefly, displayed another showing the same banner floating above what was now the Barol Temple, a shaft of heavenly light piercing the smoke of a burning Kindopol. A picture that had caused outrage, a diplomatic crisis and the Archpriest's recall. Ambassador Engiliast's clerical credentials had been carefully concealed in his letters of accreditation, and he dressed in civilian clothes. The dispensation was locked in a drawer. He sat pensive at his desk, while his senior staff stood before him.

"A pointed demonstration, gentlemen. To what end I wonder? To scare, or to provoke? The true faith is not yet well enough established here, nor is it spiritually prepared. Do they know that? Our own arms are not yet adequate on their own; that, they surely know. That weapon, that *Evaporator;* it seemed clumsy to me, but they have advanced fast since those trivial disappearances staged before. How many such devices do they have? Pollinast?"

"Your reverence. I detected no trickery. That train was effectively destroyed. The range? What they showed us falls short of our best artillery, but they may not have shown us its full extent. I would not do so in their shoes."

"It seemed to me that it was less than flexible in operation. That major of theirs was fussing about for ages."

"True, your reverence. An element of theatre may be involved, of course. But it certainly requires electricity and some complex apparatus. It could scarcely be used on the battlefield, other than at a siege. There, it might be very effective if we could not destroy it."

"On ships? Bestower be merciful, not in the hands of Outers or Easties."

"On what we saw, I would doubt it, other than on a very big one, like the *Colonel*. But who knows how fast they may refine it?"

"Numbers?" The ambassador turned to Morgon Tragopon. Officially, a Cultural Attaché, in practice the Embassy's Chief of Intelligence. Second generation refugee, grandparents killed in a Consie pogrom way in the east of Kindland. A burning hatred and a dedication to Extermination had furthered his career, for without those qualifications only a Martyrson would be posted to Kindopol.

"I cannot be sure, your reverence. It is months since they cut back on those miniatures that they evaporated in such numbers. They are certainly making something more substantial. There are new generators too."

"No insiders?"

"Only among truckers and the generator crews. They are isolated from the main buildings. There is even a separate entrance and a fence between them. That Gornik has an uncanny knack of spotting our men."

"Not arrested, surely?"

"No, he's too clever. Just that no one with true Bestowalist faith gets taken on. Reasons? *It is a military matter, and we do not have to give reasons.* That is the refrain."

"Hmm. Discrimination against Bestowalists. Get some figures, start some rumours. Sorry, that's by the by. Very well, dismissed for now."

Alone, the ambassador drummed his fingers. On the face of it, what he passed on would surely lead to the decision to strike now, before this weapon was further developed. A risk, certainly, but one worth taking, despite the doubts of the soldiers back home. He dismissed his colleagues, and started on his report. The damnable fact was that they had no inkling of what was going on. Oh, that rat

Rollo was at the bottom of it, but he seemed even to keep secrets from Congress Committees and the army. What had Tragopon found? Only some strange meetings with that diabolical Hort woman; some Consie conspiracy? Some silly story that the mad genius Galben was alive. Grumbles from the army, even openly from Bestowalist Seniors, about the reason for such diversion of resources, grumbles that subsided without any revelations.

His thoughts were interrupted by a knock. It was Tragopon again, accompanied by a very unprepossessing woman clutching at the huge Bestowalist medallion hanging at her chest.

"Your pardon, Your Re… Your Excellency. May I introduce Lara Noutten. Lara is a trusted servant of the Bestower. One who looks to the liberation of true believers. She was in His service today, near the ranges where that exhibition was staged. She has something to tell you."

Lara was overawed, and was only restrained from kneeling by the pressure of Tragopon's arm.

"May the Bestower keep you, Miss Noutten. Please sit. What is it that you have seen?"

"There were men, sir, men in and out of those huts they shoot at. And when that train disappeared, they stayed inside. There was a party came to look at it, including cameramen from the pops. Then they went away."

"That group will have caught up with Major Pollinast," said Tragopon.

"There were police around for a bit, sir. I laid down, because they were taking folk away."

The ambassador frowned. Tragopon explained.

"It is cover for our observations, sir. A group of Exterminators destroying abos around the range. They get as close as they can; the police either herd them away or arrest some. They did the same with Lara's group, but they missed her. She stayed till it got dark. Go on, Lara."

"The men came out of the huts, sir, and a truck came up from the military place, where they test all those weapons. They were loading stuff from the huts into the truck."

"Stuff? What sort of stuff?"

"That I could not see, sir, it was getting dark. But it was heavy; some took four men at once."

"Go on, Lara, there is one thing you have forgotten."

"Beg pardon, sir, he's right. There were two men with a drum, like you'd wind a rope round. They were, like, winding in something from one hut, moving down the range. They'd gone before the others had finished."

Lara sat silent. Tragopon nodded at the ambassador.

"Blessings on you, Miss Noutten. It is the Bestower's work you have done this day. Mr Tragopon will see you out, and see you rewarded." The ambassador spread his hands in the gesture of Bestowal.

Tragopon returned ten minutes later.

"Was she seen by any as she returned?"

"A policeman, when she was well away. He ignored her. That's orders, I understand, they don't pull in all they find on the road, and Extermination is not a crime off fenced land. It was a bus brought a crowd of them back."

"She'll have been seen in and out of here."

"Along with many others. They know most of the truly faithful by sight. She was not seen at the range."

"Very well. Now tell me what all this means."

"That 900 metres range? Pure fiction. They had another *Evaporator* set up less than 100 metres away. When that major pressed the button in front of us, it was firing that device through a cable."

"Miles away from any effective weapon, then?"

"Yes. We can take our time, your reverence."

Left alone, Engiliast tore up his report, and threw the pieces in a bin. He took another sheet of paper and started again. There is time, he thought, time enough to make sure the blow was fatal, time to fulfil the Bestower's will throughout the Lands.

*****

Rollo and Giffone sat comfortably in the minister's office. Both were more than a little tipsy.

"Well, Mr President," she said, raising a glass of Eastie brandy, "here's to us. Well-staged, sir, well-staged. Old Stone-em and Bush-em's face was a picture when that train vanished. Your Attaché friend, though. Kept a poker face, that one. Do you think we've fooled him?"

"Wait for Gornik, Minister, wait for Gornik. He's fooled either way as far as I'm concerned. Come early, and Morgenstrum will whip them, or so he says.

Hold off, and I promise you the transcosmos army will be at your side." He belched.

"So you say. Will you be among that number, Mr President? Will it be goodbye for ever? We'll miss you so." She hiccupped.

Rollo did not reply. The two stared vacantly into their glasses. He had played his part, as had dear Frettici. So much could have gone wrong. Now, with luck, Gornik would have played his, and they would have time to prepare, to experiment.

Two silent refills later, Gornik arrived, a smile on his face.

"Your little trick is discovered, you will be pleased to know. One little Exterminator *accidentally* overlooked, and seen in and out of the Westie's Embassy."

He saw the relief in their faces, and laughed.

"No need to have worried. Had she not spilled the beans, there were other ways of letting them know without arousing suspicion. There's always a plan B. More to the point, do you think old Morgenstrum swallowed it too? Not my business, I know, but will your colleagues let you continue with whatever it is you are contriving?"

Had Giffone been entirely sober, a sharp retort would have followed. As it was, her reply was mellow.

"We have a deadly weapon, Chief Inspector, do we not? Will the army not make the most of the terror it will inspire in our foes? He can hardly come to Congress and ask that its development be halted. The pops would have his guts. You, Chief Inspector, also have more time to deal with our indigenous rabble."

A hiccup and a belch sounded as he left them to bask in their victory.

15. Gathering Pace

Morlan Rollo stepped out of the car that had taken him to Nordgroen. He was annoyed, for the journey was tedious, and the place even more so. What was it that made them insist, them even including Galben, normally even more reluctant to travel?

The place had changed since his last visit, that very satisfactory demonstration of Kindland power, or, rather, its pretended power. Two checkpoints. Even a change of driver at the second. High screens now hid part of the range on which Frettici had staged his demonstration last year. The stands once thronged with spectators had gone. Razor wire fences surrounded the range, and were regularly patrolled. Patrolled with good reason, for both at the gates and at the fence, there were now small numbers of protesters, mainly Ultras calling for peaceful use and international co-operation. But Consies were there too.

Further, while he and Giffone knew that the Westies were aware of their limited success, Morgenstrum was not, and he had become obsessed with the need for secrecy. Those fences extended a full two kilometres east. It was for his benefit that Frettici performed even more ambitious tricks with cables and strategically placed Evaporators, while Gornik ensured that the Westies were aware of the deceit.

As far as he could see, it was working. Gornik told him that Exterminator and Ultra cells were turning more and more to recruitment rather than agitation. The man seemed more concerned about Consies, who seemed to be showing an unhealthy interest. Rollo had not enlightened him about the concerns expressed by Hort, concerns that were surely shared by her team. Giffone's agents reported a Westerland reverting to training and production, the latter slowed by the reluctance of others to trade. *The Outers and Eastland are doing a great job. The Westies have not merely stopped building the railway west of Gobinau; they are tearing it up for the metal,* she had told Rollo and Morgenstrum.

All well and good, Rollo had thought, sourly, but it was more than could be said for the project. More lifeless planets. Then, yesterday, there had been a flicker of hope, when signs of life were found, if only by indirect means. *Just micro-organisms, and the atmosphere is lethal,* they had told him. It provoked him.

"You can tell that from a transmitter?" he had asked.

If a grin could be transmitted by telephone, he had thought, it was there in the summons that followed. *Not just a transmitter, Mr President.* So, what was up? He knew already that they could send again and again to the same spot, but it had been transmitters only.

"We can make a sending, and follow it with another," Frettici had told him. "The settings can just be tweaked, and the second may arrive only minutes after the first, even if it's hours or even many days later here. Wait longer, and it often goes off course. Increase the time intervals *there,* if that's what we are doing, and we *think* that things start to go wrong rather quickly. *Think,* mind you, because that's how we interpret the vector intervals. Transfers in quick succession are safest."

At least, Rollo had thought at the time, they did get that priceless image, a picture of a transmitter lying on the ground, taken by the next, barely ten metres above it before it crashed and blacked out. Once you had a base, you could send cargo after cargo to the same place. He had never got a satisfactory answer as to how much could be moved at once. All they knew was that you could move bigger things, like the pile of boulders and the road train. These were presumably floating around in the space of another universe.

Now, as he entered the chaos of the warehouse in which they had set up their instruments, he could tell from their expressions that they had something that they just must show him. He was directed to a chair. *Look at this,* as a rather grainy picture of bare rock and rubble was put before him. In the frame was a transmitter, lying on what might be a scree, were it not apparently horizontal. Frettici put before him an old cannonball.

"We are going to send that to the same place, just a few centimetres lower."

"Underground? I thought you never got anything back. Anyway, a cannonball doesn't have cameras. How will you even know it's arrived?"

Frettici grinned, and led him to the launching area. He placed the cannonball in the arena. He pressed the button. The cannonball disappeared, but its place was filled with a shimmering sphere that instantly collapsed into a heap of stones and powdery soil. Without a word, he led an astonished Rollo back to the warehouse. Holdbo went out.

"He'll send a transmitter. Five metres above ground this time. It'll fall, of course, but the images start immediately. Mere microseconds after arrival. Printing the images takes a few minutes."

They had automated the process to a remarkable degree. No human hands were needed. Soon, the machine spat out a succession of prints. It was the first that mattered. Much the same as the original, but now the transmitter had tipped over. In the soil near it, the top of the cannonball could be seen. The ground near it appeared to be cracked.

"When we send, whatever is where it enters comes back to us."

"But you have made thousands of sendings. Nothing came back, or at least you did not tell me it had."

Frettici smiled, went to the door, and called. Very soon, a student appeared, carrying a small bag. He placed a tray on a balance, reset to zero, and spilled its contents onto the tray, contents that were revealed as the stones, soil and dust that had replaced the cannonball. 1.7 kilos. He placed an identical cannonball on the scales. 4.1 kilos. He tipped the fragments into a measuring cylinder half full of water. Volume: 655 cc.

"The cannonball has a radius of 5 cm, Rollo, volume? 522 cc. It's not mass that is transferred, but space, volume. It's not exact because a tiny amount of ground and air left with the cannonball. We can focus to within a centimetre."

"Most of our sendings have been in space, or in an atmosphere. We'd not see anything come back," added Galben.

"But some must have been into something solid or liquid, surely? Did you not see anything?"

"Not that we recognised, and we think that unless forced, the sending stops short of solid matter. Those transmitters are tiny, and we were focussed on the images, not on the point of departure. A bit of dust, a damp patch? Who knows? It was only when Holdbo wanted larger objects to discover how much power was needed that we found stuff coming back. We only had the demos for the politicians to go on, and those shot stuff into space. I think we overdid the power then. And of course, the distance matters. That's why satisfying old Morgenstrum is so hard."

"Stuff? Anything besides rock or dust?"

"Oh yes. Ice that turned out to be frozen methane. That vanished fast."

Rollo looked at the rock fragments settled at the bottom of the measuring cylinder.

"Does anything come back intact?"

"Hard to tell. Rock, not always. Dust, how can we tell? Gas or liquid the same."

"And from that planet with life?"

"We sent much larger transmitters. Each was set up to do a single, instant analysis. All in the atmosphere, of course. Organics, but no oxygen."

Rollo's mind began racing. In his imagination, transmitters from *elsewhere* located a Westie fleet. Mere air sent, and fragments of vessels sent back. Or food, minerals, uncontaminated soil were despatched from the paradise that had been developed, to face only air returning. Even soldiers could miraculously appear behind enemy lines. He had to struggle to regain a suitably rationalist approach. Cannonballs, even cannonball sized holes, were all very well. But a regiment transferred, a ship evaporated in its entirety?

"Power? You said it did not scale with size?"

"Well, it does scale with size, and that means volume, not mass. The good news is that it scales like an inverse power law. A hundred times the power and you can shift a million times the volume. It still means a lot of power when you move any large volume."

"What? How is that possible?"

"It isn't, in theory," growled Galben, who had found the whole thing ridiculous. "But then, it's not like actually moving something in space, our space. In a sense, it hasn't moved. Even so, it takes time to build up the charge. We worked on that. The transmitters take less than a second. Those rocks at the show took more than a minute. Frettici hammered that one well. Still ridiculous."

Rollo's mind turned rapidly to practicalities. The means to make the return journey, and the means, which the others had not considered, of transferring more material to the same place without overlapping what you had already sent. The arena must be cleared between each sending, or what had been sent would be returned. The level must be just so, for falling ten or twenty metres was not a good idea, still less having it entombed metres underground.

*****

The few weeks that followed threw Rollo into a mixture of fear and frustration. First, it was Minister Giffone. The rise in Bestowalist sympathy, a product of Congress' past concentration on armaments and alliances at the expense of reclamation and increased food supply was threatening the government, itself a coalition of moderate Besties and those Evolutionists more concerned with practicalities than theory. And, as Gornik told her and Rollo, the links with the Westies were growing. Her position was far from secure. It did not help that Consies were showing more militancy, despite the fact that their more extreme rivals had gone quiet. Consie support for Giffone's hard line was a mixed blessing when it involved noisy protests around Temples with Westie sympathies.

"Weapons, Rollo, weapons. That's what I need. Weapons on ships, weapons to defend the approaches to Kindopol. Something, anything, so that the use of resources can be justified. Your pet project is long term. The other side are building up steam. Two new Seniors now. Oh, they are reasonable enough in public, but Gornik tells me they've links to Exterminator cells and Westie money."

Another trick was needed to keep Morgenstrum and the Seniors on side. Rollo had to get those at Nordgroen to divert their attention. Still no planet that would meet their need, and now they must mess about again with cables and apparatus. Just when he was trying to accumulate the material for transfer, indeed for many transfers. Gornik was no better.

"Whatever you are doing, Mr President, you had better get on with it. The stories that get around? Well, you can tell me they are rubbish, but now there's a Consie faction that believe that you are out to destroy the aboriginal and start from scratch. Yes, Consie on Consie fighting now. Keeping them out of Nordgroen now is becoming a damned sight harder than dealing with Westies. I'd not put it past them to try to storm the place. We'd stop it, of course, but there would be casualties and questions asked."

Rollo had turned to go, although the Chief Inspector was still regarding him with a degree of hostility. Gornik had halted him.

"Another thing, Mr President. It's not just Westies and Consies on your back. Morgenstrum is beginning to think he's been had. Not sure, mind, but he's been probing for inside information. His plants are easy to spot, but harder to turn down or dismiss if they are with you already. I know they are all on tasks that look like weapons building, but you cannot seal off the whole site."

Rollo tried valiantly to deal with each issue. Thanks to Holdbo's ingenuity and a lot of help from a few of Giffone's hidden agents, there was a successful demonstration in the entrance of Kindopol harbour. An old ship was towed past the entrance, Frettici strutted about on the headland, crowds waiting expectantly. He pressed a button, but all that was seen was some slight disturbance in the sea a few tens of metres from the bow, while a section of tow rope disappeared. The ship slowed. Frettici could be observed frantically adjusting sights and mirrored bowls. Another shot, and a section of the stern disappeared, to cheers from all assembled. It sank rapidly. The quiet departure of a ship barely 200 metres from the target was not noticed. The kilometre from the headland was.

As darkness fell, Engiliast sat waiting in the Westerland embassy. Waiting for Tragopon to report. He had decided to avoid the demonstration, and was indeed engaged in preparing an oblique, public, criticism of these unnecessary preparations for war. It was after midnight when Tragopon returned, trying hard to look grim.

"No cable, this time, your reverence, we are quite sure. Even when all had gone, we quartered the ground. Distance at least a kilometre, though it took two shots. Only a minute between them."

Engiliast looked hard at his agent. There was more, he could tell; the man was bursting.

"A kilometre? Do we revise their rate of progress? And the aim? Was the ship moving fast?"

"No cable, your reverence, but a trick just the same." Tragopon gave a broad smile. "Radio, for sure. There was another device on a ship just out of sight from the headland. 200 metres at best; my man estimated 170."

"You are sure? Those devices give off no smoke, make no noise. And radio? You have proof?"

"Did we see the device? No, your reverence. What we saw were tarpaulins hoisted to shield the decks from landward view. What we saw was a ship in calm water, stationary. Even so, the first shot missed. What we saw was a ship that shed cables, upped anchor and was away to the north the moment after the other was hit. Radio? They needed to make sure. There was some kind of antenna on that major's apparatus at the headland. There was nothing like that at Nordgroen. A powerful transmitter."

"Your agents, Tragopon, were they noticed?"

"Possibly. After the crowd dispersed, we had a gang of Exterminators weeding on the headland, and below, where there was a view of the other ship. No cables were cleared on the headland, but there were generators set up near that anchored ship."

Dismissing Tragopon, Engiliast pondered. Another attempt to fool us into precipitate action, or a cunning attempt to incline us to delay? To make sure that we learnt of the ruse. If the latter, why? Our strength grows, theirs is diluted by internal dissension. What do they have to gain? He sighed, and prepared for bed. Next, we will try a spot of official embarrassment.

*****

Chief Senior, First Minister, Goraldon Masseter regarded Rollo with a look of distaste. Sure, the man was a nominal rationalist, but coarse and argumentative with it. An *enthusiast,* though, lets his convictions run away with him. We should really insist that those damned academicians should be Varrenians, at least if they get into positions like President. A man given to steamrolling where diplomacy would do better; a man attracting hostility from several quarters. Those flashy demonstrations, now. It had been explained to him that they were not quite what they seemed, but he had been told, *instructed* almost, to say nothing of that to Morgenstrum. Both the general and Giffone seemed to conspire together to palm him off with platitudes.

Now, the damned Westies were on his back. Such a polite note from that snake Engiliast. A note, made public of course, pleading for a global share in the technology that had such potential to shape the Lands to the advancement of the Bestowed. A desire that such powerful technology should be restricted to civil use. A demand for inspections, international inspections. Temple after temple were endorsing the Westie request. There had been *parades,* for the Bestower's sake, then more of the usual disturbances as Consies got provoked. It was all lamentably short of finesse. Now, he would have to make a response. Giffone and Morgenstrum had been adamant: no, a hundred times no, for it was their only sure way to repel or deter a Westie assault. It was with reluctance that he had summoned Rollo, and even more grudgingly, allowed Giffone to attend.

"Well, Mr President, these are the requests from High City. Defence," he nodded at Giffone, "and the military men are opposed to any of these requests. As you will have observed, those requests have attracted a measure of support elsewhere. I am wondering if there is some middle ground. A way of dispensing information and equipment that would ensure they were capable only of peaceful use?"

Rollo had not foreseen the demand, or more precisely, its airing in public and the disturbances it had provoked. A brief meeting with Gornik had been more than uncomfortable. *More and more for the sodding riot squads, fewer and fewer for intelligence. Get on with it, whatever it is, you've not much time. I'm not mowing down thousands at the gates of Nordgroen. Use the army, and there will be an open Bestowalist rising.* Indeed, it was now the Bestowalists, the Ultras, that were camped outside Nordgroen.

"First Minister. I am the first to be anxious to see peaceful use of Evaporators. There are, however, several problems with any proposal to share them with others. Perhaps the most important is that however hard we may try to avoid it, equipment designed for civilian use can easily be modified for military use."

"Which is to the point," Giffone intervened. "Our ships, Outer ships, Eastie ships, all must travel close to the Westerland coast. War, and Westerland would not need a navy to end our trade. As it is, there have been several provocations. We have halted them for the moment. Devices on land, devices we do not see until too late. Devices that leave no tell-tale smoke."

"Come, come, you are imagining whole batteries. Surely a few such apparatuses under our supervision, even operation, would not present a threat?"

"One such device alone would be a powerful deterrent," said Rollo. "But there are other reasons. First, we have very few that are operational. Each takes time to make and calibrate. Morgenstrum has made orders for more than we can make in two or more years. He requires refinements that will make their construction even harder. You would not licence others to copy our manufacture? Second, I see they ask for inspection. Again, First Minister, there are problems. Let them into Nordgroen, and they will demand to see everything. They will become aware that what is designed for civilian use can easily be adapted. Third, they will come to realise the role of the Academy's computer. They surely lack the ability to match it, but destroying it would cripple us."

Masseter had grunted at that. Both the Far Outs and Eastland were attempting to put steel in his spine, for the naval demonstration had disturbed both. Such a weapon in the hands of Westerland was terrifying. A later conversation with Giffone alone did nothing to ease his mind. *I did not probe Rollo in front of you,*

Goraldon. They are having technical difficulties in meeting Morgenstrum's specifications. On my advice, even the general is unaware. There are Westie agents everywhere. It is crucial that they do not get to know. He had pondered on that. Something, somewhere, did not add up in all this, he had thought, as he wearily started to compose a platitudinous response for public consumption.

*****

The next visit Rollo paid to Nordgroen was much better. This time, there was no hiding the jubilation among the team. The despatch arena had changed. Now, there was an absolutely flat glassy circle about 20 metres across. It was surrounded by what Rollo could only think of as distorting mirrors. Cables were everywhere.

Again, he was shown an image. More rocky ground with a transmitter lying on it. They led him outside. Holdbo pulled switches; there was a hum. Frettici placed a small canister in the centre of the circle and lit it. A cloud of dirty black smoke billowed out. Holdbo pressed a button, and the smoke was instantly contained in a neat hemisphere over the arena. He pressed another. There was a rumble, and the floor of the empty space was instantaneously filled with rocky debris. He turned everything off, and the hum ceased.

"Mr President," Frettici was unusually formal, "please inspect the material before you, material from another universe."

Rollo went forward. The rocks, rocks he did not expect to recognise, proved, many of them, to have one unnaturally smooth surface. Then, he saw it: a transmitter lying among the shattered rock.

"If we reassemble those rocks," Frettici said, "you would see that it is like a jigsaw puzzle; the smooth surfaces will fit exactly on the base of what was sent."

Frettici led him indoors while Holdbo remained to send another transmitter, Soon, they had an image; a perfectly flat circle carved out of the rock. Near its centre was the canister, on its side and extinguished. *No oxygen, of course.* He was shown a book and a coffee mug. They were taken outside. There was a short pause, and the printer again sprang to life. There, in the newly-made arena were the book and the shattered mug.

"Damn, too high," was all that Frettici said at first. It took Galben himself to explain.

"You remember, volume not mass? For transfer, yes, but for position, vertical position, mass matters when you try to hit the same spot. We were a little less than frank with you with that cannonball. A few trials showed us that mass mattered, and we had got it roughly right when we showed you. But too deep, and nothing shows on the surface; too high, and you get breakages. At a guess, we were about a metre off this time. No harm for a book, or a person, not so good for a mug."

"Even if it had been too deep, the rock would still have come back," said Rollo.

"True, but think about scale. We'd have a pile of rocks to clear here. Too high, and you get breakages. That's why a flat landing ground is vital. Uneven, and some stuff would be buried and other things would fall from a height."

"Flat? How do you manage that?"

"You saw the surface out there and the reflectors. We can shape the field. We had it as a sphere originally, but we lose focus as it gets larger. Hence, the reflectors and the base. Base flat here, base flat there. Hemisphere is the easiest, but we are working on a cylinder. Means you can use the whole base, not steer clear of the edges."

Rollo, impressed as he was, was still confused in his mind. All those transmitters? The boulder pile? The road train? Even the ship? Galben tried to explain; The default shape was a sphere, but transmitted from a distance it flattened out below. *No idea why, but you saw the ground under the train.* Rollo turned to another matter.

"That hemisphere you transmitted, it was, what, five or six metres diameter. How big can you go?"

"To the limits of the platform, 20 metres. Maybe further, but it's not cheap. 100 metres and you need five times as many reflectors. More power, too. Much more, even if it's not proportional to the volume. The generators here won't do it; we had to shut everything down to manage 18."

"You went to 18? Into rock? What have you done with it?"

"When you leave, look to the side of the office building. There's a pile. We've avoided having the whole hemisphere delivered underground. That would be a catastrophe; use the whole arena, and we'd have more than 6000 tonnes of rock appear from nowhere. Worse if it is a cylinder of the same height. We had fractures on the base as it is."

"A pity we cannot advertise," said Frettici. "Alien rocks would sell like hot cakes. You'd not have to go begging to Giffone or Morgenstrum."

As Galben and he travelled back to the Academy together, Rollo probed the practicalities.

"When we discover a habitable planet, we will need to move fast, for the news will leak. We'll need enough there to make a return even if this place is overrun. That arena is small; it would take many sendings to accumulate the gear and the manpower. Can we not make a larger one? Once there, you told me, we could take our time to plan the return."

Galben had nodded, and said little. He had been unwilling to indulge in such practical matters, and he remained envious of the way Frettici could jump to correct conclusions on the basis of intuition. Nevertheless, the problem gripped him, and back at the Academy he shut himself away with the computer, reluctantly co-opting Frettici to check his findings. Eventually, the two met with Rollo. It was a sombre assessment.

"We can make an arena a hundred metres across. It will need vastly more power. Huge capacitors to hold the charge, and an array of shaping projectors, five times as many as we have now. More generators too. It will take time. The equipment to be sent must be built from scratch. Even with a platform that size, it will need many sendings."

"There's more," added Frettici. "The first sending after transmitters will clear the site. The later ones can send, but the weight must be exact, or the load will fall from the sky or become embedded in rock. The site must be clear before another sending is made."

"How will we know?" asked Rollo.

"More transmitters. Time may move differently there."

"Can we not just send a load, once a transmitter has nailed the spot?"

"Yes, if you are willing to risk falling from the heavens, or burying your load. That first sending gives us the means to calibrate the rest. It's not exact. Too deep, and your arena will be surrounded by a cliff. Too high, and the ground will not be levelled. We need that space; we need to see that it will work. Never mind the problems of clearing and repairing the arena here. Rock would not fall, but the weight alone might damage the base. The ground must be nearly level to start with for that reason alone."

Time, too much time, had been Rollo's thought. The material needs were tough enough, but it was the fear that the transfer would be halted before completion that nagged him. Was there no short cut?

"Can we not make sendings to several places nearby, so that there is no need to clear each, no need to send transmitters to check?"

He had received a deflating answer.

"In theory, it might work. You would still need an initial clearance, a transmitter to check that you were not in an arena surrounded by cliffs. Five metres too low, and you'd have trouble getting stuff out. It might take several attempts at each site. Then there is the attractor problem. It's easy enough to arrive at the same place later, but try to be nearby, and you might overlap. Force the settings, and you might be in mid-air, or altogether underground. You might be 100 kilometres away. It would need a lot of transmitters to settle on good spots. Each one must be later than the previous, including any stuff sent."

"In any case," Galben continued, "several sites make even more problems, because each one acts as an attractor. I can't get a model that works, and I doubt even Frettici's brain can intuit a pathway through that maze. Frankly, you are safer using the same site. Clutter the area with other sendings, and we can't guarantee that stuff arrives at the right place. Just make sure it's empty."

"All that matters is that we don't make a mistake," added Frettici, "and send something back earlier, earlier *there,* than we have sent already. Or deeper, or higher. Precision is all."

Galben had been sour-faced about the whole thing. He hated incomprehension. Rollo had left him to his attempts to understand. It was dawning on him that his initial idea, so enthusiastically shared with Giffone, was a much harder job than he had anticipated. There was no possibility of an even larger arena, the team at Nordgroen had been quite clear; power, materials and time all prohibited it. As it was, even more resources would be needed, a need that would be hotly contested by nearly all. A viable colony, a settlement, would require a huge number of sendings. More to the point, it would require people, people who would disappear into the ether. All this needed time, much more time than Gornik was prepared to give him. And they had yet to find a planet on which the whole thing even entered the realm of possibility. Surely, they would, but when?

He did not look back in any spirit of self-doubt. Tense though the times were, he had not imagined either the technical or political difficulties that were now so evident. He bent his mind to a way out. Then he telephoned Minister Giffone's office.

*****

Invited to Nordgroen for the first time in more than a year, General Morgenstrum looked around the table at the people he had been invited to meet. Giffone and Rollo were, of course, familiar. The others appeared to him to be exactly the kind of mad scientists whom he had suspected of fooling him with their supposed wonder weapon. As Rollo performed introductions, he noticed an elderly man whose face was vaguely familiar. He was struggling to put a name to the face, when Rollo reached him.

"And finally, General, Professor Galben, late of the Academy. Notices of his death were a touch premature."

There was laughter at Morgenstrum's wide open eyes. Yes, that was the fellow, pictures in the papers, seizure in Rollo's office. Just what the hell is that bastard up to? He looked at Giffone, who was also smiling. Bloody woman did not think to tell me. These people are playing a game. Well, I am going to find out what it is, and put an end to it. Why am I here, now? To be convinced that they must have even more resources? He recovered his composure, and remained silent.

"General, we have to apologise for being less than frank with you," started Rollo. "We were unwilling to share an idea for which we had, at the time, no evidence, but which might transform our fortunes; our military fortunes. We were afraid that it might be starved of resources in the face of present threats."

"An idea that apparently persuaded the minister," said Morgenstrum, giving Giffone a glare. "An idea which, I am certain, has involved deceiving me as to the potential of what means of defence you have developed. I am right, am I not?"

"Indeed, General, but a necessary deception," said Giffone. "It was necessary for you to be convinced, at least for a while, that we had the means to neutralise any threat. It was equally necessary to convince Westerland that we lacked the means, as yet, to do so. Suppose that weapon worked as advertised. Would it not have led to aggression from Westerland, before we had time to produce more?"

"If they come now, it will be costly, but we will repel them. All the more certainly if our efforts had been concentrated on weapons that work. Delay, and unless your beloved Gornik can prevent it, we will face foes within as well as without."

Morgenstrum looked round the room. Except for Rollo, clearly wound up to speak, the rest, even Giffone, appeared unmoved by his words. What were they going to offer him? Fixed harbour defences, knocked out when their power supply was gone? A means to delete Exterminator nests in the city, if they could get their blasted apparatus in range? Guns would do these jobs better, and for certain at less cost. He glowered, waiting for Rollo.

"General, you saw our demonstrations. We may have deceived you as to their range, but the boulders, the train, the stern of that ship, they disappeared, did they not? Did you not wonder where they went?"

"Only what you told me; somewhere else, you said. I said space? You said yes, but not our space. I was none the wiser, but happy with the result. Happy, if it could have both range and mobility. It had neither, as it turns out."

"What if that somewhere was not space, General, but another planet, a planet capable of supporting life?"

"What of it? Some junk from our usage is scarcely going to matter. A few Westies stranded will not have much effect on any war. What planet, in any case? There are none."

"Indeed. But suppose it was not Westies that were dumped, as it were, on another planet, but our own with the means to return. To return, but not to the place from which they were sent, but to a place of your choosing. Suppose, General, that while Westie forces were gathering at Westport, a regiment, fully armed, were to appear just outside High City. A regiment that could be reinforced by as many as we could send to that other planet. Or, perhaps, one that popped up behind the lines of an invading force."

Morgenstrum regarded Rollo coolly. Was this another trick, a device to continue some obscure experiment, one that he was increasingly thinking was a product of minds frazzled by abstractions.

"You have such a planet?"

"No, but there is every chance that we will find one. In the meantime, we have the means to deliver whatever is needed for you to choose the ground on which to fight."

It was a long day. Every experiment was revealed to the general. His questions were answered in depth. He saw the photographs. He watched the images returned by transmitters, saw the rock returned as the sending was accomplished. The logistics were examined.

"First, General, we establish a base, we set up the equipment and the power plants to return. Then we send as many men, guns, equipment as you wish. Clear the drop zone, and we can make as many transfers as you wish. All we need is an estimate of how much can be carried on one 100 metre diameter launch."

Rollo saw the look on the general's face. He nodded to Galben.

"General, if I may ease an anxiety, one that is entirely rational. We can take months to prepare your base, your base *there*. Transmitters will find your designated target here. When you wish to strike, an arena will be cleared. Wave after wave of troops may be sent, at intervals spaced only by your ability to clear the site for the next arrival. Within days, your men can be pounding High City. All that is necessary is that we have calibrated the sendings correctly, so that you do not arrive here earlier than you departed. We are confident that we can do so."

"Confident? How so?"

"Because your troops and yourself are not now pounding High City, General."

There was a burst of nervous laughter. The hidden thought, that such an error would land the troops in a different universe, was not one that Morgenstrum would realise.

The general was only half convinced. He had, long ago, toyed with the idea of aerial warfare, and abandoned it. A fleet of airships was conceivable, but the few that had been made were inadequate, most especially in the face of those eternal, strong westerlies. And when the damned things were hit, not that hard to do, they exploded.

"A year," he said, "a year to find your precious planet. A year to have a base to which troops can be sent. Proof that they can be delivered back to a place of my choosing. No such result, and this place reverts to me. And you, Madam, will have no say in the matter; nor you, Mr President."

Giffone stared stonily at him, and said nothing. Travelling back to the city with Rollo, she expanded on her thoughts.

"He has you, doesn't he, even if that planet is found. No secret settlement for a triumphant return. No brave new world free of Bestowalist canting and Westie aggression. Just a transit camp. And we need it, now; Westies are using more conventional means to deploy forces behind our defences."

She handed him a single sheet of notepaper headed with the Eastland embassy's crest.

Seventy-eighth of this hundred, ESS Blenninge Maiden *was en route for Kindopol on the southern passage. There had been a violent south-south-west storm and it was well off shore. The wind veered very suddenly to the north-west and the ship sailed to get close inshore, near Cape Hollen. As it rounded the cape, just after dawn, the crew observed a Westerlander, the* Archpriest Galloniast, *at anchor in Oilboiler's Cove.*

Captain Norretile at first thought that they had taken shelter, for in the previous storm those Westerlanders would be hard put to it to avoid the rocks. Through his glasses, however, he observed a boat full of men pulling from the shore to the ship, while a small group of men on shore were carrying crates into the ruins of an old oilworming station. The crates appeared to be heavy.

It is the captain's opinion that the activities he observed were intended to take place at night, and had been delayed by the storm. The Westerlanders will have seen him pass, but he maintained speed and made no signal.

"Gun running, Rollo, without a doubt. On a coast uninhabited since the oilers abandoned the trade. A coast impossible to police. We raided, of course, but too late. The ruins were empty, but the signs of disturbance were there. The nearest villages are ten or more kilometres away. Bleak places, Rollo, and attitudes to match. A nest of Ultras and Exterminators. There were searches to no avail, searches that did nothing to make the authorities more attractive to the locals."

"Did you not expose the matter? What about that Westie ship?"

"It docked in Kindopol five days later, empty. Papers and permit to load salted beef for Westport. Log showed departure from Westport only the day before. A lie, of course, but we cannot monitor everything at that port. They know that we know; they know that our nervous First Minister will not protest without concrete evidence. They'll avoid that spot, but there are many others. We lack a fleet of any size. The Easties will not mount regular patrols two thousand kilometres from home."

16. Consie Concerns

Olden Nadder regarded his new lodgings with distaste. Effectively a single room, it was shabby, and the furnishings less than sparklingly new. The communal stairwells smelt, and not only of old cabbage. His fellow tenants were not, to put it politely, the kind of people with whom he would normally associate. The Nadder family, three generations of Congressmen and business people, were not short of the means to afford their student sons and daughters apartments in congenial surroundings and appropriate company. *I must,* Olden had thought, *be the first Old Varrenian to inhabit the place,* a pedigree he had gone to some lengths to discount with his new neighbours; the rejected black sheep reduced to poverty, and bitter with it.

It had, though, been his choice, a choice reluctantly supported by his father, Senior Markus Nadder, an Evolutionist with hidden Consie sympathies.

"They'll have their eyes on me, Father. And on you, though I guess they do that already. You can put it about that I needed teaching a lesson, that you disapprove of my Consie disruptions. And in a place like that, nobody asks questions about your visitors. Any stranger nosing around ends up on the street with some bruises. We've a few contacts there too, less conspicuous than me."

"Your friends?" His father had asked. "I know the Westie was sent back home. He'll be useful; the saner Westies are leaking, and he'll add to their number."

"Modon and Karno? They've shacked up somewhere more respectable. They will act as decoys; plenty of notionally suspicious behaviour, but nothing that matters. Absolutely no direct contact with me. It will keep Gornik's goons and the radical Besties off my back."

In the brief holiday at home after the end of his last term in the hostel, a little drama had been acted out. His father had openly told all that his wayward son needed a lesson. There had even been a formal lecture from no less than Gornik himself, with his father present. Somehow, though, the meeting had an air of the unreal. The stern warnings had been accompanied by a knowing look from the Chief Inspector, a look that said *I know that this is theatre. You know that it is theatre. Just watch it.*

As his father had said afterwards, "That man has more on his plate than Consies. If anything, he'll be landed with protecting you. Two more Temples with Westie-trained priests appointed this month. And the Eastlanders are agitating. Too many damned Heritancers being caught at Blenninge; they are threatening to search all Kindlanders unless we do something about it."

Olden Nadder had not told his father about his curiosity over Rollo. After all the man was no Bestie, and had it not been for the odd connection with Hort, he would have seen what he had learnt as military, pure and simple. And fair enough, since it would be used, if at all, against Westerland. There was just the niggle, the fact that Hort's team could not make sense of Rollo's requests.

A year went by. The clandestine Consie groups that he attended left him rather detached. The demonstrations at temples that appointed Westie-trained priests, the mobbing of amateurish Exterminator groups weeding and burning on public land, these seemed to him counterproductive. There was a subtle shift going on among the normally pious but moderate Besties. Ultras, Exterminators, had dropped their more violent protests. Instead, there were those little neighbourhood meetings. Appeals for our starving Westie brothers. Graphic pictures of stick thin mothers and their pot-bellied, malnourished children. Calls for a more vigorous clearance policy, calls that were all the more potent when food at home was hard to come by. We have the better land, was the message, the Easties even more so.

It was in vain that Consies showed equally graphic pictures of bare, burnt hillsides. In vain that there were pictures of villages wiped out by landslides. Worst of all, any hint of the Eastie efforts to adapt abo plants for bestowed consumption were countered by gruesome pictures of supposed poisoning and birth defects. The drugs derived from abo plants also featured. Here, at least, Nadder had managed a small victory, for he had talked to a few addicts, those agreeing to rehab in centres set up by his father and his friends. Dealers? He got some names. For certain, not Consies.

It had led to the only friendly exchange he had with the police, for his father had given the names to Gornik. There were busts and trials, at which a complex web of supplies by Heritancers out of Eastland was exposed. A temporary triumph for the Evolutionist and moderate cause, which moved the pops, briefly, to accusations of attempts by Westerlanders to corrupt the young. He received a note: *Thank you. More of this, and less trouble on the streets. G.*

It was, though, a drop in the bucket. The trend was steadily towards a more fundamentalist Bestie approach. The Old Varrenian Seniors might tut about stupidity, the Evolutionists to despair, but as Nadder, a Varrenian himself, came to realise, it was the character of these people that loaded the dice against them. Simple faith against the sophistries of the wealthy and out of touch. While the easy-going ways of Eastland and the romantic image of the Far Outs appealed to the young, it was the dour certainties of Westerland that appealed to the older and impoverished citizens. Nadder found himself increasingly disengaged and impotent.

It was the military demonstrations at Nordgroen that stirred him. On the face of it, reassuring, for surely only Westerland could be the intended target. Consie infiltrators told him of the interest shown by Exterminators, a sure sign that the Westies were worried. Then he started picking up a Consie backlash. Absurd stories of Rollo, even the government, preparing some kind of apocalypse. Wipe everything out, and start from scratch. It was nonsense, manifest rubbish, but his efforts to dismiss it fell on deaf ears. Consies fell out with Consies. There were stories of dismissals at Nordgroen, of evidence that the development of weapons was a cover for *something else,* though it was not clear what.

He recalled that strange conversation in the hostel, that woman from Hort's laboratory. Rollo had been wanting something from Hort. But the idea that Hort, of all people, would be a party to any kind of mass destruction was equally absurd. He probed. All he got was uncertainty. He had another meeting with Nana Selin, a meeting that involved more than the usual amount of amateur evasion and secrecy, evasions that he hoped Gornik was not tracking.

"I've nothing new, Mr Nadder," she had said. "Galla is still unaware what his aims are. The man will not spell out in what conditions he expects some colony, some self-sufficient group to face. It has become an intellectual exercise, but a rather futile one. We cannot see anything other than here, here and now. We came up with a lost continent; the sea is big enough, but we know the equatorial region is just sea from Eastland right round to the Far Outs. Anything further north or south and the best you'll find is Halfland."

"If he knows of such a place, why not just steamers? The budget for his project is huge and growing. He could hire every ship in the Far Outs and more for a quarter the price."

"We are none the wiser," Dr Selin replied. "Secrecy, perhaps? He seems to make things disappear. Perhaps he knows where they are going? We thought that perhaps he wanted to present the world with a surprise. Perhaps *Rolloland,* a rationalist's paradise with Chief Rollo its benign ruler."

"Seriously? Does he think he can conceal such a project?"

"Not really, no. But the man has directed money our way, a lot of money. So, we sit around and speculate, for we have given him the knowledge of what is needed under this or that conditions. I am sick to death with the problems of inbreeding and how to avoid them. He has not asked for the actual people, livestock or crops, though I dare say he could acquire them without our help."

"Another matter, Dr Selin. Is Professor Hort aware of all these Consie stories that Rollo is intending some apocalypse, that he is rationalist turned Exterminator? It is doing the cause no good."

"Oh yes, she is aware. Even you, Mr Nadder, might blush if you heard her language. How can he wipe the slate clean? No abo life, soon no oxygen. Save the seas, and even then, erosion would make reclamation nearly impossible. People are afraid, and fear does not make for cool heads. I have explained, again and again, at gatherings. There is a blank look in the eyes of many."

The mystery remained unsolved. Nadder began to place his hopes on Rollo really developing a weapon that worked, a weapon that kept Westies at bay if the Ultras tried anything in Kindopol. He was encouraged by the increasing interest shown by the military. Isolated though he was, he retained the ability to track funds, helped immensely by his father.

"We are holding the line there," his father had said. "Giffone has some backbone, Bestower be praised. We've kept it quiet, but the Outers are on side. Those supposed inspections? We taught the Westies a sharp lesson a while back. We have said nothing in public, but they can no longer end or divert our trade."

Another hundred came and went. The only sources of consolation for Nadder, and for those Consies who shared his scepticism, were the impressive naval demonstration, and the obvious signs of military interest in Rollo's doings at Nordgroen. It was an odd feeling, being in alliance with the powers and the military. Not so comforting, though, were the changes both in his disreputable tenement and in the attitude of the police.

His neighbours, or some of them, were perceptibly less friendly. Westie messaging was doing its work. No strangers to hunger themselves, the appeals of the notionally starving hit home. The Westie demands for universal civil use of whatever it was, those *Evaporators,* made sense, and the threat of war and the patrician character of those preparing for it added fuel to a fire. The traditional display of Westie dog-towed teams had attracted more than the usual dedicated Bestowalist following. It all made the Consie cause suspect. A few of his visitors got dirty looks as they ascended the stairwell. One was jostled and spat at. He was, he soon realised, no longer under any police surveillance, another black mark in the eyes of his observant neighbours.

The end came suddenly. A crude daub on his door one day: ABO LOVER. The next, a strange smell in the apartment, a smell he had detected in the stairwell but not recognised. He had immediately started to pack what he could carry, and to burn some papers in the tiny stove, when there was a shout outside, and with no interval, the door was rammed. Three police rushed in. One grabbed him, while the others ransacked the place. It did not take long for one to let out a whoop.

"Well, well, look what we've got here, sarge. A stash of ragebush. Thousands of doses by the weight. Enough to start quite a riot. Dealing, you Consie louse. Dealing or getting ready to drive a mob crazy. A life on the clearances for you. And I hope it's rich in painbush."

*****

Chief Inspector Gornik regarded his rather dishevelled captive with a degree of sardonic amusement.

"A year ago, even less, and I'd have been delighted to have you here on a charge that would stick. Consie shit-stirrers like you were a pain in the arse. Particularly the clever ones with Congressional connections."

Nadder scowled.

"Am I to have a lawyer, Chief Inspector? Is my father to be informed?"

"You know your rights? So I should hope, in one who has the best education money can buy. First things first; I trust you were not given a beating?"

"No, Chief Inspector. Rough handling, yes, but your men have been known to go further. I offered no resistance."

"Very well. I am glad to hear it. Now listen, and don't interrupt. I know perfectly well that ragebush was a plant. We've got the pair who brought it into the block. Just their normal trade, though they usually bring something else. Not, yet, the one who planted it on you. Skeleton keys are easily made, Master Olden, and a more streetwise person would have recognised that smell and been out the back way before even entering. You were set up. Someone other than me had a reason to get you out of the way. The question in my mind is this: Westerlanders, or a bunch of Consies who have swallowed this apocalypse nonsense?"

Nadder stared at Gornik. At least, he thought, *I am not going to clearance for life.*

"I'm not sure I can tell the difference any more, Chief Inspector. It's gone sour, and getting worse. I'm establishment, Chief Inspector. That's where the trouble lies. Did your men tell you what was painted on my door?"

"Yes," replied Gornik. "I doubt it was the same lot that dropped that ragebush on you. One lot just wanted you out, the other wanted you silenced. One way or another, you'd become a pain to more than one faction. Getting you out? Easy to see why, you've spotted it yourself. Establishment nark, am I right? Besties play on that; it's the mood on the streets, Consies not excluded. You know that. But planting a stash that puts you away for life, that's another matter, and not without its risks. Risks worth taking, evidently. So, I'm wondering just what makes disposing of you so important. But not actually killing you. Now that would have been a heap of trouble, you with a Senior father and all. Just out of the way, legally."

Gornik paused, and regarded Nadder again.

"A rush job, by the sound of it. Stash in your place, particularly there? Easy to claim a plant, though you might not be believed. Better on your person, better to set it up so that some user can claim to have bought from you, match the wrapping and so on. Even Daddy's lawyers would have a tough time with that. Even so, we have a problem. Let you go, no case to answer, and they'll try again. So, I want to know what it is that they want to prevent you doing. Your contacts, Olden, and not just any old Consie meeting."

Nadder ran through his meetings and his contacts. Gornik took no notes. Even Consie meetings that might have interested him in the past aroused no change of expression, no glint in the eye. Then he mentioned Nana Selin.

"Selin? One of Hort's team? So, that's who you were dodging and weaving to meet? We never got a name. They are Consies, right enough, but they stay just on the right side of the law. Why would she have a clandestine meeting with the likes of you? Hang on. There was some assignment with *an older woman,* when you lot were in that hostel. Was that her? You lot outsmarted us then. Quite the professionals."

"Yes. It was the same questions as at the last meeting. They were curious about President Rollo. He'd been asking them some very strange questions. What I was hearing from other Consies sounded wild. It was doing us no good. I arranged that second meeting to see if they were any the wiser."

"Rollo? I heard he'd asked for some technical advice. Why, I can't think." Gornik said nothing about what he knew. It was little enough.

"That was what was getting to them, Chief Inspector. They were asked about what was needed to start a colony from scratch. I didn't understand everything she said, other than that they all thought it was impossible, and were wondering what the hell he was playing at. We knew, way back at the hostel, that Rollo was up to something, but it did not concern us much. The man's no Bestowalist, never mind an Ultra. We determined that it was something big, and something military. Not our concern, Chief Inspector, but we'd help Hort if we could. Now, it's all Rollo is set for an apocalypse. I've seen no evidence, and Selin thinks it's nonsense. He's put a lot of money into it, she said. I can confirm that. It's got them twitching."

Gornik thought. *Who would want that avenue closed down?* If the Westies or the Ultras knew of it, they'd do better to keep watch, or drag the lad away for interrogation. He's spared that, at least. The same with the military, or any faction of the Consies. Nothing downright illegal about Rollo, though Bestowalist Seniors might make fuss about funding.

There was only one person, he realised, who might not want a two-way exchange of information, Rollo himself. Did he know about Nadder? And if he did and wanted him out of the way, who else might be inconvenient? Damnation. The answer was all too obvious. Half his career dealing with the fallout from that Hort woman's politics, and now I sodding well have to protect her. He turned to Nadder.

"Tonight, you will be locked up in *my* cells. Tomorrow, we will arrange a meeting with your father. Not here, and not at home. It may be the last time you see him, for a while at least. You will have an escorted journey to Eastland with a passport not in the name of Nadder. A long way into Eastland; too many agents in Blenninge or Varden. I hope you enjoy Gowrien; I'm told that it has some rural charm."

"And if I do not consent?"

"I will happily discharge you, and make it plain that you are innocent. At large, or even tucked up with your family, I'd not bet on you being around for more than a couple of weeks. Dead, or on a charge that sticks. I am not wasting police time providing you with round the clock protection."

"My disappearance?"

"An audacious escape. Your mugshot in every Kindopol police station. A smack in the face for our reputation, but not as hurtful as a declared death in custody. We would have no body, either. An added advantage is that it may occupy others in the futile search. Meanwhile, we will leak that the charge was concocted. Olden Nadder, a martyr to the Consie cause. Quite a welcome, when it is safe for you to return."

"Which might be when?"

"When all know, one way or another, just what it is that President Rollo is up to, other than evaporating Westie ships."

*****

The 'audacious escape' was all over the pops. At first, the line was scathing denunciation of both the degenerate old boy network that ruled, and the incompetence of the police. A saddened father, ashamed of his son, but unwilling to accept his guilt, did nothing to still the rage. Leading Bestowalists revelled in Nadder's Consie connections and the link to abo products. Gornik bided his time. The two carrying in the dreaded drug were charged; they pleaded guilty, and a connection with Ultras was revealed. Their links to Heritancer smugglers were hinted at. In the end, there was a formal police statement.

The Kindopol police wish it to be known that no charges are to be made on Mr Olden Nadder, who we believe to be innocent of any wrongdoing in connection with the quantity of illegal drugs found in his lodgings. We have good reason to believe that said drugs were placed in the lodgings by person or persons unknown for the purpose of incriminating Mr Nadder. He is free to return to his studies, and need no longer remain in hiding.

Nadder did not reappear. The police were subject to much hostile comment. *How was it that a man in custody escaped, Chief Inspector? Why should an innocent man, if he is innocent, remain in hiding? How was he treated, Chief Inspector? Has he committed suicide? If he is innocent, who placed the drugs in his lodgings?* To that last question, the police had no answer, for the two bringing the stash to the tenement denied it, and there was no evidence to prove otherwise.

All that was left, *except for our reputation*, thought Gornik, was a small shift away from the tide of sympathy for Ultras.

It was, therefore, in no good mood that Gornik met Giffone in private.

"Minister, that stash was not put in place by Ultras, by any Westie sympathisers. Those two? No, I am sure not. They did not even know Nadder lived there. They delivered regularly, but in smaller quantities. For peanuts, Minister, and to an anonymous recipient each time."

"Westies subsidising mind rotting stuff to their opponents, I suppose," replied Giffone. "And so? Your business, not mine, Chief Inspector. Good that you have exposed it. We could have wished that the whole thing involving the Nadder boy could have been avoided. But he was a known Consie troublemaker. Why might he not have been preparing some drug-fuelled outrage? A good frame, no? If not them, or any other Ultra or Exterminator, then who?"

"That is why I am here, Minister. I interrogated Nadder. There were the usual set of bone-headed Consie cell meetings, all of them known to us. There was also a meeting with a professional from Professor Hort's outfit. At Nadder's prompting. But there was another, at their request, way back when he was still in the hostel. They outsmarted us there; we caught nobody. At least we dispersed that band of agitators."

"So? Hort is an agitator too, just one clever enough and famous enough to evade your attempts to suppress her. No surprise there. Why come to me?"

"Both times, Minister, the conversations were not about staging some protest. Not even about raising funds for another of those famous expeditions. They concerned President Rollo and whatever he is doing at Nordgroen."

Giffone stiffened.

"What would the Nadder boy have to do with that, Chief Inspector? I thought Consies were all in favour of developing any defences against Westerland?"

"Consies are no longer convinced that that is what he is doing, or not only. Nor is Professor Hort. Come to that, Minister, nor am I. Olden Nadder is a remarkably well-informed young man. If I asked, I could probably get a better estimate of Rollo's expenditure from him than from the Congressional accounts. Consies are more trouble, now, in terms of whatever it is at Nordgroen, than Westies or their agents. And Hort is getting questions she cannot understand, but fears what he is up to."

Gornik paused for a moment. It was not, definitely not, his business to know the details of military readiness. It was his duty to protect and deter, most especially to deter rather than deal with the consequences of crime. He had told Rollo, more than once, *whatever you are doing get on with it, you've not much time.* Now, it was not Westies, not Ultras, but Consies that were putting on the pressure. Hort is probing, Nadder assisting. Nadder had been silenced. Not simple murder, just effective isolation, removal from the loop. Rollo is in a hurry, and not just because of mobs at the gates, but because those who have assisted him in ignorance might expose him. Minister Giffone? How much does she know? Perhaps, more to the point, how much does she understand?

"Minister, Olden Nadder, you will know, has not reappeared, even though publicly cleared of any wrongdoing. While in custody, he was clearly fearful for his life. I fear that others, others who are considered to know too much about the project, and particularly those who might have problems with its direction might be at risk. I have therefore ensured that those about whom I am concerned are protected, even if they themselves are unaware of it. I hope it will not be my duty to interrogate any who attempt to remove them."

Giffone said nothing, shocked rather than angered. As Gornik turned to leave, the thought occurred to her: *Had old Galben not agreed to join Rollo's team, would death in the president's office have been reality rather than theatre?* A small shiver took her.

*****

The conversation was going round in circles. Almar Hochast was more and more convinced that this wretched Hort woman was not being frank, while at the same time, her fears were entirely reasonable. While detached from the waves of popular passions, even he had noticed the increase in tension, and the weakening of the Consie cause. Some protection, but in what form?

"My dear Galla, I am sure you are right to plan for some disruption. Prudent, indeed, to disperse some facilities. But this is no time for me to increase expenditure for your unit at the expense of others, and I am already under pressure. Even the Evolutionist Seniors, even those you and I know are sympathetic to Conservationist arguments, are wrapped up in the need for defence."

"It is not mere disruption, Almar, and I think you know it. Oh, protests at our gates have diminished, almost faded. So have Ultra protests elsewhere, while congregations at the very best temples have increased. They are building strength. There is something brewing. No public protests, Almar, but death threats to me and others. At home too. Staff followed, rather obviously, by small groups laughing and pointing. Cats and dogs disappear. I've had two resignations, and others are thinking about it."

"But that is a matter for the police, surely, Galla? Is Gornik himself aware of this? It is his special duty."

"Gornik? He has little time for me. To be fair, and against my advice, there are Consie groups eager to scrap outside temples or to harass those pious Extermination outings for children. Even a few cells hinting at violence. Most of his attention is there, these days. There is something else. There is an idea that Rollo is planning some mass extermination. Rubbish, of course, but it's known, somehow, that he has paid us for advice. Some Consies have become much less friendly, despite our reassurance."

"Paid indeed, I see that from the private accounts. Paid surprisingly well. I confess I fail to see why his military budget should be directed to you, but, of course, I am sure it reflects some adroit accounting on your part. I cannot imagine you are designing some fiendish biological weapon."

"I will be as frank as I can, Almar. There is nothing that we see as dangerous in his requests. On the contrary, they seem a little deranged. There is no demand for some all-encompassing doomsday weapon that will exterminate the aboriginal. Just recently, both his requests and his money have faded away. Maybe he has abandoned a few ideas. We can only be grateful. It is not from him that we need protection. But it is not money, or not so much of it that is needed."

Galla Hort regarded Hochast in silence for a moment. All knew of his adventures, his escape from the Ultras in High City. On his childhood, he had remained silent, brushing aside any questions with anger. She could only speculate.

"Almar, I think a storm is coming. It is not just our work, not just Rollo, but the ideas that inspire it and the progress that will follow from them that are threatened. My people, Almar, and not just them, but the abo cultures, the knowledge, things in which we are ahead even of Eastlanders. Did Nornost not do the same for you, all those years ago? Not merely your body, but your ideas too."

Almar Hochast managed not to choke. For a moment, he could not meet Galla Hort's eyes. Eventually, he raised his head.

"Dignan Nornost, Professor Nornost. *A road accident.* You saw the obituaries? It was no accident. He was murdered. He was murdered because he arranged my escape. He was murdered because his ideas were dangerous and his pupils more so."

"I did not know, Almar. Shame on me that I did not think of it. So soon after your arrival, so unlikely an accident. Nothing was said."

"It was known. Oh, it was known! *You will say nothing, please, Dr Hochast. You have no proof. Relations are improving. We need to keep it that way.*"

There was a silence. Hochast sat for a while, head in hands. Then, it was as though a spark, an electric current had passed through him. He sat up straight, almost rigid.

"And you would do the same for yours, take the same risk."

It was not a question. Galla would face the mob, face the day-to-day knowledge that sometime, sometime soon, she might suffer a similar accident, knowing that those she had led were gone to safety. As for himself, what did it matter? His role had for years been administrative. He could run, or he could stay. Stay, and he would certainly die, if Hort's fears came true. A renegade Westie would be first on the list. Run? To do what? His work was published. There were copies all over the Lands, if concealed in Westerland.

"We are not there yet," he said. "Circumstances will not be as they were in High City. You cannot remove the whole unit now. And if the storm breaks, where to? I was a single escapee; there was a network, a resistance movement. Do our idiot Consies have any such network?"

"Eastland. Or the Far Outs. And no, not all at once. But a few at a time, all official, an academic co-operation. A last batch to take refuge in the embassy if needed, or be smuggled to Eastie or Outer ships. This you can do, Almar, I cannot. Official requests from them to you; unofficial arrangements through you. I am watched. A direct request would be blocked."

"You will stay."

"I will stay, at least until every last one is safe. We do not know how things may turn out. A direct Westie assault and many will escape east. Turmoil and the Ultras, and it will be much harder. I do not see Rollo offering any help; he seems to have all he wants, and will be concerned for his own skin. And Westie masters might be just as willing to support him in a different cause."

*****

The days rolled by. Hochast had done the necessary, and the send-off for a party of biologists to the Far Outs attracted little attention, swamped by the 'Great Nadder Escape'. The party even lined up for a group photo, to prove that none were the missing man. Talk of a mission to Eastland was treated with more attention, but had yet to happen. Westie or Exterminator agitations remained slight. To her relief, the threats to her and her colleagues also diminished. Assuming Gornik had something to do with it, she had thanked him on one of the many visits he started paying. He had given her a very strange look.

"A threat is designed to intimidate, Professor Hort, to drive away or to hinder. If your presence is itself a threat, death can come without warning."

He had not elaborated. She became aware that his plainclothes officers were around and, indeed inside the buildings. More than once, though always with a warning, she would find a policeman or woman in her home. The unnamed threat, the tensions in the city and the increasingly strident tones of Ultra priests denied her peace of mind. Wait, but wait for what, for no resolution seemed in sight.

It was, she suspected, a coincidence that Rollo ceased his inquisitions at the same time, and did so rather suddenly. No doubt, she had thought, the funding will also cease, but the statements and ledgers showed only a reduction. Reports from Nordgroen were as always, frustrating, for either Gornik or the army had ensured that her informants were excluded from those working closely with the core team. Only Scully remained. He could report that some new device was built, a circular, flat base surrounded by what resembled floodlights on stands. They never lit up, however, nor was any activity seen when he or others at the fence were able to look. Then, there were those shattered rocks by the offices. There were even photographs, for she had, with some satisfaction, used some of Rollo's funds to equip a few with the means to make them undetected. Among other things they revealed visits by Morgenstrum and an increasing number of other soldiers. She chewed it over with Jana and Nana.

"He's stopped pestering us, Galla. Do you think he has given up on this pod or capsule, or whatever?"

"We can only hope. It looks as though they have turned back to something like a weapon. But that table, that platform, or whatever it is; I don't see it on a battlefield. They managed targets before without all that clutter."

"Here's an idea," said Jana. "As far as they told us, that pile of boulders and the rest were sent into space. They cannot literally evaporate. Nor can you destroy that much matter. I asked; it would destroy half the planet. The stuff went *somewhere*. What if you can decide where to send it? Imagine a pile of rocks, bombs even, put on that base, and send it over High City."

"How could they know? And it's like a rocket then. The energy needed is surely beyond what Nordgroen can generate?"

"You'd think so. But the boulders, and that road train, wouldn't the same apply?"

"Is that pile of rocks the ammunition, do you think?" asked Nana. "For testing purposes, I mean."

"I don't see how," Galla thumbed through a set of dated prints. "It started small, got larger and has stayed the same for ages. No sign of supplies being brought in. More to the point, there are all those apparent evaporations of things too small to make out. Fifty or more in a day. What are they for? They don't bother to hide those nearly so much. They don't even use that fancy platform."

"Transmitters? Hard to see how, but suppose they are sort of mapping with them. Then they know how to send bombs or whatever. But that rock; suppose it comes from wherever whatever is on that platform goes. Maybe if you swap stuff rather than send it one way, you don't need all that energy. Like counterweights."

"But what stuff are they sending in exchange?" Nana gave a laugh. "It would be quite a thing to see a pile of rocks in High City, and some very surprised Archpriests in Nordgroen."

It was baffling. All that they could conclude was that Rollo's original demands were no longer relevant. Just in case, Galla asked the surreptitious photographers to maintain their watch. Find him dealing in livestock or crops, and it would be time to look harder.

17. The Priest

The great southern doors were closed. A bell rang, and as the assembled worthies of Westerland stilled their muffled chatter, the shutters clattered across the tall windows on either side of High Temple. In the near total darkness, a bell rang again. Suddenly, an array of spotlights illuminated the north wall, concealed, as expected, by a huge black drape. Below it, the light also shone on the familiar Table of Benevolence, reaching almost from one side of the building to the other. In front of it, backs to the congregation, were three kneeling figures. The central one appeared taller, for he knelt on a raised dais. Another single note, and the three rose to their feet and turned to face the audience.

The two on each side bowed, and retreated out of the spotlight. The central figure, in the full regalia of the Supreme Archpriest, bowed, and made the sign of the Bestower, the hands releasing before him His bounty for His people.

"May the Bestower keep you. May He preserve you from taint. May all your deeds and thoughts bend to the accomplishment of His will."

"And you also," came the muttered and irregular response from the rows of chairs before him.

"Brothers and sisters, you will know that the mosaic that adorned our north wall had given rise to strife amongst us. That scenes depicted were deemed uncanonical, and that there had been desecration. Error is all about us, brothers and sisters, even amongst those entrusted with preserving faith, even in our Holy Synod. The Adversary is with us always; honest doubt turns to heresy, even to apostasy."

"So, these last two years, the wall has been covered as it is now. A sorry matter for all who seek solace and affirmation in the depiction of the Great Bestowal. We have sought, brothers and sisters, to wrestle with the questions: What are the essentials of our faith? What are reasonable extensions, the stories that we hold dear, and which do no harm to those essentials? What, in contrast, are those stories that, when examined, perpetuate errors and incline the weak-minded or the wicked to heresy?"

Archpriest Hytoniast paused. His audience remained in darkness, but he could sense the tension. The nominally secret meetings of Synod had, inevitably, leaked. Attachment to this or that version of the Bestowal and of the Bestower's will might lead to interrogation or worse. Not a matter for his regret, for too often, far too often, arguments about doctrine had been mired in material, secular concerns.

They expected, those worthies, that the drape would be dropped to reveal the new, the authorised images that would, from now on, be canonical. But the arguments in Synod had raged for too long. Victorious at last, he intended to emphasise his authority. Now, all should be reminded of the Bestower's will.

"An example, brothers and sisters. What is the Bestower's will for our use of what was here when He bestowed this world upon us? The life that was here? His will is manifest: *Eat what is bestowed, and that alone. Destroy that which is not, for it is the creation of the Adversary.* Other uses, though, are not proscribed. Still less are we forbidden to use the non-living, the mineral of the world, to our advantage and to His glory. But it is a fine line that we draw, for dependence on such aboriginal life leads, insidiously, to its cultivation and protection. To *conservation.* To the abominations of those in other lands, to those who turn their backs on their Bestower."

"It is not only there that backs are turned on Him. Here also. The excuses, brothers and sisters, are there aplenty. And who can deny the necessity in particular cases? But we are lax; we are lazy, we are concerned with comfort. There is, or I will now say, there was, a glaring example in this, our greatest temple. The Table of Benevolence itself. Made of what? Of *aboriginal* ironwood. The aboriginal in our most holy place. It was debated. But it was said, it is the hardest, the longest lasting, the most pleasing to see. And, with the passage of time, there arose that most insidious of excuses, its age, and its intricate carvings made by our ancestors. Sanctified by tradition, antiquity and familiarity."

"Vanity. Vanity and secular pride. What is here now is unadorned and undefiled. It is made from bestowed trees only. It will perish, and be replaced, as will we all. The original? Burnt, burnt to ash and used as the Bestower intended, to fertilise fields."

There was a perceptible murmur in the congregation, too far away to have seen the change. Hytoniast had been careful. There had been no admittance to the temple for two days, and the paler wood of the eucalypts had been carefully stained, using dyes of mineral or Bestowed origin. The surprise must be complete. Now, he gave a signal, and the great black curtain was wound up.

There were gasps, for instead of the old mosaic, still less the expected replacement, there was a bare wall. Its new coat of whitewash could not disguise its rough surface, from which the hallowed images had been chiselled.

"It is gone, that hopeless miscellany of truth and lies, of scenes engraved in the minds of generations, scenes that have no authority in scripture, but were the cause of dissension among us. Fear not that we have desecrated the image of the Bestower; it is saved. It will be replaced, but only together with what is certain and canonical. The Bestower and His gifts, the landing in Bounty Bay, the journey to Rehine, the Martyrs suffering and their landing in the Cove and the establishment of High City itself. No more arguments about Halfland. No quarrels about the numbers at Bounty Bay or about the number of ships. No depiction of Kindopol, that swamp of heresy and persecution."

He made a signal. The spotlights were turned off, and the great windows freed of their shutters. The blinking people before him were silent. There had been many purges in the past; trivial events in which toys, ornaments and utensils made of abo wood had been burnt in public. Never eradicated, of course, and new ones slipped into circulation. There were few families, even among Martyrsons, that did not harbour a few heirlooms, heirlooms round which family legends were spun. Never, though, had any seen such a ripping out in any temple, still less in this one.

Even he, Hytoniast, might have hesitated had some in Synod, and still more in Council, with its ignorant laymen, not peppered the discussion with talk of cultural heritage. Cultural Heritage! There is truth, and there is error. The distinction could be hard in particular cases, but to preserve on grounds of beauty alone? There were whores in Kindopol more beautiful than many respectable women. He had been tempted to commission a panel depicting that city's sack, while reluctantly acknowledging its impossibility.

"Wait till we are in charge again, your reverence," General Norbiniast had advised him. "In your lifetime, for sure, the Bestower willing."

*****

"The man's mad," said Grahan Middenist. "Mad and dangerous with it. Yet more honest folk antagonised to no good purpose. He's all blood and thunder when it comes to overthrowing that bunch of quarrelsome weaklings in Kindopol, then undermines our strength at home."

"You'd best not say that away from present company, Grahan. There's Martyrsons have had the bush for less. At best, you'd end up in a worming station."

There was a dry note in Colonel Harritost's voice. They had known each other since childhood, though military service had given Harritost's life a variety that his friend's had not, a landowner's son who had narrowly avoided the priesthood. A life as a civil servant, a pen-pusher in the eyes of soldiers, he had been no further from High City than Westport and Martyrs' Cove.

"He's right, though, Mikki," said Julie, the colonel's wife. "Both the maids were muttering about it. News travels fast on the streets. Kollie had hidden her lucky charm, but I could see the chain round her neck. It's ironwood, of course. Way back, she told me it was her great grandmother's and went back further. It has the Gracious Hands upon it."

The three were sitting comfortably in the colonel's house, a sanctuary few were admitted to. With added reason now, since all were sat in ironwood-framed chairs upholstered in oggen, the fine yarn made from a grey-green that had been cultivated for the purpose. Using either was not in itself heretical, but cultivation had been banned for generations, while cheerfully grown in Eastland and the Far Outs. Wool, flax, hemp, were the only sources of Bestowed cloth. Artfully distressed oggen and other abo cloths were routinely smuggled in, and passed off as antiques.

"Being right and being safe are not the same thing, all the more when what was right last year is damnable heresy the next. I don't need convincing. More bloody acolytes, more monks, more Ziggara, more sent to clearance or to worming, fewer to train and fewer to farm. It's hidden a bit here, but out west there is real starvation. Even here, you send the girls away with parcels, and they are skinny kids as it is."

"It's the future puzzles me, Mikki," said Grahan. "Listen to Synod, even to Council, and they are all for the rule of the righteous from Derant to Targon. All that land to be reclaimed, once those Consies and Evolutionists are cleared out. No doubt the Far Outs and even Eastland would follow. They've stirred up the believers across Kindland; less a war of conquest, more a liberation, if we come to support them with force enough. In the meantime, we lose our own folk to disaffection or fruitless endeavour. Hunger too, not helped by the sight of lardy acolytes staggering from inn to inn. This is more of the same, isn't it?"

"You'd have allies on Council," said the colonel, "but they have a measure of protection, as does the Academy, though it's stretched pretty thin. You remember old Nornost, I guess. The most eminent to have an unfortunate accident, but there have been others since, with less reason to provoke the clerics. You have none. Nowhere to run to either, unless you've Evolutionist friends I don't know about."

"No, I'm all for the rule of the righteous. I'm no Hochast, even if I had anything like that to offer. There's one I'd have been happy to see at the Bushing Post. It's the means rather than the ends that have gone astray. Surely you military men come to the same conclusion?"

"Glad to hear it," replied Harritost. "Yes, we have our problems, but logistics take second place to doctrine when the orders come down the line. Safest for us is *keep buggering on and keep your mouth shut.* There was a captain in the Gobinaus lost it at a regimental service. We had to go right to the top to get a firing squad rather than the bush. There'd be no strings to pull for you."

The conversation turned to easier matters, and most importantly to the Dog Team Championships. To Julie's disapproval, both men were keen gamblers, a vice she devoutly wished the Bestower had pronounced upon.

*****

Council, damned Council, thought Hytoniast, as he prepared for yet another meeting at which any excuse, mere practicalities, would be put forward for delay in the Great Endeavour that he had worked on for decades. A grimace crossed his face as a spasm held him, and he reached for his bottle. Time, O Bestower, time. He looked again at the map on his wall. Three great continents, their own the largest, but the least amenable to the Bestower's will. He remembered the jibes from those smug Varrenians when he had paid his one and only visit to Kindopol.

"Sodden moorland; bogs, soils so poor. Ironic, is it not, *your reverence,* that the most devout have the hardest task."

"And botched it such that neither Bestower or Adversary reap the benefit."

Debates. Oh, those Varrenian debates, in which Evolution and Bestowal were alike treated with a detached scepticism that would warrant the bush back home. Young pups arguing for each side in turn; mere skill, mere wordplay, might win a vote without regard to truth. Two such debates were all he could stomach.

Worse, a countryside in which the aboriginal ran wild. Yes, there were clearances, but so much more could be done, would be done without thought at home. Supplies of coals and the ancient swamps that yielded oil. Things we lacked, and had little to trade for. Worst of all, these ditherers, this bunch of *rationalists,* controlled the sacred Rehine and the Founder's Trail. It had *tourists,* not pilgrims, *souvenirs,* not relics. Only his stay at Doubters' Ravine, at the Monastery of Faith Restored, had saved his composure. Returning to Holy Bay, Westport as the heathen called it, he had knelt, even on the quayside, to give thanks for his return, faith undimmed and resolve strengthened.

He had learnt of even greater evil, for Outers and Easties were there about their business. Bestowal to them was a mere convenience, an explanation for the unknown, and, as they saw it, a matter of manners and social cohesion. A story, one had said, it will do unless we learn otherwise. A coarser version of that put about by those supercilious snobs that dominated the Kindland Congress. Again, land for the taking, land that enabled them to eat in plenty without attention to the ongoing needs of his own people and the manifest command of the Bestower. The consumption of abo food, too, though he found none in Kindopol; an abomination, and one that was increasing. Toleration, that damnable rubric that allowed such foulness to pass uncontested.

Amidst that depravity, though, there were temples that preserved purity. And, most importantly, those like Barol that had survived the sack; spared then as a reminder that virtue was rewarded. There had been acolytes and priests begging for Westerland's aid, sermons that had packed the temples. Even in that despicable Congress, there were true believers. The germ of his Great Endeavour, *the Matter of Kindland,* sprouted in his mind.

In Synod, he could rely on his fellow priests. A year, more than a year, since the replacement of the Table had sparked a revival. Heretics were hounded, and his team of inquisitors gained the practice they would need when Kindopol was again subject to discipline. Bonfires of the illicit aboriginal, and of both Evolutionists and their works. The bush would have been more fitting, but the symbolism of burning both the heretics and their works together was effective.

It had been gratifying to hear the reports from that city of sin across the sea. That Tragopon; quite a find, by all accounts. Common as muck, of course, but one who could navigate that swamp in a way no true Martyrson would manage. Temple after temple turning to truth; Exterminators at work, Consies provoked into actions that alienated even those feeble Seniors, Congressmen who would compromise with heretics while remaining notionally pious.

But now, confronted by mere laymen, and in particular by the soldiers, it was problems, never solutions. Worse still, his past overriding of their caution had not had happy outcomes. Again and again, when he had pressed for action, it had been thwarted. That last Grand Tour, that monstrous exposure of the heirs of petty fiefdoms to all the vices known to man. The failure to catch them and subject them to the rigours of the faith. Then that blasphemous Hall on Lofotor, and what followed from it. Outie priests? Mere servants of their secular masters; little more than jesters. Now, the seas, even their own coasts, were not theirs to command. Almost, he had been rebuked.

"We should have been represented, your reverence. A mere spy was easily eliminated. There are no Masters or Seigneurs will serve the cause. Now Kindland guns protect Outie, Eastie and their own ships. We should have been warned. We were tricked all too easily, and the fate of the *Holy Sword* is no secret. News spreads, your reverence."

"Ships better armed than ours, and a dozen or more always at Kindopol. We'd have just the one chance to land in force. No quick victory, and there would be ships from Varden and Blenninge sinking our transports within a week."

He had protested, of course. Surely those ships in harbour would be impounded, their crews on shore detained? No, your reverence, unless the Ultras have already risen and seized power. Could not our *Swords* outgun, outmanoeuvre them? We have but six, and they have our plans. Who knows what is being made in Varden or Lofotor? More ships, your reverence, and better armed; more guns, more trained soldiers and sailors. More cells across Kindland, and more arms for them too.

"More discipline among the locals, too," said General Norbiniast. "More zeal than sense. That attempted murder of the Eastlanders, way back now. I know it was not sanctioned from here, but by those damned enthusiasts at Barol. Lucky for us it failed, for it would have turned people against us, not driven the Easties away. As it is, it merely strengthened their damned police. Too much sound and fury, your reverence, not enough recruits with patience."

There, the matter had rested. Hytoniast contained his impatience. Reluctantly, he had recalled ambassador Bokiniost when that infamous picture of Kindopol in flames had been seen by Kindland Seniors. Now it hung in his own office's reception room; each morning he would bow as he passed. The light of benevolence over Barol, while the ungodly around were consumed by fire. The ambassador's nominally secular successor was to be the model of sweet reason. Gifts to monasteries and temples; exchanges of priests and acolytes, even, with his grudging consent, more exchanges of students. A step he regretted, for even with the vetting, the priests' references, these exchanges were damaging. Even the most pious Kindlanders infected the student body with doubts, if only by their surprise at restrictions that were taken for granted here, while too many Westerlanders returned with a taste for worldly things. Cases had to be dealt with, and too quietly and too leniently for his liking. There were only so many accidents that could be arranged.

It was scant consolation to be assured by the magnates, the traders and landowners in Council, that the strategy was working. The mass of the moderate faithful was better disposed to Westerland. Appeals for help when famines were reported were enthusiastically supported. Consies were losing ground, and resorting to greater extremes. Evolutionism was increasingly associated with rulers who lacked for nothing when others went hungry.

"A virtuous circle, your reverence. The faith prospers, its enemies exposed. We have time on our side."

The Supreme Archpriest had remained silent when these *wise words* were spoken. What, pray, is a *moderately* faithful person, but one who would recoil when the necessary measures were taken? What about those so-called priests who tolerated the passively heretical? Those with mere material interests were nudging him towards a compromise, towards that loose, token service to the Bestower that was all too common at home. Love and brotherhood. He shuddered; another spasm, another draw on the precious bottle.

*****

There was a commotion in Dry Market. The Ziggara are coming. There will be a Purging. Stallholders scrambled to pack away their goods; shopkeepers pulled down shutters. The crowd parted as the leather-coated column marched to the central square. To the Bushing Post at its centre. A circle was cleared around it. Stripped to a mere loincloth, a man was tied to it, a man limp with terror. Two Ziggara placed beside it a brazier, already lit and carried there on long handles. A bag was placed beside it. There was murmuring; what was in that bag? For what purpose was the brazier?

Drums were beaten, and a silence fell. A priest raised his hands.

"In the name of the Bestower, listen well. The wages of sin?"

"The wages of sin are death," shouted the Ziggara, loud enough to obscure any deviancy among the muttering crowd. The priest bent to the sack, and pulled out a square of wood. He held it up.

"Ironwood, that most tempting of the Adversary's creations. I doubt not that the same is about the persons of many here."

A shudder in the crowd, many clutching the chains suspending the charms, the medallions, that were handed down the generations or made gifts in courtship or engagement. The priest gave a sour smile.

"Mere possession? No, that is a weakness that a gracious Bestower may overlook, for now. No, this and others in the bag are the product of a greater, a grievous sin, for they are parts of that old Table of Benevolence that was stripped from the High Temple. Stripped and burnt on the highest authority. But not all, for this wretch decided to conceal some fragments that were sawn up for the fire. How many rings, medallions, tokens of amorous passion did he hope to sell? To trade in the Adversary's products, a sin scarcely less heinous."

The wood was placed in the brazier, and other pieces followed. The priest turned to the Ziggara deacon.

"The bush and the gloves, Master deacon."

A long case was opened. The priest donned the gloves and held up a sprig of painbush tied to a handle. He walked around the post and its captive, waving the wand above him. The ritual was prescribed: one stroke, and only when the agony was on would others be given, and the victim untied to writhe upon the ground until he died, maybe two days later. He stood before the victim, and struck. The crowd swayed, and moved in a way that focussed the Ziggara's attention.

The scream was cut short. Passing him by a whisker, the priest saw a crossbow bolt embed itself in the man's face, straight between the eyes. There was a roar from the crowd, a surge that rocked the circle of leatherjackets. Then, as if by magic, the crowd dispersed, evading capture. The priest, the body and the Ziggara were left alone in the market. At his instruction, the body was cut down and removed. The market was empty. That night, a mysterious blaze destroyed the post.

Even Synod were shaken, and it was not the only instance. Where punishment was completed, crowds did not watch the agony, but overran the guards to put the victim out of his misery. Time is not on our side, your reverence. Only a victory for the faith will temper the mood.

Not on our side. But the soldiers demanded more. In Council, there was more frustration as difficulties piled up.

"Your reverence, the Outers are stifling our trade, and the Eastlanders are complicit. Subtly, for it is all *exhausted mines, bad harvests, better prices in 'Pol, a shipping shortage,* never outright refusal."

"We are tearing up the tracks west of Gobinau for iron. We are restricting civilian use of fuel, but we lack enough for any sustained transport across the narrows to 'Pol."

"Many young men, too many, are escaping service by calls to priesthood. The seminaries are backing them."

"There was a mutiny at Holle. Two for the bush, ten hanged. It went further, for there was a breakout. Two priests killed with their own bush, and the Garden of Wrath burnt."

"A bushing in Holy Bay. A soldier in the guard shot the beaten at the first stroke, then shot himself."

"Conscripts from the west: too starved to be trained, and we don't have the rations to build them up."

"A third of the fields around Gobinau uncultivated, the rest infested with higgies."

And so on, and so on, mostly complaints that Hytoniast had already heard. In full Council, he was unbending. The solution is the appropriation of Kindland for the faith, the true, unsullied faith. To one magnate, he had uttered the dread words:

"Do not go further, Master Serronost. I sense the danger of heresy. Martyrsons are not immune, Master."

The man had paled, and there was a shuffling of feet and a down-turning of eyes among the civilians. Three more had the bush that morning in Benevolence Square, one a Martyrson, for mere disrespect to a troop of passing acolytes.

Hytoniast dismissed them, and turned to the military alone. The news was not good. Ambassador Engiliast's despatches were before them.

"Kindland is up to something. What are these Evaporators, in the name of the Bestower? Pollinast's reports say there are vast resources going in." Hytoniast shuffled his papers. "Should we not strike before it is fully developed?"

"Whatever it is, you've seen Tragopon's assessment. They lack the range and mobility to be a threat. If anything, they are staging things to bring us into the open. My intelligence is that Morgenstrum is all for a scrap, and the police have penetrated many cells. They lack weapons in Kindopol. Raise the countryside, and if they beat us in the capital, many of the faithful will die in vain elsewhere."

"You could not beat him?"

"We might, your reverence, we might, but the odds are against us. There are ten Easties in the docks, at least there were last week. Large, fast and armed. Dockland is hard Consie; no way the locals can overpower them now. They might remain neutral. Or not, especially if a shell lands among them."

"Our warships?"

"Seven are ready, ten are under construction, delayed for lack of material. We will get there, but not tomorrow. When? At present, you may have two in the next hundred, and the rest in a year, assuming the materials are provided."

"Troops?"

"Five thousand camped or billeted around Holy Bay. We cannot hold more there, the logistics are strained, not to mention relationships with the city. The same again here. They could move fast enough when needed."

Norbiniast paused, and looked hard at the Archpriest. The Bestower be thanked, no living person had seen a real battle, merely the mopping up of futile mutinies and revolts. His men had trained, certainly. They were believers; the hatred of heretics was real enough. But the priests had wound them up to expect that, having sent their opponents flying, they would enter the city to cheers and bouquets. They were hungry, too.

"Your reverence, it is not the numbers that face us. Pollinast reckons four thousand at most, and they will have few elsewhere. They are not disposed to sacrifice comfort for security when there has been no war for generations. They do outgun us, though, and he says they have ammunition for months. If they command the shore, we will lose. It requires the locals to deny them that as we arrive. They may arm the Consies, and then it would be street fighting. We need those docks."

"Delay again. Tell me, General, how things will be better in a hundred, in a year, in two years. As for those accursed streets, their destruction will please the Bestower. Can we not land elsewhere and march on them from behind?"

The general was driven to extremes. The man must be told. Again.

"Under a sea cliff up which a path must be hewn? On a beach nowhere, with no road? After a voyage of two or more days in hostile waters? Where merely denying us resupply when inland will result in starvation or surrender? Men chewing grey-greens in desperation? You would like five thousand martyrs? A nice panel for your new mosaic, Hytoniast."

The Archpriest's face went white. Danger of heresy, if not heresy itself. Hytoniast, indeed. There would be a reckoning, victory or not. But not now, for he saw the unity in the soldiers' faces. The shock imposed a silence for a full minute. It took Colonel Harritost to break it.

"Your reverence, it is as the general says. For success, we need the docks, if not at once, then very soon after. We need more ships, and more men. Above all, we need a rising, an armed rising, in the city. Time is on our side, if you will cause the clergy to cease their poaching of the able-bodied, and restrain their appetites. Acolytes freed for work in the fields would be a start."

Emboldened by the Archpriest's silence, other voices were heard. Call off the Ziggara, or make them rout out Evolutionists, rather than eavesdropping on the talk of ordinary if disgruntled citizens. Withhold the bush, Evolutionists excepted. More uplift and less warnings of the danger of heresy from the army chaplains. Hytoniast gave a nod, and the soldiers left. A spasm gripped him, and he reached once more for the small bottle that was always with him. Which will come first, he wondered, the liberation of Kindland, or my passing into the Bosom of the Bestower.

*****

Derant was starving. The Outie ships were few and their cargoes sparse. The road trains that rumbled east with their loads of ore and nodules lay silent in the yards. Consul Boone did the best he could; his own vessel brought food to the academy and orphanage. The young were leaving, either recruited for the coming conflict, or simply disappearing to the Bestower only knew where. The old were quarrelsome, divided between those stirred with zeal for the Bestower, and those that cursed the authorities to the east. The bush was not used, for even the priests sensed that it would provoke revolt.

There was no such restraint in Gobinau, where monasteries and zealous acolytes were many. The Bushing Post was used almost every day. The hotel became a holding camp for those moving east, many choosing to sign up as soldiers rather than face starvation or the bush. Even in High City, things were tense. The new recruits could not be confined for ever. Acolytes, even priests, were spat at as cowards, for here, at least, there was the taste for war rather than pious words. Westport was heaving. Shipyards working all through the night, troops using the streets to learn, as best they might, the ways of urban warfare.

Then, the rumours started. Kindland has a secret weapon. Rocks could be rained on High City; Westport could be evaporated into space; ships could be cut in two. Even worse, those abo-lovers had developed plagues that would be carried through the air. Strike first, was the dominant cry, but beneath it an anxiety. The military advocated delay: We will win because we are, or will be, the stronger. The faithful in Kindland must rise up to greet us, but they lack the strength and the will.

*****

Hytoniast was being driven to desperation. Surely, the time has come. He had suspended Council, easily, for the civilians were only too pleased to be relieved of responsibility. The clergy were behind him. The soldiers, though, he could not dispense with, and they united to demand delay. It mattered not that Archpriest Bokiniost ranted, and started accusing them of being in danger of heresy. They stared back with stony faces, faces that a few years ago would have quailed before such an onslaught. Stared back as one, too; at any other time, such conspiracy would have instituted a purge.

General Norbiniast sat silent. His eyes were not on the fiery ex-ambassador, but on Hytoniast himself. The man was ill, however hard he tried to hide it. He was gaunt, gaunt in a way that made his eyes seem larger, more intense. Even now, his face tightened into a grimace.

"In the name of the Bestower, your reverence, hold back," said Norbiniast. "We cannot guarantee the docks. The faithful lack arms. That mystery weapon, that Evaporator; nothing we have heard from Engiliast so far suggests any immediate threat. Rocks? We have been deceived before. Better still, it is those damned Consies that are shouting the loudest, and losing ground as a result."

"Those stories, your reverence," added Harritost. "Let those rumours of a plague, of a doomsday weapon, gather strength. Even heretics may welcome us if they are believed. They may act against the thing themselves. Our appeal for peaceful use across the continents attracts support, even from the fragile of faith. Congregations petition their feeble government. It would not take much for it to fall, and for our aid to be asked for."

Hytoniast said nothing. Fragile of faith; a neat euphemism for the weak, the lovers of creature comforts, priests included. A purge was needed. It was not the mere establishment of a subordinate to High City that engaged him, but that image of sin purged by fire. Bokiniost looked expectantly at him, awaiting his rejection of the soldiers.

He did not. A mere nod of his head resigned the decision to the general. He waved priests and soldiers away, and sat silently on his own. Another spasm seized him, and bile rose in his throat. He reached for his bottle, but nausea overtook him. Coughing and retching, his handkerchief revealed for a second time the blood that was mixed with bile. Time, O Bestower, grant me a little more, was his unspoken prayer. He rang a bell, and two acolytes entered, helped him to his feet, and back to his rooms.

18. Yes!

It was the twentieth transmission that day. Perhaps another universe, another timeline. It was a mere technician that pressed the button, for Frettici and Holdbo had long since preferred to await the delivery of prints, so they were startled when she came running in.

"Water, Dr Frettici, water in the holder."

After the first returns of rock, they had redesigned and enlarged the small, original transmitters so that material returned fell into a small bowl. What was returned, though, was a few centilitres only, corresponding to the volume of the transmitter itself.

All waited for the printer to deliver. They were rewarded with a dim, blurry image of nothing in particular. The few that followed before the transmitter expired were much the same. Was the last just a little darker?

"Underwater, for sure," said Holdbo.

"Where there is water, there may be life. Could it be like ours?"

"Chemistry should tell us. We need more, and an analysis. We must tell Rollo; Galben too."

Tell, and fetch; no longer a simple matter, for as security had tightened, so had the siege by ragtag protesters. To Morgenstrum's fury, there was little that could be done except to keep the road and entrance clear. The village of tents and shacks erected on unclaimed, uncleared abo land was not technically illegal. Most certainly, he was told by Masseter, you are not using the army to remove them. Try that, and Congress will fall to the Ultras. Most certainly, Gornik had said, I have neither the numbers nor the will to do any such thing. Peace on the streets of Kindopol is hard enough. Workers and soldiers alike had to run a gauntlet of abuse, even stone-throwing, and that wretch Galben must be hidden on each journey.

"Bloody Consies too, now, gentlemen," said Brigadier Prevosto, the general's Chief of Staff, as the pair were driven with him past the angry mob outside the first gates. "Convinced that we are about to destroy all abo life. While the other lot are convinced that we are out to destroy our neighbours. There'll be Westie reporters and agents among them too. Get a move on, gentlemen."

Rollo was quick to grasp the significance of the find. Soon, he was presented with a larger sample. *Those old cannon balls are ideal, Mr President, we lose no time in calibration.* Now, he was faced with finding a means to get it analysed without betraying its origins. He left with a precious flask. Galben sat down with his colleagues to consider their next move.

"If it is liveable, we need to find land. If we are any guide here, there may be rather little of it. And the more we scatter transmitters, the harder it will be to guarantee returning to the same spot. We need a view from above; maybe hundreds of kilometres above."

"Which seems almost impossible, Torren. You've pointed it out before. The attraction seems to focus on or near the surface once we are near. What about Hommoz? I don't know. Maybe if the first is far off, the rest follow; we allowed no freedom then. Maybe it is easier the more similar *there* is to *here*."

Frettici fussed with the settings. One at a time, and hope, for a plethora close together would open an attraction too hard to break. They got lucky, for the next revealed a landscape clearly covered in vegetation. Of course, there were only a few pictures before the transmitter blanked out. It was frustrating, though, for another showed almost nothing.

"Night time. I will try to tune the transmitter to infra-red. A good sign, for by my reckoning, it means rotation like ours, not a face turned permanently to a sun."

Frettici bombarded the site to ensure that the attraction was strong. Galben returned to Kindopol, to the precious computer. He measured, he estimated, as the data were sent to him. Was gravity the same? How much did discernible features increase as the descent started. Soon, the transmitters were giving him more data: surface height in particular. The pictures were of a forest, a forest that looked remarkably like one made of bestowed, broad-leaved trees, though he could identify none. One returned a minute amount of soil, while another returned a piece of wood. All were now close to the ground.

"We landed in a tree trunk," said Holdbo. The sendings were put aside. The next moves would be down to the general.

*****

Rollo was having problems. Few studied the seas, for there was little to be gained from them since the need for oilworm oil had gone. Of necessity, he turned to Hort.

"It is a military matter, Professor. I have this sample of water. I think it is sea water. I wonder if it could be compared with any analyses that you know of?"

"From where, Mr President? As far as I know, the early studies in the sea showed little difference from place to place. A little dilution of salts near the polar continents, that is all."

"I was not told, Professor, so I assume it relates in some way to Westerland. Maybe it is from a river or lake, but a taste suggested salt. Simply, the Academy were asked to do this. I think the army are concerned that the Ultras have some means of contaminating our supplies. That's a guess, of course."

Galla Hort took the sample. The story sounded implausible, unless the target was Eastland or the Far Outs, for poisoning water would kill as many Bestowalists as unbelievers. She passed it to the soil scientists. She had a shock, for it was Jana Polin who reported back.

"It is sea water, not fresh, but its salinity is higher than anything they can find in the literature. There are a few salt lakes in Eastland, but they have even more salt. Not only that, but they are densely populated with abo life. No trace of that."

"Perhaps it was filtered? Or would creatures die when the water was taken?"

"I thought of that, as did they. That's why they passed it to me. We test organic matter to see the proportions of bestowed and aboriginal. It's standard to see if soils are ready for bestowed crops."

"And?"

"There was very little there. What there was is bestowed or generic. No trace of unambiguous aboriginal. Of course, there are a lot of things in common."

"But there is some. That means life. Anything else?"

"Oxygen. Not much of it, but then I do not know how that water was treated. Again, life, and life as we would expect it."

"Run off from some farm, perhaps? I imagine that the abo micro-organisms would be vanishingly rare?"

"With that amount of salt? A strange crop indeed. Did Rollo give no hint as to its origin?"

"A military matter. I assumed that Westerland came into it somehow. I cannot see how."

Galla Hort puzzled for a while. Was it some concoction planted on Kindland agents in order to confuse? She composed a report, and had it delivered. The phrase *Not known at this address* came to mind, as she turned her mind to other things.

*****

Frettici was happy. He could calibrate precisely. As a final test, he sent another cannon ball in the presence of Galben. Soil and leaf litter returned. To their astonishment a small creature, buzzing angrily, flew off before it could be captured. Worse, when they examined the sample indoors, others crawled out. Some were captured.

"Look like higgies, don't they? And those dead leaves; I don't recognise them, but they are more like bestowed than abo."

"So, time to summon the general. Looks like we've found him his base, unless Rollo tells us otherwise from that water. See what Mr President says. He should be here in the morning."

Scully the technician locked up behind them. Galben, to his distaste, would be obliged to spend yet another night. Morgenstrum was adamant.

"The trouble at the gates is getting worse, Professor. We had a car stopped and its occupants dragged out and beaten. Oh, they were rescued, and arrests made, but if you are recognised, there will be hell to pay. Everybody will be on our backs. Gornik simply does not have enough men on the ground to deal with it. I start shooting, and we'll have riots. And I will be out. Come to that, so will the government."

*****

The girl who turned up at Hort's laboratories the following morning was hard to follow.

"I am to give you these, Professor, from Scully. They arrived yesterday evening. He has a network, because he is kept on site these days. It is a picture of where they are sending to and some of what comes back. There is more, so the message said."

The girl pulled out a crumpled photograph and three dead leaves, each different. Hort examined them. A forest; indeed, a forest like none she had seen or knew of. The leaves, evidently bestowed, but not of species she recognised.

"Does he know where?"

"Everybody in the chain asks the same. He says he is sure they come from *somewhere else.* Said in a peculiar way."

"Somewhere else? What did he mean, Letti? Of course, it must come from somewhere else. More like Rehine."

"Didn't make sense, and he was scared, I think, when he passed them on. Best we could understand, he meant another world. But there isn't one, is there, Professor? At least not with stuff like this. There was soil too, and creatures that ran off, like higgies, he said. He didn't dare take any more."

Galla Hort went to the window. By choice, her room overlooked the main entrance. Yes, the supposedly inconspicuous police were lounging about, as usual. Letti would have been seen. And, as with other visitors, she would be questioned.

"You were not stopped on the way in? Good. How old are you, Letti? Do you have a job?"

"Sixteen, Professor. No, or not regular. I'd not have been able to come otherwise."

"Very well," Hort sat for a few moments composing a note. Not the first time a messenger needed cover.

"Now, Letti, you are to do as I say. Go to Dr Nidolf's office with this note. Tell him that I want to consider employing you as an apprentice technician. He is to get you to fill in a form, an application. He is to give you a slip with a date and time for a formal interview. When the police stop you, you will show them the slip."

It was a matter of minutes to summon Tamon Guterri, Jessa Reboud and Kallan Gort. She laid the picture and dead leaves before them.

"From Nordgroen. A product of Rollo's mysterious project. And before this, as you know, the man himself had brought us seawater. Seawater with no trace of the aboriginal. This looks like Bestowed, but I have seen nothing like this. You have all been on Halfland; do you recognise anything?"

"Nothing like Halfland. The forests there are all needle-leaf, at least as far as we know. There are a few here, by the look of the photo. The others look more like those in the city parks, or at Rehine."

"These leaves. I know they are decayed, but they are very flimsy. I'll check, but I don't recognise any right now. We don't have that many species to compare."

"It was Scully passed these on down the chain. The message was that they came from *somewhere else*. There was soil, and there were things like higgies ran off. He did not catch any."

"Higgies? There are Bestowed higgy-like creatures on Halfland, Professor. We'd need some actual animals to make comparisons."

"Well, I am sure he will try, if they get any more. What worries me is the *somewhere else*. Scully seems to mean another planet, but there are none in our system could support life; at least not life like this."

Hort sent the three away. After a while, she picked up the photo and the leaves and called on Jana Polin.

"Suppose, Jana, that the man really has found another planet with life like ours. What happens if material, living material, is exchanged between them?"

"Strange. I had the same idea. That, or some land here we have not discovered. I asked Becca. Here, she thinks there is none, and if there was, it would be like Halfland or worse. She said that the most likely result is that the newcomers can't compete with the locals. At least, not without help. A bit like here; some of the first-run do well in a cold climate, like Halfland, but we have to work hard to make the first-run work in the Lands."

"So, no danger, either way, just a bit of effort if you were out to colonise. And by the look of these, easier than dealing with our own abos."

"Most likely, not certain, that was what Becca said. Sometimes, the newcomer has some advantage. She quoted some abo plant, I forget the name, that arrived in Eastland accidentally from the Far Outs. Carried on a ship, I guess. It overran large tracts of abo land near Varden. It was a curiosity, nothing more, until some of it reached an experimental station and outcompeted their selected strains. Now, it is a pest; they have to weed the fields."

"So, there is a risk, either way. I think the Easties imposed some kind of sanitary regime on ships carrying food or timber. But there is something else: disease. I'd be worried if micro-organisms were even only marginally compatible. It only takes one, one the host has no experience of, and you could have a plague. Remember your history? All those plagues up until the last big one, when was it, in the 1300s?"

"Yes. I was taught it was all bad hygiene. But I suppose we developed resistance too?"

"Yes, we did. My colleagues argue about it, but some of those plagues could have been abo in origin. Some higgies have adapted to eat the bestowed, so why not bacteria? Not proven, but it makes sense. We have adapted, at a cost. But if we exchanged with a world more like our first-run, there might be many such, and not only for us. There are plant diseases too. An exchange might be devastating either way."

The conversation left Galla Hort in a quandary. At no time had Rollo shown any interest in disease, and his plans, whatever they were, had not seemed to require it. With the exception of the seawater sample, he had given up, as it seemed, on gaining more information from her. Now, though, he was importing life, even if accidentally. He was surely going to export it too. Who knew what people carried with them? At the very least, there needed to be some safeguards. She drafted a very cautiously worded letter, cautious, for she had no evidence that she could reveal as to his actions. The seawater had to carry a heavy burden.

*****

The general was in high spirits. At last, those weirdos had done the necessary. There was life, there was oxygen. They could clear a patch; he could ferry the material and the men, and he could be confident. He brushed aside warnings from the team.

"There are problems, General. First, it is a while since we firmed up a location. Settings seem to drift with time. There is always a risk that we will get there *before.* Particularly with a massive sending. The whole lot would vanish. That is, possibly."

"Yes, yes, you have explained this at least ten times. I am none the wiser. You are the experts. Set your instruments for thousands of years later if you like. I think it makes no difference to the return journey?"

"No. Once we have cleared an arena, we can send all the material you need for the return journey, in many loads. You will be able to calibrate, if you have given us your targets beforehand. That is not all. Clearing the arena is not simple. It is not all at the same level, although the differences are slight."

"But your sending will flatten it, won't it?"

"Yes. But we have to balance off too much material returning against some parts remaining with the stumps of trees. A second sending would land on those."

"Too much material? Clear in stages, a metre lower each time?"

"General, the area of such an arena is more than 7,500 square metres. Take away soil or rock a mere one metre thick, and at least 20,000 tonnes will return here. Never mind possible damage to our arena; how long would it take to clear? Be obliged to do it several times, and the logistics are near impossible. It could not be concealed. As it is, we will get some huge amount of timber. Best estimate is 200 tonnes. It must be cleared from the arena before your sending can happen."

Activity was intense. Protesters outside the gates recorded more and more trucks entering. Consie photos revealed new buildings. Soon, it became clear that new, bigger generators were being assembled. The daytime sending of the minute *thingies* largely ceased, while the assembly of equipment around a new, huge, arena advanced rapidly. Some of the strange reflectors, dark spotlights as the Consie observers called them, were being mounted on scaffolding towers around the new arena.

"Nearly ready, General. We are sure we can avoid digging some hole, but we cannot tell you until after what remains in the way of stumps. You are prepared? How fast can you clear the arena?"

"We've done trials. It depends on how long it takes to get stuff past the trees around. We have nothing as dense to use for practice. First drop will have to be for the means of clearance. You will have to send a transmitter to check, for we won't be able to send anything back until we have at least three loads, and time to assemble the kit."

If the general was satisfied, the team were not. Those trees; they were up to twenty-five metres high. Not only must the sending be a cylinder, not a hemisphere, but it must reach to that height with room to spare. Frettici and Holdbo were out with the technicians, erecting yet more shaping reflectors, some now mounted on taller scaffolds. Structures impossible to conceal even from those held beyond the perimeter. They needed a test.

It worked. As the accumulators and the reflectors buzzed, Holdbo placed a smoke generating machine in the centre. A cloud of dark smoke emerged, and drifted in the wind. Frettici pulled switches, and the movement ceased. A boiling cloud of smoke was contained in a massive cylinder. Another switch, and it disappeared. There was a bang as air filled the vacuum.

"Into space, General, *other* space, of course. We can remove all. No jumble of tree tops to hinder your sendings. It will all come here."

Then there was the letter from Hort. It niggled Rollo, even if he was not minded to halt. Stuff coming here, living stuff, that could be burnt while the general's plan was carried out. But the thought that the troops, or the colonists he hoped to send later, might catch or carry infection had not occurred to him. He put it to one side, thinking vaguely that as long as it was only humans that came or went, all would be well. He wrote a short letter of thanks, full of assurances.

*****

It was raining. Rollo and Galben, umbrellas over them, stood to one side in the near total darkness. Unseen now night had fallen, there was a massive bar at one side of the arena. Its ends were attached by chains to stationary engines, now only audible in the darkness. Opposite the bar, and clear of the arena, parties of soldiers stood ready to fire what was cleared from the arena.

It was Morgenstrum who had devised the scheme, and Holdbo who had reset the reflectors to accommodate it. The ground had been smoothed flat and flush with the arena surface. The general had been firm.

"Fast, and in the dark. The fewer see clearly what you have brought, the better. There will be a great pile of trees and the Bestower only knows what else. They must disappear as fast as possible, Picked men for you, gentlemen. Never mind the bonfire. It's all over then."

Rollo was thankful. At least, this way, there is little chance of anything from *there* being able to infect anything *here.* We will find out soon enough if we get anything *there.* Surprising how that Hort woman gets under the skin. He peered, futilely into the dark. The rumble of the engines was now overlain by the buzzing of the accumulators building the charge, a charge so massive that nearly the whole of Nordgroen was in darkness. Only the faint outline of Frettici was visible from the glow of his instrument panel.

It was to the general that the honour of despatch was given, an inspired notion from Galben that had flattered the general's vanity. A short flash across the arena, and Morgenstrum would pull a lever.

The flash came. Morgenstrum hesitated for perhaps a second. The lever was pulled, and there was a crashing as trees cut off at the stump came crashing down.

It was not all, for at the centre was a fire, a fire that blazed up as what was clearly a needle-leaf fell on it. The rumble of motors drowned out any other noise. The fire was extinguished as the bar moved forward, carrying with it trees, soil and who knew what else. Clear of the arena, and it was pulled back.

The pyre was immense, a linear bonfire fed by flamethrowers and by whole cans of petrol and pitch hurled into the blaze. The roar drowned out all other noise. Bit by bit, lights came on in Nordgroen. Frettici turned to a smaller arena and despatched a transmitter, his actions illuminated by the blaze behind him.

The party waiting around the printer had but a few minutes to wait. Triumph, for there was a clearing, the perfect circle. Only the smouldering remains of a fire caused comment.

"Maybe a lightning strike, General," said Galben. "Did you see the needle-leaf blaze. It will not be there when you are ready for the real sending."

"Thank you, gentlemen. A couple of metres lower would have been better, but if you get it right, those stumps should be no problem."

The morning, however, revealed problems. Falling trunks had dented the surface, even cracked it in places. There was fire damage near the centre, and the intense heat of the pyre had warped one edge. A week, General Holdbo told him; give us a week.

"No problem, I expected as much. If I understand you right, though, the sending will arrive mere minutes later? We don't want anything that has wandered onto it brought here. And those following as soon as the arena is clear? Good."

The pyre was a mere pile of ash. Mechanical scoops were already at work. Workers repairing the centre of the arena did not notice the small, darkened patches nearby. The whole thing was washed clean when they had finished.

The activity at Nordgroen had not gone unseen. At the Westerland embassy, Ambassador Engiliast found Pollinast's and Tragopon's accounts disturbing.

"First that smoke, then whatever it was that arrived in the night and was burnt. Burnt very thoroughly by the sound of it. Where did that smoke go, in the name of the Bestower? Where did whatever arrived come from? 100 metres across? Suppose the next lot is poison gas or time bombs for the centre of High City, or the fleet at Westport? Or, the other way, most of the Great Temple, or the docks at Westport materialising here."

"I don't know, your reverence, neither does Pollinast. Nothing came back from the smoke, as far as we know. It would disperse wherever it went. As to what arrived, the only clue was what the fire in the centre revealed. Our observer said that what looked like a needle-leaf caught fire. It must be trees, for everything was burnt to ashes. The only place that could come from is Halfland."

"Where we have no observers. No chance of anyone seeing the place from which the material came, only Kindlanders there, all a bunch of Evolutionists. Think about it; send smoke, which will leave no sign within minutes, receive trees or something from where we cannot see."

"There is more, your reverence," said Pollinast. "Their army has been moving in a lot of men and equipment. All covered, of course. They hardly need all that to operate an Evaporator. I've been fobbed off with talks of exercises, but I've seen no sign."

"Whatever it is," said the ambassador, "they are testing it. Whatever it is clearly works. Take stuff from Halfland? Why not from our own country? We face terror either way or both at the same time. Swap the High Temple for a regiment with artillery. A regiment that can be reinforced. How much will fit on a platform that large? We are in danger, and it must be stopped. Tragopon, can we sabotage anything? They seem to need vast amounts of power. That at least limits the speed."

"No, your reverence, not from inside. The army has taken over nearly everything, and Gornik has been vetting everybody. It can be done only from outside, by a riot, by breaking the perimeter. There will be casualties. The place is full of soldiers, too. It might not succeed."

"Either way, we win, I think. We set them back, or the casualties are sufficient to justify an ultimatum. The temples will be in uproar."

"But war itself? Are we ready to intervene?"

"No, we are not, not sufficiently. At least, not without a successful rising here. We are obstructed by Eastland and the Far Outs, and our arms production is behind. We might win, at a cost, but we have our own subversives to deal with too. But provoke a massacre, and their wretched government may fall. Friendly faces here. There might even be a formal plea for help if real Bestowalists take charge. At the least, it would put a stop to whatever is going on at Nordgroen. No need for secrecy then, the preachers can bellow defiance. Gornik will not be able to halt the tide. A few more editorials about peaceful use, the common cause, eh? Wind them up, Tragopon, wind them up. I'll give you the word."

"A minor puzzle, your reverence; it's the Consies. They seem less than happy. All this apocalyptic stuff about a doomsday weapon. They will have seen the smoke and the arrival that followed too."

"Encourage them, Tragopon. In fact, if they lead the charge, then there will be fewer left to mop up afterwards. You have the wherewithal to drive them crazy."

His cipher clerk was kept busy for a while before a transmission could be sent. The return message was simple and uncoded: *Agreed.*

*****

Galla Hort and her colleagues were equally perplexed. The smoke had aroused Consie fears. If smoke could be sent, why not plagues. She was accosted the following day. The whole doomsday picture was reignited. In vain, she pointed out to anxious contacts that there was no evidence of a pod or refuge for survivors, no request for plants, animals or even seeds and soil. Illogical though it might be, the sighting of a needle-leaf in the mass of material burnt a few days later merely shifted the argument.

"A refuge, Professor? They can use Halfland. When they have killed all, they will return."

"Impossible. They cannot send from there, and there is no protection at Nordgroen for those who are sending. Why would they bring Halfland plants here, if that is their plan? A test? But there are no crops, no cattle, no sheep on Halfland. They could only be kept in small numbers under cover. I would have heard if any such thing was happening."

"They could return by ship, Professor, when extinction is complete."

The irony struck her; rationalists, so called, planning what amounted to a new Bestowal, but one onto sterile ground. It was no use. Her team sensed both the withdrawal of support and the evidence that many Consie groups were planning violence, violence even when it was alongside Ultras. Violence that would serve the Ultra cause all too well. She turned to speeding up the plans to evacuate what was left of her team.

She was interrupted by a commotion outside, and had barely time to move to the window when the door was thrown open, and three police entered. One was Gornik himself.

"Scully, Professor, where is he?"

"Scully, Chief Inspector, who is he? We have no Scully here."

"An end to games, Professor. We are searching the buildings now. No, you have no Scully, but you certainly know of him. A technician at Nordgroen. He did not report for work this morning. All of them were supposed to stay overnight. No trace."

Hort returned to her chair; the police remained silent. The sounds of doors banging, of protests from disturbed staff could be heard through her open door. A sergeant appeared.

"Nothing, sir. All are staff here. There are three students in the lobby. All legit. We have searched them. Nothing to the point, and not on our list."

Gornik turned back to Hort.

"You spent the night here, I know. Any of your staff still travelling from home?"

"No, Chief Inspector. Their choice, not my order. There have been incidents. You can protect our homes, but too many are recognised on the street, and I cannot afford taxis for all. There are plenty of empty rooms here now. But you must know that; your men have been at the entrance for days. Those students? There should be ten at least. They are being threatened too, Chief Inspector. Kindopol is less than safe for the likes of them."

Gornik noted the implied rebuke. Damned Consies, though, were out of control, never mind the Ultras. A problem he could not lay at that Hort woman's door, for his agents had recorded the attempts by her staff to dismiss the apocalyptic nonsense that had gripped so many. The Consies who had visited her earlier, before he had entered? Clean; presumably just reporting from the perimeter. They would know only what was already common knowledge.

"No further requests from Rollo, Professor?"

"Only a request to analyse some water. It turned out to be sea water of a sort. I was told it was given him by the military. I assume you recorded his visit?"

The police left, though there were now more of them outside, and two in the foyer, ready to interrogate any arrivals let in. It was not long before Jana Polin and the three students came to Galla Hort.

"These three have more to tell us, Galla. That Letti girl dug Gorsten here out. A message from Scully. Gorsten's rather well known to the police, so he repeated it to Flarana and Toggen, in case the police would keep him out. They let all three in, as it happened."

Scully had been among those standing by to help with the clearance of what was delivered. Remembering the escape of higgy-like creatures, he had armed himself with a jar. At first, he had seen nothing but the blaze in the centre, which flared up as the presumed needle-leaf caught fire. But when the pyre was lit, he again saw creatures on the ground, creatures that were off the arena before the great bar had passed. He had caught a few, and some soil that had spilled over the edge.

"There were dead leaves too, Professor. Letti said they were like the ones she brought you."

"Scully. He's missing. How did he get out? Does he have that jar?"

"He has the jar, according to Letti. Would not let anyone get caught with bringing it here. He has a picture, too. Letti told me it showed a felled area. There were trees all around, but only the trunks showed in the picture. Something about infra-red, that she didn't understand. I think it was dark there as well."

"Letti was pretty vague about how he got out. I think there was some kind of disturbance at the gates as an army truck left. I think there is a group the police have not penetrated. It took them some time to get all the lights back on."

There was little more to say. Hort gathered that Scully would try to get his catch to her, but she could not see how. In any case, it was evident that living material from *there* was now *here,* and in greater quantities than in the first sending that Scully had reported. She thanked the students, and sent them away.

"What sort of risk is there, Jana? There is not much of Bestowed life around Nordgroen. I'd think those creatures would die of starvation, if nothing else."

"Probably. We don't know what they are capable of. Are they really like our Bestowed? Looks can deceive. Think of the higgies. One creature flew away from that first sending, the small one. Where did it go? It's not from Halfland, nor are the leaves. That pyre at least suggests that Rollo has paid some attention. Is it enough? It's what might go the other way that bothers me, the more so if Rollo still intends to move some kind of capsule. Worse, if he just dumps a collection of the bestowed into the open air. And what might come back if he is successful?"

The two sat silent. The evidence pointed to some kind of exchange. A directed exchange with a known location. Here or *there,* even if *there* was here, on some undiscovered island, caution was needed; quarantine, testing in secure conditions, trial after trial. The hard-won gains of reclamation should not be put at risk. Nor, for that matter, the risk of devastating some pristine planet. Eventually, Galla brought the reflection to a close.

"They are mending the arena. I think it will take days at least. Rollo has stopped asking for advice. I think whatever is going on is military now. We must watch what is happening, I think. Without Scully, of course."

*****

Jarpen Stagg had taken the news of Olden Nadder's arrest, escape and disappearance badly. At the time, he had been resentful of the rather brusque treatment he had received at his meeting in the hostel. Now, he felt some relief that he had not been summoned again, although, in truth, he could have told Nadder little. The two cosmology students had not talked to him again, and later they had disappeared completely, seemingly putting in only night time sessions on the computer, time off limits to all others.

As time went by, he and his fellow Consies among the physics students had lost their interest in whatever it was that Rollo, Galben for that matter, were doing. All the news, including the military demonstrations, suggested some means of confounding Westie and Ultra plans. They could only approve, at least in principle, for the evidence of increasing Ultra strength was mounting.

It was only when the weird idea that Rollo was planning some doomsday weapon began to circulate that he reflected back. At first, all of them in physics had dismissed it as a nonsense, even a piece of false news designed by Ultras. But it had taken hold, and they had been pressed by others to explain what was going on, a task that they found impossible. He remembered that woman from Hort's lab. She'd said nothing in his presence. Given Hort's reputation, he had assumed it was normal Consie business, even fundraising for another of her famous expeditions. Now, he started to wonder; Nadder had been a marked man, whereas Hort and her team were open and operated just within the law. Get caught together, and they put a lot at risk.

It would have remained a mere niggle in his mind, had luck not favoured him. He and a few others arrived for precious time at the computer. The two Rollo students were wrapping up a mass of disordered papers, in a state that appeared half way between drunk and exhausted. Six o'clock in the morning, Bestower's Backside; their only allocation, and a scant two hours.

"What cosmological mysteries have you two been plumbing?" he had asked, jokingly. The reply astonished him.

"Just this, Jarpen, just this," said Rigal. He looked around, and saw a glass of water on a desk. He fished in his pocket and pulled out a coin. He dropped it into the water.

"What just happened, Jarpen? And what happens when you load a ship?"

He had laughed, laughed with a hint of hysteria, as his colleague frowned and led him away. As the team settled down, Jarpen noticed a piece of paper underneath a desk. There were scribbles. He folded it and put it away.

Back in the Institute, he discussed it later with Hellica and Delia. The theme appeared to be displacement.

"The coin displaces water. The same volume of water, not the same mass."

"Only because it is denser. Oh, wait. What about that ship? Part of it stays above the water; it's only the volume of what is below that's moved."

"They disappeared stuff. So, it displaced whatever was there where it went. But all the talk was sending it into space. Nothing to displace. Of course, air rushed in to fill the space left behind."

"What if there was something at the other end, not just space or air?"

"It would be displaced. It would just move stuff out of the way. Like the coin."

"If just air arrived in something solid, it would just compress. At most, it would explode something. But they sent nothing that we know of at Nordgroen and got rock back. And all that stuff that got burnt."

"The story is it came from Halfland. Hard to imagine; the place is nearly vertical everywhere."

"That's the point though. Stuff isn't just shifted; it replaces what has been sent, even though the distance is great. Like a pulley: one goes up, the other goes down."

They looked at the paper. It had scribbles and drawings, cartoon-like. One showed a gaggle of Westie archpriests in their robes, speech bubbles containing some choice blasphemies, standing in a crudely drawn circle. A mass of to-and-fro arrows connected it to an image of a monstrous Morgenstrum backed by sketchily drawn soldiers in some place surrounded by trees.

"Time to play games," said Delia, bitterly, "while we get a few miserable slots per hundred at crack of dawn."

Jarpen said nothing more. Clearly, it was a weapon of some sort, and the idea of the pulley burrowed into his mind. What if what was displaced was not pushed aside, but channelled in some way? If just a weapon, why Hort's involvement?

No Nadder with whom to consult, damn the idiot. Then there was that pyre, that destruction of a mass of what was said to be trees. Trees arriving from where? It took ingenuity and not a little risk to get a message to Hort. Unknown to him, the message also reached Scully, a fugitive barely two safe houses ahead of Gornik.

19. No!

Scully sank to the floor in the derelict house, a burnt-out shell that had once been a House of Pleasure. Unknown to him, it was the remains of that run by Gornik's mother many years ago. A last resort, as the police had been tracked moving from refuge to refuge, intent on his capture. There were weak links in the network, but this last refuge was known to few.

He pulled out the jar in which he had put the creatures captured at Nordgroen, and opened the lid. To his despair, all were dead, even starting to decompose. Several appeared to have been half-eaten by others. *I have nothing*, he thought, *with which to preserve them.* But there had been no way to get them to Professor Hort; as Letti had made clear, the police were searching everybody.

It had been something of a miracle that the physicists he had worked for had assumed his incomprehension. Only in the last days had they begun to confine him to Nordgroen overnight. At first, he had conceived of the project as teleportation, a useful weapon indeed, but one that seemed not to satisfy the Consie network around Hort. He had heard Frettici trying to explain things to the general. All this *somewhere else,* not *here,* but *there.* Whatever had come from *there* had been destroyed, very thoroughly, and very much at Rollo's insistence; at Morgenstrum's too.

It had been dark already when he reached his sanctuary, and as the night advanced, his mind revolved around what he had learnt, and what his comrades were saying. *It is a doomsday weapon, Scully.* He had dismissed the notion, for if no less a person than Professor Hort dismissed it, he was not disposed to think otherwise. In the cold, in the dark, he conjured up possibilities. The select few safely set up *there*, then plagues to eliminate all *here.* They had cleared a space. Stuff, he knew, could leave here also. It made a grim picture. Hort could be deceived.

He fell asleep in a corner. He was wakened by a mixture of shouting, singing and laughter in the street outside. A student birthday outing, perhaps, not a stag night for the voices of both sexes were there. Then, he realised that someone had entered his refuge. He got up, looking to hide before he was seen. Perhaps just to piss; the place stank of it.

"Scully. Scully. It's me, Letti. We have someone to see you. A physicist, Scully, Jarpen Stagg. He's safe. He has info. Time to go, now."

"How? And where? We will be seen," Scully whispered.

"No, there are too many, and some come and go. Oh, the police are watching, we are all Consies after all, but they can't keep count, and we are pushing each other from one pavement to another. We will leave in the crowd. You can't stay here for ever."

"Where, for heaven's sake? The police will search out everywhere now."

"It's beyond that now. There are Bestie gangs on the streets too. Somewhere really safe, somewhere defended, from police and Besties both. A citadel, Scully. You know the plans."

The riotous crowd moved away, out towards the city's edge. There were police on the streets, but they watched impassively as the singing, swaying mob passed by. Only when they met a smaller, more determined crowd of Besties were there scuffles. Scully knew the strategy, but was still impressed by its effectiveness. A small group from his crowd engaged the Besties; real fights broke out and the police charged in to make arrests. The majority moved on, and were soon in a quiet side street, the noise of battle fading behind them. He found himself escorted by a mere handful, as others checked the streets ahead and on either side. He was led down an alley, through backyards, in and out of houses through back doors. Finally, passing several masked figures with guns or crossbows, he was guided up some stairs to a dimly lit room, its windows firmly sealed with blankets.

Besides himself, Letti, and the two others who had come with him, there were others he recognised, leading Consies, some of whom had done time on clearance. There were two he did not know, a young man dressed more smartly than the rest, and a much older man, a man whose insignia marked him out as a Senior. A dull, grey cloak hung over his chair. Then there was Nana Selin, partly disguised by the clothes of a typical working woman of the district. A woman he had not met for weeks. She made the introductions.

"Scully, this is Jarpen Stagg. He has things to tell you. This is Senior Markus Nadder, Olden's father. He also has things to tell you."

"Dr Selin," Letti broke in. "How are you here? Do the police not know you have left Professor Hort's lab? Were you not followed?"

Selin gave a sour grin.

"No, I was not followed, Letti. But I cannot return. As far as the police were concerned, I was one of those evacuated to Eastland. I have only now managed to get smuggled back from the station at Kindopol Swinery. All who enter our lab now are searched; searched very thoroughly. By now, Gornik will have realised that I am no longer on the train to Targon."

The conversation that followed was long and tortuous, for there had to be repeated explanations for those who lacked knowledge of Rollo's project. The Senior reported on the vast sums of money that had been spent, and his son's conviction that Rollo was doing more than merely developing a weapon.

"Someone was trying to silence my son, and it was not Besties. Gornik was not explicit, but it was Rollo, for certain. We were left wondering why, for none of us would object to a weapon that saved us from Westerland and the Ultras." The Congressman saw the looks.

"Oh, he's safe enough. I might even see him again if the crisis is over. The police were protecting him. He'd not be safe here, innocent though he is."

"We have the same threat," said Selin. "Oh, Gornik hates us right enough. He'd be happy to see the lot of us in a penal colony or departing to Eastland or the Far Outs. But he is protecting us too; even men in our homes before we all decided to camp out in the labs. Not from Besties, we are sure."

Scully handed her the container with his decaying catch. Selin opened it, wrinkled her nose, and quickly closed it.

"It was inevitable. They cannot destroy everything that they bring back from *somewhere else.* Stuff that may be lethal to us. Who knows what escaped the flames at Nordgroen?"

There was a muttering among the other Consies. A voice rose above it.

"So, he is intent on doomsday. Kill all but those in his pod, capsule or whatever. Is it too late, Dr Selin? If not, we must destroy his machinery."

"No, that pod or capsule, that assembly of Bestowed life, is something he seems to have given up on. But he has material from that place that could be a danger to us. A place that seems to be full of life like our Bestowed. A place, equally, that might harbour micro-organisms that could kill us or our crops and livestock. A place that might suffer similarly from whatever he sends there. He does not intend destruction, but it may be a consequence of his actions. A perverse consequence, for it would probably leave the aboriginal untouched here, while devastating whatever is there."

"That would please the Diabolists, for sure," said a voice from the Consies listening. "But surely Rollo is not of their number?"

"No. He just ignores the risks, assuming he understands them. I think he was intent on setting up a colony, a place free of the confrontations that plague us here," said Selin. "It does not matter what his motives are. He must be stopped."

"It is no longer a matter for Rollo, I think. He has lost control to the soldiers," said the Senior. "For ages, Morgenstrum was opposed, and he was protected only by Giffone. Now, the general is pouring in men and materials; he is backed by Giffone. It is a weapon that is being prepared. Not that it changes the risks Dr Selin has pointed out."

The room fell silent. It was time for Jarpen to speak. Even as the others turned to him, there was an explosion outside, followed by shots. The tacked-up blankets billowed in and then out, and glass from the shattered windows cascaded on the floor. Some moved to extinguish the lights. More shots, and the sounds of a battle outside. Gradually, the noise subsided as the fighting moved down the street.

"Besties," said a woman sent to tell them. "Ultras, organised, and intending to disperse us. We will wait until they are driven off. Stay here."

"Do they know we are here?"

"We don't think so. These attacks are happening elsewhere, wherever there are defended Consie districts. It's all over the city. We cannot move you safely now. Never mind the Besties, it will be fatal for Scully and the Senior to be taken by the police."

She left. Someone restored the light, and in its feeble glow, the others saw the face of Markus Nadder, white with fear, and his fists clenched tightly on the table.

"It is beginning. A civil war here. Riots, murder, a sign that Ultras are in danger, while disrupting any Consie groups. What better excuse for an appeal for Westie assistance? All the more so since Morgenstrum has half the army tied up in Nordgroen. Take the port, and the Westies will land unopposed."

The sounds of shots and yelling had faded. It was Selin who broke the silence.

"Morgenstrum and Rollo must be stopped. The only person who can do it without wholesale destruction is Scully. The only one who can guide him is

Jarpen. Abort the mission, the sending, but not the equipment. Keep the Ultras out, even if there is shooting, and Westerland will remain in doubt. Buy time."

"And if we do? Will Morgenstrum not simply try again? And how is this to be done?"

Markus Nadder looked around the room. Excepting Selin, they were all young. Not just young, but armed with the passion and righteousness of youth. Martyrdom, many would be prepared for; murder would come harder, the more so if the victims were notionally on the same side.

"Morgenstrum can do nothing on his own. In any case, he will be ordered to bring forces back to the city if the plan fails. It is the team that enable him. The same for Rollo. Neutralise the team; in particular, neutralise Galben and Frettici, and it will be years, if ever, that anything like it can be tried again. If we are spared from the Westies, time enough for any future sendings to be under the closest supervision."

Jarpen Stagg stared at the Senior. Did the man mean us to kill?

"If you wish to prevent further sendings, there are simpler ways to do it, Senior. That sending that they burnt required all the energy they could generate. Deny Nordgroen the power, and they will send or receive much less. Better still, destroy that computer, or the team's data and algorithms alone, and keep the team under guard. Done silently, and Westies and Ultras will remain uncertain. Even Frettici will not be able to send accurately. Morgenstrum can give orders; they will not be fulfilled."

He turned to Scully.

"What do you know about the preparations for each sending? I guess you do not make the calibrations, or just follow instructions?"

"Usually, it is Dr Frettici that sets the co-ordinates, yes. We actually trigger the tiny sendings, the ones that send back images. With larger objects, we weigh them, and give him the data."

"You weigh them? Why? Does it need more power? What about the stuff that comes back?"

"Not more power. That seems to be needed for volume, even if it's just air. I don't know whether how much comes back matters. Frettici would get cross if he did not get back what he expected. It seemed that the weight affected the settings. Get it wrong, and what you send may end up underground or high up. Obviously too high up, and whatever you send comes down with a crash. Still in the same place, though; they've got that down to a fine art."

"So, if the weight is wrong, the mission fails. How would they know? How does it work: lighter than expected, more deeply buried, or dropped from a height?"

"I don't know. But they would check by sending a transmitter straight afterwards. I think the idea is to send enough men to clear the arena for more loads to arrive without hitting what is already there, or simply swapping it. I see what you mean. No one could alter the settings, but it might be possible to change the weight. I don't see how, unless something was removed at the last minute, and it was not noticed."

Scully looked hard at Stagg, and then at Selin.

"If it worked, it would be murder, wouldn't it? And perhaps in vain, because corpses could still carry disease. In any case, how is anyone to alter the weight? I have no idea how much change affects the height."

Dr Selin nodded.

"It would protect us, at that cost, if no further attempts were made. Not there, though. Is there no other way?"

"Power failure. It would have to be more than just cutting a cable, though. Generation needs to be sabotaged, badly. Even if I were still there, it would need more people, and there are none. It would mean storming the gates."

"That means Ultras, for we don't have the numbers. They are all round the gates. Morgenstrum would surely shoot to kill."

Markus Nadder looked again round the table. The silent Consies would not baulk at the killing of Ultras, the more so since they would not be the killers. Allow the generators to be destroyed, but then expel the Ultras? All well and good, provided the arena and its mechanisms were not also destroyed. Allow that, and the Ultras would rise, and the Westies would strike. Morgenstrum could not be told. We would rely on his ability to protect the arena, but not the generators. It was not enough.

"Do we have any idea when this sending will occur?" He asked Scully.

"Soon, is all I know, sir," replied Scully. "The arena was damaged by fire. I think the troops and equipment are merely waiting on its repair. They'll send at night though; those at the fence will know because all the generators will be going full blast, and they'll be turning off all the lights to build up the charge."

"You know the layout. If you were there, unseen, could you cut the power if they were about to send, and the generators were working?"

"I know where the cables run. I might reach one unseen in the dark. It would abort the sending, I think. I hope might be a better way of putting it, for it might simply be sent, but not as intended. It would be a last-minute dash through the fence while others cause distractions. Take a couple with me, too, to divert attention."

"Finally," the Senior turned to Jarpen Stagg. "You are to stay here in the city. If the sending succeeds, you will get a message. The computer must be sabotaged. Preferably merely disabled, or Galben's data erased. In fact, it would be good to do the erasing anyway, if that can be done with no other damage. If not, then the thing must be crippled."

As dawn broke, the streets became silent. The Senior was seen safely home, while Scully and his Consie companions set out for Nordgroen. Only Nana Selin remained; getting her to safety would have to wait.

*****

"For pity's sake, can someone get that man off our backs," said Holdbo, after Morgenstrum had paid yet another visit to the workshops where elements of the arena were being repaired, rewired and tested. "It's hard enough without Scully, and he looks at the lads as though they are all about to abscond. He's added at least a day to our efforts."

It was a rhetorical question, for their workshop was guarded on the outside by soldiers. They were prisoners in all but name, for only Rollo, always with a soldier at his side, had been allowed to come and go. The fitting and wiring of each piece at the arena necessitated an escort and working behind a screen that remained in place when they were done. All quite pointless, as Frettici observed.

"Anybody with any sense will know that we are repairing damage. What else would we be doing? Any spying from the perimeter, or from the main enclosures will tell them nothing, even with those cameras the soldiers keep confiscating. He won't be able to hide it when they start trundling the delivery onto the arena."

"Carefully, at that," said Holdbo. "Drop one those crates, and the surface will crack. And I cannot get it into his head that the weight has to be as he asked for, no more, no less. Change it, and we have to recompute. Took us ages to get the settings right for such a heavy load. He still keeps changing his mind about what is to go, how it should be packed, how many are to travel with it. And I have to chivvy him about weights each time. Every damned crate is to be weighed in my presence, marked and sealed, and to be checked off on the arena before his men get in position. They'll need weighing too, complete with all their equipment. He gave me a set of weights from the medical records to start with. Naked men. I will keep them in line to be weighed until I have the totals from the crates. One by one, and when we reach the limit, the rest stay behind."

"It's worse than that," Galben chuckled. "He actually thought that if we sent the gear first, but marked their positions, we could send the men later outside them, and far more of them, to the same weight, and that would solve the problem. The fact that the crates would all come back here had not penetrated."

"He could send the men first. They'd move out."

"He did not think of that. In any case, judging by the gear he wants to move, he'd be sending the best part of a regiment to match the weight. Anything went wrong, and they'd be stuck there while the Westies sacked the city. I thought of sending a few technicians first. But if the equipment did not follow, he'd lose all those we have trained. In any case, we'd have a different weight to work to, and that means time. He doesn't have it."

"Anyway," said Holdbo, "we are actually nearly ready to go. Next time he comes stomping around, tell him tomorrow night. I'll be checking the crates and watching the placements. Their training runs were a shambles; less weight in each, and they still managed to drop a few. Now I have them all on trolleys, and the trolleys will go with them. He has to cut down the weight to compensate."

*****

The journey to Nordgroen had done nothing to soothe Chief Inspector Gornik's temper. He needed troops to support him in the city; he needed to recall his men from Nordgroen. Morgenstrum had been obdurate. Even Minister Giffone had not prevailed. Very well, there was trouble there. In the city, though, things had become far worse. Effectively, it was now partitioned into no go areas for his force, some Consie, some Bestie. He had, just, deterred them from open warfare. Seniors demanded personal escorts; demonstrations outside each embassy had required hundreds to protect them. Even so, most Eastland and Far Out diplomats and staff had been packed into a train for Rehine.

He had gone straight to Masseter, Giffone in tow. The man was in a funk. The Westerland embassy were already at work. *The faithful are being persecuted. Can we not assist you to restore order? High City will respond promptly to any such call. Our citizens in your country are in peril.* That damned Engiliast parading about on visits to temples, shedding crocodile tears at the hardships of believers. Masseter's known pragmatism, his Varrenian detachment, once of value in calming faction, was now derided, even in Congress. *Action not words, First Minister. Where are the police? Where is the army?* Sweet reason and patrician disdain served him no longer. At least, though, Gornik thought, I got what I wanted from the man, a letter, a direct order to Morgenstrum, to release all the police from Nordgroen, and make the army alone responsible for its security. Two companies of soldiers to come with them. Authority to shoot if needed to defend the site.

It was a large convoy that made its way on the road to the testing ground, for many empty trucks and buses would be needed to bring his forces back to the city. At first, the going, slow as always, was unremarkable. Then it became noticeable that there were many on the road, all headed northwards like themselves. Many on foot, too, though it was a two-day hike to Nordgroen. Most paid little attention, but as they neared the place, there were shouts; stones were thrown, and only the firing of shots in the air prevented direct obstruction. Around the outer gates there was a dense crowd, facing nervous soldiers. To the right, Gornik saw, there was a struggle of some sort, a struggle that was edging away from the gate along the fencing that marked the perimeter.

It was no small feat to get the convoy inside, for the space between outer and inner gates was far too small to hold it, and there was no way the captain in charge would allow both to be open at once. Each opening of the outer gate provoked a rush, repelled with rifle butts and tear gas, while soldiers had to line up to protect the waiting convoy.

"Leave it another day, and you'd have been lucky to get in without bloodshed. It will be worse going out. They've thrown a few fire-bombs."

"There was some kind of fight going on outside?"

"Oh, Ultras and the idiot Consies screaming doomsday. Each wanting the glory of overrunning us. It's the Ultras here, there are far more of them. The Consies try to cut the fence, but they are easily dealt with. There are a few of them protesting the protest too: death to Westerland, and save our brave boys. All a lot more squeamish when it comes to violence, other than scrapping with Ultras."

The meeting with Morgenstrum was tense. Besides the general, there were two colonels, presumably on his staff, and a rather dejected Rollo, sitting apart to one side. To make sure that the message was not suppressed, he read it out before handing it to the general.

"All police, General, and now. Two companies of your men, with full kit. We have the transport. An escort until we are clear of that mob outside. That is not all. Two battalions are to be ready to leave if ordered by Giffone. At once, General, when the order is given. The docks must be defended or destroyed if they are threatened by Ultras."

It was as well, Gornik realised, that he had spelled it out. Morgenstrum had glanced at his aides, who stared stonily ahead. Disobey, and they would refuse his orders. Rollo had slumped in his chair.

"See to it, Narutan," the general said to one of his aides. "Round up the police too. The First Targons to provide an escort and clear the gates."

Morgenstrum and the other colonel left, brushing past Gornik without a look. Gornik looked down at Rollo, who refused to meet his eyes, and said nothing. The Chief Inspector shrugged, and left to rejoin his convoy.

*****

"All zeal and no bloody discipline," Major Pollinast muttered, as he was left with Tragopon in the makeshift headquarters they had set up in the Ultra camp outside the gates of Nordgroen. Smuggled there by gangs of Ultras assembling to protest and obstruct, they found the priests in charge incapable of coherent command. Piecemeal assaults led merely to arrests and injuries, without serious effect on whatever devilment was going on inside.

"What's worse," he continued, "is that sooner or later they will catch someone who knows we are here before the job is done. We're screwed right royally then. The army will be all over us, and the waverers in their damned Congress will flip."

"Damned Consies don't help," said Tragopon. "There are too many seeing them as the target, when they are actually a help, so long as they draw force along the fence. But they are the same; just stupid attempts to cut the fence. Manage it, and they get a beating. More often, they just get gassed and retreat. I'm not dishing out the ragebush until we are ready to go."

"A few more days. I want to hear that we are ready to take the docks; I want more here, too, and more guns, guns that are not used until we go in."

Tragopon was about to reply when there was a tap on the door of the old bus that had been stripped to accommodate them. An Ultra sentry, bedecked with bandoliers, an impressive array of pistols and knives at his belt and a carefully cultivated military moustache awaited Tragopon.

"A Consie, sir. Came to us of his own accord. Father Giraud interviewed him, told us to bring him here."

Tragopon sighed. Idiot priest. This was one Consie would not see the light of day once he knew who he was talking to. At the least, their accents would betray their origin.

"Does he know who he will meet? No? Very well, bring him in. Hands bound, and two of you, one on each side."

The Consie was brought in and placed roughly on a seat.

"To what do we owe this honour, Mr Heretic? Too much to expect a conversion, I assume?"

The Consie stared at the two before him. If the tones of Westerland surprised him, he gave no sign. The voice that replied was educated, almost Varrenian in its cadence.

"No. But there is a saying, is there not: *my enemy's enemy is my friend.* Your *nation,* Mr Tragopon, and those here who support you, wish to remove a supposed military threat. We are concerned to prevent a potential ecological disaster. Just now, we have an aim in common, to prevent whatever it is that is happening here. We have information that may help us achieve that goal."

"Us?" Tragopon was contemptuous. "Oh, a little disturbance along the fence might distract a number of the soldiers within when we choose to act. Mission accomplished, and we might, note might, allow a little time for your rabble to disperse. But it is unbelievers and the weak of faith that set this up, and it will not be forgotten."

"Information?" said Pollinast, with some irritation, and an angry glance at Tragopon. "Explain."

"Information that will tell you when to act, if you wish for success. Follow our instructions, and *we* have a chance. Act otherwise, and you may fail. We know something of the workings of this place, you do not."

The Consie turned to Tragopon.

"A little disturbance, you say. No doubt aided by drugging us with ragebush. Your agents have been eliminated, Mr Tragopon, and their supplies burnt. There will be no disturbance along the fence. Indeed, we will be giving the appearance of declining in numbers and enthusiasm. It will be up to you to divert attention from the fence, not the other way round. We can derail the operation and be well away while you deal with the army."

Pollinast managed to remain composed, though he was obliged to press hard on Tragopon's arm to command silence. The man was known to all, it would appear.

"You can prevent the operation? We are to take your word for it, only to find that you have laid a trap, and the army is ready for us? I need convincing, my enemy's enemy."

"Did you observe the huge sending, and the fire that followed? When all lights went out, and remained out for many minutes? That darkness means a sending, a big sending. Too late to destroy the generators, and the arena will be protected with overwhelming force. We can sabotage the sending. One that goes wrong will do more to prevent another than a simple failure to send. You should move when the lights go out and we signal. Aim for the generators, not the arena. Succeed or fail, you will provide a distraction, and we will go, silently, for the arena."

"And if we go straight for the generators, or the arena, at a time of our own choosing?"

"We will leave you to it. Or not quite, for I am sure that some of us will take the opportunity to crack a few skulls in your rear. You might take the generators, but you would be repelled sooner or later. Head for the arena and you have no chance. Nor would we, were we minded to try."

The Consie looked from one to the other, a sardonic grin on his face. He stood up, standing clear of the guards on either side.

"There is one last thing, gentlemen. If I do not return to my friends before dawn, you will find that the army is exceptionally well-prepared, and that your rear will be attacked with vigour the moment you are fully engaged. Now, if you would be so kind, cut my bonds and escort me to the dead ground between us."

*****

As dusk drew near, Holdbo was in a state of suppressed fury. Already he had unloaded the contents of three crates, to find one containing far more than that specified. He had nearly insisted on each crate being loaded under his personal supervision. Another had slipped off its trolley, scratching the surface of the arena. I need Scully, was his recurring thought, as he dashed between scales by the warehouses and the arena itself. His irritation infected others, including those scheduled to accompany the crates. A few had dropped out. Against his feelings, which were murderous, Morgenstrum was making substitutions without censure. Others were calling for a priest.

The activity did not go unnoticed, despite the screens. Scully and his small team checked their gear. In full view, Consies could be seen leaving the fence where it ran closest to the arena, moving east towards the far end of the ranges themselves. Troops were deployed in response. Ultra numbers were increasing around the gates, but traffic in and out was unmolested bar the shouting of obscenities.

There was, however, a small scuffle at the outer gate, leaving one woman trapped inside. While still visible, she screamed and spat at the two soldiers holding her. In the guardhouse, she fell silent and passive.

"What shall we do with her, sarge?" asked one. "We've run out places to secure the bastards. Kick her out to join her friends? She can't do much harm."

The woman's reaction astonished them, for she tugged at a string and brought out a medallion with the unmistakeable Consie symbol of the grey-green tree-fern.

"Don't do that, Sergeant. I was sent to mix with that rabble. The talk is that they will make for your generators, keep you occupied, then break for the arena. There's some with sledgehammers to smash it."

"Brave woman," said Colonel Narutan, when she had been brought before the general and his staff. "That is, assuming she is what she claims. Anyone out there see that medallion and she'd be for it. I'm told there are Westies in there with painbush carriers. Unless, of course, it's a disguise."

"No, she's the real thing. Those idiots outside have not thought to cut the telephone. She gave a name. Gornik has her on the books, and the description matches. Genuine Consie; done time for it too."

"Still be meant to deceive us though. Bloody Consies are building up at the far end, and we don't know how many. We could put too much here, and they make a rush for it."

"Consies can be held off easily enough, and they'd have a way to run before they got anywhere that matters. No, she wants us to kill as many Ultras as possible. More to the point, when? That she seemed not to know. I'm told there are more on the road, and they know we've pulled some out on that piece of shit

Masseter's orders. Hoping for more to save their sorry hides. Still, we should be prepared."

The general looked around the room.

"Let them come, gentlemen, and give them a good thrashing. Masseter will not be able to stop us clearing the whole area. A couple of weeks and we can be burning High City."

The Consie encampment, so stupidly sited far from the arena from Morgenstrum's perspective, had one important feature: from the high ground where it was placed, screens might conceal the arena itself, but not the space between it and the warehouses. Even before dusk had descended, watchers could see crates and pallets being trundled out of sight. There were already fewer lights coming on in the complex than usual, and the smoke from many stacks indicated that generators were building up to full power.

A signal was given, a flare from the Consie camp. As Besties below stirred themselves for action, soldiers behind the fence watched carefully, as a party of Consies moved along it towards the gates. A party of Besties set out to confront them. Soon, a small battle was in progress, moving downhill, while at the gates themselves, there were fire-bombs thrown and the sound of gunfire. Uphill, Consies were struggling to batter down the fence. Here, there were no shots, and soldiers repelled the assaults with tear gas and rifle butts. Captured Consies, sat in disconsolate groups, were guarded by others.

Unseen in the near total darkness, Scully and his two companions had dropped out of the party moving downhill. They cut the wires and crept towards the arena, pausing in the shelter of the screens that surrounded it. Scully peered through a gap. Crates were still being run onto the arena, and he saw that each was on a trolley; only a pair of soldiers were needed to move them into place.

"Change of plan, comrades. Cut the cables; they will abort the mission, repair it and try again. But it is easy to roll a few off the arena. In the dark, they won't see it. There will be chaos at the other end. Wait till I give the word."

The noise of battle could be heard either side of them. The outer gates had already fallen, but the mass of Ultras was temporarily trapped between the inner and outer gates, while others were attempting to destroy the fences on either side. The soldiers retained their discipline. Ultras were falling, falling in numbers that would have halted the sane. Tragopon had foreseen this; the fumes of ragebush, originally intended to stir the Consies, now dulled the senses of the protesters.

Darkness was complete. At the triggering podium, Morgenstrum, Rollo and Frettici were waiting for the charging to complete. Holdbo was still checking the weights of each man to be sent, and a column were waiting to enter the arena at his signal.

"Bestower's Bollocks, can we not go?" asked Morgenstrum. "There are just too many of them, and they'll reach the generators or overrun us here."

"When Holdbo gives the signal, General."

Scully and his partners were on the arena. At the edge, two crates had already been moved. On the edge, he was heaving at another, bent almost double. There was a roar from the gatehouses, and a mob of Ultras broke through towards the arena. The soldiers still contained them, but were steadily forced back.

"Run, Scully, they are nearly on us."

"Just this one," panted Scully. "The more we shift, the greater the error."

A dial on Frettici's console wavered.

"They've got a generator."

"But the charge, it is enough?"

Frettici had scarcely time to nod, when Morgenstrum pushed him aside and pulled the lever. The load on the arena vanished. An explosion towards the warehouses took out another generator. Rollo sank to his knees, head in hands. The idiot had destroyed the material they had so arduously assembled. Who knew from what height it had fallen?

"Better a wreck there, than in the hands of Westies here," was all the general said, as he left the console and headed towards his men, who were now holding the line in hand-to-hand combat, a mere 100 metres from the arena. Frettici stood, paralysed, as the Ultras advanced. Almost at the stage itself, the firepower and discipline of the soldiers prevailed, and their opponents turned and ran. Many fell as the soldiers continued firing. Among the many corpses left as the soldiers advanced was that of the general himself.

The rout was complete. Among the many captives were the two Westerlanders. No longer obstructed, both gates destroyed, a convoy soon moved out, carrying troops to the capital.

Scully felt just a tug. Then he was falling, his descent broken by branches as his backward momentum flung him away from the sending arena. Still numb, but without the use of his legs, he hauled himself up against a tree trunk. As the pain hit him, he stared out at an inferno, where smashed crates and pallets blazed in the release of fuel sent to power the machinery. In the glare of the flames, he looked up. The trees around him were nearly leafless, and his hands felt the dense accumulation of dead leaves around him. Hort was right, but too late; they had already contaminated this new world. A deep despair overtook him as his vision dimmed and all went black.

20. Encyclopaedia Kindlandica

Extracts from the 13th Edition (3037)

Bestowalist Reformation (The Doctrine of Material Cause). A belief, now orthodox, that the Bestowal was not supernatural, but the result of a transcosmos exchange from another universe in which the notionally bestowed were aboriginally evolved. The idea was first suggested by the ardent Conservationist **Galla Hort**. At the **Synod of Rehine** (3025), she pointed to the similarities between the anomalous status of the Rehine Basin and the project of **Morlan Rollo**, later taken over by the army, to exploit the development of the **Evaporator** and the theoretical work of **Torren Galben**. The doctrine neatly solved the long-running dispute between those (**Evolutionists**) who regarded the Bestowed, or first-run, as of natural origin, and those (**Bestowalists**) who believed in a divine plantation. While solving many problems (cf: The **Hochast Hypothesis**), however, it failed to convince all, because of the obscurity of **Galben's** theories and the inability to continue his work after the **Nordgroen Incident**. The disorder of the presumed transfer, with the legendary placing of humans in the ocean rather than at Rehine, also remained problematic.

Bokiniost, Pieton (2977–3024). A Westerland Archpriest, seconded for a short period as Ambassador to Kindland. Recalled after displaying a provocative picture of the **Sack of Kindopol** (2735) in the embassy. A loyal disciple of Archpriest **Hytoniast,** he succeeded him as Supreme Archpriest for a mere sixty-three days, before being deposed by the **Committee for Reconstruction and Restitution** in 3023. He was found murdered in his monastic retreat a year later.

Committee for Reconstruction and Restitution. A self-appointed group of soldiers and civilian councillors in Westerland, led by General **Huegren Norbiniast**, who deposed **Archpriest Bokiniost** when the sailors at Westport defied his order to attack the intercontinental fleets. They were signatories to the **Memorandum of Reconciliation** with the other powers. As the **High Council**, the Committee constitutes the ruling body of Westerland today.

Evaporator, the. A weapon alleged to transfer material between parallel universes, a concept developed by **Torren Galben.** So-called, because matter did disappear, with no explosion, and in certain trials it seemed capable of 'evaporating' hostile targets. The subject of intensive development at **Nordgroen**, work was abandoned after the **Nordgroen Incident**. The underlying theory was understood only by **Galben** himself. With his death in 3023, and a malfunction in the great **Kindopol Computer**, the whole concept was abandoned. The collapse of the project resulted in the dismissal of **Morlan Rollo** as President of the Kindland Academy of Arts and Sciences, as investigations established the unorthodox ways in which he had appropriated funds for the project.

Hochast Hypothesis. The idea, developed by Professor Almar Hochast (2948–3029) that it was possible to trace the evolution of the Bestowed, or first-run, prior to their known arrival in the Lands by means of detailed comparisons of many characters and their separation into ancestral and 'derived'. The idea, first developed when Professor Hochast was in Westerland, and related to the less controversial evolution of aboriginal life, was less widely accepted for the Bestowed, not least because of the formidable statistical analyses involved. With the widespread acceptance of the **Doctrine of Material Cause** at the **Synod of Rehine**, recent work has tended to support it.

Hytoniast, Grindoln (2962–3022). Supreme Archpriest of the Bestowal in High City. A celibate cleric who rose through the ranks of priesthood to be both the spiritual and secular ruler of Westerland. Noted for his piety, his Exterminator credentials and his uncompromising hatred of heresy, he is generally held responsible for inciting the Ultra-Bestowalists in Kindland, and seeking to establish a theocratic government on both continents. Already very ill, the news of the Nordgroen Incident and the subsequent collapse of the Ultra cause in Kindland precipitated his early death.

Kindopol, the sack of (2735). The final battle of the Westerland War (2733–35), in which the retreating Westerland forces fired the city, sparing only the major Bestowalist Temples. The war was an attempt by Westerland to overrun Kindland, and in particular to take control of the Rehine Basin. Aided by the recent development of steamships, the initial invasion was successful, but the superior resources of Kindland and the decisive Battle of Brund forced the Westerlanders to retreat. The sack left lasting animosity between Westerland and the other nations of the Lands.

Martyrs, the. The name given to the strict, Exterminator Bestowalists who left Kindland in 1157 to settle in northern Westerland, outside the region ruled by Kindopol. They established a theocratic republic, and later (1201) established High City as their capital. Despite the name, used ironically by others, they were not killed for their faith, but many died in the harsh conditions in which they established their first settlement. Their landing place on Westerland, **Martyrs' Cove,** is a place of pilgrimage.

Martyrsons. The descendants of the original **Martyrs**, held in high esteem and with preferential access to public office in Westerland. Typically, names end in -ist, -ost, or -ast (-iast), the reasons for which are obscure. In the present population of Westerland, they constitute a substantial minority (c. 22%), the numbers diluted both by the conquest of east Westerland in the Holy War (1355), and by the immigration of devout Bestowalists over many centuries.

Memorandum of Reconciliation (44/1/3023). The intercontinental settlement that followed from the **Nordgroen Incident** and the defeat of Ultra-Bestowalist factions in Kindland. The involvement of Westerland in supporting those factions exposed the clear intention of the Westerland government to impose theocratic rule 'from Derant to Targon'. Briefly defiant under the leadership of **Archpriest Bokiniost**, the Westerland government was overthrown by a military coup, led by the **Committee for Reconstruction and Restitution**, after a blockade of Westport by the combined fleets of both other continents and that of the Far Outs. The overthrow followed starvation in much of Westerland and a rise in anticlericalism. In return for the destruction of its warships, Westerland was supplied with food and with the means to improve its production, means previously banned on grounds of doctrine.

Nordgroen Incident, the (35/4/3022) A violent attempt by various factions to destroy or disrupt the development of the **Evaporator,** a weapon based on the theories of **Torren Galben**. It was the culmination of many days of increasingly disorderly demonstrations outside the military complex, which was heavily defended by the Kindland army. On the night of the 35th, a large body of armed protesters breached the gates and overran a large part of the complex. They were repelled with great loss, and the army's subsequent return to Kindopol ended the increasingly violent clashes between armed bands of **Ultra-Bestowalists** and **Conservationists**. It was notable for the death of General **Ivanen Morgenstrum**, the Commander-in-Chief of Kindland's armed forces, and for the capture of two diplomats from Westerland who were instrumental in provoking the assault. Their involvement, and the subsequent **Memorandum of Reconciliation** (44/1/3023) ended the long period in which war with Westerland had threatened.

Painbush. A low shrub in the grey-green family Agonistacea. While all members of the family exude toxins when touched, painbush is the most harmful. Even an accidental contact, while not usually fatal, causes agonising pain that causes many sufferers to call for death. A rare plant, generally eliminated when found, it was for centuries the chosen form of punishment for heresy in Westerland, several strokes resulting in a period of agony before death occurred. Until very recently, it was cultivated in **Gardens of Wrath** attached to certain monasteries in Westerland. These have now been destroyed.

Lands, the. The traditional name for the three continents and the Far Out Islands, the lands fit for human occupation. The term excludes **Halfland** and the massive, ice-covered Polar Continents.

Halfland. The name given to a row of islands situated between 14° and 20° West and 36° and 40° North. It was discovered by accident by Vascon the Navigator in 2577. Area, 19,680 km². A desolate archipelago, sustaining temperatures only a few degrees above freezing most of the time, and with very high rainfall brought about by the high, volcanic mountains, the highest of which exceeds 4500 metres. The smaller islands at the eastern end have active volcanos, the only such known. Notable for the richness of its Bestowed or first-run fauna and flora, most of which are endemic and flourish in the absence of human intervention. Politically the property of Kindland, its only inhabitants are those running a research station, but it was for a time the site of a penal colony (2789–2934), abandoned on grounds of cost and humanitarian concern. Halfland is the subject of folklore relating to the Bestowal, and recent evidence supports the idea that humans occupied it for a short while around the time of the Bestowal Event. It appears that this population died out or evacuated not long after its arrival.

Kindland. The central and smallest of the three continents of the Lands. Area, 1,430,984 km². Its name derives from its 'kindness' to the first human occupiers. A continent with very subdued topography; the highest hills rise only to 1100 metres. Even excluding the Rehine Basin, it is the most amenable to clearance and cultivation, with the added advantage of substantial deposits of coal and oils. Despite its size, it carries the largest population (c. 15 million) and the largest city, Kindopol, in the Lands. Despite periodic revolts, it has remained a single political entity, governed by a Congress (whose members are called

Seniors) elected on a very restricted franchise. Potentially dominant throughout the Lands, its influence was diminished by turbulent politics and religious disputes.

Eastland. The second largest of the continents (area, 2,048,760 km^2), as also in population (12 million), its development is hindered by a more rugged topography than that of Kindland, holding the highest mountain in the Lands (Kolumba, 2100 metres). Its eastern end has been subject to recent tectonic disturbance, and shows biotic relationships to the Far Outs, 23,000 kilometres away to the east. A frequent destination for refugees and dissidents, it developed a more maritime culture, and was responsible for the discovery and colonisation of the Far Outs, despite the vast distances involved. Its eastern provinces, *the Wild East,* retain a variety of aboriginal life unmatched other than on the more remote Far Outs, and have a culture of rugged individualism. Its government is similar to that of Kindland, though with a broader franchise and much weaker central control. Prior to the **Memorandum of Reconciliation**, its people and culture were anathema to the theocrats of Westerland.

Westerland. The largest (Area, 3,341,654 km^2) of the three continents of the Lands, both its position and its topography make it the least amenable to human life. Heavy rainfall, especially in the far west, and eroded, acidic, igneous rocks forming two chains of low hills along the north and south coasts give rise to vast areas of moor and bog covered with stunted grey-green shrubs. Even in the central raised plain, clearance and plantation face severe difficulties, and erosion on cleared land frequently leads to landslides and floods. Its population (9.5 million) is concentrated mainly in the far east of the continent, between High City and Westport, where conditions are more favourable.

Its political history is more complex than that of the other continents. The east was colonised directly from Kindland, but few wished to advance into the inhospitable west. It was the sailing of the **Martyrs** that established settlements further west, leading to the establishment of High City, and later to the **Holy War** (1355) that ended Kindland rule in Westport. Thereafter, the continent was ruled mainly by a priesthood and the most powerful Martyrson families, the relative power of the secular and spiritual fluctuating over time. At high points of priestly rule, the doctrine of Exterminationism resulted both in famines and in an increasingly aggressive approach to others. Priestly rule was ended by the consequences of the **Nordgroen Incident** and the establishment of the **Committee of Reconstruction and Restitution.**

Far Outs, the. The name given to two different archipelagos to the west of Westerland. The Inners (total area, 14,071 km^2) contain 23 inhabited islands. The largest island, Killet, is also the nearest to the Westerland shore (250 km). Some of the uninhabited islands hold untouched aboriginal fauna and flora, including the spectacular giant octopods. The Outers (total area, 9,982 km^2) all more than 600 km from the Westerland shore, are mainly composed of sedimentary rocks. They are more fertile than the Inners; in some, Bestowed vegetation is now dominant.

Among ten inhabited islands, Greater and Lesser Lofotor are the wealthiest and most populated, though not the largest. Both archipelagos are rich in minerals scarce elsewhere, and their climate is less severe than that of Westerland nearby. Discovered by Goden the Navigator in 1479, they were initially colonised by mariners from Eastland. Mineral wealth, and abundance of food enabled the inhabitants to become wealthy and very independent-minded. Most islands are ruled by a hereditary chief, Master on the Inners, Seigneur on the Outers. Nominally independent, these chiefs acknowledge a senior in dealing with the outside world, the Ombro family on Killet for the Inners, the Denno family from the Lofotors in the Outers. The Outers trade mainly with Kindland and Eastland, while the Inners trade mainly with the nearby Westerland ports.

Total population believed to be around 600,000. The rising tide of fundamentalist Bestowalism in Westerland in the thirty-first century brought the rulers of the two archipelagos closer together, and they were signatories to the **Memorandum of Reconciliation** in 3023. The Anasman Memorial on Greater Lofotor is now the place where the Masters and Seigneurs meet to decide their relationship with the outside world.

Prologue

The screen that had blanked out intermittently died completely. The other three sitting in Mariusz Sulikowski's laboratory remained silent while he tried to re-establish contact. They stared at the map that adorned the wall above the terminal, the map that displayed the world that had preoccupied them for so long. Eventually, Maniklal Chatterjee spoke, "Did Ponta Delgada get the message?"

"I think so. More to the point, did they, could they, act on it?" replied Mariusz.

"Would it matter if they did? Gothenburg is finished, and you know it. No gear, no fuel, just the damned livestock. Nothing with the party other than is what is on their backs. The poor bastards are screwed, just like the guardians before them and those on Vulcania. We should have kept it all together. You should have cancelled the *Arethusa*."

Heike Götz glared at her colleagues as she spoke. Spreading the sending sites across the globe had supposedly concealed their plan; A farm here, a depot there, a sailing school, a boot camp, an arboretum, all at least notionally uncontentious. *And if one link in your chain fails,* she had asked, repeatedly. Now, not just one link broken, but all, with no hope of repair as the tide of chaos engulfed them. Not only chaos, for the agents of several powers were closing in.

"You know why we didn't, Heike, even though you joined us late," said Satoshi Myakama, quietly. "The scale needed to settle the tropics was vast. Our stuff could not compete without transforming the soils. We tried, again and again. Little patches over two continents. We went for Vulcania instead, and it failed. Too damned cold, too rugged, too few resources. A land near enough like Alaska, nothing more. Even so, we were attracting attention, and those up top were doubting the whole teleportation cover. Our sendings returned far too much stuff, some of it living. All that rubble, all those phytosanitary inspections at Anchorage when someone brought in specimens. The military asked some awkward questions. We had to shut down sending for a while and hope they survived. Made play of unsuccessful teleportation. Back to Maniklal's bicycle. It needed his triangulation to avoid stuff coming back here. Then, too late, perhaps, the Large Field Transform. But we had to conceal it."

"And now we've left the poor sods up there with a hopeless struggle for survival while we were taking longer to set things up. The last lot on Vulcania would have perished before Colonel Anson could reach them. The guardians in Great Circle perished too, when we could not resupply them. Now we will have more deaths on our hands."

"We can only hope that's not so. They were building ships on Vulcania; some may have left, and they knew where to go. Thanks to Maniklal we could tell the *Arethusa*. They skipped Vulcania, which saved them at least a week. If Ponta Delgada has managed to send, at least there will be food and the means of maintaining it in Great Circle. They were only a few hours away."

"Food and what else? At best they will be back to the Stone Age in a generation or two. Ponta Delgada will have nothing else to send them, and it's probably been occupied. Not even horses, for the love of God. Murder, Mariusz, and you know it."

Mariusz did not reply. All had been ready for the final sendings. The crisis had developed too fast, and the prospect of total failure had turned to near certainty. Site after site for sending had fallen, either to the mounting chaos of unstable climate, economic dislocation, pandemics and cyberwarfare, or to direct occupation by government agencies. The military had lost confidence, and were questioning the operations. Aside from their own transmitters, easily concealed, only two survived, their activities so manifestly innocent as to escape suspicion. Who could worry about an experimental farm in the Azores? Who would think a training ship marketed as a boot camp of sorts for the delinquent sons and daughters of the wealthy was a training ground for trans-universe pioneers? A sailing ship at that, both because such things were familiar, and because Mariusz had foreseen the difficulties of fuelling.

It had been a scramble, and one that had cut more than a few moral corners. Colonel Anson had said go, send us, but it was clear that he had not explained to the rest what might face them. Mariusz had not told his colleagues until the deed was done, nor that the co-ordinates had been out. Not fatally, but enough to make the task harder. To the outside world, yet another disaster at sea. A ship lost with all hands, a matter that would have provoked intensive coverage in less troubled times.

So near, they had been. Triangulation had sent anything they removed off into some other dimension, rather than here. Large Field Transform had cleared Great Circle with minimal power. Cleared, then reconstituted. Forests and pastures had developed in a hundred years there, but settlers and stock could be sent a mere few months after the initial sending from here. All attuned to the climate, at that. On Vulcania, the bloody climate had defeated them, even though they had shipped whole chunks of forest onto the less toxic soils. Just dandy for Sitka Spruce; not so much for anything else.

Satoshi broke the silence, holding up his doomsday key, "It's time, isn't it? They must know where we are."

There were nods. Satoshi keyed in his password and clicked. The lights flickered briefly. Decades of research and development turned to dust. Mariusz tore down the map, and went outside briefly to burn it. Then they sat in silence, awaiting the arrival of the authorities.

*****

"Visitor for you, Doc," said the prison guard, as he unlocked Mariusz' cell. "Up you come."

"Not another," groaned Sulikowski. Two whole years, and the bastards did not give up trying to co-opt him. CIA, a few Europeans, even someone acting on behalf of the Chinese. The same every time: *Do you want to rot here forever? A whole team to work with you. A comfortable life.* All convinced that teleportation was just around the corner.

At the beginning, of course, it had been more coercive, moderated only by the need to keep him alive and mentally fit. It eased off rather suddenly, and it was only later that he learnt that Heike had hanged herself under pressure. They had not parted on good terms. Maniklal had broken down into incoherence. A psychiatric case, they said. Well, no Maniklal, no progress, thank the Lord, he had thought at the time, for it was only he who could make anything really functional. No news of Satoshi, probably sent back to Japan.

"Not the usual, this one. An elderly Brit, don't know how the hell he got here these days. Scruffy with it. In with the governor for a while. I'm to watch you, and anything said will be recorded, as if you didn't know that. There's some piece of paper you are allowed to see. Seems the governor thought it might loosen your tongue."

Todd was old-fashioned. Doc was no criminal in his eyes, and he had developed a liking for the man. As for those smarmy spooks that pestered him, they were just full of it.

Arnie, Mariusz' cellmate, snorted. "Tongue, Mr Todd. The man lost his way back. I'd appreciate someone a bit more sociable."

Arnie, a rapist, had been paired with Mariusz in the hope that rough company would indeed loosen his tongue. No luck, for Arnie bore his companion's silence with restraint.

Elderly, now there was an understatement, thought Mariusz, as a tall, stooped man rose from his chair to greet him from behind a screen.

"Dr Sulikowski? I am Arthur Wright. I was a journalist. I came here to show you something."

"And you are acting on behalf of which gang of bastards? MI6? That would be a novelty."

The aggression in Mariusz' tone shook the old man, who simply shook his head.

"On your own? So, how the hell did you get here these days? And how did you find me? I understood the big wide world did not know where I was held. Afraid someone would try to spring me."

"No, not MI6, or not directly. Official assistance, I'll admit. I was showing too keen an interest in mysterious disappearances, and they hauled me in. Time passes, Dr Sulikowski. Once upon a time, what I knew, and what my source knew, could have resulted in a couple more, if you get my meaning. It was my following up on your pal Chatterjee that got me some unwanted attention, him and his disappearing bicycle. Ages ago, I know, and I only came across the reports last year. It was the only one that really stood out. All set up, lots of reliable witnesses. All the others, well, there could be any number of rational explanations."

Mariusz examined the man's face. An agent? He measured his words.

"Oh, yes. It did attract some interest. We were trying to achieve teleportation. The bicycle did disappear. It was a joke that took us by surprise. We never knew where it went, and it never worked again. We spent ages afterwards trying to find out why. Don't tell me it turned up in Britain?"

"No." Wright laughed. "But we did have a disappearance in Britain, a rather strange one. It was all hushed up, but I got a first-hand account, handed on anonymous, like. I'd sat on it for years, but it nagged at me. I spent years poking around for more examples when I came across that bicycle, I thought, why not ask that Chatterjee fellow."

Wright saw the look on Sulikowski's face.

"I read that it was done at the Institute of Theoretical Cosmology near Toronto. Strange outfit. And there was a list of members, with your name among them. Boss Man. I started digging. It brought the spooks down on me like a ton of bricks. Yours, ours, the bleeding CIA. I'll not lie; they've seen what I have, and they know I'm here. Got me here in fact. Outfit closed down, they told me, and all of you banged up for sabotage or sedition, trial in camera. That wasn't all. They told me the poor bugger had gone mad, and another topped herself. Just you and that Japanese fellow, and he'd been sent back."

"Why send you, if they have whatever it is? They could have sent another operative." Mariusz uttered the last word with exaggerated contempt. "Must have been quite a trial for you."

"Would you have believed it, coming from a spook? I'm not here to question you, just to pass on the info. I am what I seem to be."

Wright laid out a set of documents and cuttings. A long-expired press pass, and printouts with his byline. Todd leant over Mariusz' shoulder to examine them, and stepped back with a satisfied grunt. Mariusz nodded, and Wright gathered them up.

"OK? Remember, this is second-hand. A mate who thought he might cop it if they knew what he held."

The pages were handed over. *Arthur, I'm dumping this on you as insurance. They will have no reason to come calling, and good old-fashioned snail mail escapes their notice, especially up here. Too much of it, these days. I've cleared my files…*

Mariusz read. With an eye to any camera, he read again, holding the papers up to his face. With an effort, he put them down and looked at Wright with an air of emphatic puzzlement. "Weird indeed. Did they give you any more info on the corpse?"

"I asked. DNA and all that made him bog standard north European. I was told that he was darker-skinned than they expected, that's all. Oh, there was something about a high level of homozygosity. I got them to spell it."

"And they think we had something to do with it? Some teleportation trick? No, that bicycle was the limit of our achievements. And we'd not send anyone dressed like that from a Canadian November. Half his arse missing too. Something not right there."

"True, but there's more. That incident, it was years before your vanishing bicycle, before your institute was set up. Time travel, I was told; that's what got them worked up. Something you lot had done on the quiet. Think about it. Trees disappeared. Your mate's bicycle disappeared. A body appears, along with a lot else. Machinery, I gathered. Could as well be Canadian as anything else. I start nosing around; they latch on, see my stuff and put two and two together. You telling me they made five?"

"Pretty much. Certainly not us. We never knew what the Chinese were up to, but I don't think they'd have sent a scantily-dressed European. What about the source; he's OK?"

"In the way you mean, yes, but the poor bugger died a few years ago. Natural causes for sure. Dead nervous at the time though. You can see why."

"Yes. Well, thanks for the info. Sorry I can't shed any light."

*****

The rain was relentless. Huddled under his leaking coat, Mariusz passed through the cemetery gates, now swinging in the wind with a clatter. It took a while to find the small plot where the remains of prisoners with none to care for them were buried. The small, horizontal stones and their laconic inscriptions spoke of miserable lives ended in futility. There were not so many, and soon he found it:

Heike Götz
b.4/6/2032 d.16/10/2089

Stupidly, he looked around, checking for any watcher. He brought out a trowel and excavated a small hole underneath the stone. From a pocket, he pulled a small brass plate, a plate he had engraved in the prison workshop before his release.

THEY MADE IT

He slipped it into the hole and stamped the soil back with his foot. Then he turned and left. Just one among millions, drifting in a world that was falling apart.